PENGUIN BOOKS
Assassin's Creed

Assassin's Creed
Brotherhood

OLIVER BOWDEN

PENGUIN BOOKS

PENGUIN BOOKS

Published by the Penguin Group
Penguin Books Ltd, 80 Strand, London WC2R ORL, England
Penguin Group (USA) Inc., 375 Hudson Street, New York, New York 10014, USA
Penguin Group (Canada), 90 Eglinton Avenue East, Suite 700, Toronto, Ontario, Canada M4P 2Y3
(a division of Pearson Penguin Canada Inc.)
Penguin Ireland, 25 St Stephen's Green, Dublin 2, Ireland (a division of Penguin Books Ltd)
Penguin Group (Australia), 250 Camberwell Road,
Camberwell, Victoria 3124, Australia (a division of Pearson Australia Group Pty Ltd)
Penguin Books India Pvt Ltd, 11 Community Centre,
Panchsheel Park, New Delhi – 110 017, India
Penguin Group (NZ), 67 Apollo Drive, Rosedale, North Shore 0632, New Zealand
(a division of Pearson New Zealand Ltd)
Penguin Books (South Africa) (Pty) Ltd, 24 Sturdee Avenue,
Rosebank, Johannesburg 2196, South Africa

Penguin Books Ltd, Registered Offices: 80 Strand, London WC2R ORL, England

www.penguin.com

First published 2010
1

Typeset by Penguin Books Ltd
Printed in Great Britain by Clays Ltd, St Ives plc

A CIP catalogue record for this book is available from the British Library

ISBN: 978-0-241-95171-2

www.greenpenguin.co.uk

Contents

Prologue

The events of the past extraordinary fifteen minutes – which might have been fifteen hours, even days, so long had they seemed – ran through Ezio's head once more as he stumbled, his brain reeling, from the vault beneath the Sistine Chapel.

He remembered, though it seemed like a dream, that in the depths of the vault he had seen a vast sarcophagus made of what looked like granite. As he'd approached it, it had begun to glow, but with a light that was welcoming.

He touched its lid and it had opened, as if as light as a feather. From it a warm, yellow light glowed, and from within that glow a figure rose, whose features Ezio could not make out, although he knew he was looking at a woman. A woman of unnatural stature, who wore a helmet, and on whose right shoulder sat a tawny owl.

The light that surrounded her blinded him.

'Greetings, O Prophet,' she said, calling him by the name which had been mysteriously assigned to him. 'I have been waiting for you for ten thousand thousand seasons.'

Ezio dared not look up.

'Show me the Apple.'

Humbly, Ezio proffered it.

'Ah.' Her hand caressed the air over it but she did not touch it. It glowed and pulsated. Her eyes bore into him. 'We must speak.' She tilted her head, as if considering something, and Ezio, raising his head, thought he could see the trace of a smile on her iridescent face.

'Who are you?'

'Oh – many names have I. When I . . . died, it was Minerva.'

Ezio recognized the name. 'Goddess of Wisdom! The owl on your shoulder. The helmet. Of course.' He bowed his head.

'We are gone now. The gods your forefathers worshipped. Juno, queen of the gods, and my father, Jupiter, their king, who brought me forth to life through his forehead. I was the daughter, not of his loins, but of his brain!'

Ezio was transfixed. He looked at the statues ranged round the walls. Venus. Mercury. Vulcan. Mars . . .

There was a noise like glass breaking in the distance, or the sound a falling star might make – it was her laughter. 'No – not gods. We simply came before. Even when we walked the world, humankind struggled to understand our existence. We were just more advanced in time.' She paused. 'But, although you may not comprehend us, you must take note of our warning.'

'I do not understand.'

'Don't be frightened. I wish to speak to you but also *through* you. You are the Chosen One for your time. The *Prophet*.'

Ezio felt a mother's warmth embrace all his weariness.

Minerva raised her arms and the roof of the vault became the firmament. Her glittering face bore an expression of inexpressible sadness.

'Listen and see.'

Ezio could hardly bear the memory: he had seen the whole earth and the heavens surrounding it as far as the Milky Way, the galaxy, and his mind could barely comprehend his vision. He saw a world – his world – destroyed by Man, and a windswept plain. But then he saw people – broken, ephemeral, but undismayed.

'We gave you Eden,' said Minerva, 'but it became Hades. The world burned until naught remained but ash. But we created you in our image, and we created you, whatever you did, however much cancerous evil was in you, by choice, because we gave you choice, to survive. And we rebuilt. After the devastation, we rebuilt the world and it has become, after aeons, the world you know and inhabit. We endeavoured to ensure that such a tragedy would never again be repeated.'

Ezio looked at the sky again. A horizon. On it, temples and shapes, carvings in stone like writing, libraries full of scrolls, and ships, and cities, and music and dancing. Shapes and forms from ancient civilizations he didn't know, but recognized as the work of his fellow beings.

'But now my people are dying,' Minerva was saying. 'And time will work against us . . . truth will be turned into myth and legend. But Ezio, prophet and leader, though you have the physical force of a mere human, your will ranks with ours, and in you shall my words be preserved.'

Ezio gazed at her, entranced.

'Let my words also bring hope,' Minerva continued. 'But you must be quick, for time grows short. Guard against the Borgia. Guard against the Templar Cross.'

The vault darkened. Minerva and Ezio were alone, bathed in a fading glow of warm light.

'My people must now leave this world. But the message is delivered. It is up to you now. We can do no more.'

And then there was darkness and silence, and the vault became a mere underground cellar again, with nothing in it at all.

And yet . . .

Ezio made his way out, glancing at the writhing body of Rodrigo Borgia, the Spaniard, Pope Alexander VI, Leader of the Templar faction – bloody in his apparent death agonies; Ezio could not bring himself, now, to deliver a *coup de grâce*. The man seemed to be dying by his own hand. From the look of him, Rodrigo had taken poison, no doubt the same cantarella he had administered to so many of his enemies. Well, let him find his own way to the *Inferno*. Ezio would not give him the mercy of an easy death.

He made his way out of the gloom of the Sistine Chapel into the sunshine. Once on the portico, he could see his friends and fellow Assassins, members of the Brotherhood, at whose side he had lived so many adventures and survived so many dangers, waiting for him.

PART ONE

Yet it cannot be called prowess to kill fellow
citizens, to betray friends, to be treacherous,
pitiless, irreligious. These ways can win a prince
power, but never glory.

Niccolò Machiavelli, *The Prince*

I

Ezio stood for a moment, dazed and disorientated. Where was he? What was this place? As he slowly regained his senses, he saw his uncle Mario detach himself from the group of his fellow Assassins and approach him, taking his arm.

'Ezio, are you all right?'

'Th . . . th . . . there was a fight – with the Pope, with Rodrigo Borgia. I left him for dead.'

Ezio trembled violently. He could not help himself. Could it be real? Minutes earlier – though it seemed like one hundred years ago – he had been involved in a life-and-death struggle with the man he most hated and feared – the Leader of the Templars, the vicious organization bent on the destruction of the world Ezio and his friends in the Brotherhood of the Assassins had fought so hard to protect.

But he had beaten them. He had used the great powers of the mysterious artefact, the Apple, the sacred Piece of Eden vouchsafed to him by the old gods to ensure that their investment in humanity did not vanish in bloodshed and iniquity. And he had emerged triumphant.

Or had he?

What had he said? 'I left him for dead?' And indeed Rodrigo Borgia, the vile old man who had clawed his way to the head of the Church and ruled it as Pope had indeed seemed to be dying. He had taken poison.

But now a hideous doubt gripped Ezio. In showing mercy, mercy which was at the core of the Assassin's Creed and which should, he knew, be granted to all but those whose life would endanger the rest of mankind, had he in fact been *weak*?

If he had, he would never let his doubt show, not even to his uncle Mario, leader of the Brotherhood. He squared his shoulders. He had left the old man to die by his own hand. He had left him with time to pray. He had not stabbed him through the heart to make sure of him.

A cold hand closed over his heart as a clear voice in his mind said, *You should have killed him.*

He shook himself to get rid of his demons as a dog shakes off water after a swim. But still his thoughts dwelt on his mystifying experience in the strange vault beneath the Sistine Chapel in Rome's Vatican; the building from which he had just emerged into the blinking, unfamiliar sunlight. Everything around him seemed strangely calm and normal – the buildings of the Vatican stood just as they always had, resplendent in the bright light. The memory of what had just passed in the vault came back to him, great surges of recollection overwhelming his consciousness. There had been a vision, an encounter with a strange goddess – for there was no other way of describing the being – whom he now knew as Minerva, the Roman goddess of Wisdom. She had shown him both the distant past and the far future in such a way as to make him loathe the responsibility that the knowledge he had gained placed on his shoulders.

With whom could he share it? How could he explain *any* of it? It all seemed so unreal.

All he knew for sure after his experience – better to call it an ordeal – was that the fight was not yet over. Perhaps one day there would be a time when he could return to his home town of Florence and settle down with his books, drinking with his friends in winter and hunting with them in autumn, chasing girls in spring and overseeing the harvests on his estates in summer.

But this was not it.

In his heart he knew that the Templars and all the evil they represented were not finished. In them he was pitted against a monster with more heads than the Hydra, and like that beast, which it had taken no less a man than Hercules to slay, all but immortal.

'Ezio!'

His uncle's voice was harsh, but served to make him snap out of the reverie that held him in its clutches. He had to get a grip and think clearly.

There was a fire raging in Ezio's head. He said his

name to himself as a kind of reassurance: I am Ezio Auditore da Firenze. Strong, a master of the traditions of the Assassin.

He went over the ground again: He didn't know whether or not he'd been dreaming. The teaching and the revelations of the strange goddess in the vault had shaken his beliefs and assumptions to the core. It was as if time itself had been stood on its head. Emerging from the Sistine Chapel, where he had left the evil Pope, Alexander VI *apparently* dying, he squinted again in the harsh sunlight. His fellow Assassins were gathered around, their faces grave and set with a grim determination.

The thought pursued him still: *should he have killed Rodrigo – made sure of him?* He had elected not to – and the man had seemed bent on taking his own life, having failed in his final goal.

But that clear voice still rang in Ezio's mind.

And there was more: a baffling force seemed to be drawing him back to the chapel – he sensed that there was something left undone.

Not Rodrigo. Not *just* Rodrigo. Though he would finish him now. Something *else*.

'What is it?' Mario asked.

'I must return,' Ezio said, realizing afresh, and with a lurching stomach, that the game *wasn't* over and that the Apple should not yet pass from his hands. As the thought struck him, so he was seized by an overwhelming sense of urgency. Tearing himself free of his uncle's sheltering arms, he hurried back into the gloom. Mario, bidding the others to stay where they were and keep watch, followed.

Ezio quickly reached the place where he'd left the dying Rodrigo Borgia – but the man wasn't there! A richly decorated papal damask cope lay in a heap on the floor, flecked with gore, but its owner was gone. Once again the hand, clad in an icy steel gauntlet, closed over Ezio's heart and seemed to crush it.

The hidden door to the vault was, to all intents and purposes, closed and almost invisible, but as Ezio approached the point where he remembered it had been, it swung open gently at his touch. He turned to his uncle and was surprised to see fear on Mario's face.

'What's in there?' said the older man, fighting to keep his voice steady.

'The Mystery,' Ezio replied.

Leaving Mario on the threshold, he walked down the dimly lit passage, hoping he was not too late and that Minerva would have foreseen this and therefore show mercy. Surely Rodrigo would not have been allowed entry here. Nevertheless, Ezio kept his Hidden Blade, the blade his father had bequeathed him, at the ready.

In the vault, the great *human*, yet at the same time *super-human* figures – were they statues? – stood holding the Staff.

One of the pieces of Eden.

The Staff was apparently welded to the figure that held it, and as Ezio tried to pry it loose, the figure seemed to glow and tighten its grip, as did the Runic inscriptions on the walls of the vault.

Ezio remembered that no human hand should ever touch the Apple unprotected. The figures then turned away, and sank into the ground, leaving the vault void of anything save the great sarcophagus and its surrounding statues.

Ezio stepped back, looking round briefly and hesitating before taking what he instinctively knew would be his final leave of this place. What was he expecting? Was he hoping that Minerva would once more manifest herself to him? But hadn't she told him all there was to tell? Or at least all that it was safe for him to know? The Apple had been vouchsafed him. In combination with the Apple, the other pieces of Eden would have accorded Rodrigo the supremacy he craved, and Ezio understood in the fullness of his years that such united power was too dangerous for the hands of Man.

'All right?' Mario's voice, still untypically nervous, floated down to him.

'All's well,' replied Ezio, making his way back to the light with a curious reluctance.

Once reunited with his uncle, Ezio wordlessly showed him the Apple.

'And the Staff?'

Ezio shook his head.

'Better in the hands of the Earth than in the hands of Man,' said Mario with immediate understanding. 'But you don't need me to tell you that. Come on, We shouldn't linger.'

'What's the hurry?'

'Everything's the hurry. Do you think Rodrigo is just going to sit back and let us stroll out of here?'

'I left him for dead.'

'Not quite the same as leaving him good and dead, is it? Come on!'

They made their way out of the vault then, as quickly as they could, and a cold wind seemed to follow them as they did so.

2

'Where did the others go?' Ezio asked Mario, his mind still reeling from his recent experiences, as they made their way back to the great nave of the Sistine Chapel. The gathered Assassins were no longer there.

'I told them to go. Paola has returned to Florence; Teodora and Antonio to Venice. We need to keep ourselves covered throughout Italy. The Templars are broken but not destroyed. They will regroup if our Assassin Brotherhood is not vigilant. Eternally vigilant. The rest of our company have gone ahead and will await us at our headquarters in Monteriggioni.'

'They were keeping watch.'

'So they were, but they knew when their duty was done. Ezio, there is no time to waste. We all know that.' Mario's face was earnest.

'I should have made sure of Rodrigo Borgia.'

'Did he harm you in the fight?'

'My armour protected me.'

Mario clapped his nephew on the back. 'I spoke hastily before. I think you were right not to kill needlessly. I have always advised moderation. You thought him as good as dead, by his own hand. Who knows?

Perhaps he was faking – or perhaps he failed to give himself a fatal dose of poison. Either way, we must deal with the situation as it is now and not waste energy pondering what might have been. In any case, we sent you – one man against an entire army of Templars. You've more than done your part. And I am still your old uncle, and I've been worried about you. Come on, Ezio. We have to get out of here. We have work to do, and the last thing we need is to get cornered by Borgia guards.'

'You wouldn't believe the things I've seen, Uncle.'

'Just be sure to stay alive, then, that I may hear of them. Listen: I've stabled some horses just beyond Saint Peter's, outside the precincts of the Vatican. Once we reach them we'll be able to make our way safely from here.'

'The Borgia will try to stop us, I expect.'

Mario flashed a broad grin. 'Of course they will – and *I* expect the Borgia to mourn the loss of many lives tonight!'

In the chapel, Ezio and his uncle were surprised to find themselves faced with a number of priests, who had returned to complete the Mass interrupted by Ezio's confrontation with the Pope as he and Rodrigo had battled for control of the Pieces of Eden they had discovered.

The priests confronted them angrily, surrounding them and clamouring, *'Che cosa fate 'qui?* – What are you doing here?' They yelled, 'You have desecrated the sanctity of this Holy Place!' And: '*Assassini!* God will see that you pay for your crimes!'

As Mario and Ezio pushed their way through the angry throng, the bells of Saint Peter's began to ring the alarm.

'You condemn what you do not understand,' said Ezio to a priest who was trying to bar their way. The softness of the man's body repelled him and he shoved him aside as gently as possible.

'We must go, Ezio,' said Mario urgently. '*Now!*'

'His is the voice of the Devil,' another priest's voice rang out.

And another said, 'Turn away from them.'

Ezio and Mario pushed their way through the mob and out into the great courtyard of the church. There they were confronted by a sea of red robes. It seemed that the entire college of cardinals was assembled, confused, but still under the dominion of Pope Alexander VI, Rodrigo Borgia, captain of the Association of the Templars.

'For we wrestle not against flesh and blood,' the cardinals were chanting, 'but against principalities, against powers, against the rulers of the darkness of this world, against spiritual wickedness in high places. Wherefore take unto you the whole armour of God, and the shield of Faith, wherewith you shall be able to quench all the fiery darts of the wicked.'

'What's the matter with them?' Ezio asked.

'They are confused. They seek guidance,' Mario replied grimly. 'Come on. We must get away before the Borgia guards take notice of our presence. He looked back towards the Vatican. There was a glitter of armour in the sunlight.

'Too late. Here they come. Hurry!'

3

The billowing vestments of the cardinals formed a sea of red that parted as four Borgia guards pushed through in pursuit of Ezio and Mario. Panic overtook the crowd as the cardinals started shouting in fear and alarm, and Ezio and his uncle found themselves encircled by a human arena. The cardinals, not knowing where to turn, had inadvertently formed a barrier; perhaps their courage was unconsciously bolstered by the arrival of the heavily armoured guards, their breastplates gleaming in the sunlight. The four Borgia soldiers had unsheathed their swords and stepped into the circle to face Ezio and Mario, who in turn drew their blades.

'Lay down your weapons and surrender, Assassins. You are surrounded and outnumbered!' shouted the lead soldier, stepping forward.

Before he could utter another word, Ezio had sprung from his stance, energy returning to his weary limbs. The lead guard had no time to react, not expecting his opponent to be so bold in the face of such overwhelming odds. Ezio's sword arm circled in a blur, the blade whistling as it sliced through the air. The guard tried in vain to raise his sword to parry, but Ezio's movement was simply too quick. The Assassin's sword hit its mark with unfaltering accuracy, slicing into the guard's exposed neck, a plume of blood fol lowing its impact. The three remaining guards stood motionless, astonished at the speed of the Assassin and idiotic in the face of such a skilled foe. It was a delay that was to prove their death. Ezio's blade had barely finished its first lethal arc when he raised his left hand, the mechanism of his hidden blade clicking as the lethal spike appeared from his sleeve. It pierced the second guard between the eyes before he could even twitch a muscle in defence.

Meanwhile Mario, unnoticed, had taken two steps sideways, closing the angle of attack on the two remaining guards, whose attention was still entirely focused on the shocking display of violence unfolding before them. In two more steps, he closed in and heaved his sword under the breastplate of the nearest guard, the point rising up sickeningly into the man's torso. The guard's face contorted with confused agony. One man left. With horror in his eyes he turned as if to flee – but too late. Ezio's blade struck his right flank as Mario's sword sliced into his thigh. The man fell to his knees with a grunt and Mario kicked him over.

The two Assassins looked around – the blood of the guards spread across the paved ground, soaking into the scarlet hems of the cardinals' vestments.

'Let's go before more of Borgia's men reach us.' They brandished their swords at the now terrified cardinals, who quickly fled the Assassins, clearing a path that would lead them from the Vatican. They heard the sound of approaching horses – no doubt more soldiers – as they pushed their way forcefully towards the south-east, running at full speed across the expanse of the plaza, away from the Vatican in the direction of the Tiber. The horses Mario had organized for their escape were tethered just outside the purlieus of the Holy See. But first they had to turn to those Papal Guards who had followed on horseback and who were bearing down on them fast, their thundering hooves echoing on the cobbles. Using their falchions, Ezio and Mario managed to strike away the halberds the guards thrust at them.

Mario cut one guard down just as he was about to stab Ezio from behind with his spear.

'Not bad for an old man,' Ezio cried gratefully.

'I expect you to return the favour,' returned his uncle. 'And not so much of your "old man"!'

'I haven't forgotten everything you taught me.'

'I should hope not. Look out!' Ezio whirled round just in time to slice the legs of a horse from under a guard who'd galloped up wielding a vicious-looking mace.

'*Buona questa!*' shouted Mario. 'Good one!'

Ezio leapt sideways, avoiding two more of his pursuers and managing to unsaddle them as they careered past, carried forward by their own momentum. Mario, heavier and older, preferred to stand his ground and cut at his enemies before leaping out of their reach. But once they had gained the edge of the broad square that faced the great cathedral church of St Peter, the two Assassins quickly clambered to the safety of the rooftops, scaling the crumbling house walls as nimbly as geckos, and scampering across them, leaping over the gaps where the streets between them made canyons. It wasn't always easy, and at one point Mario nearly didn't make it, his fingers scrabbling for the gutters as he fell just short. Panting hard, Ezio doubled back to pull him clear, succeeding just as the crossbow bolts fired by their pursuers rattled uselessly past them into the sky.

But their going was far faster than that of the guards, who, more heavily armoured and lacking the skills of the Assassins, tried in vain to keep up by running though the pathways beneath until gradually they fell back.

Mario and Ezio clattered to a halt on a roof overlooking a small square on the edge of Trastevere. Two large, tough-looking chestnut horses were saddled and ready outside a lowly-looking inn, its battered sign declaring it to be The Sleeping Fox, while being watched over by a wall-eyed hunchback with a bushy moustache.

'Gianni!' hissed Mario.

The man looked up and immediately undid the reins by which the horses were tethered to a huge iron ring set into the wall of the inn. Mario instantly leapt down from the rooftop, landing in a crouch, and from there sprang into the saddle of the nearer, and larger, of the two horses. It whinnied and trod the earth in nervous anticipation.

'Shh, *Campione*,' said Mario to the animal, and then, looking up to where Ezio still stood on the parapet, he yelled, 'Come on! What are you waiting for?'

'Just a minute, *Zio*,' said Ezio, turning to face two Borgia guards who had managed to struggle up to the roof and who were now facing him with – to his astonishment – cocked pistols of a type that was new to him. Where the hell had they got those from? This was no time for questions, though, so he whirled through the air at them, unleashing his Hidden Blade and slicing each neatly through the jugular before they had a chance to fire.

'Impressive,' said Mario, reining in his impatient horse. 'Now, get a move on! *Cosa diavolo aspetti?*'

Ezio threw himself off the roof to land close by the second horse, which was being held firmly by the hunchback, then he rebounded off the ground to spring into the animal's saddle. It reared excitedly under his weight but he immediately had it under control and wheeled it round to follow his uncle as he rode fast towards the Tiber. At the same time Gianni disappeared into the inn, and a detachment of Borgia cavalry tore round the corner into the square. Digging his heels into the horse's flanks, Ezio sped after his uncle as they made their way at breakneck speed through the broken-down streets of Rome towards the dirty, sluggish river. At their backs they could hear the shouts of the mounted Borgia guards, cursing their prey as Mario and Ezio galloped through the maze of ancient streets, slowly pulling further away.

Having reached Tiber Island they crossed the river by a rickety bridge that trembled beneath their horses' hooves, then they doubled back, turning north to ride up the main street leading out of the squalid little town that had once been the capital of the civilized world. They did not stop until they were in the depths of the countryside, and had assured themselves they were out of reach of their pursuers.

Near the settlement of Settebagni, in the shade of a massive elm tree by the side of the dusty road that ran parallel to the river, they reined their horses in and took time to draw breath.

'That was too close, Uncle.'

The older man shrugged and smiled a little painfully. From a saddlebag Mario produced a leather flagon of rough red wine and proffered it to his nephew.

'Here,' he said, slowly catching his breath. 'Good for you.'

Ezio drank, then grimaced. 'Where did you get this?'

'It's the best they can do at The Sleeping Fox,' said Mario, grinning broadly. 'But once we get to Monteriggioni you'll fare better.'

Ezio smiled and passed the flask back to his uncle, but then his features became troubled.

'What is it?' asked Mario in gentler tones.

Slowly, Ezio produced the Apple from the pouch in which he'd stowed it. 'This. What am I to do with it?'

Mario looked grave. 'It is a heavy responsibility. But it is one you must shoulder alone.'

'How can I?'

'What does your heart tell you?'

'My heart tells me to be rid of it. But my brain . . .'

'It was vouchsafed you . . . by whatever powers you encountered in the vault,' said Mario solemnly. 'They would not have given it back to mortals if there was not a purpose devised for it.'

'It is too dangerous. If it fell into the wrong hands again . . .' Ezio looked ominously at the slothful river flowing nearby. Mario watched him expectantly.

Ezio hefted the Apple in his gloved right hand. But still he hesitated. He knew he couldn't throw such a great treasure away, and his uncle's words had swayed him. Surely Minerva would not have allowed him to take back the Apple without reason.

'The decision must be yours alone,' said Mario. 'But if you feel unhappy having custody of it now, give it to *me* for safekeeping. You can take it back later when your mind is calmer.'

Ezio hesitated still, but then they both heard, in the distance, the sound of thundering hooves and the baying of hounds.

'Those bastards don't give up easily,' said Mario through gritted teeth. 'Come, give it to me.'

Ezio sighed, but replaced the Apple in its leather pouch and threw it over to Mario, who quickly stowed it in his saddlebag.

'And now,' said Mario, 'we must jump these nags into the river and swim them across. That'll put the damned dogs off our scent, and even if they're bright enough to ford the Tiber themselves, we'll be able to lose them in the woods over there. Come on. I want to be in Monteriggioni by this time tomorrow.'

'How hard do you expect to ride?'

Mario dug his heels into his mount's flanks and the beast reared, foam at the corners of its mouth.

'Very hard,' he said. 'Because from now on we don't simply have Rodrigo to contend with, his son and daughter are with him – Cesare and Lucrezia.'

'And they are . . . ?'

'The most dangerous people you are ever likely to meet.'

4

It was the afternoon of the following day when the little walled town of Monteriggioni, dominated by Mario's *rocca*, appeared on its hill on the horizon. They had made better time than they'd expected and had now eased their pace to spare the horses.

'. . . and then Minerva told me about the sun,' Ezio was saying. 'She told of a disaster that happened long ago, and foretold of another which is to come . . .'

'But not until some time in the future, *vero*?' said Mario. 'Then we need not fret about it.'

'*Sì*,' Ezio replied. 'I wonder how much more work we have to do.' He paused reflectively. 'Perhaps it will soon be finished.'

'Would that be so bad?'

Ezio was about to reply when he was interrupted by the sound of an explosion: cannon fire from the direction of the town. He drew his sword, rising in his saddle to scan the ramparts.

'Don't worry,' said Mario, laughing heartily. 'It's only exercises. We've upgraded the arsenal here and installed new cannon all along the battlements. We have training sessions daily.'

'As long as they aren't aiming at us.'

'Don't worry,' said Mario again. 'It's true that the men still need to get their eye in, but they have enough sense not to fire at the boss!'

A short while later they were riding through the open principal gate of the town and up the main thoroughfare that led to the citadel. As they did so, crowds gathered to line the street, looking at Ezio with a mixture of respect, admiration and affection.

'Welcome back, Ezio!' one woman called.

'*Grazie, Madonna,*' Ezio smiled back, inclining his head slightly.

'Three cheers for Ezio!' a child's voice rang out.

'*Buongiorno, fratellino,*' Ezio said to him. Turning to Mario, he added, 'It's good to be home.'

'I think they're more pleased to see you than me,' said Mario, but he was smiling as he spoke, and in fact much of the cheering, especially from the older townsmen, was for him.

'I'm looking forward to seeing the old family seat again,' said Ezio. 'It's been a while.'

'It has indeed, and there are a couple of people there who'll be looking forward to seeing you.'

'Who?'

'Can't you guess? You can't be that preoccupied with your duties to the Brotherhood.'

'Of course. You mean my mother and my sister. How are they?'

'Well, your sister was very unhappy when her husband died, but time heals most things, and I think she's much better now. In fact, there she is.'

They had ridden into the courtyard of Mario's fortified residence, and, as they dismounted, Ezio's sister, Claudia, appeared at the top of the marble staircase that led up to the main entrance and flew down it and into her brother's arms.

'Brother!' she cried, hugging him. 'Your return home is the best birthday present I could have wished for.'

'Claudia, my dearest,' said Ezio, holding her close. 'It is good to be back. How is our mother?'

'Well, thanks be to God. She's dying to see you – we've been on tenterhooks ever since the news reached us that you were returning. And your fame goes before you.'

'Let's go in,' said Mario.

'There's someone else who'll be glad to see you,' continued Claudia, taking his arm and escorting him up the staircase. 'The Countess of Forlì.'

'Caterina? Here?' Ezio tried to keep the excitement out of his voice.

'We did not know when exactly you would arrive. She and Mother are with the Abbess, but they will be here by sunset.'

'Business first,' said Mario knowingly. 'I am calling a meeting of the Council of the Brotherhood here tonight. Machiavelli, I know, is especially keen to talk to you.'

'Is it finished, then?' asked Claudia intently. 'Is the Spaniard truly dead?'

Ezio's grey eyes hardened. 'I will explain everything at the meeting this evening,' he told her.

'Very well,' replied Claudia, but her eyes were troubled as she took her leave.

'And please give my greetings to the Countess when she returns,' Ezio called after her. 'I will see her, and Mother, this evening. First I have business to attend to with Mario which will not wait.'

Once alone, Mario's tone became serious. 'You must prepare well for tonight, Ezio. Machiavelli will be here by sunset and I know he has many questions for you. We will discuss matters now, and then I advise you to take some time off – it won't hurt you to get to know the town a little again.'

After a session of deep conversation with Mario in his study, Ezio made his way back into Monteriggioni. The question of the Pope's survival hung heavily over him and he sought distraction from it. Mario had suggested he visit his tailor to order some new clothes to replace his travel-stained ones, so first he made his way to the tailor's shop, where he found the tailor sitting cross-legged on his workbench, sewing a brocade cloak of a rich emerald green.

Ezio liked the tailor, who was a good-natured fellow a little older than Ezio himself. The tailor greeted him warmly.

'To what do I owe the honour?' he asked.

'I think I'm due some new clothes,' said Ezio a little ruefully. 'Tell me what you think. Be honest.'

'Even if it were not my job to sell you clothes, *signore*, I would have to advise you that a new suit would be the making of you.'

'I thought as much! Very well!'

'I'll measure you now. Then you can pick out the colours you'd like.'

Ezio submitted himself to the tailor's ministrations and chose a discreet dark grey velvet for the doublet, with matching hose in wool.

'Can it be ready by tonight?'

The tailor smiled. 'Not if you want me to do a good job of it, *signore*. But we can try for a fitting towards midday tomorrow.'

'Very well,' replied Ezio, hoping that the meeting he was to attend that evening would not result in his having to leave Monteriggioni immediately.

He was making his way across the town's main square when he noticed an attractive woman struggling with an unwieldy box of red and yellow flowers that was clearly too heavy for her to lift. At that time of day there were few people around, and Ezio had always found it difficult to resist a damsel in distress.

'Can I lend you a hand?' he asked, coming up to her.

She smiled at him. 'Yes, you're just the man I need. My gardener was supposed to pick these up for me, but his wife's sick so he had to go home. As I was passing this way I thought I'd fetch them, but this box is way too heavy for me. Do you think you could . . . ?'

'Of course.' Ezio stooped and hefted the box onto his shoulder. 'So many flowers. You're a lucky woman.'

'Even luckier now that I've run into you.'

There was no doubt that she was flirting with him. 'You could have asked your husband to fetch them for you, or one of your other servants,' he said.

'I have only one other servant and she isn't half as strong as I am,' replied the woman. 'And as for a husband – I have none.'

'I see.'

'I ordered these flowers for Claudia Auditore's birthday.' The woman looked at him.

'That sounds like fun.'

'It will be.' She paused. 'In fact, if you'd like to help me out some more, I'm looking for someone with a bit of class to escort me to the party.'

'Do you think I have enough class?'

She was bolder now. 'Yes! No one in this entire town walks with greater bearing than you, sir. I am sure Claudia's brother, Ezio himself, would be impressed.'

Ezio smiled. 'You flatter me. But what do you know of this Ezio?'

'Claudia – who is a particular friend of mine – thinks the world of him. But he rarely visits her, and from what I can gather he's rather distant.'

Ezio decided it was time to come clean. 'It's true, alas – I have been . . . distant.'

The woman gasped. 'Oh no! *You* are Ezio! I don't believe it. Claudia did say you were expected back. The party's supposed to be a surprise for her. Promise you won't say a word.'

'You'd better tell me who you are now.'

'Oh, of course. I am Angelina Ceresa. Now promise.'

'What will you do to keep me quiet?'

She looked at him archly. 'Oh, I'm sure I can think of several things.'

'I'm longing to hear what they are.'

They had reached the door of Angelina's house by this time. Angelina's elderly housekeeper opened it to them and Ezio placed the box of flowers on a stone bench in the courtyard. He faced Angelina and smiled.

'Now, are you going to tell me?'

'Later.'

'Why not now?'

'*Signore*, I assure you it will be worth the wait.'

Little did either of them know that events would overtake them, and that they would not meet again.

Ezio took his leave and, seeing that the day was drawing in, directed his walk back towards the citadel. As he was approaching the stables he noticed a little girl wandering down the middle of the street, apparently alone. He was about to speak to her when he was interrupted by the sound of frantic shouting and the thunder of horse's hooves. Quicker than thought, he snatched up the child and moved her to the shelter of a doorway. He was in the nick of time, too, as around the corner galloped a powerful war horse, fully harnessed but riderless. In less than hot pursuit, and on foot, came Mario's stable master, an elderly man called Federico, whom Ezio recognized.

'*Torna qui, maledetto cavallo!*' yelled Federico helplessly after the disappearing horse. Seeing Ezio, he said. 'Can you help me please, sir? It's your uncle's favourite steed. I was just about to unsaddle and groom him but something must have scared him; he's very highly strung.'

'Don't worry, I'll try and get him back for you.'

'Thank you, thank you.' Federico mopped his brow. 'I'm getting too old for this.'

'Don't worry. Just stay here and keep an eye on this child – I think she's lost.'

'Surely.'

Ezio raced off after the horse, which he found without difficulty. It had calmed down and was grazing on some hay that had been loaded onto a parked wagon. It baulked slightly when Ezio approached, but then recognized him and didn't run. Ezio laid a comforting hand on its neck and patted it reassuringly before taking its bridle and leading it gently back the way they had come.

On the way, he had the opportunity to do another good deed when he encountered a young woman, frantic with anxiety, who turned out to be the mother of the lost little girl. Ezio explained what had happened, taking care to tone down the degree of danger the little girl had been in. Once he'd told her where the girl was, she ran ahead of him, calling out her child's name – 'Sophia! Sophia!' – and Ezio heard an answering cry of 'Mamma!' Minutes later he had rejoined the little group and handed the reins over to Federico who, thanking him again, begged him not to say anything to Mario. Ezio promised not to and Federico led the horse back to the stables.

The mother was still waiting with her daughter and Ezio turned to them with a smile.

'She wants to say thank you,' said the mother.

'Thank you,' said Sophia dutifully, looking up at him with a mixture of awe and trepidation.

'Stay with your mother in future,' said Ezio kindly. 'Don't leave her like that, *capisco*?'

The little girl nodded mutely.

'We'd be lost without you and your family to watch over us, *signore*,' said the mother.

'We do what we can,' Ezio said, but his thoughts were troubled as he entered the citadel. Even though he was pretty sure he could stand his ground, he wasn't looking forward to his encounter with Machiavelli.

*

There was still time enough before the meeting, so to avoid brooding on the course it might take, and from natural curiosity, Ezio climbed the ramparts to take a closer look at the new cannon Mario had installed and of which he was so proud. There were several of them, all beautifully chased in cast bronze and each with a pile of iron cannonballs neatly stacked beside its wheels. The biggest cannon had barrels ten feet long, and Mario had told him that these weighed as much as 20,000 pounds, but there were also lighter, more easily manoeuvrable culverins interspersed with them. In the towers that punctuated the walls were saker cannon on cast-iron mounts, as well as lightweight falconets on wooden trolleys.

Ezio approached a group of gunners who were clustered round one of the bigger guns.

'Handsome beasts,' he said, running a hand over the elaborately chased decoration around the touch hole.

'Indeed they are, *Messer* Ezio,' said the leader of the group, a rough-hewn master sergeant whom Ezio remembered from his first visit to Monteriggioni as a young man.

'I heard you practising earlier. May I try firing one of these?'

'You can indeed, but we were firing the smaller cannon earlier. These big 'uns are brand new. We don't seem to have got the trick of loading 'em yet, and the master armourer who's supposed to be installing them seems to have taken off.'

'Have you got people looking for him?'

'Indeed we have, sir, but no luck so far.'

'I'll have a look round, too. After all, these things aren't here for decoration and you never know how soon we'll need them.'

Ezio set off, continuing his rounds of the ramparts. He hadn't gone more than another twenty or thirty yards when he heard a loud grunting from a wooden shed that had been erected on the top of one of the towers. Near by, outside, lay a box of tools, and as he approached the grunts resolved themselves into snores.

It was dark and hot inside the shed, and smelled appallingly of stale wine. As his eyes grew accustomed to the dim light, Ezio quickly made out the form of a large man in his none-too-clean shirtsleeves spread-eagled on a pile of straw. He gave the man a gentle kick, but its only effect was to make the man splutter, come half awake, then turn over with his face to the wall.'

'*Salve, Messere,*' Ezio said, jostling the man again, less gently this time, with the toe of his boot.

The man twisted his head round to look at him and opened one eye. 'What is it, friend?'

'We need you to fix the new cannon on the battlements.'

'Not today, chum. First thing.'

'Are you too drunk to do your job? I don't think Captain Mario would be very happy if he got wind of that.'

'No more work today.'

'But it's not that late. Do you know what time it is?'

'No. Don't care either. Make cannon, not clocks.'

Ezio had squatted down to speak to the man, who in turn had pulled himself into a sitting position and was treating Ezio to a gale of his breath, pungent with garlic and cheap Montalcino, as he belched luxuriously. Ezio drew himself to his feet.

'We need those cannon ready to be fired and we need them ready now,' he said. 'Do you want me to find someone else who's more capable than you?'

The man scrambled to his feet. 'Not so fast, friend. No other man's going to lay a hand on my guns.' He leaned on Ezio as he got his breath back. 'You don't know what it's like – some of these soldiers, they got no respect for artillery. New-fangled stuff for a lot of 'em, of course, grant you that, but I ask you. They expect a gun to work like magic, just like that! No sense of coaxing a good performance out of 'em.'

'Can we talk as we walk?' said Ezio. 'Time isn't standing still, you know.'

'Mind you,' the master armourer continued, 'these things we've got here, they're in a class of their own. Nothing but the best for Captain Mario – but they're still pretty simple. I've got hold of a French design for a hand-held gun. They call it a wrought-iron murderer. Very clever. Just think, hand-held cannon. That's the future, chum.'

By now they were approaching the group surrounding the cannon.

'You can call off the hunt,' said Ezio cheerfully. 'Here he is.'

The master sergeant eyed the armourer narrowly. 'Up to it, is he?'

'I may be a little the worse for wear,' retorted the armourer, 'but I am a peaceful man at heart. In these times, encouraging the sleeping warrior in my gut is the only way to stay alive. Therefore it is my duty to drink.' He pushed the sergeant aside. 'Let's see what we've got here . . .'

After examining the cannon for a few moments, the master-armourer rounded on the soldiers. 'What have you been doing? You've been tampering with them, haven't you? Thank God you didn't fire one: you could have got us all killed. They're not ready yet. Got to give the bores a good clean first.'

'Perhaps with you around we won't need cannon after all,' the sergeant told him. 'We'll just get you to breathe on the enemy!'

But the armourer was busy with a cleaning rod and wads of coarse, oily cotton. When he'd finished, he stood up and eased his back.

'There, that's done it,' he said. Turning to Ezio, he

continued, 'Just get these fellows to load her – that's something they can do, though God knows it took 'em long enough to learn – and you can have a go. Look over there on the hill. We set some targets up on a level with this gun. Start by aiming at something on the same level, that way, if the cannon explodes, at least it won't take your head off with it.'

'Sounds reassuring,' said Ezio.

'Just try it, *Messer.* Here's the fuse.'

Ezio placed the slow match on the touch hole. For a long moment nothing happened, then he sprang back as the cannon bucked and roared. Looking across to the targets, he could see that his ball had shattered one of them.

'Well done,' said the armourer. '*Perfetto!* At least one person here, apart from me, knows how to shoot.'

Ezio had the men reload and fired again, but this time he missed.

'Can't win 'em all,' said the armourer. 'Come back at dawn. We'll be practising again then and it'll give you a chance to get your eye in.'

'I will,' said Ezio, little realizing that when he next fired a cannon, it would be in deadly earnest.

5

When Ezio entered the great hall of Mario's citadel, the shadows of evening were already gathering and servants were beginning to light torches and candles to dispel the gloom. The gloom accorded with Ezio's increasingly sombre mood as the hour of the meeting approached.

So wrapped up in his own thoughts was he that he didn't at first notice the person hovering by the massive fireplace, her slight but strong figure dwarfed by the giant caryatids that flanked the chimney. So he was startled when the woman approached him and touched his arm. As soon as he recognized her, his features softened into an expression of pure pleasure.

'*Buonasera*, Ezio,' she said, a little shyly for her, he thought.

'*Buonasera*, Caterina,' he replied, bowing to the Countess of Forlì. Their former intimacy was some way in the past, though neither of them had forgotten it, and when she'd touched his arm, both of them, Ezio thought, had felt the chemistry of the moment. 'Claudia told me you were here, and I have been looking forward to seeing you. But...' he hesitated.

'Monteriggioni is far from Forlì, and . . .'

'You needn't flatter yourself that I have come all this way just on your account,' she said with a trace of her former sharpness, though he could see by her smile that she was not entirely serious. It was then he realized he was still drawn to this fiercely independent and dangerous woman.

'I am always willing to be of service to you, *Madonna* – in any way I can.' He meant it.

'Some ways are harder than others,' she countered, and now there was a tough note in her voice.

'What is it?'

'It is not a simple matter,' continued Caterina Sforza. 'I come in search of an alliance.'

'Tell me more.'

'I am afraid your work is not over yet, Ezio. The papal armies are marching on Forlì. My dominion is small, but fortunately – or unfortunately for me – it lies in an area of the utmost strategic importance to whomever controls it.'

'And you desire my help?'

'My forces on their own are weak – your *condottieri* would be a great asset to my cause.'

'This is something I will have to discuss with Mario.'

'He will not refuse me.'

'And nor will I.'

'By helping me you will not just be doing me a good deed, you will be taking a stand against the forces of

43

evil against which we have always been united.'

As they spoke, Mario appeared. 'Ezio, *Contessa*, we are gathered and await you,' he said, his face unusually serious.

'We will talk more of this,' Ezio told her. 'I am bidden to a meeting which my uncle has convened. I am expected to explain myself, I think. But let us arrange to see each other afterwards.'

'The meeting concerns me, too,' said Caterina. 'Shall we go in?'

6

The room was very familiar to Ezio. There, on the now-exposed inner wall, the pages of the Great Codex were arranged in order. The desk, usually littered with maps, was cleared, and around it, on severe straight-backed chairs of dark wood, sat those members of the Assassin Brotherhood who had gathered at Monteriggioni, together with those of the Auditore family who were privy to its cause. Mario sat behind his desk, and at one end sat the sober, dark-suited man, still young looking, but with deep lines of thought etched into his forehead, who had become one of Ezio's closest associates, as well as one of his most unremitting critics: Niccolò Machiavelli. The two men nodded guardedly at one another as Ezio greeted Claudia and his mother, Maria Auditore, matriarch of the family since his father's death. Maria hugged her only surviving son hard, as if her life depended on it, and looked at him with shining eyes as he broke free and took a seat near Caterina and opposite Machiavelli, who now rose and looked questioningly at him. Clearly there was going to be no polite prologue to the matter in hand.

'First, perhaps, I owe you an apology,' began Machiavelli. 'I was not present in the vault and urgent business took me to Florence before I could truly analyse what happened there. Mario has given us his account, but yours alone can be the full one.'

Ezio rose and spoke simply and directly. 'I entered the Vatican, where I encountered Rodrigo Borgia, Pope Alexander VI, and confronted him. He was in possession of one of the Pieces of Eden, the Staff, and used it against me. I managed to defeat him and, using the combined powers of the Apple and the Staff, gained access to the secret vault, leaving him outside. He was in despair and begged me to kill him. I would not.' Ezio paused.

'What then?' prompted Machiavelli as the others watched silently.

'Within the vault were many strange things – things not dreamt of in our world.' Visibly moved, Ezio forced himself to continue in level tones. 'A vision of the goddess Minerva appeared to me. She told of a terrible tragedy that would befall mankind at some future time, but she also spoke of lost temples which may, when found, aid us and lead us to a kind of redemption. She appeared to invoke a phantom, which had some close connection with me, but what that was I cannot tell. After her warning and predictions, she vanished. I emerged to see the Pope dying – or so it seemed; he appeared to have taken poison. Later something compelled me to return. I seized the Apple, but the Staff, which may have been another Piece of Eden, was swallowed up by the earth. I am glad of it: the Apple alone, which I have given in custody to Mario, is already more than I personally wish to have responsibility for.'

'Amazing!' cried Caterina.

'I cannot imagine such wonders,' added Claudia.

'So the vault did not house the terrible weapon we feared – or at any rate, the Templars did not gain control of it. This at least is good news,' said Machiavelli evenly.

'What of this goddess – Minerva?' Claudia asked. 'Did she appear . . . like us?'

'Her appearance was human, and also superhuman,' Ezio said. 'Her words proved that she belonged to a race far older and greater than ours. The rest of her kind died many centuries ago. She had been waiting for that moment for a long time. I wish I had the words to describe the magic she performed.'

'What are these temples she spoke of?' put in Mario.

'I know not.'

'Did she say we should search for them? How do we know what to look for?'

'Perhaps we should . . . perhaps the quest will show us the way.'

'The quest must be undertaken,' said Machiavelli crisply. 'But we must clear the path for it first. Tell us of the Pope. He did not die, you say?'

'When I returned to the vault, his cope lay on the chapel floor. He himself had disappeared.'

'Had he made any promises? Had he shown repentance?'

'Neither. He was bent on gaining the Power. When he saw he was not going to get it, he collapsed.'

'And you left him to die.'

'I would not be the one to kill him.'

'You should have done so.'

'I am not here to debate the past. I stand by my decision. Now, we should discuss the future. What we are to do.'

'What we are to do is made all the more urgent by your failure to finish off the Templar leader when you had the chance.' Machiavelli breathed hard, but then relaxed a little. 'All right, Ezio. You know in what high esteem we all hold you. We would not have got anything like this far without the twenty years' devotion you have shown to the Assassin Brotherhood and our Creed. And a part of me applauds you for not having killed when you deemed it unnecessary to do so. That is also in keeping with our code of honour. But you misjudged, my friend, and that means we have an immediate and dangerous task ahead of us.' He paused, scanning the assembled company with eagle eyes. 'Our spies in Rome report that Rodrigo is indeed a reduced threat. He is at least somewhat broken in spirit. There is a saying that it is less dangerous to do battle with a lion's whelp than with an old, dying lion; but in the case of the Borgia the position is quite otherwise. Rodrigo's son, Cesare, is the man we must match ourselves against now. Armed with the vast fortune the Borgia have amassed by fair means and foul – but mostly foul' – here Machiavelli allowed himself a wry smile – 'he heads a large army of highly trained troops, and with it he intends to take over all Italy – the whole peninsula – and he does not intend to stop at the borders of the Kingdom of Naples.'

'He would never dare – he could never do it!' Mario roared.

'He would and he could,' snapped Machiavelli. 'He is evil through and through, and as dedicated a Templar as his father the Pope ever was, but he is also a fine though utterly ruthless soldier. He always wanted to be a soldier, even after his father made him Cardinal of Valencia when he was only seventeen years old. As we all know he resigned from that post, making him the first cardinal in the Church's history to do so. The Borgia treat our country and the Vatican as if they were their own private fiefdom. Cesare's plan now is to crush the north first, to subdue the Romagna and isolate Venice. He also intends to extirpate and destroy all of us remaining Assassins, since he knows that in the end we are the only people who can stop him. "Aut Cesar, Aut Nihil" – that's his motto – "either you're with me or you're dead". And do you know I think the madman actually believes it.'

'My uncle mentioned a sister,' Ezio began.

Machiavelli turned to him. 'Yes. Lucrezia. She and Cesare are . . . how shall I say? Very close. They are a very close-knit family; when they are not killing those other brothers and sisters, husbands and wives, whom they find inconvenient to them, they are . . . coupling with each other.'

Maria Auditore could not suppress a cry of disgust.

'We must approach them with all the caution we would use to approach a nest of vipers,' Machiavelli concluded. 'And God knows where and how soon they will next strike.' He paused and drank half a glass of wine. 'And now, Mario, I leave you. Ezio, we will meet again soon, I trust.'

'You're leaving this evening?'

'Time is of the essence, good Mario. I ride for Rome tonight. Farewell.'

The room was silent once Machiavelli had left. After a long pause, Ezio said bitterly, 'He blames me for not killing Rodrigo when I had the chance.' He looked round at them. 'You all do.'

'Any of us might have made the decision you made,' said his mother. 'You were sure he was dying.'

Mario came and put an arm round his shoulders. 'Machiavelli knows your value; we all do. And even with the Pope out of the way, we'd still have had to deal with his brood.'

'But if I had cut off the head, could the body have survived?'

'We must deal with the situation as it is, good Ezio, not with it as it might have been.' Mario clapped him on the back. 'And now, as we are in for a busy day tomorrow, I suggest we dine and prepare for an early night!'

Caterina's eyes met Ezio's. Did he imagine it, or was there a flicker of lust there? He shrugged inwardly. Perhaps he was just imagining it.

7

Ezio ate lightly – just *pollo ripieno* with roasted vegetables – and he drank his Chianti cut half and half
with water. There was little conversation at dinner, and
he answered his mother's string of questions politely
but laconically. After all the tension that had mounted
in anticipation of the meeting, and which had now
melted away, he was very tired. He had barely had a
chance to rest since leaving Rome, and it looked now
as if it would be a long time still before he could realize
his long-cherished ambition of spending some time
back in his old home in Florence, reading and walking
in the surrounding gentle hills.

As soon as he decently could, Ezio made his excuses
to the company and set off for his bedroom, a large,
quiet, dimly lit space on one of the upper floors, with
a view across the countryside rather than the town.
Once he'd reached it and dismissed the servant, he let
go of the steeliness that had supported him throughout the day; his body slumped, his shoulders sagged
and his walk eased. His movements were slow and
deliberate. He moved across the room to where the
servant had already drawn him a bath. As he approached

it, he tugged at his boots and took off his clothes and, once naked, he stood for a moment, his clothes bundled in his hands, before a full-length mirror on a stand near the copper tub. He looked at his reflection with weary eyes. Where had the last four long decades gone? He straightened. He was older, stronger even, certainly wiser, but he could not deny the profound fatigue he felt.

Ezio threw his clothes onto the bed. Under it, in a locked elm chest, were the secret Codex weapons that Leonardo da Vinci had fashioned for him. He would check them over first thing in the morning, after the council of war he'd be holding with his uncle. The original Hidden Blade never left him except when he was naked, and even then he kept it within arm's reach. He wore it always; it had become part of his body.

Sighing with relief, Ezio slipped into the bath. Immersed up to his neck in the hot water, breathing in the gently scented steam, he closed his eyes and let out a long, slow breath of relief. Peace at last. He had better make the most of the few short hours he had of it.

He had just dozed off and begun to dream when the softest of noises – the door opening and closing behind its heavy, tapestry hanging – caused him to wake. He was instantly alert, like a wild animal. Silently his hand sought the blade and with a practised movement he attached it to his wrist. Then, in one fluid motion, he turned and stood upright in the tub, poised for action and looking in the direction of the door.

'Well,' said Caterina, grinning as she approached. 'You certainly haven't lost any inches with the years.'

'You have the advantage of me, *Contessa*,' smiled Ezio. 'You are fully clothed.'

'I expect we could arrange something to change that. But I am waiting.'

'Waiting for what?'

'For you to say that you don't really need to see for yourself. For you to say that you are sure, even without seeing my naked body, that Nature has been as kind to me, if not kinder, as she has been to you.' Her grin broadened at Ezio's confusion. 'But I remember you were never as good at paying compliments as you were at ridding the world of Templars.'

'Come here!'

He drew her to him, pulling at the girdle of her skirt as her fingers flew first to the blade, detaching it, and then to the laces of her bodice. Seconds later he had lifted her into the bath with him, their lips glued to one another's and their naked limbs entwined.

They did not linger long in the bath, but soon got out, drying each other on the rough linen towels the servant had left. Caterina had brought a phial of scented massage oil with her and drew it from a pocket in her dress.

'Now, lie on the bed,' she said. 'I want to make sure you are good and ready for me.'

'Surely you can see that I am.'

'Indulge me. Indulge yourself.'

Ezio smiled. This was better than sleep. Sleep could wait.

Sleep, Ezio found, was obliged to wait three hours, at which point Caterina curled up in his arms. She fell asleep before him and he watched her for a while. Nature had indeed been kind to her. Her slender yet curvaceous body, with its narrow hips, broad shoulders and small but perfect breasts, was still that of a twenty-year-old, and her cloud of fine light red hair that tickled his chest as she laid her head on it carried the same scent that had driven him wild all those years ago. Once or twice in the depths of the night, he woke to find he had rolled away from her, and when he took her in his arms again, she nestled up to him without waking, giving a tiny sigh of joy and closing her hand around his forearm. Ezio wondered later if this hadn't been the best night of love in his life.

They overslept, of course, but Ezio was not about to forego another bout in favour of cannon practice, even though a part of his mind reproved him for this. In the background he could distantly hear the sounds of marching – clattering men moving at a running march – and shouted orders, followed by the boom of cannon.

'Target practice with the new cannon,' said Ezio when, for a moment, Caterina stopped and looked at him quizzically. 'Manoeuvres. Mario's a hard taskmaster.'

The heavy brocade curtains across the windows shut out most of the light and the room remained cocooned in comfortable dimness; no servant came to disturb them. Soon, Caterina's moans of pleasure drowned out any other noise to his ear. His hands tightened around her strong buttocks, and she was pulling him up urgently towards her when their lovemaking was interrupted by more than just the roar of cannon.

Suddenly the peace and the softness of the room was shattered. The windows blew away with a mighty roar, taking a part of the stone outer wall with them, as a gigantic cannonball smashed in and landed, boiling hot, inches from the bed. The floor sagged under its weight.

Ezio had instinctively thrown himself protectively over Caterina at the first sign of danger, and in that moment the lovers transformed themselves into professionals and colleagues – if they were to remain lovers, they first had to survive.

They leapt from the bed, throwing on their clothes. Ezio noticed that apart from the delicious phial of oil, Caterina touted a very useful jagged-edged dagger beneath her skirts.

'What the hell . . . ?' Ezio cried.

'Go and find Mario,' said Caterina urgently.

Another ball flew in, shattering the beams over their recently vacated bed and smashing it to pieces.

'My troops are in the main courtyard,' said Caterina.

'I'll find them and get around the back of the citadel to see if we can't outflank them. Tell Mario that's what I've decided.'

'Thank you,' said Ezio. 'Stay out of sight.'

'I wish I'd had time to change,' she said, laughing. 'We'd better book into an *albergo* next time, eh?'

'Let's make damned sure there *is* a next time,' rejoined Ezio, laughing too, but nervously, as he strapped on his sword.

'You bet! *Arrivederci!*' cried Caterina, rushing from the room without forgetting to blow him a kiss.

He looked at the ruins of the bed. The Codex weapons – the Double Blade, the Poison Blade and the Pistol – were buried beneath it, in all probability destroyed. At least he still had his Hidden Blade. Even *in extremis* he would never forget that – his murdered father's last bequest.

8

Ezio had no idea what time it was, but experience told him attacks usually began at dawn, when the victims were still confused and wiping the sleep from their eyes. He was lucky that his training had bestowed on him, even having reached the age of forty, the alertness and agility of a wildcat.

Once outside and on the battlements he scanned the surrounding landscape. The town below him was in flames in many quarters. He saw the tailor's shop burning, and Angelina's house too. There would be no birthday party for poor Claudia tonight.

He ducked as another cannonball smashed into the ramparts. For God's Love, what guns were their attackers bringing to bear? How could they reload and fire so fast? And who was behind this?

Through the smoke and dust he made out Mario, dodging crumbling masonry as he came towards him. Ezio leapt off the ramparts, landing in a crouch near Mario, and ran to join him.

'Uncle! *Che diavolo . . . ?*'

Mario spat. 'They've caught us on the back foot. It's the Borgia!'

'*Fottere!*'

'We underestimated Cesare. They must have massed to the east during the night.'

'What must we do?'

'The main thing is to get all the townspeople clear – those who haven't already been killed. We've got to hold them off until we've done that. If they take the town with the people still inside it, they'll kill them all: everyone in Monteriggioni is either an Assassin or an Assassin's abettor, in their eyes.'

'I know the route out. Leave it to me.'

'Good man. I'll muster our defenders and give them everything we've got.' Mario paused. 'Look. Let's take them on first. You go and command the cannon on the ramparts.'

'And you?'

'I'll lead a frontal assault. Take the battle to the bastards.'

'Caterina is going to try to take her forces around the flank.'

'Good. Then we are in with a chance. Now hurry!'

'Wait!'

'What is it?'

Ezio lowered his voice. 'Where is the Apple?' He did not tell his uncle that the Codex weapons had been destroyed by one of the first cannonades. Inwardly he prayed that, by some miracle, his path would cross Leonardo's again, for he did not doubt that the Master

59

of all the arts and sciences would help him reconstruct them, in case of need. In the meantime, he had the Hidden Blade still, and he was a past master in the use of conventional weapons.

'The Apple is safe,' Mario reassured him. 'Now go. And if you see that the Borgia show the slightest chance of breaching the walls, shift your attention to evacuating the town. Do you understand?'

'*Si, zio mio.*'

Mario placed his hands on Ezio's shoulders and looked at him gravely for a long moment. 'Our fate is only partially in our own hands. There is only a certain amount of it that we can control. But never forget – *never* forget, nephew – that whatever happens to you or me this day, there is never a feather lost by a sparrow that is not brushed away by the finger of God.'

'I understand, *Capitano.*'

There was a brief moment of silence between them, then Mario extended his hand.

'*Insieme per la vittoria!*'

Ezio took his uncle's hand in his and wrung it fervently. '*Insieme!*'

As Mario turned to go, Ezio said, '*Capitano*, be careful.'

Mario nodded grimly. 'I'll do my best. And you – take my best horse and get to the outer walls as fast as you can.' He drew his sword and, with a great war cry to rally his men, ran towards the foe.

Ezio watched him briefly, then ran towards the stable, where the old groom whose runaway horse he'd saved the day before was waiting. The huge chestnut was saddled and ready.

'*Maestro* Mario had already sent orders,' the old man said. 'I may be past my prime, but no one could ever accuse me of being inefficient. *Ma attenzione*, this horse is full of spirit!'

'I brought him to heel yesterday. He'll know me today.'

'True enough. *Buona fortuna*. We all depend on you.'

Ezio swung himself into the saddle and urged the eager horse towards the outer walls.

He rode through the already devastated town. The tailor was dead and mutilated in front of his shop — what harm had he ever done anyone? — And Angelina was weeping in front of her burned-down house; what was the point of not showing her pity?

War — that was all. Brutalizing and cruel. Vicious and infantile. Ezio's gorge rose at it.

Freedom, mercy and love — these were the only things worth fighting and killing for — and these were the prime elements of the Assassin's Creed. Of the Brotherhood.

As Ezio rode forth, he encountered scenes of terrible desolation. Devastation and chaos surrounded him as his horse carried him through the burning town.

'My children! Where are my children?!' a young mother screamed as he passed by, helplessly.

'Just pack what you can and let's get out of here.' A man's voice rang out.

'Shit, my leg! My leg's been shot away!' yelled a townsman.

'How can we escape?' shrieked several people, rushing around in panic.

'I can't find my mother! Mamma! Mamma!' rang out the voice of a little child.

Ezio had to steel his heart. He could not go to the rescue of individuals – there was no time – but if he could organize the defence properly, more people would be saved than lost.

'*Aiuto! Aiuto!*' a teenaged girl, mobbed by Borgia troops, cried out as they forced her down.

Ezio rode grimly on. He would kill them. Kill them all, if he could. Who was this heartless Cesare Borgia? Could he be worse than the Pope? Could there ever be a more evil Templar?

'Water! Water! Bring water!' a man's voice bellowed despairingly. 'Everything is burning!'

'Where are you, please, oh God? Where are you, Marcello?' a woman's voice sang out.

Ezio rode on, his mouth set, but the cries for help still rang in his ears: '*Comè usciamo di qui?*'

'Run! Run!' Voices were raised against the sound of the bombardment. There were screams and sobs, desperate pleas for help, for a means of getting out of the beleaguered town as the pitiless Borgia troops piled cannonade upon cannonade.

Please God they do not breach the walls before our own guns have been brought into play, Ezio thought, and though he could hear the explosions as the sakers and falconets spat shot at the attackers, he could not yet hear the boom of the big guns he had encountered the day before, the only cannon that might be able to smash the huge wooden siege towers the Borgia forces were trundling towards the city walls.

He goaded the chestnut up the ramp to the walls and leapt off as he reached the point where he had last seen the drunken master armourer beside the ten-foot cannon. He was perfectly sober now and directing gunners to bring the gun to bear on a tower which their highly trained attackers were pushing slowly but surely towards the ramparts. Ezio could see that its top matched the height of the crenellations at the top of the walls.

'The wretches,' he muttered. But how could anyone have predicted the speed and – even Ezio had to admit this to himself – masterly perfection of the attack?

'Fire!' yelled the grizzled master sergeant who was in command of the first big gun. The great cannon boomed and sprang back, but the ball was just wide and only nicked a splattering of wood off a corner of the siege tower's roof.

'Try to hit the fucking towers, you fools!' yelled the sergeant.

'Sir, we need more ammunition!'

'Then go down to the stores and make it snappy! Look! They're storming the gate!'

Meanwhile the other cannon bellowed and spat. Ezio was pleased to see a tranche of attackers smashed into a sea of blood and bone.

'Reload!' yelled the sergeant. 'Fire again at my command!'

'Wait until the tower's closer,' ordered Ezio, 'then aim for the bottom. That'll bring the whole thing down. Our crossbowmen can finish off any survivors.'

'Yes, sir.'

The armourer came up. 'You learn tactics fast,' he said to Ezio.

'Instinct.'

'Good instinct's worth a hundred men in the field,' returned the armourer. 'But you missed target practice this morning. No excuse for that.'

'And what about you?' said Ezio.

'Come on,' grinned the armourer, 'we've got another of these cannon covering the left flank, and the commander of its gun crew is dead: crossbow bolt bang in his forehead. Dead before he hit the ground. You take over. I've got my work cut out for me making sure none of the guns overheats or cracks.'

'All right.'

'But watch how you aim. Your girlfriend's troops are out there fighting the Borgia. We wouldn't want to take any of them out.'

'What girlfriend?'

The armourer winked. 'Do me a favour, Ezio. This is a very small town.'

Ezio made his way to the second big gun. A gunner was sponging it down to cool it after firing as another was muzzle-loading it with tamped-down powder and a 50-pound iron ball. A third man prepared the slow match, lighting it at both ends so there would be no delay if one end accidentally burnt out at the moment of touch.

'Let's go,' said Ezio as he came up.

'*Signore!*'

He scanned the field beyond the wall. The green grass was splattered with blood, and the fallen lay strewn among the wheatsheaves. He could see the yellow, black and blue livery of Caterina's men interspersed with the mulberry and yellow of the Borgia tunics.

'Get some of the smaller guns to pick out those individuals. Tell them to aim for the black and gold,' Ezio snapped. 'And let's get this gun trained on the siege tower over there. It's getting too close for comfort; we need to take it out.'

The gunners heaved the cannon round and dipped the barrel so that it was aimed at the base of the approaching tower, which was no more than fifty yards from the walls by now.

Ezio was busy directing aim when a nearby saker was hit. It exploded, flinging red-hot bronze in every direction. Ezio's gunner, who was inches away from him, had his head and shoulders sliced off by shards. The man's arms fell to the floor, and the remains of his body followed suit, spewing blood like a fountain. The pungent smell of burnt meat filled Ezio's nostrils as he leapt to take the gunner's place.

'Keep your nerve,' he yelled to the rest of the crew. He squinted along the gunsight. 'Steady now . . . and . . . *fire*!'

The cannon thundered as Ezio jumped to one side and watched as the ball smashed into the base of the tower. Had that one shot been enough? The tower lurched badly, seemed to steady, and then – by God! – crashed to the earth, seemingly in slow motion, throwing some of the men it contained clear whilst crushing others. The screams of the wounded mules that had been dragging it forward added to the cacophony of panic and death – the attendants of all battles. Ezio watched as Caterina's troops moved in swiftly to wipe out the wounded and bemused Borgia survivors. She herself was at the head, her silver breastplate flashing in the cold sunlight. Ezio saw her plunge her sword straight through a Borgia captain's right eye and into his brain. The soldier's body squirmed in the agony of death for a long moment, pivoted by its point, his hands uselessly trying to clutch the firmly held blade and pull it out.

There was no time to take pleasure in their triumph or rest on their laurels, though. Looking down over the ramparts, Ezio could see Borgia troops bringing massive battering rams up to the main gate, and at the same time he heard Caterina's warning cry. We'll send a thousand men to Forlì to help her against this bastard Cesare, he said to himself.

'If they get in, they'll kill us all,' said a voice at his shoulder. Ezio turned to see the old master sergeant. He had lost his helmet and an ugly head wound seeped blood.

'We must get the people out. Now.'

'Some have already been able to leave, but those less able to help themselves are stranded.'

'I'll deal with it,' said Ezio, recalling Mario's admonition. 'Take over here, Ruggiero. Look! Over there! They've got a tower right up to the ramparts! Their men are storming the wall! Get some more of our men over there before they overpower us.'

'Sir!' And the sergeant was gone, yelling orders, at the head of a platoon that gathered swiftly at his command and which, within seconds, was locked in hand-to-hand combat with the vicious Borgia mercenaries.

Ezio, sword in hand and slashing his way past the oncoming enemy troops, made his way down to the town. Quickly organizing a group of Caterina's men who had been forced to retreat into the town as the tide of battle turned once more in the Borgia's favour, he did his best to round up the remaining vulnerable townspeople and shepherd them into the relative safety of the citadel. As he completed the task, Caterina joined him.

'What news?' he asked her.

'Bad news,' she rejoined. 'They've smashed down the main gate. They're moving into the town.'

'Then we haven't a minute to lose. We must all retreat into the citadel.'

'I'll muster the rest of my men.'

'Come quickly. Have you seen Mario?'

'He was fighting outside the walls.'

'And the others?'

'Your mother and sister are already in the citadel. They've been guiding the citizens through the escape tunnel that leads to the north, beyond the walls, and safety.'

'Good. I must go to them. Join us as fast as you can. We'll have to fall back.'

'Kill them all,' yelled a Borgia sergeant as he rounded the corner at the head of a small troop of men. All held bloodied swords aloft, and one man brandished a pike on which he had stuck the head of a girl. Ezio's throat went dry as he recognized the face – it was Angelina's. With a roar, he fell on the Borgia soldiers.

Six against one was nothing to him. Slicing and stabbing, within seconds he stood amidst a circle of maimed and dying men, his chest heaving as he breathed hard with the exertion

The blood cleared from his eyes. Caterina was gone. Wiping sweat, blood and grime from his face, he made his way back up to the citadel, telling the men guarding it to open up only to Mario and Caterina. He climbed the inner tower and looked down over the burning town.

Apart from the crackle of the flames and the isolated moans of the wounded and dying, things had gone ominously quiet.

9

The quiet did not last for long, however. Just as Ezio was checking that the cannon on the ramparts were correctly aligned and loaded, a mighty explosion threw the citadel's massive wooden gates aside, hurling its defenders backwards into the courtyard, below where Ezio stood on the battlements, and killing many.

As the smoke and dust cleared, Ezio made out a group of people standing in the gateway. His Uncle Mario appeared to be at their head, but evidently something was badly wrong. His face was grey and drained of blood. He also looked far older than his sixty-two years. His eyes locked with Ezio's as his nephew leapt down from the battlements to confront the new danger. Mario fell to his knees, then onto his face. He struggled to rise, but a long, thin, thrusting sword – a Bilbao – projected from between his shoulder blades. The young man behind him shoved him back into the gravel with the toe of his black boot and a trail of blood formed at the corner of the old man's mouth.

The young man was dressed in black, and a black mask partially covered his vicious face. Ezio recognized the pustules of the New Disease on the man's skin. He shuddered inwardly. There was no doubt whom he was confronting.

Flanking the man in black were two others, both in early middle age; and a beautiful blonde woman with cruel lips. Another man, also dressed in black, stood apart and a little to one side. He held a bloodstained falchion in his right hand, and in his left he held a chain, which was attached to a heavy collar around Caterina Sforza's neck, who was bound and gagged. Her eyes flashed unquenchable rage and defiance. Ezio's heart stopped – he couldn't believe that just this morning he'd held her once again, and now she'd been captured by the vile Borgia leader. How could this be happening? His eyes met hers for an instant across the courtyard, sending her a promise that she would not be a prisoner for long.

With no time to figure out all that was unfolding around him, Ezio's soldier's instinct took control. He must act now or lose everything. He strode forward, closed his eyes and stepped off the battlement, his cape flowing out behind him – it was a leap of faith to the courtyard below. With practised grace he landed on his feet and stood tall to confront his enemies, cold determination etched on his face.

The master armourer staggered up, struggling with a wounded leg, and stood by Ezio. 'Who are these people?' he breathed.

'Oh,' said the young man in black, 'we haven't

introduced ourselves. How remiss of us. But I course I know you, Ezio Auditore, if only by repute. Such a pleasure. At last I shall be able to remove the biggest thorn in my side. After your dear uncle, of course.'

'Step back from him, Cesare!'

One eyebrow went up and the dark eyes blazed in the handsome, flawed face. 'Oh, how flattered I am that you've guessed my name correctly. But let me present my sister, Lucrezia.' He turned to nuzzle the blonde in a most unbrotherly way as she squeezed his arm and pressed her lips dangerously close to his mouth. 'And my close associates Juan Borgia, cousin, friend and banker; my dear French ally, General Octavien de Valois, and, last but not least, my indispensable right-hand man, Micheletto da Corella. What would I do without my friends?'

'And your father's money.'

'Bad joke, my friend.'

As Cesare spoke, his troops moved like ghosts into the citadel. Ezio was powerless to stop them as his own men – hopelessly outnumbered – were swiftly overcome and disarmed.

'But I'm a good soldier, and part of the fun is choosing efficient support,' Cesare continued. 'I must admit I didn't think you'd be quite such a pushover. But of course, you aren't getting any younger, are you?'

'I'll kill you,' Ezio said evenly. 'I'll wipe you and your kind from the face of the earth.'

'Not today you won't,' said Cesare, smiling. 'And just look what I've got, courtesy of your uncle.' A gloved hand delved into a pouch at his side and from it he produced, to Ezio's horror, the Apple!

'Useful gadget,' said Cesare, smiling thinly. 'Leonardo da Vinci, my new military advisor, tells me he already knows quite a lot about it, so I'm hoping he'll enlighten me further, which I'm sure he will if he wants to keep his head on his shoulders. Artists! Ten a penny, as I'm sure you'd agree.'

Lucrezia sniggered unfeelingly at this.

Ezio looked across at his old friend, but da Vinci refused to meet his gaze. On the floor, Mario stirred and groaned. Cesare pushed his face into the ground with his boot and produced a gun – it was a new design, as Ezio immediately recognized, regretting again the destruction of most of his Codex weapons at the out-set of the attack.

'That's not a matchlock,' said the armourer keenly.

'It's a wheel-lock,' said Cesare. 'You're clearly no fool,' he added, addressing the armourer. 'It's much more predictable and efficient than the old guns. Leonardo designed it for me. Reloads fast, too. Would you like a demonstration?'

'Indeed!' the armourer replied, his professional interest overcoming any other instinct.

'By all means,' said Cesare, levelling the pistol at him and shooting him dead. 'Reload, please,' he continued, passing the gun to General Octavien and producing its twin from his belt. 'We've had so much bloodshed,' he went on, 'so it's distressing to reflect that a little more cleansing is in order. Never mind. Ezio, I'd like you to take this in the spirit it's meant – from my family to yours.'

Stooping slightly and placing one foot in the centre of Mario's back, he drew the sword out, letting the blood ooze forth. Mario's eyes went wide with pain as he struggled to crawl towards his nephew.

Cesare leaned forward and fired the pistol at point-blank range into the back of Mario's cranium, which burst apart.

'No!' shouted Ezio as the memory of the brutal murder of his father and brothers flashed through his mind. 'No!' He lunged towards Cesare, the agony of loss surging through him uncontrollably.

As Ezio leapt forward, General Octavien, having reloaded the gun. Ezio staggered back, choking, and the world went black.

10

By the time Ezio came to, the tide of battle had turned again and the Borgia attackers had been chased back outside the walls of the citadel. He found himself being dragged to safety as the soldiers who had retaken the *rocca* closed the broken gate with a barricade, gathered all the remaining citizens of Monteriggioni within its walls and began organizing their escape to the countryside beyond. There was no knowing how long they could hold out against the determined forces of the Borgia, whose strength seemed limitless.

All this Ezio learned from the grizzled master sergeant as he was recovering.

'Stay still, my Lord.'

'Where am I?'

'On a stretcher. We're taking you to the sanctuary. The inner sanctum. No one will reach there.'

'Put me down. I can walk.'

'We have to dress that wound.'

Ignoring him, Ezio shouted an order at the stretcher-bearers. But when he stood up his head reeled.

'I cannot fight like this.'

'Oh God, here they come again,' bellowed the sergeant as a siege tower crashed into the upper castellations of the citadel, disgorging yet another fresh troop of Borgia soldiers.

Ezio turned to face them, his head slowly clearing from the darkness, his steely self-control overcoming the searing pain of the gunshot wound. Assassin *condottieri* quickly surrounded him and fought off Cesare's men. They managed to beat a retreat with few casualties, but as they made their way into the inner vastness of the castle, Claudia shouted from a doorway, eager to hear of her brother's well-being. As she stepped into the open, a Borgia captain rushed towards her, bloodied sword in his hand. Ezio looked on in horror, but recovered his composure enough to yell at his men. Two Assassin fighters ran towards Ezio's sister, only just managing to put themselves between her and the flashing blade of the Borgia murderer. Sparks shot from the contact of the three blades as both Assassins raised their swords simultaneously to block the killing blow. Claudia stumbled to the ground, her mouth open in a silent scream. The stronger of the Assassin soldiers, the master sergeant, pushed the enemy's sword skywards, locking the hilts at the hand-guards, while the other Assassin pulled back his blade and stabbed forward into the guts of the Borgia captain. Claudia regained her composure and rose slowly to her feet. Safely in the fold of the Assassin troop, she rushed towards Ezio, ripping a strip of cotton from her skirts and pressing it to his shoulder; the white cloth quickly bloomed red with blood from the wound.

'Shit! Don't take risks like that!' Ezio told her, thanking the sergeant as his men pushed the enemy back, hurling some from the high battlements while others fled.

'We must get you inside the sanctuary,' cried Claudia. 'Come on!'

Ezio allowed himself to be carried again – he had lost a lot of blood. In the meantime, the remaining citizens of the town, who had not yet been able to escape, crowded round them. Monteriggioni itself was deserted and under the complete control of the Borgia force. Only the citadel remained in Assassin hands.

Finally they reached their goal: the cavernous fortified room beneath the castle's northern wall, linked to the main building by a secret passage leading from Mario's library. But only in the nick of time. One of their men, a Venetian thief called Paganino who had once been under Antonio de Magianis's control, was in the act of closing the secret door to the stairwell as the last of the fugitives passed through it.

'We thought you had been killed, *Ser* Ezio!' he cried.

'They haven't got me yet,' returned Ezio grimly.

'I don't know what to do. Where does this passage lead?'

'To the north, outside the walls.'

'So it's true. We always thought it was a legend.'

'Well, now you know better,' said Ezio, looking at the man and wondering if, in the heat of the moment, he had said too much to a man he knew little of. He ordered his sergeant to close the door, but at the last moment Paganino slipped through it, back to the main building.

'Where are you going?'

'I have to help the defenders. Don't worry, I'll lead them back this way.'

'I must bolt this door behind us. If you don't come now you are on your own.'

'I'll manage, sir. I always do.'

'Then go with God. I must ensure the safety of these people.'

Ezio took stock of the crowd gathered in the sanctuary. In the gloom he could make out amongst the fugitives the features not only of Claudia, but of his mother. He breathed an inward sigh of relief.

'There is no time to be lost,' he told them, jamming the door shut behind him with a sizeable iron bar.

Ezio's mother and sister quickly dressed and bandaged his wound properly, and got him to his feet, then Ezio directed the master sergeant to twist the hidden lever that had been built into the statue of the Master Assassin, Leonius, which stood by the side of the giant chimney piece at the centre of the northern wall of the sanctuary. The concealed door swung open, revealing the corridor through which the people could escape to the safety of the countryside half a mile beyond the city limits.

Claudia and Maria stood by the entrance, shepherding townsfolk through it. The master sergeant had gone ahead with a platoon, bearing torches, to guide and protect the refugees as they made their escape.

'*Hurry!*' Ezio urged the citizens as they entered the dark maw of the tunnel. 'Don't panic. Be quick but don't run. We don't want a stampede in the tunnel.'

'And what of us? What of Mario?' asked his mother.

'Mario – how can I tell you this? – Mario has been killed. I want you and Claudia to make your way home to Florence.'

'Mario dead?' cried Maria.

'What is there in Florence for us?' asked Claudia.

Ezio spread his hands. 'Our home. Lorenzo de' Medici and his son undertook to restore the Auditore mansion to us, and they were as good as their word. Now the city is in the control of the *Signoria* again, and I know that Governor Soderini watches over it well. Go home. Put yourselves in the care of Paola and Annetta. I will join you as soon as I can.'

'Are you sure? The news we've heard about our old house is very different. *Messer* Soderini was too late to save it. In any case, we want to stay with you. To help you.'

The last remaining townspeople were filing into the dark tunnel now, and as they did so, a great hammering and crashing of blows fell on the door that divided the sanctuary from the outside world.

'What is that?'

'It's the Borgia troops. Make haste! Make haste!'

He ushered his family into the tunnel, bringing up the rear with the few surviving Assassin troops.

It was a tough haul through the tunnel, and when they were halfway through Ezio heard a crash as the Borgia men broke through the door into the sanctuary. Soon, they would be in the tunnel themselves. He urged his charges forward, shouting at the stragglers to hurry and he heard the stamping of armed soldiers running down the tunnel behind them. As the group rushed past a gateway that ended one section of the passage, Ezio grabbed at a lever on the wall and, as the last of the Assassin fugitives rushed through, he yanked hard, releasing the portcullis gate. When it came crashing down, the first of their pursuers had caught up, only to be pinned to the floor by the heavy ironwork of the gate. His screams of agony filled the passage. Ezio had already run on, safe in the knowledge that he'd bought his people precious time to make good their escape.

After what seemed like hours, but can only have been minutes, the passage's incline seemed to change, levelling out and rising slightly. The air seemed less stale now that they were nearly out. Just at that moment they heard a heavy rumbling of sustained cannon fire – the Borgia must have unleashed their firepower on the citadel, a final act of desecration. The passage shook and eddies of dust fell from the ceiling; the sound of cracking stones could be heard, quiet at first but getting ominously louder.

'*Dio, ti prego, salvaci* – the roof is coming down!' sobbed one of the townswomen. The others began to scream as the fear of being buried alive flooded through the crowd.

Suddenly, the roof of the tunnel seemed to open up and a torrent of rubble cascaded down. The fugitives rushed forward, trying to escape from the falling rock, but Claudia reacted too slowly, disappearing in a cloud of dust. Ezio wheeled round in alarm, hearing his sister scream, but unable to see her. 'Claudia!' he shouted, panic in his voice.

'Ezio!' came the reply, and as the dust cleared Claudia picked her way carefully across the debris.

'Thank God you're all right. Did anything fall on you?' he asked. 'No, I'm fine. Is mother all right?'

'I'm fine,' answered Maria.

They dusted themselves down, thanking the gods they had survived this far, and made their way along the final stretch of the escape passage. At last they broke out into the open air. Never had grass, and the earth itself, smelled sweeter.

The mouth of the tunnel was separated from the countryside by a series of rope bridges swung across ravines. It had been designed like this by Mario as part of a master escape plan. Monteriggioni would survive the Borgia desecration. Once the Borgia had razed it, it would be of no further interest to them, but Ezio would return in time and rebuild it once more as the proud stronghold of the Assassins. Of that Ezio was certain. It would be more than that, he promised himself; it would be a monument to his noble uncle, who had been so pitilessly slain.

He had had enough of the depredations wrought on his family by pointless villainy.

Ezio planned to cut the bridges down behind them as they fled, but their progress was slow as they were shepherding elderly and wounded stragglers. At his back he heard the yells and footsteps of their pursuers approaching rapidly. He was scarcely able to carry anyone on his back, but he managed to haul a woman whose leg had given out onto his good shoulder, and staggered forward across the first rope bridge, which swung dangerously under his weight.

'Come on!' he yelled, encouraging the rearguard who were already engaging with the Borgia soldiers. He waited on the far side until the last of his men had reached safety, but a couple of Borgia had also made it across. Ezio stepped into their path and, using his good arm to wield his sword, engaged the enemy. Even hampered by his wound, Ezio was more than a match for his opponents; his sword parried their attacks in a blur of steel, taking on both blades at once. Stepping to one side, he crouched low under a wild swing from one man, while using his weapon to slice at the knee joint of the man's leg armour. The soldier toppled, his left leg useless. The other attacker lunged down, thinking Ezio off balance, but Ezio had rolled aside as the blade clanged off the rocks, sending shards of stone skittering into the ravine. The man winced as the blow vibrated along his sword, jarring the bones of his hand and arm. Ezio saw his chance and, heaving himself upright, raised his sword above his foe's lowered arm and across his face. The man went down, and in a single fluid movement Ezio brought his blade to bear on the ropes supporting the bridge. They severed instantly, slashing violently backwards across the ravine. The bridge concertinaed away from the rocks, and the Borgia men who had begun to cross fell screaming into the abyss below.

Looking back across the ravine, Ezio saw Cesare. Next to him was Caterina, still in chains, which were held by a vicious-looking Lucrezia. Juan Borgia, the deathly pale Micheletto and the sweaty Frenchman, General Octavien, stood beside him.

Cesare was waving something at Ezio.

'Yours next!' he screamed in fury.

Ezio could see that it was his uncle's head.

I 2

There was only one place for Ezio to go now. The way forward for Cesare's troops was cut off and it would take them days to work their way around the ravine and catch up with the Assassin survivors. He directed the refugees to towns outside Borgia control, at least for the moment – Siena, San Gimignano, Pisa, Lucca, Pistoia and Florence – where they would find sanctuary. He also tried to impress upon his mother and sister the wisdom of returning to the safety of Florence, whatever had happened to Villa Auditore and despite the sad memories the city held, and the fact that both were seized with a compulsive desire to avenge Mario's death.

Ezio himself was bound for Rome, where, he knew, Cesare would go to regroup. It might even be that Cesare in his arrogance would think Ezio beaten, or dead on the road, like carrion. If so, then that could only be to the Assassin's advantage. Something else was haunting Ezio, though. With Mario dead, the Brotherhood was leaderless. Machiavelli was a powerful force within it, and at present he did not seem to be Ezio's friend. This was something that had to be resolved.

Along with the human survivors of the town was a

number of livestock, including the great chestnut war-horse Mario had loved so much. Ezio mounted the steed, held for him by the old stable master, who had also managed to escape, though most of his horses had been captured by the Borgia.

Reining his horse in, he took leave of his mother and sister.

'Must you really go to Rome?' asked Maria.

'Mother, the only way to win this war is to take it to the enemy.'

'But how can you possibly succeed against the forces of the Borgia?'

'I am not their only enemy. And besides, Machiavelli is already there. I must make my peace with him so that we can work together.'

'Cesare has the Apple,' Claudia said soberly.

'We must pray that he does not master its powers,' Ezio replied, though privately he felt great misgivings. Leonardo was in Cesare's pay now, and Ezio was well aware of of his former friend's intelligence. If Leonardo taught Cesare the mysteries of the Apple – worse still, if Rodrigo got hold of it again . . .

He shook his head to rid himself of these thoughts. Time enough to confront the threat of the Apple when it presented itself.

'You shouldn't be riding now. Rome is miles to the south. Can't you at least give it a day or two?' asked Claudia.

'The Borgia will not rest and the evil spirit of the Templars rides within them,' rejoined Ezio drily. 'No one will be able to sleep easily until their power is broken.'

'What if it never is?'

'We must never give up the fight. The minute we do that, we have lost.'

'*È vero.*' His sister's shoulders slumped, but then she straightened them again. 'The fight must *never* be given up,' she said firmly.

'Until death,' said Ezio.

'Until death.'

'Take care on the road.'

'Take care on the road.'

Ezio leaned down from the saddle to kiss his mother and sister before wheeling the horse round and onto the road south. His head was pounding with the pain of his wound and the exertions of battle. More than this was the aching of his heart and soul at the loss of Mario and the capture of Caterina. He shuddered at the thought of her in the clutches of the evil Borgia family; he knew all too well what fate might befall her in their hands. He would have to skirt around the Borgia troops, but his heart told him that now his main objective had been achieved – to break the Assassin stronghold – Cesare would head home. There was also the question of Caterina's safety, though Ezio knew that if ever a person would go down fighting, it was she.

The most important thing was to lance the boil that was infecting Italy, and lance it soon, before it could infect the whole land.

Ezio dug his heels hard into the horse's flanks and galloped south down the dusty road.

His head was swimming with exhaustion, but he willed himself to keep awake. He vowed he would not rest until he arrived in the broken-down capital of his beleaguered country. He had miles to go before he would be able to sleep.

13

How stupid had he been to ride for so long wounded, and so far south, only breaking the ride for the horse's sake. A post horse would have been more sensible, but the chestnut steed, Agnella, was his last link to Mario.

Where was he? He remembered a crumbling, dingy suburb and then, rising out of it, a once-majestic yellow stone arch, an erstwhile gateway that pierced a formerly magnificent city's walls.

Ezio's impulse had been to rejoin Machiavelli – to right the wrong he had committed by not making sure that Rodrigo Borgia was dead.

But by God, he was tired.

He lay back on the pallet he found himself on. He could smell the dry straw, its odour carrying with it a hint of cow dung.

Where was he?

An image of Caterina came suddenly and strongly into his mind. He must free her. They had to be together at last.

But perhaps he should also free himself *from* her, though part of his heart told him that this was not what he really wanted. How could he trust her? How could a simple man ever understand the subtle labyrinths of a woman's mind? Alas, the torture of love didn't seem to get any less acute with age.

Was she using him?

Ezio had always maintained an inner room within his heart, a *sanctum sanctorum* that was kept locked, even to his most intimate friends, his mother — who knew of it and respected it — his sister, and his late brothers and father.

Had Caterina broken in? He hadn't been able to prevent the killing of his father and brothers, and by Christ and the Cross he had done his best to protect Maria and Claudia.

Caterina could look after herself — she was a book that kept its covers closed — and yet . . . and yet, how he longed to read it.

'I love you,' his heart cried out to Caterina in spite of himself. The woman of his dreams at last, this late in life. But his duty, he told himself, came first, and Caterina . . . Caterina never truly showed her cards. Her enigmatic brown eyes, her smile, the way she could twist him round her long, expert fingers. The closeness. The closeness. But also the keen silence of her hair, which always smelled of vanilla and roses . . .

How could he ever trust her, even when he laid his head on her breast after they had made passionate love, and wanted so much to feel secure?

No! The Brotherhood. The Brotherhood. The Brotherhood! His mission and his destiny.

I am dead, Ezio said to himself. I am already dead inside, but I will finish what I have to do.

The dream dissolved and his eyelids flickered open, revealing a view of an ample but elderly cleavage descending on him, the chemise the woman was wearing parting like the Red Sea.

Ezio sat up rapidly. His wound was properly dressed now, and the pain was so dull as to be almost negligible. As his eyes focused, they took in a small room with walls of rough-hewn stone. Calico curtains were drawn across the small windows, and in a corner an iron stove burned, the embers from its open door giving the place its only light. The door was shut, but whoever was with him in the room lit the stump of a candle.

A middle-aged woman, who looked like a peasant, knelt beside him, just within the frame of his vision. Her face was kindly as she tended to his wound, rearranging the poultice and bandage.

It was sore! Ezio winced in pain.

'*Calmatevi*,' said the woman. 'The pain will end soon.'

'Where's my horse? Where's Campione?'

'Safe. Resting. God knows she deserves it. She was bleeding from the mouth. A good horse like that. What were you doing to her?'

The woman put down the bowl of water she was holding and stood.

'Where am I?'

'In Rome, my dear. *Messer* Machiavelli found you fainting in your saddle, your horse frothing, and brought you both here. Don't worry, he's paid me and my husband well to look after you both. And a few more coins for our discretion. But you know *Messer* Machiavelli – cross him at your peril. Anyway, we've done this kind of job for your organization before.'

'Did he leave me any message?'

'Oh yes. You're to meet him as soon as you're fit at the Mausoleum of Augustus. Know where that is?'

'It's one of the ruins, isn't it?'

'Dead right. Not that it's much less of a ruin than most of this awful city nowadays. To think it was once the centre of the world. Look at it now – smaller than Florence; half the size of Venice. But we do have one boast.' She cackled.

'And that is?'

'Only fifty thousand poor souls live in this shanty town of a city that once was proud to call itself Rome; and seven thousand of them are prostitutes. That's got to be a record.' She cackled some more. 'No wonder everyone's riddled with the New Disease. Don't sleep with anyone here', she added, 'if you don't want to fall apart with the pox. Even cardinals have it – and they say the Pope himself, and his son, are sufferers.'

Ezio remembered Rome as if in a dream. A bizarre place now, whose ancient, rotting walls had been designed to encompass a population of one million. Now most of the area was given over to peasant farming.

He remembered too the ruined wasteland of what had once been the Great Forum in ancient times, but where sheep and goats now grazed. People stole the ancient carved marble and porphyry stones, which lay higgledy-piggledy in the grass, to build pigsties or to grind down for lime. And out of the desolation of slums and crooked, filthy streets, the great new buildings of Popes Sixtus IV and Alexander VI rose obscenely, like wedding cakes on a table where there was nothing else to eat but stale bread.

The aggrandisement of the Church was confirmed, back at last from the Papal exile at Avignon. The Pope – the leading figure in the international world, outclassing not only kings but the Holy Roman Emperor Maximilian himself – had his seat in Rome once more.

Hadn't it been Pope Alexander VI who'd divided, in his great judgment, the southern continent of the New Americas between the colonizing countries of Portugal and Spain in the Treaty of Tordesillas in 1494? It was the same year the New Disease broke out

in Naples in Italy. They called it the French Disease –
morbus gallicus – but everyone knew it had come back
from the New World with Columbus's Genoese sailors. It was an unpleasant affliction. People's faces and
bodies bubbled up in pustules and boils, and their
faces were often pressed out of all recognizable shape
in the last stages.

Here in Rome, the poor made do on barley and
bacon – when they could get bacon – and the dirty
streets harboured typhus, cholera and the Black Death.
As for the citizens, on the one hand there were the
ostentatiously rich, whilst the majority looked like
cowherds and lived just as badly.

What a contrast to the gilded opulence of the Vatican. The great city of Rome had become a rubbish
heap of history. Along the filthy alleys that passed for
streets, in which feral dogs and wolves now roamed,
Ezio remembered churches which today were falling
apart, rotting deserted palaces that reminded him of
the probable wreck of his own family seat in Florence.

'I must get up. I must find *Messer* Machiavelli,' said
Ezio, urgently flinging the visions from his mind.

'All in good time,' replied his nurse. 'He left you a
new suit of clothes. Put them on when you are ready.'

Ezio stood, but as he did so his head swam. He
shook himself to clear it, then donned the suit Machiavelli had left him. It was new and made of linen, with
a hood of soft wool that had a peak like an eagle's

beak. There were strong, soft gloves and boots of Spanish leather. He dressed himself, fighting the pain the effort caused him, and when he was done, the woman guided him to a balcony. Ezio realized then that he had not been in some shrunken hovel, but in the remains of what had once been a great palace. They must have been on the *piano nobile*. He drew in his breath as he looked at the desolate wreck of the city spread out below him. A rat scuttled boldly over his feet. He kicked it away.

'Ah, *Roma*,' he said ironically.

'What's left of it,' the woman repeated, cackling again.

'Thank you, *Madonna*. To whom do I owe . . . ?'

'I am the *Contessa* Margherita deghli Campi,' she said, and in the dim light Ezio could see at last the fine lines of a once beautiful face. 'Or what's left of her.'

'*Contessa*,' Ezio said, trying to keep the sadness out of his voice as he bowed.

'The *Mausoleo* is over there,' she replied, smiling and pointing. 'That is where you are to meet.'

'I can't see it.'

'In that direction. Unfortunately, you cannot see it from my *palazzo*.'

Ezio squinted into the dark. 'What about from the tower of that church?'

She looked at him. 'Santo Stefano's? Yes. But it's a ruin. The stairs to the tower have collapsed.'

Ezio braced himself. He needed to get to his meeting place as safely and as quickly as possible. He did not want to be delayed by the beggars, tarts and muggers who infested the streets by day and night.

'That shouldn't be a problem,' he told the woman. '*Vi ringrazio di tutto quello che avete fatto per me, buona Contessa. Addio.*'

'You are more than welcome,' she replied with a wry smile. 'But are you sure you're fit enough to go so soon? I think you should see a doctor. I'd recommend one, but I can't afford them any more. I have cleaned and dressed your wound, but I am no expert.'

'The Templars won't wait and nor can I,' he replied. 'Thank you again, and goodbye.'

'Go with God.'

He leapt from the balcony down to the street, wincing at the impact, and darted across the square, which was dominated by the disintegrating palace, in the direction of the church. Twice he lost sight of the tower and had to double back. Three times he was accosted by leprous beggars and once confronted by a wolf, which slunk off down an alley with what may have been a dead child between its jaws. At last he was in the open space before the church. It was boarded up, and the limestone saints that adorned its portal were deformed by neglect. He didn't know whether he could trust the rotten stonework, but there was nothing for it; he had to climb.

He managed it, though he lost his footing on several occasions and once his feet fell free over an embrasure that collapsed beneath them, leaving him hanging by the tips of his fingers. He was still a strong man, despite his injuries, and he managed to haul himself up and out of danger until at last he was on top of the tower that was perched on its lead roof. The dome of the Mausoleum glinted dully in the moonlight several blocks away. He'd go there now and wait for Machiavelli to arrive.

He adjusted his Hidden Blade, sword and dagger, and was about to make a leap of faith down to a hay-wain parked in the square below when his wound caused him to double up in pain.

'The *Contessa* dressed my shoulder well, but she was right, I must see a doctor,' he said to himself.

Painfully, he clambered down the tower to the street. He had no idea where to find a *medico*, so he made his way to an inn, where he obtained directions in exchange for a couple of ducats, which also bought him a beaker of filthy Sanguincus, which assuaged his pain somewhat.

It was late by the time he reached the doctor's surgery. He had to knock several times, and hard, before there was a muffled response from within, then the door opened a crack to reveal a fat, bearded man of about sixty, wearing thick eyeglasses. He looked the worse for wear – Ezio could smell drink on his breath – and one of his eyes seemed larger than the other.

'What do you want?' said the man.

'Are you *Dottore* Antonio?'

'And if I am . . . ?'

'I need your help.'

'It's late,' said the doctor, but his gaze had wandered to the wound on Ezio's shoulder, and his eyes became cautiously more sympathetic. 'It'll cost extra.'

'I am not in a position to argue.'

'Good. Come in.'

The doctor unchained his door and stood aside. Ezio staggered gratefully into a hallway whose beams were hung with a collection of copper pots and glass phials, dried bats and lizards, mice and snakes.

The doctor ushered him through to an inner room containing a huge desk, untidily covered with papers, a narrow bed in one corner, a cupboard whose open doors revealed more phials, and a leather case, also open, containing a selection of scalpels and miniature saws.

The doctor followed Ezio's eyes and barked out a short laugh. 'We *medici* are just jumped-up mechanics,' he said. 'Lie down on the bed and I'll have a look. Before you do, it's three ducats – in advance.'

Ezio handed over the money.

The doctor undressed the wound and pushed and shoved until Ezio virtually passed out with the pain.

'Hold still!' the doctor grumbled. He poked around some more, poured some stinging liquid from a flask over the wound, dabbed at it with a cotton wad, produced some clean bandages and bound it firmly once more.

'Someone your age cannot recover from a wound like this with medicine.' The doctor rummaged about in his cupboard and produced a phial of treacly-looking stuff. 'But here's something to dull the pain. Don't drink it all at once. It's another three ducats, by the way. And don't worry, you'll heal over time.'

'*Grazie, dottore.*'

'Four out of five doctors would have suggested leeches, but they haven't proven effective against this sort of wound. What is it? If they weren't so rare, I'd say it was from a gunshot. Come back if you need to. Or I can recommend several good colleagues around the city.'

'Do they cost as much as you do?'

Doctor Antonio sneered. 'My good sir, you've got off lightly.'

Ezio stomped out into the street. A light rain had begun to fall and the streets were already turning muddy.

'"Someone your age,"' grumbled Ezio. '*Che sobbalzo!*'

He made his way back to the inn as he'd noticed they had rooms for rent. He'd stay there, eat something, and make his way to the Mausoleum in the morning. Then he'd just have to wait for his fellow

Assassin to show up. Machiavelli might at least have left some kind of rendezvous time with the *Contessa*. Ezio was aware of Machiavelli's passion for security, though. He'd no doubt turn up at the appointed spot every day at regular intervals. Ezio shouldn't have too long to wait.

Ezio picked his way through the wretched streets and alleys, darting back into the darkness of doorways whenever a Borgia patrol – easily recognized by their mulberry and yellow livery – passed by.

It was midnight by the time he reached the inn again. He took a swig from the phial of dark liquid – it was good – and hammered on the inn door with the pommel of his sword.

14

The following day Ezio left the inn early. His wound felt stiff, but the pain was duller and he was better able to use his arm now. Before leaving he practised a few strokes with the Hidden Blade and found he could use it without difficulty, as well as more conventional sword-and-dagger work. It was just as well he hadn't been shot in the shoulder of his sword-arm.

Not being sure whether the Borgia and their Templar associates knew that he had escaped the battle of Monteriggioni with his life, and noting the high number of soldiers armed with guns and dressed in the dark mulberry red and yellow livery of the Borgia, he took a roundabout route to the Mausoleum of Augustus, and the sun was high by the time he reached it.

There were fewer people about, and after having scouted round, assuring himself that no guards were watching the place, Ezio cautiously approached the building, slipping through a ruined doorway into the gloomy interior.

As his eyes accustomed themselves to the darkness, he made out a figure dressed in black, leaning against a stone outcrop and still as a statue. He glanced to each side to ascertain that there was somewhere to duck behind before it noticed him, but apart from tussocks of grass among the fallen stones of the ancient Roman ruin, there was nothing. He decided on the next best thing and swiftly but silently started to move towards the deeper darkness of the Mausoleum's walls.

He was too late. Whoever it was had seen him, probably as soon as he'd entered, framed by the light from the doorway, and moved towards him. As it approached, he recognized the black-suited figure of Machiavelli, who placed a finger on his lips as he came closer. Beckoning him discreetly to follow, Machiavelli made his way into a deeper, darker area of the ancient Roman Emperor's tomb, built almost one and half millennia earlier.

At last he stopped and turned.

'Shh,' he said and, waiting, listened keenly.

'Wha—?'

'Voice down. Voice very low,' admonished Machiavelli, listening still.

At last he relaxed. 'All right,' he continued. 'There's no one.'

'What do you mean?'

'Cesare Borgia has eyes everywhere.' Machiavelli relaxed a little. 'I am glad to see you here.'

'But you left me clothes at the *Contessa*'s . . .'

'She had word to watch for your arrival in Rome.' Machiavelli grinned. 'Oh, I knew you'd come here.

Once you'd assured yourself of the safety of your mother and sister. After all, they are the last of the Auditore family.'

'I don't like your tone,' said Ezio, bridling slightly.

Machiavelli allowed himself a thin smile. 'This is no time for tact, my dear colleague. I know the guilt you feel about your lost family, even though you are not remotely to blame for that great betrayal.' He paused. 'News of the attack on Monteriggioni has spread across this city. Some of us were sure that you had died there. I left the clothes with our trusted friend because I knew you better than that you would go and die on us at such a crucial time – or at any rate, just in case.'

'You still have faith in me then?'

Machiavelli shrugged. 'You blundered. Once. Because fundamentally your instinct is to show mercy and trust. Those are good instincts. But now we must strike, and strike hard. Let's hope the Templars never know that you are still alive.'

'But they must already know.'

'Not necessarily. My spies tell me there was a lot of confusion.'

Ezio paused for thought. 'Our enemies will know soon enough that I am alive – and very much so. How many do we fight?'

'Oh, Ezio, the good news is that we have narrowed the field. We have wiped out many Templars across Italy and across many of the lands beyond its boundaries.

The bad news is that the Templars and the Borgia family are now one and the same thing, and they will fight like a cornered lion.'

'Tell me more.'

'We are too isolated here. We need to lose ourselves in the crowds in the centre of town. We will go to the bullfight.'

'The bullfight?'

'Cesare excels as a bullfighter. After all, he is a Spaniard. In fact he's not a Spaniard, but a Catalan, and that may one day prove to be to our advantage.'

'How?'

'The king and queen of Spain want to unify their country. They are from Aragon and Castile. The Catalans are a thorn in their side, though they are still a powerful nation. Come, and be cautious. We must both use the skills of blending in that Paola taught you so long ago in Venice. I hope you have not forgotten them.'

'Try me.'

They walked together through the half-ruined, once-imperial city, keeping to the shadows and slipping in and out of the crowds as fish hide in the rushes. At last they reached the bullring, where they took seats on the more expensive, crowded, shady side, and watched for an hour as Cesare and his many backup men despatched three fearsome bulls. Ezio watched Cesare's fighting technique: he used the banderilleros and the picadors to break the animal down before delivering the *coup de grâce* after a good deal of showing off. But there was no doubting his courage and prowess during the grim ritual of death, despite the fact that he had four junior matadors to support him. Ezio looked over his shoulder at the box of the *Presidente* of the fight: there he recognized the harsh but compellingly beautiful face of Cesare's sister, Lucrezia. Was it his imagination or had he seen her bite her lip until it bled?

At any rate, he had learned something of how Cesare would behave in the field of battle – and how far he could be trusted in any kind of combat.

Everywhere, Borgia guards watched the throng, just as they did in the streets, all of them armed with those lethal-looking new guns.

'Leonardo . . .' he said involuntarily, thinking of his old friend.

Machiavelli looked at him. 'Leonardo was forced to work for Cesare on pain of death – and a most painful death it would have been. It's a detail – a terrible detail, but a detail nonetheless. The point is, his heart is not with his new master, who will never have the intelligence or the facility to control the Apple fully. Or at least I hope it isn't. We must be patient. We will get it back, and we will get Leonardo back with it.'

'I wish I could be so sure.'

Machiavelli sighed. 'Perhaps you are wise to be doubtful,' he said at last.

'Spain has taken over Italy,' said Ezio.

'Valencia has taken over the Vatican,' Machiavelli replied, 'but we can change that. We have allies in the College of Cardinals, some of whom are powerful. They aren't all lapdogs. And Cesare, for all his vaunting, depends on his father Rodrigo for funds.' He gave Ezio a keen look. 'That is why you should have made sure of this interloping Pope.'

'I didn't know.'

'I'm as much to blame as you are. I should have told you. But as you said yourself, it's the present we have to deal with, not the past.'

'Amen to that.'

'Amen.'

'But how do they afford all this?' Ezio asked as another bull foundered and fell under Cesare's unerring and pitiless sword.

'*Papa* Alexander is a strange mixture,' Machiavelli replied. 'He's a great administrator and has even done the Church some good, but the evil part of him always defeats the good. He was the Vatican's treasurer for years and found ways of amassing money – the experience has stood him in good stead. He sells cardinal's hats, creating dozens of cardinals virtually guaranteed to be on his side. He has even pardoned murderers, provided they have enough money to buy their way off the gallows.'

'How does he justify that?'

'Very simple. He preaches that it is better for a sinner to live and repent than to die and forego such pain.'

Ezio couldn't help laughing, though his laugh was mirthless. His mind returned to the recent celebrations to mark the year 1500 – the Great Year of the Half-Millennium. True, there had been flagellants roaming the country in expectation of the Last Judgement, and hadn't the mad monk Savonarola – who'd briefly had control of the Apple, and whom he himself had defeated in Florence – not been duped by that superstition?

1500 had been a great jubilee year. Ezio remembered that thousands of hopeful pilgrims had made their way to the Holy See from all parts of the world. The year had even been celebrated in those small outposts across the far seas to the west, in the New Lands discovered by Colombus and, a few years later, by Amerigo Vespucci, who had confirmed their existence. Money had flowed into Rome as the faithful bought indulgences to redeem themselves from their sins in anticipation of Christ returning to earth to judge the quick and the dead. It had also been the time when Cesare had set out to subjugate the city states of the Romagna, and when the king of France had taken Milan, justifying his actions by claiming to be the rightful heir – the great-grandson of Gian Galeazzo Visconti.

The Pope had then made his son, Cesare, Captain-General of the Papal Forces, and *Gonfaloniere* of the

Holy Roman Church in a great ceremony on the morning of the fourth Sunday of Lent. Cesare was welcomed by boys in silk gowns and four thousand soldiers wearing his personal livery. His triumph had seemed complete: the previous year, in May, he'd married Charlotte d'Albret, sister of John, King of Navarre; and King Louis of France, with whom the Borgia were allied, gave him the dukedom of Valence. Having already been Cardinal of Valencia, no wonder the people gave him the nickname Valentino.

Now this viper was at the peak of his power.

How could Ezio ever defeat him?

He shared these thoughts with Machiavelli.

'In the end, we will use their own vainglory to bring them down,' said Niccolò. 'They have an Achilles heel. Everyone does. I know what yours is.'

'And that is?' snapped Ezio, needled.

'I do not need to tell you her name. Beware of her,' rejoined Machiavelli, but then, changing the subject, he continued, 'Remember the orgies?'

'They continue?'

'Indeed they do. How Rodrigo – I refuse to call him Pope any more – loves them. And you've got to hand it to him, he's seventy years old.' Machiavelli laughed wryly, then suddenly became more serious. 'The Borgia will drown under the weight of their own self-indulgence.'

Ezio remembered the orgies well. He had been

witness to one. There'd been a dinner, given by the Pope in his Nero-like, over-decorated, gilded apartments and attended by fifty of the best of the city's army of whores. Courtesans, they liked to call themselves, but whores for all that. When the eating – or should it be called feeding? – was over, the girls danced with the servants who were in attendance. They were clothed at first, but later they shed their garments. The candelabra that had been on the tables were set down on the marble floor, and the nobler guests threw roasted chestnuts among them. The whores were then told to crawl about the floor on all fours like cattle, buttocks high in the air, to collect the chestnuts. Then almost everyone had joined in. Ezio remembered with distaste how Rodrigo, together with Cesare and Lucrezia, had looked on. At the end, prizes were given – silk cloaks; fine leather boots, from Spain of course; mulberry-and-yellow velvet caps encrusted with diamonds; rings; bracelets; brocade pouches each containing 100 ducats; daggers; silver dildoes; anything you could imagine – to those men who had had sex the most number of times with the crawling prostitutes. And the Borgia family, fondling each other, had been the principal judges.

The two Assassins left the bullfight and made themselves invisible in the crowds that thronged the early-evening streets.

'Follow me,' Machiavelli said, an edge to his voice. 'Now you have had a chance to see your principal opponent at work, it would be well to purchase any equipment you are missing. And take care not to draw any undue attention to yourself.'

'Do I ever?' Ezio found himself once more needled by the younger man's remarks. Machiavelli wasn't the Brotherhood's leader – after Mario's death, no one was – and this interregnum would have to be concluded soon. 'In any case, I have my Hidden Blade.'

'And the guards have their guns. These things Leonardo has created for them – you know his genius cannot control itself – are fast to reload, as you've seen, and moreover they have barrels filed in a cunning way on the inside to make the shot more accurate.'

'I'll find Leonardo and talk to him.'

'You may have to kill him.'

'He's worth more to us alive than dead. You said yourself his heart wasn't with the Borgia.'

'I said that is what I hope.' Machiavelli stopped. 'Look. Here is money.'

'*Grazie*,' said Ezio, taking the proffered pouch.

'While you are in my debt, listen to reason.'

'As soon as I hear more reason from you, I shall.'

Ezio left his friend and made his way to the quarter of the armourers, where he provided himself with a new breastplate, steel cuffs, and a better-balanced, higher-quality sword and dagger than those he already possessed. Above all he missed the old Codex Bracer, made of a secret metal, which had staved off so many blows that otherwise would have been fatal. But it was too late to regret that now. He'd just have to rely on his wits and his training. No one, and no accident, could take them from him.

He returned to Machiavelli, who was waiting for him at an inn, their pre-appointed rendezvous.

He found him in a prickly mood.

'*Bene*,' said Machiavelli. 'Now you can survive the journey back to *Firenze*.'

'Perhaps. But I am not going back to Florence.'

'No?'

'Perhaps you should. It is where you belong. I have no home there any more.'

Machiavelli spread his hands. 'It's true that your old home has indeed been destroyed. I didn't want to tell you. But surely your mother and sister are safe there now. It is a city safe from the Borgia. My master, Piero Soderini, guards it well. You can recoup there.'

Ezio shuddered at having his worst fears confirmed. Then he pulled himself together and said, 'I stay here. You said yourself, there will be no peace until we rise up against the entire Borgia family and the Templars who serve them.'

'Such brave talk! And after Monteriggioni.'

'That is cheap of you, Niccolò. How could I have

known that they would find me so quickly? Or that they would kill Mario?'

Machiavelli spoke earnestly, taking his companion by the shoulders. 'Look, Ezio, whatever happens we must prepare ourselves carefully. We must not hit out in rash anger. We are fighting *scorpioni* – worse, serpents! They can coil around your neck and bite your balls in one movement. They know nothing of right and wrong; they only know their goal. Rodrigo surrounds himself with snakes and murderers. Even his daughter Lucrezia has been sharpened into one of his most artful weapons: she knows all there is to know about the art of poisoning.' He paused. 'However, even she pales by comparison with Cesare.'

'Him again.'

'He is ambitious, ruthless and cruel beyond – thank God! – your imagination. The laws of men mean nothing to him. He has murdered his own brother, the Duke of Gandía, to claw his way towards absolute power. He will stop at nothing.'

'I'll pluck him down.'

'Only if you are not rash. He has the Apple, don't forget. Heaven help us if he really learns its powers.'

Ezio's mind flashed nervously to Leonardo, who understood the Apple all too well . . .

'He recognizes neither danger nor fatigue,' Machiavelli continued. 'Those who do not fall by his sword clamour to join his ranks. Already the powerful Orsini and Colonna families have been brought down and made to kneel at his feet, and King Louis of France stands by his side.' Machiavelli paused again, thoughtful. 'But at least King Louis will only remain his ally as long as he is useful to him . . .'

'You overestimate the man.'

Machiavelli appeared not to have heard him; he was lost in his own thoughts. 'What does he intend to do with all that power and money? What drives the man? That, I still do not know. But, Ezio,' he added, fixing his gaze on his friend, 'Cesare has set his sights on all *Italia*, and at this rate he will have it.'

Ezio hesitated, shocked. 'Is that . . . is that *admiration* I hear in your voice?'

Machiavelli's face was set. 'He knows how to exercise his will – a rare virtue in the world today – and he is the kind of man who could make the world bend to that will.'

'What do you mean, exactly?'

'Just this: people need someone to look up to – to adore even. It may be God, or Christ, but better yet, someone you can really see, not just an image. Rodrigo, Cesare, even a great actor or singer, as long as they're dressed well and have faith in themselves. The rest follows quite logically.' Machiavelli drank a little wine. 'It's part of us, you see. It doesn't interest you or me or Leonardo, but there are people out there who have a hunger to be followed, and they are the dangerous ones.' He finished his drink. 'Fortunately, they can also be manipulated by people like me.'

'Or destroyed by people like me.'

They sat in silence for a long moment.

'Who will lead the Assassins now that Mario is dead?' asked Ezio.

'What a question! We are in disorder and there are few candidates. It's important, of course, and the choice will be made in time. In the meantime, come on. We have work to do.'

'Shall we take horses? Half of it may be falling down, but Rome's still a big city,' suggested Ezio.

'Easier said than done. As Cesare's conquests in the Romagna increase – and he controls most of the region now – and the Borgia grow in power, they've taken the best areas of the city for themselves. We're in a Borgia *rione* now. We won't get horses from the stables here.'

'So the will of the Borgia is the only law here now?'

'Ezio, what are you implying? That I approve of it?'

'Don't play dumb with me, Niccolò.'

'I don't play dumb with anyone. Do you have a plan?'

'We'll improvise.'

They made their way towards the place where the local stables with horses for hire were located, walking down streets where, Ezio noticed, many of the shops that should have been open had their shutters down. What was the matter? Sure enough, the closer they got, the more numerous and menacing were the guards in mulberry-and-yellow livery. Machiavelli, Ezio noticed, was becoming increasingly nervous.

It wasn't long before a burly sergeant, at the head of a dozen or so tough-looking thugs in uniform, blocked their path.

'What's your business here, friend?' he said to Ezio.

'Time to improvise?' whispered Machiavelli.

'We want to hire some horses,' Ezio replied evenly to the sergeant.

The sergeant barked out a laugh. 'Not here you won't, friend. On your way.' He pointed back in the direction they'd come.

'Isn't it allowed?'

'No.'

'Why not?'

The sergeant drew his sword as the other guards followed suit. He held the point of his blade against Ezio's neck and pushed slightly, so that a drop of blood appeared. 'You know what curiosity did to the cat, don't you? Now, fuck off!'

With an almost imperceptible movement, Ezio swept out his Hidden Blade and with it severed the tendons of the wrist holding the sword, which clattered uselessly to the ground. With a great cry the sergeant buckled over, grasping his wound. At the same time Machiavelli leapt forward and slashed at the nearest three guards with his sword in a great sweeping motion – they all staggered back, astonished at the sudden boldness of the two men.

Ezio swiftly withdrew the Hidden Blade, and in one fluid movement unsheathed his sword and dagger. His weapons were clear and poised just in time to cut down the first two of his attackers who, having recovered some of their composure, had stepped forward to avenge their sergeant. None of the Borgia men had the skill at arms required to take on either Ezio or Machiavelli – the Assassin's training was of a wholly different class. Even so, the odds were against the two allies, who were heavily outnumbered. However, the unexpected ferocity of their attack was enough to give them an unassailable edge.

Taken almost wholly by surprise, and unused to coming off worse in any encounter, the dozen men were soon dispatched. But the commotion of the scuffle had raised the alarm, and more Borgia soldiers were quick to come – over two dozen men all told. Machiavelli and Ezio were nearly overwhelmed by the sheer weight of numbers, and with the effort of taking on so many at once. The flourishes of style that they were capable of were set aside for a quicker, more efficient form of swordsmanship – the three-second kill, a single thrust sufficing. The two men stood their ground, grim determination set on their faces, and finally all their enemies had either fled, or lay wounded, dead or dying at their feet.

'We'd better hurry,' said Machiavelli, breathing hard. Just because we've sent a few Borgia henchmen to their Maker doesn't mean we'll get access to the stables. The ordinary people remain afraid. That's why so many of them won't even open their shops.'

'You're right,' agreed Ezio. 'We need to send them a signal. Wait here.'

A fire was burning in a brazier nearby. From it, Ezio seized a brand, then leapt up onto the wall of the stable, where the Borgia flag with the black bull in a golden field flew in the light breeze. Ezio set it on fire, and as it burned, one or two shop doors cautiously opened, as did the gates of the stables.

'That's better!' cried Ezio. He turned to address the small but doubtful crowd that had gathered. 'Do not fear the Borgia. Do not be in thrall to them. Their days are numbered, and the hour of reckoning is at hand.'

More people came up, raising a cheer.

'They'll be back,' Machivelli said.

'Yes they will, but we've shown these people that they are not the all-powerful tyrants they took them to be.'

Ezio leapt down from the wall into the stable yard, where Machiavelli joined him. Swiftly, they picked two sturdy mounts and had them saddled.

'We'll come back,' Ezio promised the head ostler. 'You might like to get this place cleaned up a bit – now that it belongs to you again, as it rightfully should.'

'We will, my Lord,' said the man. But he still looked fearful.

'Don't worry. They won't harm you now that you've seen them bested.'

'How do you figure that, my Lord?'

'They need you. They can't do without you. Just show them you won't be bullied and pushed around and they'll have to cajole you into helping them.'

'They'll hang us – or worse.'

'Do you want to spend the rest of your lives under their yoke? Stand up to them. They'll have to listen to reasonable requests. Even tyrants can't function if enough people refuse to obey them.'

Machiavelli, already on his horse, took out a small black notebook and wrote in it, smiling absently to himself. Ezio swung himself into the saddle.

'I thought you said we were in a hurry,' said Ezio.

'We are. I was just making a note of what you said.'

'I hope I should be flattered by that.'

'Oh yes, you should be. Come on.'

'You excel at opening wounds, Ezio,' Machiavelli continued as they rode. 'But can you also close them?'

'I intend to heal the sickness that is at the heart of our society, not merely tinker about with the symptoms.'

'Bold words. But you don't have to argue with me; we're on the same side, don't forget. I'm just putting across another point of view.'

'Is this a test?' Ezio was suspicious. 'If so, let us talk openly. I believe that Rodrigo Borgia's death would not have solved our problem.'

'Really?'

'Well, I mean, look at this city. Rome is the centre of Borgia and Templar rule. What I just said to that stable-man holds true. Killing Rodrigo won't change things – cut off the head of a man and he is dead, sure. But we are dealing with a Hydra.'

'I see what you mean – like the seven-headed monster Hercules had to kill – and even then the heads grew back until he learned the trick of stopping that happening.'

'Precisely.'

'So – you suggest that we appeal to the people?'

'Maybe. How else?'

'Forgive me, Ezio, but the people are fickle. Relying on them is like building on sand.'

'I disagree, Niccolò. Surely our belief in humanity is at the heart of the Assassin's Creed.'

'And that's something you intend to put to the test?'

Ezio was about to reply, but at that instant a young thief ran alongside them and, with his knife, swiftly and surely cut through the leather strings that attached Ezio's money pouch to his belt.

'What the—!' Ezio shouted.

Machiavelli laughed. 'He must be from your inner circle. Look at him run! You might have trained him yourself. Go, get back what he's stolen. We need that money.

I'll meet you at the Campidoglio on the Capitoline.'

Ezio wheeled his horse round and galloped off in pursuit of the thief. The man ran down alleys too narrow for the horse and Ezio had to go round, worried that he might lose his quarry but at the same time knowing, to his chagrin, that on foot the younger man would surely outrun him. It was almost as if the man had had some Assassin training. But how could that be?

At last he cornered the man in a blind alley and used the body of the horse to pin him up against the wall of the dead end.

'Give it back,' he said evenly, drawing his sword.

The man still seemed bent on escape, but when he saw how hopeless his situation was, his body slumped and, mutely, he raised the hand that held the pouch. Ezio snatched it back and stowed it away safely. But in doing so he let his horse move back a fraction, and in the wink of an eye the man had scrambled up the wall with almost extraordinary speed and disappeared over the other side.

'Hey! Come back! I haven't finished with you yet!' Ezio yelled, but all he got in reply was the receding sound of running feet. Sighing, and ignoring the small crowd that had gathered, he steered the horse in the direction of the Capitoline Hill.

Dusk was falling as he rejoined Machiavelli.

'Did you liberate your money from our friend?'

'I did.'

'A small victory.'

'They add up,' said Ezio. 'And in time, with work, we'll have a few more.'

'Let's hope we make it before Cesare's gaze falls on us and we are broken again. He damned nearly succeeded at Monteriggioni. Now let's get on with things.' Machiavelli spurred on his horse.

'Where are we going?'

'To the Colosseum. We have a rendezvous with a contact of mine, Vinicio.'

'And—?'

'I'm expecting him to have something for me. Come on.'

As they rode through the city towards the Colosseum, Machiavelli commented drily on the various new buildings that had been erected by Pope Alexander VI during his administration.

'Look at all these façades, masquerading as government buildings. Rodrigo is very clever in the way he keeps this place in business. It fools your friends the "people" quite easily.'

'When did you become so cynical?'

Machiavelli smiled. 'I'm not being cynical at all. I'm just describing *Roma* as she is today. But you're right, Ezio, perhaps I am a little too bitter, a little too negative sometimes. All may not be lost. The good news is that we do have allies in the city. You will meet them.

And the College of Cardinals is not completely under Rodrigo's thumb, much as he'd like it to be, although it is touch and go . . .'

'What's touch and go?'

'Our ultimate success.'

'We can only try. Giving up is a sure way to failure.'

'Who said anything about giving up?'

They rode on in silence until they reached the gloomy hulk of the ruined Colosseum, a building over which, for Ezio, the remembered horrors of the Games that had taken place there a thousand years ago, still hung. His attention was immediately caught by a group of Borgia guards with a Papal courier. Their swords drawn, halberds pointing threateningly and bearing flickering red torches, they were jostling a small, harassed-looking man.

'*Merda!*' said Machiavelli softly. 'It's Vinicio. They've got to him first.'

Silently, the two men slowed their horses, approaching the group quietly and with as much caution as possible in order to gain the greatest element of surprise. As they neared, they picked up snatches of conversation.

'What you got there?' one guard was asking.

'Nothing.'

'Attempting to steal official Vatican correspondence, eh?'

'*Perdonatemi, signore.* You must be mistaken.'

'No mistake, you little thief,' said another guard, prodding the man with his halberd.

'Who are you working for, *ladro*?'

'No one.'

'Good, then no one will care what happens to you.'

'I've heard enough,' said Machiavelli. 'We've got to save him and get the letter he carries.'

'Letter?'

'Come on!'

Machiavelli dug his heels into his mount's flanks, and the surprised horse bolted forward as Machiavelli tugged hard on the reins. The beast reared, forelegs kicking wildly and slamming into the temple of the nearest Borgia guard, caving his helmet into his skull. The man fell like a stone. Meanwhile, Machiavelli had swivelled himself to his right, leaning low out of his saddle. Reaching down he slashed viciously at the shoulder of the guard threatening Vinicio. The man dropped his halberd instantly and collapsed with the pain flaming through his shoulder. Ezio spurred his steed forward, careening past two other guards and using the pommel of his sword to strike fatally hard down on the first man's head and slapping the second across the eyes with the flat of his blade. One more guard was left. Distracted by the sudden attack, he didn't notice Vinicio grabbing the shaft of his halberd and suddenly felt himself yanked forward. Vinicio's dagger was waiting and pierced the man's throat. He fell with a sickening gargling sound as blood flooded his lungs. Once again, the element of surprise gave the Assassins the edge; the Borgia soldiers were clearly not used to such effective resistance to their bullying. Vinicio wasted no time and gestured to the main thoroughfare leading from the central plaza. A horse could be seen clattering away from the plaza – the courier standing hard in the stirrups urging on his steed.

'Give me the letter. Be quick about it!' ordered Machiavelli.

'But I haven't got it; he has,' Vinicio cried, pointing towards the fleeing horse. 'They took it from me.'

'Get after him!' Machiavelli shouted to Ezio. 'Whatever it costs, get that letter and bring it to me at the *Terme di Diocleziano* by midnight. I'll be waiting.'

Ezio rode off in pursuit.

It was easier than catching the thief had been. Ezio's horse was better than the courier's, and the man he was pursuing was no fighter. Ezio pulled him from the horse with ease. He didn't like to kill the man, but he couldn't afford to let him go and raise the alarm. '*Requiescat in Pace*,' he said softly as he slit his throat. He put the letter, unopened, in his belt pouch and made a tow rope from the horse's bridle so he could take the courier's steed with him. He then turned his own mount and made for the ruins of the Baths of Diocletian.

It was now almost pitch dark, except for where the

occasional torch guttered in a wall-mounted sconce. To reach the baths, Ezio had to cross a sizeable stretch of wasteland, and halfway across, his horse reared and neighed in fear. The other horse followed suit and Ezio had his hands full calming them. Suddenly a blood-curdling sound came to his ears, like the howling of wolves, and yet not quite the same. Possibly worse. It sounded more like human voices imitating the animals. He spun his horse round in the dark, loosening the tow rope he'd made. Once free, the courier's horse turned tail and galloped off into the night. Ezio hoped it would find its way home in one piece.

He didn't have much time to reflect on that as he reached the deserted baths. Machiavelli had not yet arrived – no doubt he was off again on one of his mysterious private missions in the city – but then . . .

From among the hillocks and tussocks of grass that had grown over the remains of the ancient Roman city, figures appeared and surrounded him. Feral-looking people who were hardly human in appearance at all. They stood upright, but they had long ears, snouts, claws and tails, and they were covered in rough grey hair. Their eyes seemed to glint red. Ezio drew a sharp breath – what on earth were these devilish creatures? His eyes darted around the ruins; he was encircled by at least a dozen of these wolfmen. Ezio unsheathed his sword once more. This was not turning out to be the best of days.

With wolf-like snarls and howls, the creatures fell upon him. As they came close, Ezio could see that these were indeed men like him, only seemingly mad, like creatures in some kind of holy trance. Their weapons were long, sharp steel talons sewn firmly into the tips of heavy gloves, and with these they slashed at his legs and at the horse's flanks, trying to bring him down.

He was able to keep them at bay with his sword and, as their disguises seemed to have no chain mail or other protection under the wolfskins, he was able to wound them with the keen edge of his sword. He cut one creature's arm off at the elbow and it slunk away, wailing horribly in the darkness. The strange creatures seemed to be more aggressive than skilful, and their weapons were no match for the point of Ezio's flashing blade. He quickly pressed forward, splitting the skull of another and pierced the left eye of a third. Both wolfmen fell on the spot, mortally injured by Ezio's blows. By then the other wolfmen seemed to be having second thoughts about continuing their attack, melting into the darkness or into hollows and caves formed by the overgrown ruins surrounding the baths. Ezio gave chase, gouging the thigh of one of his would-be assailants, while another fell under the hooves of his horse, only to have his back broken. Overtaking a sixth, Ezio leant down and, turning backwards, ripped the man's stomach open so that his guts spilled onto the ground and he stumbled over them as he fell and died.

Finally, all was silent.

Ezio calmed his horse and stood up in his stirrups, willing his eyes to penetrate the darkness and his ears to pick up signals his eyes could not see. Presently he thought he could make out the sound of laboured breathing not far off, though nothing was visible. He urged his horse into a walk and softly made his way in the direction it was coming from.

It seemed to be coming from the blackness of a shallow cave, formed by the overhang of a fallen archway and festooned with creepers and weeds. Dismounting and tying his horse firmly to a tree stump, he rubbed the blade of his sword with dirt so that it would not glint and give his location away and gingerly made his way forward. For a brief second he thought he saw the flickering of a flame in the bowels of the cave.

As he inched forward, bats swooped over his head and out into the night. The place stank of their droppings. Unseen insects and doubtless other creatures clattered and scuttled away from him. He cursed them for the noise they made as it seemed as loud as thunder to him, but the ambush – if there was one – still did not come.

Then he saw the flame again, and heard what he could have sworn was a faint whimpering. He saw that the cave was less shallow than the fallen arch suggested, and that its corridor curved gently, and at the same time narrowed, leading into a deeper darkness. As he followed the curve, the flickers of flame he had glimpsed earlier resolved themselves into a small fire, in the light of which he could make out a hunched figure.

The air was slightly fresher here. There must be some airway in the roof which he could not see. That would be why the fire could breathe. Ezio stood stock still and watched.

Whimpering, the creature reached out a skinny left hand, grubby and bony, and plucked at the end of an iron bar, which was stuck in the fire. Its other end was red hot, and, tremblingly, the creature drew it out and, bracing itself, applied the end to the bloody stump of its other arm, stifling a shriek as it did so, in an attempt to cauterize the wound.

It was the wolfman Ezio had maimed.

In the moment when the wolfman's attention was bound up in his pain and the job in hand, Ezio surged forward. He was almost too late, for the creature was fast and nearly got away, but Ezio's fist closed hard around its good arm. It was difficult, for the limb was slippery with grease, and the stench the creature released as it moved was all but overpowering, but Ezio held on firmly. Catching his breath and kicking the iron bar away, Ezio said, 'What the fuck are you?'

'Urgh,' was all the reply he got. Ezio slapped the man hard round the head with his other fist, which was still sheathed in a mailed glove. Blood spurted close to the man's left eye and he moaned in pain.

'What are you? Speak!'

'Ergh.' His open mouth displayed a broken, greyish set of teeth, and the smell that came from it made that of a drunken whore seem sweet.

'Speak!' Ezio drove the point of his sword into the stump and twisted it. He hadn't time to mess about with this wreck of a person. He was worried about his horse.

'Aargh!' Another cry of pain, then a rough, almost incomprehensible voice emerged from the inarticulate grunting, speaking good Italian. 'I am a follower of the *Secta Luporum*.'

The Sect of the Wolves? What the hell is that?'

'You will find out. What you did tonight—'

'Oh, shut up.' Tightening his grip, Ezio stirred up the fire to gain more light and glanced around. Now he saw that he was in a kind of domed chamber, possibly hollowed out deliberately. There was little in it but a couple of chairs and a rough table with a handful of papers on it, weighted down with a stone.

'My brothers will return soon, and then . . .'

Ezio dragged him to the table, pointing with his sword at the papers. 'And these? What are these?'

The man looked at him and spat. Ezio placed his sword point close to the bloody stump again.

'No!' wailed the man. 'Not again!'

'Then tell me.' Ezio looked at the papers. The moment would come when he would have to put his sword down, however briefly, to pick them up. Some of the writing was in Italian, some in Latin, but there were other symbols, which looked like writing, but which he could not decipher.

Then he heard a rustling, coming from the direction he had come. The wolfman's eyes gleamed. 'Our secrets,' he said.

At the same moment two more of the creatures bounded into the room, roaring and clawing at the air with their steel claws. Ezio's prisoner wrenched himself free and would have joined them if Ezio had not slashed his head from his shoulders and sent it rolling towards his friends. He tore round to the other side of the table, seizing the papers, and hurling the table over towards his enemies.

The firelight dimmed. The fire needed stirring again – either that or more fuel. Ezio's eyes strained to pick out the two remaining wolfmen. They were like grey shadows in the room. Ezio dropped back into the darkness, stashed the papers in his tunic and waited.

The wolfmen may have had the strength of the insane, but they couldn't have been very skilled, except in the art, perhaps, of scaring people to death. They certainly couldn't keep quiet or move silently. Using his ears more than his eyes, Ezio managed to circle them, skirting the walls until he knew he was behind them, while they thought he was still somewhere in the darkness ahead of them.

There was no time to lose. He sheathed his sword, unleashed his Hidden Blade, came up, silent as a real wolf behind one of them and, holding him firmly from behind, cut his throat. He died instantly and silently, and Ezio eased the body quietly to the floor. He considered trying to capture the other, but there was no time for interrogation. There might be more of them, and Ezio wasn't sure he had enough strength to fight any more. Ezio could sense the other man's panic, which was confirmed when he left off his impersonation and called anxiously into the silent darkness, 'Sandro?'

It was a simple matter then to locate him, and again the exposed throat was Ezio's hoped-for target. This time, however, the man spun round, frantically tearing at the air in front of him with his claws. He could see Ezio, but Ezio remembered that these creatures wore no mail under their fancy dress. He withdrew the Hidden Blade, and with his larger and less subtle dagger, which had the advantage of a serrated edge, opened the man's breast. The exposed heart and lungs glistened in the dying firelight as the last wolfman fell forward, his face in the fire. A smell of burning hair and flesh threatened to overcome Ezio, but he sprang back and made his way as fast as he could, fighting down panic, to the kindly night air outside.

Once outside, he saw that the wolfmen hadn't touched his horse. Perhaps they had been too sure of trapping him to bother to kill it or drive it away. He untied it and realized he was trembling too much to mount. Instead, he took its bridle and led it back to the Baths of Diocletian. Machiavelli had better be there and he had better be well-armed. By God, if only he still had his Codex gun, or one of those things Leonardo had fashioned for his new master. At least Ezio had the satisfaction of knowing he could still win fights by using his wits and his training – two things they couldn't deprive him of until the day they caught him and tortured him to death.

He remained fully alert on the short journey back to the baths, and found himself occasionally starting at shadows – something that would not have happened to him as a younger man. The thought of a safe arrival brought him no comfort. What if there were another ambush awaiting him there? And what if these creatures had surprised Machiavelli. Was Machiavelli himself aware of the *Secta Luporum*?

Where were Machiavelli's loyalties anyway?

He reached the dim, vast ruin – a memorial to the lost age when Italy had ruled the world – in safety. There was no sign of life that he could see, but then Machiavelli himself emerged from behind an olive tree and greeted him soberly.

'What kept you?'

'I was here before you. But then I was . . . distracted.'
Ezio looked at his colleague evenly.

'What do you mean?'

'Some jokers in fancy dress. Sound familiar?'

Machiavelli's gaze was keen. 'Dressed as wolves?'

'So you do know about them.'

'Yes.'

'Then why suggest here as a meeting place?'

'Are you suggesting that I—?'

'What else am I to think?'

'Dear Ezio.' Machiavelli took a step forward. 'I
assure you, by the Sanctity of our Creed, that I had no
idea they would be here.' He paused. 'But you are right.
I sought a meeting place remote from men, little realizing that they too might choose such a place.'

'Unless they'd been tipped off.'

'If you are impugning my honour . . .'

Ezio made an impatient gesture. 'Oh, forget it,' he
said. 'We've enough to do without quarrelling with
each other.' In truth, Ezio knew that for the moment
he would have to trust Machiavelli. And so far he had
had no reason not to. He would play his cards closer to
his chest in future, though. 'Who are they? What are
they?'

'The Sect of the Wolves. Sometimes they call themselves the Followers of Romulus.'

'Shouldn't we move away from here? I managed to

133

grab some papers of theirs and they might be back to collect them.'

'First, tell me if you got the letter back, and tell me quickly what else has happened to you. You look as if you've been in the wars,' said Machiavelli.

After Ezio had done so, his friend smiled. 'I doubt that they will return tonight. We are two trained, armed men and it sounds as if you well and truly thrashed them. But that in itself will have incensed Cesare. You see, although there is little proof as yet, we believe that these creatures are in the Borgia's employ. They are a band of false pagans who have been terrorizing the city for months.'

'To what purpose?'

Machiavelli spread his hands. 'Political. Propaganda. The idea is that people will be encouraged to throw themselves under the protection of the Papacy, and in return a certain loyalty is exacted from them.'

'How convenient. But even so, shouldn't we be getting out of here now?' Ezio felt suddenly and unsurprisingly tired. His very soul ached.

'They won't be back tonight. No disparagement to your prowess, Ezio, but the wolfmen aren't fighters or even killers. The Borgia use them as trusted go-betweens, but their main job is to frighten. They are poor, deluded souls whom the Borgia have brainwashed into working for them. They believe their new masters will help them rebuild ancient Rome from its very beginnings. The founders of Rome were Romulus and Remus, and they were suckled as babies by a she-wolf.'

'I remember the legend.'

'For the wolfmen, poor creatures, it is no legend. But they are a dangerous enough tool in the Borgia's hands.' He paused briefly. 'Now – the letter! And those papers you say you grabbed from the wolfmen's lair. Well done, by the way.'

'If they're of any use.'

'We'll see. Give me the letter.'

'Here it is.'

Hastily, Machiavelli broke the seal on the parchment. '*Cazzo*,' he muttered. 'It's encrypted.'

'What do you mean?'

This one was supposed to be in plain text. Vinicio is – was – one of my moles among the Borgia. He told me he had it on good authority. The fool! They are transmitting information in code. Without their code sheet we have nothing.'

'Perhaps the papers I got hold of will help.'

Machiavelli smiled. 'By heaven, Ezio, sometimes I thank God we are on the same side. Let's have a look.'

Quickly he sifted through the pages Ezio had seized, and his troubled face cleared.

'Any good?'

'I think . . . perhaps . . .' He read on, his brow furrowed once more. 'Yes! By God, yes! I think we have it!' He clapped Ezio on the shoulder and laughed.

Ezio laughed, too. 'You see? Sometimes logic is not the only way to win a war. Luck can play a part, too. *Andiamo!* You said we had allies in the city. Come on, bring me to them.'

'Follow me.'

15

'What about the horse?' Ezio asked.

'Turn her loose. She'll find her way back to her stable.'

'I can't abandon her.'

'You must. We are going back to the city. If we let her go there, they'll know you got back. If they find the horse out here, they'll think – with luck – that you're still wandering around this area and divert their search here.'

Ezio reluctantly did as he was told, and Machiavelli led him to a concealed flight of stone steps leading underground. At the foot of them a torch was burning, which Machiavelli seized.

'Where are we?' asked Ezio.

'This leads to a system of ancient underground tunnels that criss-cross the city. Your father discovered them and they have remained the Assassin's secret ever since. We can use this route to avoid any guards who are out looking for us, because you may be sure that the wolfmen who escaped will raise the alarm. They're big, because they were used for transport and troops in ancient times, and they're well built, too, as everything was in those days. Many of the outlets within the city have collapsed now and are blocked, so we must pick our way carefully. Stay close – it would be fatal for you to get lost down here.'

For two hours they passed through a labyrinth that seemed never-ending. On the way Ezio glimpsed side tunnels, blocked entranceways, strange carvings of forgotten gods over archways and the occasional flight of steps, some leading upwards, some leading into blackness, a few others showing a glimmer of light at their heads. Finally Machiavelli, who had kept up a steady but hurried pace all along, paused at one such flight.

'We're here,' he announced. 'I'll go first. It's almost dawn. We must be careful.' He vanished up the steps.

After what seemed an age, during which Ezio wondered if he had been abandoned, he heard a whispered 'All clear' from Machiavelli.

Despite his fatigue, Ezio ran up the steps, glad to be back in the fresh air. He'd had enough of tunnels and caves to last a lifetime.

He emerged from a kind of big manhole into a large room, large enough to have been a warehouse of sorts once.

'Where are we?'

'On an island in the Tiber. It was used years ago as a depot. No one comes here now, except us.'

'Us?'

'Our Brotherhood. It is, if you like, our hideout in Rome.'

A burly, confident young man rose from a stool by a table, on which lay papers and the remains of a meal, and came to greet them. His tone was open and friendly.

'Niccolò! *Ben trovato!*' He turned to Ezio. 'And you – you must be the famous Ezio! Welcome!' He took Ezio's hand and shook it warmly. 'Fabio Orsini at your service. I've heard a lot about you from my cousin – an old friend of yours – Bartolomeo d'Alviano.'

Ezio smiled at the name. 'A fine warrior,' he said.

'It was Fabio who discovered this place,' put in Machiavelli.

'Every convenience here,' said Fabio. 'And outside it's so overgrown with ivy and whatnot, you wouldn't even know it existed.'

'It's good to have you on our side.'

'My family has taken a few bad blows from the Borgia of late, and my one aim is to kick their stall in and restore our patrimony.' He looked around doubt-fully. 'Of course, this may all seem a bit shabby to you, after your accommodations in Toscana.'

'This is perfect.'

Fabio smiled. '*Bene*. Well, now that you have arrived, you must forgive me but I must leave you – immediately.'

'What are your plans?' asked Machiavelli.

Fabio's face became serious. 'I am off to begin prep-arations for Romagna. Today, Ceasare has control of my estate and my men, but soon, I hope, we will be free again.'

'*Buona fortuna.*'

'*Grazie.*'

'*Arriverderci.*'

'*Arriverderci.*'

And, with a friendly wave, Fabio was gone.

Machiavelli cleared a space on the table and spread out the encypted letter, together with the wolfmen's decoding page. 'I have to get on with this,' he said. 'You must be exhausted; there's food and wine there, and good, clear Roman water. Refresh yourself while I work, for there is still much to be done.

'Is Fabio one of the allies of whom you spoke?'

'Indeed. And there are others. One very great indeed.'

'And he is? Or is it a "she"?' Ezio asked, thinking, despite himself, of Caterina Sforza. He could not get her out of his mind. She was the Borgia's prisoner still. His own private priority was to free her. But was she playing games with him? He could not rid his mind of a grain of doubt. She was a free spirit, though; he did not own her. Only he did not relish the thought of being played for a fool. And he did not want to be used.

Machiavelli hesitated, as if he had already divulged too much, but then he spoke: 'It is the Cardinal, Giuliano della Rovere. He was in competition with Rodrigo for the Papacy, and lost; but he is still a powerful man, and he has powerful friends. He has potentially strong connections with the French, but he bides his time – he knows that King Louis is only using the

Borgia for as long as it suits him. Above all, he hates the Borgia with a deep and enduring loathing. Do you know how many Spaniards the Borgia have placed in positions of power? We are in danger of having them control Italy.'

'Then he's the man for us. When can I meet him?'

'The time is not yet ripe. Eat while I work.'

Ezio was glad of the hour's respite, but found that hunger and even thirst – at least for wine – had abandoned him. He drank some water gratefully, and toyed with a chicken leg as he watched Machiavelli pore over the papers in front of him.

'Is it working?' he asked at one point.

'Shhh!'

The sun had reached the church towers of Rome by the time Machiavelli put down his quill and drew towards him the spare sheet of paper on which he'd been writing.

'It's done.'

Ezio waited expectantly.

'It's a directive to the wolfmen,' said Machiavelli. 'It states that the Borgia will provide their usual payment and orders the wolfmen to attack – that is, to create terrifying diversions – in various parts of the city not yet under full Borgia control. The attacks are to be timed with the "fortuitous" appearance of a Borgia priest, who will use the Powers of the Church to "banish" the attackers.'

'What do you propose?'

'If you agree, Ezio, I think we should begin planning our own assault on the Borgia. Carry on the good work you started at the stables.'

Ezio hesitated. 'You think we are ready for such an attack?'

'*Sì.*'

'I'd like to know where the Borgia are holding Caterina Sforza first. She'd be a powerful ally.'

Machiavelli looked nonplussed. 'If she is their prisoner, she'll be held at the Castel Sant'Angelo. They've turned it into a stronghold.' He paused. 'It is too bad they have control of the Apple. Oh, Ezio, how could you have let that happen?'

'You were not at Monteriggioni.' It was Ezio's turn to pause after an angry silence. 'Do we *really* know what goes on with our enemies? Do we at least have an underground network here to work with?'

'Hardly. Most of our mercenaries, like Fabio, are tied up in battle with Cesare's forces. And the French still back him.'

Ezio remembered the French general at Monteriggioni – Octavien.

'What have we got?' he asked.

'One solid source. We have girls working at a brothel. It's a high-class joint, frequented by cardinals and other important Roman citizens, but there's a snag. The madam we have in place is lazy, and seems rather to enjoy parties for their own sake than to further our cause by gathering information.'

'What about the city's thieves?' asked Ezio, thinking about the adroit robber who'd almost cost him his purse.

'Well, *sì*, but they refuse to talk to us.'

'Why?'

Machiavelli shrugged. 'I have no idea.'

Ezio rose. 'You'd better tell me how to get out of here.'

'Where are you going?'

'To make some friends.'

'May I ask what friends?'

'I think, for the moment, you had better leave that to me.'

16

It was nightfall by the time Ezio had found the head-quarters of the Roman Thieves' Guild. He'd spent a long day asking questions discreetly in taverns, getting suspicious looks and misleading answers, until, finally, word must have got round that it was all right to let him know the secret location, at which point a raga-muffin boy had led him into a rundown district, through a maze of alleys, and left him at a door, only to disappear immediately the way he had come.

It wasn't much to look at: a large, broken-down-looking inn, whose sign, showing a fox, either asleep or dead, hung awry, whose windows were shrouded with tattered blinds and whose woodwork was in need of repainting.

Unusually for an inn, its door was shut fast, and Ezio hammered on it in vain.

He was surprised by a voice coming from behind him, speaking softly. Ezio spun round. It wasn't like him to allow himself to be approached noiselessly from behind like that. He must ensure that it didn't happen again.

Fortunately, the voice was friendly, if guarded.

'Ezio.'

The man who'd spoken stepped forward from the shelter of a tree and Ezio recognized him immediately. It was his old ally, Gilberto, La Volpe – the Fox – who had led the thieves in Florence in alliance with the Assassins some time previously.

'La Volpe! What are you doing here?'

Gilberto grinned as they embraced. 'Why am I not in Florence, do you mean? Well, that's simply answered. The thieves' leader here died and they elected me. I felt like a change of air, and my old assistant, Corradin, was ready to take over back home. Besides' – he lowered his voice conspiratorially – 'just at the moment, Rome presents me with a little bit more of a . . . challenge, shall we say?'

'Seems a good enough reason to me. Shall we go in?'

'Of course.' La Volpe knocked at the door – obviously using a coded knock – and the door swung open almost immediately to reveal a spacious courtyard with tables and benches laid out, just as you'd expect at an inn, but all very dingy. A handful of people, men and women, bustled about, in and out of doors that led from the courtyard into the inn itself, which was built around it.

'Doesn't look like much, does it?' said La Volpe, ushering him to a seat and calling for wine.

'Frankly—'

'It suits our purposes. And I have plans. But what brings you here?' La Volpe held up a hand. 'Wait! Don't tell me. I think I know the answer.'

'You usually do.'

'You want to put my thieves to work as spies for you.'

'Exactly,' Ezio said, leaning forward eagerly. 'Will you join me?'

La Volpe raised his beaker in a silent toast and drank a little of the wine that had been brought, before replying flatly, 'No.'

Ezio was taken aback. 'What? Why not?'

'Because that would only play into Niccolò Machiavelli's hands. No, thank you. That man is a traitor to our Brotherhood.'

This did not come as a surprise, though Ezio was very far from convinced of the truth of it. He said, 'That's a very serious allegation, coming from a thief. What proof do you have?'

La Volpe looked sour. 'He was an ambassador to the Papal Court, you know, and he travelled as a personal guest of Cesare himself.'

'He did those things on our behalf.'

'Did he? I also happen to know he abandoned you just before the attack on Monteriggioni.'

Ezio made a gesture of disgust. 'Pure coincidence. Look, Gilberto, Machiavelli may not be to everyone's taste, but he *is* an Assassin, *not* a traitor.'

La Volpe looked at him with a set face. 'I'm not convinced.'

At that point in their conversation, a thief whom Ezio recognized as the man who'd tried to steal his purse scuttled up and whispered in La Volpe's ear. La Volpe stood as the thief scuttled off. Ezio, sensing trouble, stood too.

'I apologize for Benito's behaviour yesterday,' said La Volpe. 'He did not know who you were then, and he had seen you riding with Machiavelli.'

'To hell with Benito. What's going on?'

'Ah, Benito brought news. Machiavelli is meeting someone in Trastevere very soon. I'm going to check what's going on. Care to accompany me?'

'Lead on.'

'We'll use one of the old routes – the rooftops. It's a bit tougher here than it was in Florence. Do you think you're up to it?'

'Just lead on.'

It was hard going. The roofs of Rome were spaced further apart than in Florence, and many were crumbling, making it harder to gain a footing. More than once, Ezio sent a loose tile crashing to the ground. But there were few people about in the streets, and they moved so fast that by the time any Borgia guards could react, they were already out of sight. At last they reached a market square, its stalls closed up except for one or two brightly lit wine booths, where a number of people were gathered. Ezio and La Volpe paused on a roof overlooking it, concealing themselves behind chimney stacks, and watched.

Soon afterwards, Machiavelli walked into the square, first glancing around carefully. Ezio watched keenly as another man, wearing the Borgia crest on his cloak, approached Machiavelli, discreetly handing him what looked like a note, before walking on, barely breaking his stride. Machiavelli also moved on, out of the square.

'What do you make of that?' La Volpe asked Ezio.

'I'll follow Machiavelli, you follow the other guy,' snapped Ezio tersely.

At that moment a brawl broke out at one of the wine booths. They heard angry cries and saw the flash of weapons.

'Oh, *merda*! That's some of my men. They've picked a fight with a Borgia guard,' cried La Volpe.

Ezio glimpsed Machiavelli's retreating back as he fled down a street that led towards the Tiber, then he was gone. It was too late to follow him now so he turned his attention back to the brawl. The Borgia guard lay prostrate on the ground. Most of the thieves had scattered, scrambling up the walls to the rooftops and safety, but one of them, a young man, scarcely more than a boy, lay groaning on the ground, his arm spurting blood from a flesh wound.

'Help! Help! My son has been injured!' an anguished voice rang out.

'I recognize that voice,' said La Volpe with a grimace. 'It's Trimalchio.' He looked at the wounded thief. 'And that's Claudio, his younger son!'

Borgia guards armed with guns had appeared on the parapets of two roofs on either side of the far wall of the market and were taking aim.

'They're going to shoot him,' Ezio said urgently.

'Quickly then, I'll take the group to the left, you take the one to the right.'

There were three guards on each side. Moving as unobtrusively as shadows but as swiftly as panthers, Ezio and La Volpe swept around the connecting sides of the square. Ezio saw his three gunmen raise their weapons and take aim at the fallen boy. He sprinted along the spine of the roof, his feet barely touching the tiles, and with one huge leap sprang towards the three gunmen. His jump had sufficient height for him to be able to crumple the middle gunman with the heel of his foot by connecting with the nape of the man's neck. In one movement, Ezio landed on his feet, crouched to absorb the impact of the landing, and then straightened his knees – arms outstretched on either side of him. The two remaining gunmen fell at that instant – a dagger piercing one man's right eye from the side, the blade pushing deep into his skull, while the other gunman was felled by the needle-like point of Ezio's Hidden Blade, which punctured his ear, causing dark viscous liquid to trickle down his neck. Ezio looked up to see that La Volpe had felled his opponents with similar efficiency. After a minute of silent slaughter, all the guards with firearms were dead. But there was a fresh danger, as a platoon of halberdiers charged into the square, weapons lowered and rushing towards the unfortunate Claudio. The people in the wine booths shrank back.

'Claudio! Get out!' La Volpe yelled.

'I can't! Too much . . . pain . . .'

'Hang on.' Ezio, who was fractionally closer to where the boy lay, shouted. 'I'm coming!'

He leapt down from the rooftops, breaking his fall on the canvas roof of one of the market stalls, and was soon by the boy's side. Quickly, he checked the wound, which looked more serious than it was.

'Get up,' he ordered.

'I can't.' Claudio was clearly in a state of panic. 'They're going to kill me.'

'Look. You can walk, can't you?' The boy nodded. 'Then you can also run. Pay attention and follow me. Do exactly what I do. We've got to hide from the guards.'

Ezio drew the boy to his feet and made his way to the nearest wine booth. Once there, he melted into the crowd of nervous drinkers, and was surprised to see how easily Claudio was able to do the same. They eased their way through the booth to the side nearest the wall, while on the other side some of the halber-diers started to push their way in. Just in time, they made it to an alleyway leading off the square to safety. La Volpe and Trimalchio were waiting for them.

'We guessed you'd come this way,' said La Volpe as the father hugged his son. 'Get going,' he said to them. 'We've no time to lose. Get back to headquarters fast and have Teresina dress that wound. Go!'

'And you, keep out of sight for a while, *intesi*?' Ezio added to Claudio.

'*Molte grazie, Messere,*' said the departing Trimalchio, his arm around the boy, guiding him as he admonished him: '*Corri!*'

'You're in trouble now,' said La Volpe once they'd reached the safety of a quiet square. 'Especially after this. I've already seen posters up for you after that business at the stables.'

'None for Machiavelli?'

La Volpe shook his head. 'No. But it's quite possible they didn't get a good look at him. Not many people know how handy he is with a sword.'

'But you don't believe that?'

La Volpe shook his head.

'What to do about the "Wanted" posters?'

'Don't worry. My people are already ripping them down.'

'Glad some of them are more disciplined than to start picking fights for no reason with Borgia guards.'

'Listen, Ezio, there's a tension in this city that you haven't experienced.'

'Really?' Ezio hadn't yet told his friend about the episode with the wolfmen.

'As for the heralds, a few ducats each should be enough to shut them up,' La Volpe continued.

'Or . . . I could eliminate the witnesses.'

'It needn't come to that,' said La Volpe more lightly. 'You know how to "disappear". But be very careful, Ezio. The Borgia have many other enemies apart from you, but none quite so irritating. They won't rest until they have you hanging from hooks at Castel Sant'Angelo.'

'They'll have to catch me first.'

'Keep your guard up.'

They returned by a circuitous route to the Thieves' Guild, where Claudio and his father had already arrived safely. Teresina was dressing the boy's wound, and once the bleeding had been staunched, it turned out to be nothing more than a deep cut into an arm muscle – it hurt like hell but would do no serious harm – and Claudio himself was much more cheerful.

'What a night,' said La Volpe, tiredly, as they sat down over a glass of Trebbiano and a plate of coarse salami.

'You're telling me. I could do with a few less of them.'

'You won't get many while the fight goes on.'

'Listen, Gilberto,' Ezio said. 'I know what we saw, but

I am sure you have nothing to fear from Machiavelli. You know his methods.'

La Volpe looked at him evenly. 'Yes. Very devious.' He paused. 'But I have you to thank for saving Claudio's life. If you believe Machiavelli remains loyal to the Brotherhood, then I am inclined to trust your judgment.'

'So, how do I stand with your thieves? Will you help me?'

'I told you I had plans to do something about this place,' La Volpe said thoughtfully. 'Now that you and I seem to be working together again, I'd like to know what you think, too.'

'Are we working together?'

La Volpe smiled. 'Looks like it. But I'm still keeping an eye on your black-suited friend.'

'Well, it'll do no harm. Just don't do anything rash.'

La Volpe ignored that. 'So tell me, what do you think we should do with this place?'

Ezio considered. 'We need to make sure the Borgia stay away at all costs. Perhaps we could turn it into a proper working inn.'

'I like that idea.'

'It'll need a lot of work – repainting, re-shingling, a new sign.'

'I've got a lot of men. Under your direction . . .'

'Then I will make it so.'

*

A month of respite, or at least semi-respite, followed for Ezio as he busied himself with the business of renovating the Thieves' Guild headquarters, helped by many willing hands. Between them, the thieves represented a variety of skills, since many were tradesmen who'd been put out of work when they'd refused to kowtow to the Borgia. At the end of that time, the place had been transformed. The paintwork was bright, the windows clean and with new blinds. The roof was no longer rickety and the new sign showed a young male fox, still sleeping but certainly not dead. He looked as if, the moment he awoke, he'd be capable of raiding fifty hen coops at a stroke. The double doors gleamed on new hinges and stood open to reveal an immaculate yard.

Ezio, who'd had to go on a mission to Siena during the last week of work, was delighted by the end product when he returned. It was already up and running when he arrived.

'I've kept the name,' La Volpe said. 'I like it. *La Volpe Addormentata*. Can't think why.'

'Let's hope it lulls the enemy into a false sense of security,' grinned Ezio.

'At least all this activity hasn't drawn any undue attention to us. And we run it like a regular inn. We even have a casino. My own idea. And it's turned out to be a great source of income, since we ensure that the Borgia guards who patronize us always lose!'

'And where——?' said Ezio, lowering his voice.

'Ah. Through here.' La Volpe led the way to the west wing of the inn, through a door marked *Uffizi – Privato,* where two thieves stood guard without making it too obvious.

They passed along a corridor, which led to a suite of rooms behind heavy doors. The walls were hung with maps of Rome, the desks and tables covered with neatly stacked papers at which men and women were already working, even though it was only just past dawn.

'This is where our real business is done,' said La Volpe.

'It looks very efficient.'

'One good thing about thieves – good ones, at least,' said La Volpe – 'they're independent thinkers and they like a bit of competition, even amongst themselves.'

'I remember.'

'You'd probably be able to show them a thing or two, if you took part yourself.'

'Oh, I will.'

'But it wouldn't be safe for you to stay here,' said La Volpe. 'For you or for us. But visit me whenever you like – visit me often.'

'I will.' Ezio thought of his own lonely lodgings – lonely, but comfortable and very discreet. He'd have been happy nowhere else. He turned his mind to the business in hand. 'Now that we are organized, the most important thing is to locate the Apple. We have to get it back.'

'*Va bene.*'

'We know the Borgia have it, but despite our best efforts we still haven't been able to track it down. So far, at least, they seem to have made no use of it. I can only think they are still studying it and getting nowhere.'

'Have they sought . . . expert advice?'

'Oh, I'm pretty sure they will have, but he may be pretending to be less intelligent than he is. Let's hope so. And let's hope the Borgia don't become impatient with him.'

La Volpe smiled. 'I won't pursue you on that. But in the meantime, rest assured we already have people scouring Rome for its location.'

'They'll have hidden it well. Very well. Maybe even from one another. There's an increasingly rebellious streak in young Cesare, and his father doesn't like it.'

'What are thieves for but to sniff out well-hidden valuables?'

'*Molto bene.* And now I must go.'

'A last glass before you do?'

'No. I have much to do now. But we will see each other again soon.'

'And where shall I send my reports?'

Ezio considered and replied, 'To the rendezvous of the Assassin Brotherhood on Tiber Island.'

17

It was high time now, Ezio decided, to look up his old friend Bartolomeo d'Alviano, Fabio Orsini's cousin. He'd fought shoulder-to-shoulder with the Orsini against the papal forces back in 1496 and had recently returned from mercenary service in Spain.

Bartolomeo was one of the greatest of the *condotierri*, and an old companion-in-arms of Ezio's. He was also, despite his sometimes oafish manner and a tendency to alarming fits both of anger and depression, a man of unbending loyalty and integrity. Those qualities made him one of the mainstays of the Brotherhood, those and his adamantine hatred of the Templar Sect.

But how would Ezio find him now? He would soon know. He had learned that Bartolomeo had just returned from fighting, to the barracks of his private army, on the outskirts of Rome. The barracks were well outside town, in the countryside to the northeast, but not far from one of the fortified watchtowers the Borgia had erected at various vantage points in and around the city. The Borgia knew better than to tangle with Bartolomeo — at least, not until they felt powerful enough to crush him like the cockroach they considered him to be. And their power, Ezio knew, was growing daily.

He arrived at his destination soon after the hour of *pranzo*. The sun was past its peak and the day was too hot, the discomfort mitigated by a westerly breeze. Arriving at the huge gate in the high palisade that surrounded the barracks, he pounded it with his fist.

A judas set in the gate opened and Ezio sensed an eye appraising him. Then it closed and he heard a brief, muffled conversation. The judas opened again. Then there was a joyous, baritone bellow, and after much drawing of bolts, the gate was flung open. A large man, slightly younger than Ezio, stood there, his rough army clothes in slightly less than usual disarray, with his arms held wide.

'Ezio Auditore, you old so-and-so! Come in. Come in. I'll kill you if you don't.'

'Bartolomeo.'

The two old friends embraced warmly, then walked across the barracks square towards Bartolomeo's quarters.

'Come on. Come on,' Bartolomeo said with his usual eagerness. 'There's someone I want you to meet.'

They'd arrived inside a long, low room, well lit from large windows facing the inner square. It was a room that clearly served both for living and for dining, and it was spacious and airy. But there was something very unlike Bartolomeo about it. There were clean blinds on the windows. There was an embroidered cloth spread on the table, from which the remains of lunch had already been cleared. There were pictures on the walls. There was even a bookcase. Bianca, Bartolomeo's beloved great sword, was nowhere to be seen. Above all, the place was unbelievably tidy.

'Wait here,' said Bartolomeo, snapping his fingers at an orderly for wine, and clearly in a state of high excitement. 'Now just guess who I want you to meet?'

Ezio glanced around the room again. 'Well, I've met Bianca . . .'

Bartolomeo made a gesture of impatience. 'No, no! She's in the map room – it's where she lives nowadays. Guess again.'

'Well,' Ezio said slyly, 'could it possibly be . . . your wife?'

Bartolomeo looked so crestfallen that Ezio almost felt sorry for having made so accurate a deduction, not that it had been hard, exactly. But the big man cheered up quickly and continued, 'She's such a treasure. You wouldn't believe it.' He turned and bellowed in the direction of the inner rooms, 'Pantasilea! Pantasilea!' The orderly appeared again with a tray bearing sweetmeats, a decanter and glasses. 'Where is she?' Bartolomeo said.

'Have you checked under the table?' Ezio asked, tongue-in-cheek.

Just then, Pantasilea appeared, descending a staircase that ran along the western wall of the room.

'Here she is!'

Ezio stood to greet her.

He bowed. 'Auditore, Ezio.'

'Baglioni, Pantasilea – now Baglioni-d'Alviano.'

She was still young – in her mid- to late twenties, Ezio judged. By her name she was from a noble family, and her dress, though modest, was pretty and tasteful. Her face, framed by fine blonde hair, was oval; her nose tip-tilted like a flower; her lips generous and humorous, as were her intelligent eyes – a deep, dark brown – which were welcoming when she looked at you, and yet seemed to withhold something of herself. She was tall, reaching Bartolomeo's shoulders, and slender, with wide shoulders and narrow hips; long, slim arms and shapely legs. Bartolomeo had clearly found a treasure. Ezio hoped he'd be able to hang onto her.

'*Lieta di conoscervi,*' Pantasilea was saying.

'*Altrettanto a lei.*'

She glanced from one man to the other. 'We will have time to meet properly on another occasion,' she said to Ezio, with the air of a woman not leaving men to their business, but of having business of her own.

'Stay a little, *tesora mia.*'

'No, Barto, you know I have to see the clerk. He always manages to bungle the accounts, somehow. And there is something wrong with the water supply.

I must see to that, too.' To Ezio she said, '*Ora, mi scusi, ma . . .*'

'*Con piacere.*'

Smiling at both, she remounted the stairs and disappeared.

'What do you think?' Bartolomeo asked.

'Charmed, truly.' Ezio was sincere. He'd also noticed how his friend reined himself in in her presence. He imagined there'd be very little barrack-room swearing around Pantasilea. He did wonder what on earth she saw in her husband, but then, he didn't know her at all.

'I think she'd do anything for me.'

'Where did you meet her?'

'We'll talk about that some other time.' Bartolomeo seized the decanter and two glasses and put his free arm round Ezio's shoulders. 'I am very glad you've come. I've just got back from campaigning as you must know, and as soon as I heard you were in Rome I was going to send men out to locate you. I know you like to keep your lodgings secret and I don't blame you, especially in this nest of vipers, but luckily you've beaten me to it. And that's good, because I want to talk to you about the war. Let's go to the map room.'

'I know Cesare has an alliance with the French,' Ezio said. 'How goes the fight against them?'

'*Bene.* The companies I've left out there, who'll be campaigning under Fabio, are holding their own. And I've more men to train here.'

Ezio considered this. 'Machiavelli seemed to think things were . . . more difficult.'

Bartolomeo shrugged. 'Well, you know Machiavelli. He—'

They were interrupted by the arrival of one of Bartolomeo's sergeants. Pantasilea was at his side. The man was in a panic While she was calm.

'*Capitano*,' said the sergeant urgently. 'We need your help now. The Borgia have launched an attack.'

'What? I hadn't expected that so soon. Excuse me, Ezio.' To Pantasilea, Bartolomeo cried, 'Throw me Bianca.'

She immediately tossed the great sword across the room to him and, buckling it on, Bartolomeo ran out of the room, following his sergeant. Ezio made to follow, but Pantasilea held him back, grasping his arm firmly.

'Wait!' she said.

'What is it?'

She looked deeply concerned. 'Ezio, let me get straight to the point. The fight is not going well – either here or out in the Romagna – we've been attacked on both sides. The Borgia are on one flank, the French under General Octavien on the other. But know this: the Borgia position is weak. If we can defeat them, we can concentrate our forces on the French front. Taking this tower would help. If someone could get round the back . . .'

Ezio inclined his head. 'Then I think I know a way I can help. Your information is invaluable. *Mille grazie, Madonna d'Alviano.*'

She smiled. 'It's the least a wife can do to help her husband.'

18

The Borgia had launched a surprise attack on the barracks, choosing the hour of the siesta to do so. Bartolomeo's men had fought them off using traditional weapons, but as they drove them back towards the tower, Ezio could see Cesare's gunmen massing on its battlements, all armed with their new wheel-locks, which they were training on the *condottieri* swarming below.

He skirted the melee, managing to avoid any confrontation with the Borgia troops. He circled and made his way around to the back of the tower. As he'd expected, everyone's attention was focused on the battle going on at the front. He clambered up the outer walls, easily finding footholds in the rough-hewn stones from which it had been built. Bartolomeo's men were armed with crossbows, and some had matchlocks, for long-range work, but they would not be able to withstand the deadly fire of the sophisticated new wheel-lock guns.

Ezio arrived at the top, some forty feet above the ground, in less than three minutes. He heaved himself over the rear parapet, sinews straining, and silently lowered himself onto the roof of the tower. He stalked behind the musketeers, moving one quiet step after another closer to the enemy. He silently drew his dagger and unleashed his Hidden Blade. He stole up behind the men, and in a sudden frenzy of killing, dispatched four gunmen with the two blades. It was only then that the Borgia sharpshooters realized the enemy was amongst them. Ezio saw a man turn his wheel-lock towards him; he was still some 15 feet away, so Ezio simply launched his dagger through the air. It pirouetted three times before embedding itself between the man's eyes with a sickening thud. The man fell, but not before he'd squeezed the trigger of his musket – luckily for Ezio the barrel had slipped away from its intended aim, and the ball shot to the man's right, hitting his nearest colleague and passing clean through his Adam's apple before embedding itself in the shoulder of the man behind him. Both men fell, leaving only three Borgia gunmen on the tower roof. Without pausing, Ezio leapt sideways, and with the flat of his hand slapped the nearest man across the face with such force he toppled backwards over the battlements. Ezio grabbed his weapon by the barrel as the man fell and swung the gun butt into the next soldier's face. He followed his colleague over the wall with an agonized yell. The last man raised his hands in surrender, but it was too late – Ezio's Hidden Blade had already found its way between his ribs.

Ezio grabbed another rifle and bounded down the stairs to the floor below. There were four men here, firing through narrow slits in the thick stone walls. Ezio squeezed the trigger, holding the musket at waist height. The furthest went down with the impact of the shot, his chest exploding with red gore. Taking two strides forward, Ezio swung the gun like a club, barrel first this time, connecting with another man's knee so that he crumpled. One of the remaining men had turned sufficiently to take a shot. Ezio rolled forwards instinctively and felt the air searing as the ball missed his cheek by a matter of inches and embedded itself in the wall behind. Ezio's momentum sent him crashing into the gunman and the man lurched backwards, his head crunching into the thick stone battlement. The last soldier had also swivelled round to tackle the unexpected threat. He looked down as Ezio sprang up from the floor, but only for an instant, as the Hidden Blade skewered the man's jaw.

The man who's knee Ezio had shattered stirred and tried to reach his dagger, but Ezio simply kicked the man's temple and turned, unbothered, to watch the battle unfolding down below. It was resolving itself into a rout. With no overwhelming firepower on their side any more, the Borgia soldiers fell back fast, and soon turned tail and fled, abandoning the tower to the *condottieri*.

Ezio descended the staircase to the tower's main

gate, encountering a handful of guards who put up fierce resistance before succumbing to his sword. Ensuring that the tower was clear of Borgia men, he flung open the gate and went out to join Bartolomeo. The battle was over and Pantasilea had joined her husband.

'Ezio, Well done! Together, we sent those *luridi codardi* running for the hills.'

'Yes, we did.' Ezio exchanged a secret, conspiratorial smile with Pantasilea. Her sound advice had won the fight as much as anything.

'Those new-fangled guns,' said Bartolomeo. 'We've managed to capture a few, but we're still working out how to use them.' He beamed. 'Anyway, now that the Pope's dogs have fled, I'll be able to draw more men to the fight on our side. But first, and especially after this business, I want to reinforce our barracks.'

'Good idea. But who's going to do it?'

Bartolomeo shook his head. 'I'm not much good with these things. You're the one with an education, why don't you approve the plans?'

'You got some drawn up?'

'Yes. I engaged the services of a brilliant young man. A Florentine like you by the name of Michelangelo Buonarotti.'

'Never heard of him, but, *va bene*. In return I need to know Cesare's and Rodrigo's every move. Can some of your men shadow them for me?'

'One thing I'll soon have no shortage of is men. At least, I've enough to give you a decent workforce for the rebuilding work, and a handful of skilled scouts to cover the Borgia for you.'

'Excellent!' Ezio knew that Machiavelli had spies in place, but Machiavelli tended to play his cards close to his chest and Bartolomeo didn't. Machiavelli was a closed room; Bartolomeo the open sky. And while Ezio didn't share La Volpe's suspicions – which he hoped he'd now allayed – there was no harm in having a second string to his bow.

He spent the next month supervising the strengthening of the barracks, repairing the damage done in the attack, building taller and stronger watchtowers, and replacing the palisades with stone walls. When the work was complete, he and Bartolomeo took a tour of inspection.

'Isn't she a thing of beauty?' beamed Bartolomeo.

'Very impressive, I think.'

'And the even better news is, more and more men are joining us every day. Of course, I encourage competition between them: it's good for morale and it's good training too, for when they go out and fight for real.' He showed Ezio a large wooden board with his crest at the top, mounted on an easel. 'As you can see, this board shows the ranking of our top warriors. The better they become, the higher they move up the board.'

'And where am I?'

Bartolomeo gave him a look and waved at the air above the board. 'Somewhere up here, I should think.'

A *condottiero* came up to tell him that one of his best men, Gian, had begun his fight down in the parade ground.

'If you want to show off, we have sparring matches too. Now, if you'll excuse me, I've got money on this boy.' Laughing, he took his leave.

Ezio made his way to the new, improved map room. The natural light was better and the room had been enlarged to accommodate broader map tables and easels. He was poring over a map of the Romagna when Pantasilea joined him.

'Where is Bartolomeo?' she asked.

'At the fight.'

Pantasilea sighed. 'He has such an aggressive view of the world. However, I think strategy is just as important. Don't you agree?'

'I do.'

'Let me show you something.'

She led the way from the room to a wide balcony overlooking an inner courtyard of the barracks. On one side of it was a sizeable new dovecote, alive with birds.

'These are carrier pigeons,' Pantasilea explained. 'Each one, sent from Niccolò Machiavelli in the city, brings me the name of a Borgia agent in Rome. The Borgia grew fat on the Jubilee of 1500. All that money from eager pilgrims, willing to buy themselves absolution. And those that would not pay were robbed.'

Ezio looked grim.

'But your various attacks have unsettled the Borgia badly,' Pantasilea continued. 'Their spies comb the city, seeking out our people and exposing them where they can. Machiavelli has uncovered some of their names as well, and these too he is often able to send me by pigeon post. Meanwhile, Rodrigo has added even more new members to the Curia, in an attempt to maintain his balance of power among the cardinals. As you know, he has decades of experience in Vatican politics.'

'Indeed he has.'

'You must take these names with you when you return to the city. They will be useful to you.'

'I am lost in admiration, *Madonna*.'

'Hunt these people down, eliminate them if you can, and we will all breathe more easily for it.'

'I must return to Rome without delay. And I will tell you something that makes *me* breathe more easily.'

'Yes?'

'What you have just disclosed proves that Machiavelli is undoubtedly one of us.' But then Ezio hesitated. 'Even so . . .'

'Yes?'

'I have a similar arrangement with Bartolomeo. Give it a week, then ask him to come to the island in the Tiber – he knows the place and I daresay you do, too – bringing me what he has gleaned about Rodrigo and Cesare.'

'Do you doubt Machiavelli still?'

'No, but I am sure you'll agree that it is good to double-check *all* the information one gets, especially in times like these.'

A shadow seemed to pass across her face, but then she smiled and said, 'He will be there.'

19

Back in Rome, Ezio made his first port of call the brothel Machiavelli had mentioned as another source of information – perhaps some of the names he was sending Pantasilea by carrier pigeon came from there. He needed to check on how the girls collected their information, but he'd decided to go there incognito. If they knew who he was, they might just give him the information they thought he wanted.

He arrived at the address and checked the sign: The Rosa in Fiore. There was no doubt of it, and yet it didn't look like the kind of place the Borgia *nomenklatura* might frequent – unless they went in for slumming. It certainly wasn't a patch on Paola's establishment in Florence, at least from the outside. But then, Paola's place had kept a pretty discreet shop front. He knocked dubiously on the door.

It was opened immediately by an attractive, plump girl of about eighteen, wearing a tired-looking silk dress.

She flashed him a professional smile. 'Welcome, stranger. Welcome to the Rosa in Fiore.'

'*Salve*,' he said, as she let him pass. The entrance hall

was certainly a step up, but even so there was an air of neglect about the place.

'And what did you have in mind for today?' the girl asked.

'Would you be kind enough to get your boss for me?'

The girl's eyes became slits. '*Madonna* Solari isn't in.'

'I see.' He paused, uncertain what to do. 'Do you know where she is?'

'Out.' The girl was distinctly less friendly now.

Ezio gave her his most charming smile, but he wasn't a young man any more and he could see that it cut no ice with the girl. She thought he was an official of some sort. Damn! Well, if he wanted to get any further, he'd have to pretend to be a client. And if pretending to be one meant actually becoming one, so be it.

He had just decided on this course of action when the street door suddenly burst open and another girl ran in, her hair awry, her dress disarranged. She was distraught.

'*Aiuto! Aiuto!*' she cried urgently. '*Madonna* Solari—' she sobbed, unable to continue.

'What is it Lucia? Pull yourself together. What are you doing back so soon? I thought you'd gone off with *Madonna* and some clients.'

'Those men weren't clients, Agnella. They . . . they . . . said they were taking us to a place they knew down by the Tiber, but there was a boat there and they started to slap us about and drew knives. They took Madonna Solari on board and chained her up.'

'Lucia! *Dio mio!* How did you get away?' Agnella put an arm round her friend and guided her to a couch set along one wall. She took out a handkerchief and dabbed at a red weal that was starting to rise on Lucia's cheek.

'They let me go – sent me back with a message – they're slave traders, Agnella. They say they'll only let her go if we buy her back. Otherwise they'll kill her.'

'How much do they want?' Ezio asked.

'A thousand ducats.'

'How much time do we have?'

'They'll wait an hour.'

'Then we have time. Wait here. I'll get her back for you.' *Cazzo!* Ezio thought. *This looks bad. I need to talk to that woman.* 'Where are they?'

'There's a jetty, *Messere.* Near Isola Tiberina. Do you know the place?'

'Very well.'

Ezio made haste. There was no time to get to Chigi's bank and none of its three branches was on his route, so he resorted to a moneylender, who drove a hard bargain, but made up the sum Ezio already carried to the one thousand required. Armed with this, but determined not to part with a penny of it if he could possibly avoid it, and swearing to exact interest from the bastards who'd taken the one person he most needed to talk to, he hired a horse and rode recklessly through the streets towards the Tiber, scattering the people, chickens and dogs that cluttered them as he went.

He found the boat – more of a small ship really – without difficulty, thank God, and, dismounting, ran to the end of the jetty on which it was moored, yelling Madonna Solari's name.

Her captives were prepared for him. There were two men already on deck and they trained pistols on him. Ezio's eyes narrowed. Pistols? In the hands of cheap little villains like these?

'Don't come any closer.'

Ezio backed off, but kept his finger on the release trigger of his Hidden Blade.

'Brought the fuckin' money, have you?'

Ezio slowly produced the pouch that contained the thousand ducats with his other hand.

'Good. Now we'll see if the captain's in a good enough mood *not* to slit her fuckin' throat.'

'The captain! Who the hell do you think you are? Bring her out! Bring her out now!'

The rage in Ezio's voice subdued the slave trader who'd spoken. He turned slightly and called to someone below deck, who must already have heard the interchange because two men were on their way up the companionway, manhandling a woman of perhaps thirty-five. Her makeup was badly smeared, both by tears and rough treatment, and there were ugly bruises on her face, shoulders and breasts, which were exposed where her lilac dress had been ripped apart, revealing the bodice beneath. There was blood on her dress, lower down, and she was manacled hand and foot.

'Here's the little treasure now,' sneered the trader who'd first spoken.

Ezio breathed hard. This was a lonely bend of the river, but he could see Tiber Island only fifty yards in the distance. If only he could get word to his friends. If they had heard anything, they'd assume it was just a bunch of drunken sailors – God knows, there were enough of them along the riverbank – and if Ezio raised his voice or called for help, La Solari would be dead in an instant, and himself, too, unless the gunmen were bad shots, for the range was negligible.

As the woman's desperate eyes caught Ezio's, a third man, sloppily dressed in the sad remains of a naval captain's jacket, came up the ladder. He looked at Ezio, then at the bag of money.

'Throw it over,' he said in a rough voice.

'Hand her over first. And take off those manacles.'

'Are you fuckin' deaf? Throw. Over. The. Fuckin'. Money!'

Involuntarily, Ezio moved forward. Immediately the guns were raised threateningly, the captain drew a falchion and the two others took a tighter grip on the woman, making her moan and wince with pain.

'Don't come any closer. We'll finish her if you do.'

Ezio stopped, but did not retreat. He measured the distance between where he stood and the deck with his eyes. His finger trembled over the trigger of the Hidden Blade.

'I have the money; it's all here,' he said, waving the bag and edging one step closer while their eyes were on it.

'Stay where you are. Don't test me. If you take one step more, she dies.'

'You won't get your money then.'

'Oh, won't we? There's five of us and one of you, and I don't think you'd get a fuckin' toe on board before my friends here had shot you in the mouth and in the balls.'

'Hand her over first.'

'Look, are you stupid or what? Nobody gets near this fuckin' boat unless you want this *puttana* dead!'

'*Messere! Aiutateme!*' whimpered the wretched woman.

'Shut the fuck up, you bitch!' snarled one of the men holding her, hitting her across the eyes with the pommel of his dagger.

'All right!' yelled Ezio, as he saw fresh blood spurt from the woman's face. 'That's enough. Let her go. Now.'

He threw the bag of money over to the captain so it landed at his feet.

'That's better,' said the slave trader. 'Now, let's finish this business.'

Before Ezio could react, he placed the blade of his sword against the side of the woman's throat and drew it across, down and deep, half-severing her head from her body.

'Any objections, take it up with *Messer* Cesare,' sneered the captain as the body slumped to the deck under a fountain of blood. Almost imperceptibly, he nodded to the two men with pistols.

Ezio knew what was coming next, and he was ready. With lightning speed he dodged both bullets, and in the same instant that he threw himself into the air, he released the Hidden Blade. With it he stabbed the first of the men who'd been holding the prisoner deep in the left eye. Before the man had even fallen to the deck, Ezio, dodging a swinging blow from the captain's falchion and, coming up from underneath, he plunged the blade low down into the other man's belly, ripping as he thrust. The blade wasn't designed for slicing, and bent a little, tearing rather than cutting, but no matter.

Now for the gunmen. As he'd expected, they were frantically trying to reload their weapons, but panic had made them clumsy. He rapidly withdrew the blade and unsheathed his heavy dagger. The fighting was too close for him to be able use his sword, and he needed the dagger's serrated edge and heavy blade. He sliced off the weapon hand of one gunman, then jabbed the point hard into the man's side. He hadn't time to finish the job, though, because the other gunman, coming from behind, clubbed him with the butt of his pistol. Luckily the blow didn't find its mark, and Ezio, shaking his head to clear it, swung round and drove his dagger into the man's chest as he raised his arms to attempt another blow.

He looked round. Where was the captain?

Ezio caught sight of him stumbling along the river-bank, clutching the bag as coins spilled from it. *Fool*, thought Ezio, *he should have taken the horse*. He bounded after him, easily catching up, for the bag was heavy. He seized the captain by the hair and kicked his legs away, forcing him to kneel with his head back.

'Now for a taste of your own medicine,' he said, and severed the captain's head exactly as he had done to *Madonna* Solari.

Letting the body fall writhing to the ground, he picked up the bag and made his way back to the boat, collecting fallen coins as he went. The wounded slave trader squirmed on deck. Ezio ignored him and went below, ransacking the meagre cabin he found there and quickly locating a small strongbox, which he wrenched open with the bloody blade of his dagger. It was full of diamonds.

'That'll do,' said Ezio to himself, tucking it under his arm and running up the companionway again.

He loaded the bag of coins and box of diamonds into the saddlebags of his horse, along with the pistols, then he returned to the wounded man, nearly slipping on the blood in which the slave trader slithered. Bending down, Ezio cut one of the man's hamstrings, keeping a hand over his mouth to stop him howling. That should slow him up. For good.

He pressed his mouth close to the man's ear.

'If you survive,' he said, 'and get back to that pox-ridden louse you call your master, tell him all this was done with the compliments of Ezio Auditore. If not, *Requiescat in Pace.*'

Ezio didn't return to the brothel immediately. It was late. He returned the horse, bought a sack from the ostler for a few coins, and stowed his spoils, and the money, in it. He slung the sack over his shoulder and made his way to the moneylender, who seemed surprised and disappointed to see him back so soon, and gave him what he owed. Then he returned to his lodgings, taking care to blend in with the evening crowds whenever he sighted Borgia guards.

Once there, he had them bring him water to bathe, undressed, and washed himself wearily, wishing that Caterina would once again appear at the door and surprise him. This time there was no one to interrupt him so pleasantly. He changed into fresh clothes and shoved the ones he'd been wearing – ruined by the day's work – into the sack. He would get rid of them later. He cleaned the pistols and put them in a satchel. He'd thought of keeping them, but they were heavy and unwieldy, so he decided to hand them over to Bartolomeo. Most of the diamonds would go to Bartolomeo, too, but after examining them, Ezio selected five of the largest and best and put them in his own wallet. They'd ensure that he wouldn't have to waste time scraping around for money for a while, at least.

Everything else he'd get La Volpe to send to the barracks. If you can't trust a friendly thief, who can you trust?

Soon he was ready to go out again. The satchel was slung over his shoulder and his hand was on the latch when he was overcome by tiredness. He was tired of the killing; tired of the greed, and the grasping for power, and tired of the misery that all that led to.

He was almost tired of the fight.

He let his hand fall from the door and unslung the satchel, placing it on his bed. He locked the door and undressed once more, then he snuffed out the candle and all but fell onto the bed. He just had time to remember to place a protecting arm around the bag before he fell asleep.

He knew the respite wouldn't be long.

At The Sleeping Fox, Ezio handed over the satchel with precise instructions. He didn't like to delegate this job, but he was needed elsewhere. The reports La Volpe's spies had brought in were few, but the results coincided with those Machiavelli had sent by carrier pigeon to Pantasilea, which assuaged most of Ezio's remaining misgivings about his friend, though La Volpe remained reserved. Ezio could understand it. Machiavelli came across as remote, even cold. Although they were fellow Florentines, and Florence had no love for Rome, and especially not for the Borgia, it seemed that La Volpe, despite all the evidence to the contrary, still harboured doubts.

'Call it a gut feeling,' was all he said, gruffly, when Ezio pressed the point.

There was no news of the Apple, except that it was still in the possession of the Borgia, though whether Cesare or Rodrigo had it was uncertain. Rodrigo well knew its potential, though to Ezio it seemed unlikely that he would confide much of what he knew to his son, given the tension between them. As for Cesare, he was the last person seen in control of it, but there was no sign that he was using it. Ezio prayed that whoever he had given it to for study – if indeed he *had* done so – was either stumped by its mysteries or was concealing them from his master.

Machiavelli was nowhere to be found. Even at the Assassin's secret headquarters on Tiber Island he had left no news. The best information Ezio could get was that he was 'away', but he wasn't reported to be in Florence either. The two young friends who were temporarily in Rome at the time – Baldassare Castiglione and Pietro Bembo – and running the hideout were completely reliable, and already associate members of the Brotherhood, not least because one had connections with Cesare and the other with Lucrezia. It was a pity, Ezio thought, that the first had to return to Mantua soon and the other to Venice. He consoled himself with the thought that they would nonetheless be useful to him in their home towns.

Satisfied that he had done what he could on those fronts, Ezio turned his thoughts back to The Rosa in Fiore.

This time, when he paid a visit to the brothel, the door was open. The place seemed airier somehow, and lighter. He'd remembered the names of the girls he'd met on the day of Madonna Solari's abduction, and after having given them to the older and more sophisticated woman in the entrance hall, who, he noticed, had two well-dressed, young, polite, but tough-looking men standing guard, he was ushered through to the inner courtyard, where, he was told, he'd find the girls.

He found himself in a rose garden, surrounded by high red-brick walls. A pergola, almost hidden under luxuriant pink climbing roses, ran along one wall, and in the centre was a small fountain with white marble benches around it. The girls he sought were with a group of others, talking to two older women whose backs were to him. They turned on his approach.

He was about to introduce himself – he'd decided to try another tack this time – when his jaw dropped.

'Mother! Claudia! What are you doing here?'

'Waiting for you. *Ser* Machiavelli told us we might find you here. Before he left.'

'Where is he? Did you see him in Florence?'

'No.'

'But what are you doing here in Rome?' he repeated dumbly. He was filled with shock and anxiety. 'Has Florence been attacked?'

'No, nothing like that,' said Maria. 'But the rumours were true: our *palazzo* has been destroyed. There is nothing for us there.'

'And even if it were not in ruins, I would never go back to Mario's *rocca* at Monteriggioni,' put in Claudia. Ezio looked at her and nodded. He understood what a backwater that place would seem to a woman like her, but his heart was troubled.

'So we have come here. We have taken a house in Rome,' continued Maria. 'Our place is with you.'

Thoughts raced through Ezio's mind. In his innermost heart, though he scarcely admitted it to his conscious mind, he still felt that he might have prevented the deaths of his father and brothers. He had failed them. Maria and Claudia were all that was left of his family. Might he not fail them in the same way? He did not want them to be dependent on him.

He attracted danger. If they were near him, would they not attract danger too? He didn't want their deaths on his head. They'd have been better off in Florence, where they had friends, where their safety, in a city once again stable under the wise management of Piero Soderini, would have been ensured.

'Ezio,' said Claudia, interrupting his thoughts. 'We want to help.'

'I sought to keep you safe by sending you to Firenze.' He tried to keep the impatience out of his voice, but found that he was snapping as he spoke. Maria and Claudia looked shocked, and although Maria let it go quickly, Ezio could see that Claudia was wounded and offended. Had she picked up something of his thoughts?

Luckily, they were interrupted by Agnella and Lucia. '*Messer*, excuse us, but we are anxious. 'We still have no news of Madonna Solari. Do you know what has become of her?'

Ezio's thoughts were still on Claudia and the expression in her eyes, but his attention switched at the question. Cesare must have done a good cover-up job. But then again, bodies were found in the Tiber practically every day, and some of them had been there for some time.

'She's dead,' he said abruptly.

'What?' cried Lucia.

'*Merda*,' said Agnella succinctly.

The news spread quickly among the girls.

'What do we do now?' asked one.

'Will we have to close?' asked another.

Ezio deduced the undercurrent of their anxiety. Under Madonna Solari, however inefficient Machiavelli had said she was, these girls had been collecting information for the Assassins. Without protection, and if, as Solari's death suggested, Cesare had his suspicions about The Rosa in Fiore, what might their fate be? On the other hand, if he had thought that Solari wasn't the *only* spy in the place, wouldn't he have made a move by now?

That was it. There was still hope.

'You cannot close,' he told them. 'I need your help.'

'But *Messere*, without someone to run things, we are finished.'

A voice near him said decisively, 'I'll do it.'

It was Claudia.

Ezio wheeled on her. 'You do not belong *here*, sister!'

'I know how to run a business,' she retorted. 'I ran Uncle Mario's estates out in the sticks for years.'

'This is quite different.'

His mother's calming voice intervened. 'What alternative do you have, Ezio? You need someone fast, evidently, and you know you can trust your sister.'

Ezio saw the logic of this, but it would mean putting Claudia on the front line – the very place he most dreaded her being. He glared at her, and she returned the look with defiance.

'You do this, Claudia, and you are on your own. You'll get no special protection from me.'

'I've done perfectly well without that for twenty years,' she sneered.

'Fine,' he returned icily. 'Then you'd better get down

to work. First of all, I want this place thoroughly cleaned up, redecorated and improved in every way. Even this garden needs a good job done on it. I want this place to be the best establishment in town. And God knows you've got competition. And I want the girls clean – this new disease no one seems to know much about, it's rife in all the ports and in the biggest cities, so we all know what that means.'

'We'll see to it,' replied Claudia coldly.

'You'd better. And there's another thing. While you're at it, I want your courtesans to find out the whereabouts of Caterina Sforza.' He remained stony-faced.

'You can count on us.'

'You're in this now, Claudia. Any mistakes and they're on your head.'

'I can take care of myself, Brother.'

'I hope you can,' growled Ezio, turning on his heel.

21

Ezio was busy for the next few weeks, consolidating the remaining forces of the Brotherhood gathered in Rome, and deciding what use to make of the initial information he had gathered from La Volpe, and from the early reports sent by Bartolomeo. He hardly dared hope that the tide was turning against the Borgia, but it could be that he was looking at the beginning of the end. He remembered, however, the old adage about how much easier it is to handle a young lion than to approach an old, experienced one. Set against his cautious optimism was the fact that Cesare's grip on the Romagna was tightening, while the French held Milan. Nor had the French withdrawn their support from the Papal Commander. Years earlier, the Cardinal of San Pietro in Vincula, Giuliano della Rovere, the Pope's great enemy, had tried to turn the French against the Borgia and topple Alexander from his seat, but Alexander had outwitted him. How could Ezio succeed where della Rovere had failed? At least no one had poisoned the cardinal – he was too powerful for that – and he remained Ezio's trump card.

Ezio had also decided, though this he kept to himself,

that his mission should be to encourage the Brotherhood to relocate their headquarters permanently to Rome. Rome was at the centre of world affairs – and the centre of world corruption. Where else could be better suited, especially now that Monteriggioni was no longer a viable option. Ezio had plans for a system of distribution of the Brotherhood's funds, in response to individual Assassins' successfully completed missions. Those diamonds he'd taken from the slave traders had come in very handy and been a welcome addition to the campaign fund.

One day . . .

But 'one day' was still a long way off. The Brotherhood still had no new elected leader, though by common consent, and by virtue of their actions, he and Machiavelli had become its temporary chiefs. This was only temporary, though, and nothing had been ratified in formal council.

Caterina still preyed on Ezio's mind.

He had left Claudia to oversee the renovation of The Rosa in Fiore without any supervision or interference. Let her sink or swim in her own overweening confidence. It would be no fault of his if she sank. The brothel was an important link in his network, however, and he admitted to himself that if he really had no faith in her, he might have leaned on her harder in the first place. Now was the time to put her work – what she had achieved – to the test.

When he returned to The Rosa in Fiore, he was as surprised as he was pleased. It was just as successful as his other transformations in the city and at Bartolomeo's barracks, though he was modest and realistic enough not to take all the credit for those. He hid his delight as he took in the sumptuous rooms hung with costly tapestries, the wide sofas, the soft silk cushions and the white wines chilled with ice – an expensive luxury.

The girls looked like ladies, not whores, and from their manner someone had evidently taught them to be more refined. As for the clientele, the least he could infer was that business was booming, and though he'd had his reservations about the nature of their standing earlier, there could be no doubt now. Looking around the central salon, he could see at least a dozen cardinals and senators, as well as members of the Apostolic Camera and other officers of the Curia.

They were all enjoying themselves, all relaxed, and all – he hoped – unsuspecting. But the proof of the pudding would lie in the value of the information Claudia's courtesans were able to extract from this venal bunch of slobs.

He caught sight of his sister – modestly dressed, he was glad to see – talking rather too affectionately (to his mind) to Ascanio Sforza, the former Vice-Chancellor of the Curia and now in Rome again after his brief disgrace, trying to wheedle his way back into Papal favour. When Claudia caught sight of Ezio, her expression changed. She excused herself from the cardinal and came towards him, a brittle smile on her face.

'Welcome to The Rosa in Fiore, Brother,' she said.

'Indeed.' He did not smile.

'As you can see, it is the most popular brothel in Rome.'

'Corruption is still corruption, however well dressed it is.'

She bit her lip. 'We have done well. And don't forget why this place *really* exists.'

'Yes,' he replied. 'The Brotherhood's money seems to have been well invested.'

'That's not all. Come to the office.'

To Ezio's surprise, he found Maria there, doing some paperwork with an accountant. Mother and son greeted each other guardedly.

'I want to show you this,' said Claudia, producing a book. 'Here is where I keep a list of all the skills taught to my girls.'

'*Your* girls?' Ezio could not keep the sarcasm out of his voice. His sister was taking to this like a duck to water.

'Why not? Take a look.' Her own manner had tightened.

Ezio leafed through the proffered book. 'You aren't teaching them much.'

'Think you could do better?' she answered sarcastically.

'*Nessun problema*,' Ezio said unpleasantly.

Sensing trouble, Maria abandoned her accounts and came up to them. 'Ezio,' she said, 'the Borgia make it difficult for Claudia's girls. They keep out of trouble, but it's hard to avoid suspicion. There are several things you could do to aid them . . .'

'I'll keep that in mind. You must let me have a note of them.' Ezio turned his attention back to Claudia. 'Anything else?'

'No.' She paused, then said, 'Ezio?'

'What?'

'Nothing.'

Ezio turned as if to go. Then he said, 'Have you found Caterina?'

'We are working on it,' she replied coldly.

'I'm glad to hear it. *Bene*. Come to see me at Isola Tiberina the minute you have found out *exactly* where they are holding her.' He inclined his head towards the sounds of merriment coming from the central salon. 'With this lot to milk, you shouldn't find it *that* difficult.'

He left them to it.

Outside in the street, he felt guilty about the way he'd behaved. They seemed to be doing a great job. But would Claudia be able to hold her own?

Inwardly, he shrugged. He acknowledged once again that the true source of his anger was his own anxiety about his ability to protect those he held most dear. He needed them, he knew, but he was aware that his fear for their safety made him vulnerable.

22

Ezio's long-awaited reunion with Machiavelli finally took place on Tiber Island soon after the encounter at the brothel. Ezio was reserved at first – he didn't like any of the Brotherhood disappearing without his knowing where they had gone – but he recognized in his heart that, for Machiavelli, he must make an exception. The Brotherhood itself was an association of free-minded, free-spirited souls, acting together not from coercion or obedience, but from a common concern and interest. He didn't own, or have any right to control, any of them.

Serious and determined, he shook hands with his old colleague – Machiavelli shunned the warmth of an embrace. 'We must talk,' he said.

'We certainly must.' Machiavelli looked at him. 'I gather you know about my little arrangement with Pantasilea?'

'Yes.'

'Good. That woman has more sense of tactics in her little finger than her husband has in his whole body – not that he isn't the best man in his own field.' He paused. 'I've been able to secure something of great worth from one of my contacts. We now have the names of nine key Templar agents whom Cesare has recruited to terrorize Rome.'

'Just tell me how I may find them.'

Machiavelli considered. 'I suggest looking for signs of distress within any given city district. Visit the people there. Perhaps you'll uncover citizens who can point you in the right direction.'

'Did you get this information from a Borgia official?'

'Yes,' said Machiavelli carefully, after a pause. 'How do you know?'

Ezio, thinking of the encounter he had witnessed with La Volpe in the market square, wondered if that might not have been the initial contact. Machiavelli must have been following it up ever since.

'Lucky guess,' he said. '*Grazie*.'

'Look, Claudia, Bartolomeo and La Volpe are waiting for you in the inner room here.' He paused. 'That *was* a lucky guess.'

'*Virtù*, dear Niccolò, that's all,' said Ezio, leading the way.

'Virtue?' said Machiavelli to himself, as he followed.

His companions in the Brotherhood stood as he entered the hideout's inner sanctum. Their faces were sombre.

'*Buona sera*,' Ezio said and got straight down to business. 'What have you discovered?'

Bartolomeo spoke first: 'We've ascertained that that

bastardo Cesare is now at the Castel Sant'Angelo – with the Pope.'

La Volpe added, 'And my spies have confirmed that the Apple has indeed been given to someone for secret study. I am working on determining his identity.'

'We can't guess it?'

'Guesswork's no good. We need to know *for sure*.'

'I have news of Caterina Sforza,' Claudia put in. 'She will be moved to the prison within the Castel next week, on Thursday towards dusk.'

Ezio's heart involuntarily skipped a beat at this, but it was all good news.

'*Bene*,' said Machiavelli. 'So, the Castel it is. Rome will heal quickly once Cesare and Rodrigo have gone.'

Ezio held up a hand. 'Only if the right opportunity to assassinate them arises will I take it.'

Machiavelli looked irritated. 'Do not repeat your mistake in the vault. You must kill them now.'

'I'm with Niccolò,' said Bartolomeo. 'We shouldn't wait.'

'Bartolomeo is right,' agreed La Volpe.

'They must pay for Mario's death,' said Claudia.

Ezio calmed them: 'Do not worry, my friends; they will die. You have my word.'

23

On the day appointed for Caterina's transfer to Castel Sant'Angelo, Ezio and Machiavelli joined the crowd that had gathered in front of a fine carriage, its windows closed with blinds, whose doors bore the Borgia crest. Guards surrounding the carriage kept the people back, and it was no wonder, because the mood of the people was not unanimously enthusiastic. One of the coachmen leapt down from his box and hastened round to open the nearside carriage door, pulled down the steps, and stood ready to assist the occupants down.

After a moment, the first figure emerged, wearing a dark blue gown with a white bodice. Ezio recognized the beautiful blonde with the cruel lips immediately. He had last seen her at the sacking of Monteriggioni, but it was a face he could never forget. Lucrezia Borgia. She stepped down to the ground, all dignity, but this was lost as she reached back into the carriage, seized hold of something – or someone – and pulled hard.

She dragged Caterina Sforza out by her hair and flung her to the ground in front of her. Bedraggled and in chains, wearing a coarse brown dress, Caterina in defeat still had greater presence and spirit than her captor would ever know. Machiavelli had to put a restraining hand on Ezio's arm as he automatically started forward. Ezio had seen enough loved ones maltreated, but this was time for restraint. A rescue attempt now would be doomed to failure.

Lucrezia, one foot on her prostrate victim, started to speak, '*Salve, cittadini de Roma*. Hail, citizens of Rome. Behold a sight most splendid. Caterina Sforza, the she-whore of Forlì! Too long has she defied us. Now she has, at last, been brought to heel.'

There was little reaction from the crowd at this, and in the silence Caterina raised her head and cried, 'Ha! No one stoops as low as Lucrezia Borgia. Who put you up to this? Was it your brother? Or your father? Perhaps a bit of both? Perhaps at the same time, eh? After all, you all pen in the same sty.'

'*Chiudi la bocca!* Shut your mouth!' screamed Lucrezia, kicking her. 'No one speaks ill of the Borgia.' She bent down, dragging Caterina up to her knees, and slapped her hard, so that she fell into the mud again. She raised her head proudly. 'The same will happen to any – *any* – who dare to defy us.'

She motioned to the guards, who seized the hapless Caterina, dragged her to her feet, and manhandled her in the direction of the Castel gates. Still, Caterina managed to cry out, 'Good people of Rome, stay strong. Your time will come. You will be free of this yoke, I swear it.'

As she disappeared, and Lucrezia got back into her carriage to follow, Machiavelli turned to Ezio: 'Well, the *Contessa* hasn't lost any of her spirit.'

Ezio felt drained. 'They're going to torture her.'

'It is unfortunate that Forlì has fallen. But we will get it back. We will get Caterina back, too. But we must concentrate. You are here, now, for Cesare and Rodrigo.'

'Caterina is a powerful ally, one of us indeed. If we help her now, while she is weak, she will aid us in return.'

'Perhaps. But kill Cesare and Rodrigo first.'

The crowd was beginning to disperse and, apart from the sentries at the gate, the Borgia guards withdrew into the Castel. Soon only Machiavelli and Ezio were left, standing in the shadows.

'Leave me, Niccolò,' said Ezio as the shadows lengthened. 'I have work to do.'

He looked up at the sheer walls of the ancient, circular structure, the Mausoleum of the Emperor Hadrian built over a thousand years earlier and now an unassailable fortress. Its few windows were high up and its walls sheer. Connected to St Peter's Basilica by a fortified stone corridor, it had been a great Papal stronghold for nearly two hundred years.

Ezio studied the walls. Nothing was completely impregnable. By the light of the torches flickering in their sconces, as night fell, his eyes began to trace the slight ridges, fissures and imperfections which, however small, would enable him to climb. Once he'd planned his route, he leapt up like a cat to the first hand- and footholds, digging fingers and toes in, steadying his breath, and then, deliberately, unhurriedly, started to scale the wall, wherever possible keeping away from the light cast by the torches.

Halfway up, he came to an opening – an unglazed window in a stone frame, beneath which, on the inner side of the wall, was a walkway for guardsmen. He looked each way along it, but it was deserted. Silently, he swung himself over and looked down, on the other side of the walkway, over a railing into what he quickly saw was the stable yard. Four men were walking there, and he recognized every one of them. Cesare was holding some kind of conference with three of his chief lieutenants: the French general, Octavien de Valois; Cesare's personal banker and close associate, Juan de Borgia Lanzol de Romaní; and a lean man in black with a cruel, scarred face: Micheletto da Corella, Cesare's right-hand man and most trusted killer.

'Forget the Pope,' Cesare was saying, 'you answer only to me. Rome is the pillar that holds our entire enterprise aloft. She cannot waver. Which means, neither can you.'

'What of the Vatican?' asked Octavien.

'What? That tired old men's club?' answered Cesare contemptuously. 'Play along with the cardinals for now, but soon we shall have no more need of them.'

With that, he went through a door leading from the stable yard, leaving the other three alone.

'Well, it looks as if he's left Rome for us to manage,' said Juan after a pause.

'Then the city will be in good hands,' said Micheletto evenly.

Ezio listened for a while longer, but nothing more was said that he didn't already know, so he continued his climb around the outer wall, in a quest to locate Caterina's whereabouts. He saw light coming from another window, glazed this time, but open to the night air, and with an outer sill on which he could partially support himself. Doing so, he looked cautiously through the window into a candlelit corridor with plain wooden walls. Lucrezia was there, sitting on an upholstered bench, writing in a notebook, but every so often she looked up, as if she were expecting someone.

A few minutes later, Cesare came through a door at the far end of the corridor and made his way hurriedly towards his sister.

'Lucrezia,' he said and kissed her. It was no fraternal kiss.

Once they had greeted one another, he took her hands from round his neck and, still holding them and looking into her eyes, said, 'I hope you are treating our guest with kindness.'

Lucrezia grimaced. 'That mouth on her . . . How I'd love to sew it shut.'

Cesare smiled. 'I rather like it open, myself.'

'Oh, really?'

Ignoring her archness, he continued, 'Have you talked to our father about the funds requested by my banker?'

'The Pope is at the Vatican just now, but he might need some convincing when he returns. As will his own banker. You know how cautious Agostino Chigi is.'

Cesare laughed briefly. 'Well, he certainly didn't get rich by being rash.' He paused. 'But that shouldn't be a problem, should it?'

Lucrezia wound her arms round her brother's neck again, nuzzling against him. 'No, but . . . it gets quite lonely sometimes without you here. You and I spend so little time together these days, busy as you are with your *other* conquests.'

Cesare held her to him. 'Don't worry, kitten. Soon, once I have secured the throne of Italy, you are going to be my queen, and your loneliness will be a thing of the past.'

She withdrew a little and looked him in the eye. 'I cannot wait.'

He ran his hand through her fine blonde hair: 'Behave yourself while I am gone.'

Then, after another lingering kiss, Cesare left his sister by the door through which he'd entered, while Lucrezia, looking downcast, went in the opposite direction.

Where was Cesare going? Was he leaving immediately? From that leave-taking, it looked likely. Quickly, Ezio manoeuvred himself around the circumference of the wall until he could take up a position that overlooked the Castel's main gate.

And not before time. As he watched, the gate was being thrown open amid cries from the guards of, 'Attention! The Captain-General is leaving for Urbino!' And shortly afterwards, on a black horse, Cesare rode forth, accompanied by a small entourage.

'*Buona fortuna, Padrone* Cesare!' cried one of the officers of the Watch.

Ezio watched his arch-enemy ride off into the night. *That was a flying visit*, he thought to himself. *And no chance to kill him at all. Niccolò will be very disappointed.*

24

Ezio turned his attention back to the task in hand: finding Caterina. High up on the western side of the Castel he noticed a small window set deep in the wall, from which a faint light came. He made his way to it. When he reached it, he saw that there was no sill on which to rest; instead there was a narrow transom projecting above the window, which he could cling to securely with one hand.

He looked into the room. It was empty, though a torch burned on one wall. It looked like a guardroom, though, so Ezio hoped he was on the right track.

Further along on the same level was another, similar window. Ezio made his way to it and peered through the bars, though there seemed no reason for them. No one slim enough to escape through this window would be able to climb down a good 150 feet to the ground and then make it across the open ground to the river and possible safety. The light was dimmer here, but Ezio could see immediately that it was a cell.

He drew in his breath sharply. There, still in chains, was Caterina! She sat on a rough bench against one wall, but Ezio could not see if she was chained to it. Her head was down, and Ezio did not know if she was awake or asleep.

Whatever the case, she raised her head at a thunderous hammering on the door.

'Open up!' Ezio heard Lucrezia cry.

One of the two guards outside the door, who had both been dozing, hastened to obey. 'Yes, *Altezza*. At once, *Altezza*.'

Once inside the cell, and followed by one of the guards, Lucrezia wasted no time at all. From the conversation Ezio had already heard, he could guess the reason for her fury: jealousy. Lucrezia believed that Caterina and Cesare had become lovers. He could not believe that to be true. The thought of Caterina being defiled by such a monster of depravity was something his mind refused to accept.

Lucrezia rushed across the cell and pulled Caterina to her feet by her hair, bringing her face close to her prisoner's. 'You bitch! How was your journey from Forlì to Rome? Did you ride in Cesare's private carriage? What did you get up to?'

Caterina looked her in the eye. 'You're pathetic, Lucrezia. Even more pathetic if you think I'd live by the same standards as you.'

Enraged, Lucrezia threw her to the floor. 'What did he talk about? His plans for Naples?' She paused. 'Did you . . . enjoy it?'

Wiping blood from her face, Caterina said, 'I really can't remember.'

Her quiet insolence drove Lucrezia into a blind fury. Pushing the guard aside, she seized an iron bar used for securing the door and brought it down heavily across Caterina's back. 'Perhaps you will remember *this*!'

Caterina screamed in intense pain and Lucrezia stood back, satisfied.

'Good. That's put you in your place at last.'

She threw the iron rod onto the floor and strode out of the cell. The guard followed her and the door slammed shut. Ezio noticed that there was a grille set into it.

'Lock it, and give me the key,' ordered Lucrezia from the outside.

There was a rattle and a rusty creak as the key turned, then a chain clattered as the key was handed over.

'Here it is, *Altezza*.' The man's voice was trembling.

'Good. Now, if I come back and catch you asleep at your post, I'll have you flogged. One hundred lashes. Understood?'

'Yes, *Altezza*.'

Ezio listened to Lucrezia's footsteps as they grew fainter. He considered. The best way to reach the cell would be from above.

He climbed up until he came to another opening, which gave onto a guard's walkway. This time, sentries were on duty, but it seemed that there were only two, patrolling together. He calculated that it must take them five minutes to complete the circuit, so he waited until they had passed, then swung himself inside once again.

Crouching low, Ezio followed the guards at a distance until he came to a doorway in the wall from which a stone stairway led downwards. He knew that he'd climbed into the Castel two floors above where Caterina's cell was located, and so, two flights down, he left the stairway and found himself in a corridor similar to the one in which he'd seen the encounter between Cesare and Lucrezia, only this time it was clad in stone, not wood. He doubled back in the direction of Caterina's cell, encountering no one but passing a number of heavy doors, each with a grille, suggesting they were cells. As the wall curved following the line of the Castel, he heard voices ahead and recognized the Piedmontese accent of the guard who'd been talking to Lucrezia.

'This is no place for me,' he was grumbling. 'Did you hear the way she spoke to me? I wish I was back in fucking Torino.'

Ezio edged forward. The guards were facing the door when Caterina appeared at the grille. She spotted Ezio behind them as he withdrew into the shadows.

'Oh, my poor back,' she said to the guards. 'Can you give me some water?'

There was a jug of water on the table near the door,

which the two guards had been sitting at. One of them picked it up and brought it close to the grille.

'Anything else you require, princess?' he asked sarcastically.

The guard from Turin sniggered.

'Come on, have a heart,' said Caterina. 'If you open the door, I might show you something worth your while.'

The guards immediately became more formal. 'No need for that, *Contessa*. We have our orders. Here.'

The guard with the water jug unlatched the grille and passed it through to Caterina, closing the grille again afterwards.

'About time we were relieved, isn't it?' said the Piedmontese guard.

'Yes, Luigi and Stefano should have been here by now.'

They looked at each other.

'Do you think that bitch Lucrezia will be back any time soon?'

'Shouldn't think so.'

'Then why don't we take a look in the guard room and see what's keeping them?'

'All right. It'll only take us a couple of minutes.'

Ezio watched as they disappeared round the curve of the wall, and then he was at the grille.

'Ezio,' breathed Caterina. 'What the hell are you doing here?'

'Visiting my tailor – what do you think?'

'For Christ's sake, Ezio, do you think we have time for jokes?'

'I'm going to get you out. Tonight.'

'If you do, Cesare will hunt you down like a dog.'

'He's already trying to do that, but, judging by these two, his men don't seem all that fanatical. Do you know if the guards have another key?'

'I don't think so. The guards handed theirs to Lucrezia. She paid me a visit.'

'I know. I saw.'

'Then why didn't you do anything to stop her?'

'I was outside the window.'

'Out *there*? Are you mad?'

'Just athletic. Now, if Lucrezia has the only key, I'd better go and get it. Do you know where she is?'

Caterina considered. 'I heard her mention that her quarters are at the very top of the Castel.'

'Excellent. That key is as good as mine. Now stay here until I get back.'

Caterina gave him a look, glanced at her chains and then at the cell door. 'Why, where do you think I *might* go?' she said with a dry smile.

25

He was getting used to the contours of the outer walls of the Castel Sant'Angelo by now, and he found that, the higher he climbed, the easier it was to find hand and footholds. Clinging like a limpet, his cape billowing slightly in the breeze, he soon found himself on a level with the highest parapet, and silently hauled himself up onto it.

The drop on the other side was slight – four feet to a narrow brick walkway, from which stairs led down, at occasional intervals, to a rooftop garden, in the centre of which was a one-storey stone building with a flat roof. The building had broad windows, so it wasn't an additional fortification, and the light of many candles blazed within, revealing opulent and tastefully decorated rooms.

The walkway was deserted, but the garden was not. On a bench under the spreading bows of a button-wood tree, Lucrezia sat demurely, holding hands with a handsome young man whom Ezio recognized as one of Rome's leading romantic actors, Pietro Benintendi. Cesare wouldn't be too pleased if he knew about this! Ezio, a mere silhouette, crept along the walkway to a point as close to the couple as he dared, grateful for the moon, which had risen by now, providing not only light but also confusing, camouflaging pools of shade. He listened.

'I love you so, I want to sing it to the heavens,' Pietro said ardently.

Lucrezia shushed him. 'Please, you must whisper it only to yourself. If Cesare found out, who knows what he would do.'

'But you are free, are you not? Of course I heard about your late husband and I am very sorry, but—'

'Quiet, you fool!' Lucrezia's hazel eyes glittered. 'Do you not know that Cesare had the Duke of Bisceglie murdered – my husband was strangled.'

'What?'

'It's true.'

'What happened?'

'I loved my husband, and Cesare grew jealous. Alfonso was a handsome man, and Cesare was conscious of the changes the New Disease had made to his own face, though God knows they are slight. He had his men waylay Alfonso, and beat him up. He thought that would act as a warning. But Alfonso was no puppet. He hit back and, while he was still recovering from Cesare's attack, had his own men retaliate. Cesare was lucky to escape the fate of St Sebastiano! But then, cruel man, he had Micheletto da Corella go to his bedchamber where he lay nursing his wounds, and strangle him there.'

'It isn't possible.' Pietro looked nervous.

'I loved my husband. Now, I make-believe to Cesare, to allay his suspicions, but he is a snake – always alert, always venomous.' She looked into Pietro's eyes. 'Thank God I have you to console me. Cesare has always been jealous of where I place my attentions, but that should not deter us. Besides, he has gone to Urbino to continue his campaigning. There is nothing to hinder us.'

'Are you sure?'

'I will keep our secret – if you will,' said Lucrezia intensely. She disengaged one hand from his and moved it to his thigh.

'Oh, Lucrezia,' sighed Pietro. 'How your lips call to me.'

They kissed, delicately at first, then more and more passionately. Ezio shifted his position slightly and inadvertently kicked a brick loose, which fell into the garden. He froze.

Lucrezia and Pietro sprang apart.

'What was that?' she said. 'No one is allowed access to my garden and my apartments without my knowledge – no one!'

Pietro was already on his feet, looking around fearfully. 'I'd better go,' he said hastily. 'I have to prepare for my rehearsal – scan my lines for the morning. I must go.' He stooped to give Lucrezia a last kiss. 'Farewell, my love.'

'Stay, Pietro, I'm sure it was nothing.'

'No, it's late. I must go.'

Putting on a melancholy expression, he slipped away across the garden and vanished through a door set into the wall on the far side.

Lucrezia waited a moment, then stood and snapped her fingers. Out of the shelter of some tall shrubs growing nearby, one of her personal guard emerged and bowed.

'I heard the entire exchange, *mia signora*, and can vouch for it.'

Lucrezia pursed her lips. 'Good. Tell Cesare. We shall see how he feels when the boot is on the other foot.'

'Yes, s*ignora*.'

Bowing again, the guard withdrew.

Left alone, Lucrezia picked a marguerite from a clump of flowers that was growing nearby, and started to pluck its petals off, one by one.

'He loves me; he loves me not; he loves me; he loves me not . . .'

Ezio slipped down the nearest staircase and made his way towards her. She had sat down again and looked up at his approach, though she showed no fear, only slight surprise. Well, if she had any more guards concealed in the garden, Ezio would give them short shrift.

'Please continue. I do not mean to interrupt,' Ezio

said, bowing, though in his case the bow was not made without irony.

'Well, well. Ezio Auditore da Firenze.' She gave him her hand to kiss. 'How pleasant to meet you properly at last. I've heard so much about you, especially recently. That is, I imagine no one else can have been responsible for the little upsets we have been experiencing here in Rome?' She paused. 'It's a pity Cesare is no longer here. He would have enjoyed this.'

'I have no quarrel with you personally, Lucrezia. Free Caterina and I will stand down.'

Her voice hardened slightly. 'I'm afraid that is impossible.'

Ezio spread his hands. 'Then you leave me no choice.' He closed in on her, but cautiously. She had long fingernails.

'Guards!' she shrieked, turning in an instant from noblewoman to harpy, and slashing at his eyes as – just in time – he caught her wrists. Pulling a length of twine from his leather pouch he twisted her wrists behind her and tied them swiftly, before flinging her to the ground and placing one foot firmly on a fold of her dress so that she could not rise and run. Then he drew his sword and dagger and stood his ground, ready to face the four or five guards who came running from the direction of the apartments. Luckily for Ezio they were lightly armed and heavily built, and wore no chain mail. Though unable to change his position – for above all he could not afford to have Lucrezia escape, even though she was trying to bite his ankle through his boot – he ducked below the swinging blade of the first guard and hacked at the man's exposed flank. One down. The second guard was more cautious, but conscious of the now snarling Lucrezia on the floor, he stepped forward to attack Ezio. He lunged at Ezio's chest, but Ezio parried upwards, locking the guards of both blades and swinging his left hand, dagger pointing forward, at the man's head. Two down. The final man, hoping to take advantage of the fact that both of Ezio's blades were engaged, rushed forward. Ezio flicked his right arm hard – sending the blade of the second guard spiralling up towards the new foe. The final guard had to raise his sword to deflect the blow – but just too late and the flying blade nicked his bicep. He winced with pain but came forward again, sword swinging at Ezio. Ezio had recovered his stance and deflected the attack with his dagger, freeing his sword hand to slash viciously at the man's torso. It was over. The guards lay dead around him – and Lucrezia was silent for the first time. Breathing hard, Ezio pulled his captive to her feet.

'Now come on,' he said. 'And don't scream. If you do, I will be forced to take your tongue.'

He dragged her towards the door through which Pietro had left, found himself in a corridor, and half-pushed, half-dragged Lucrezia back down the tower, in the direction of the cells.

'Rescuing princesses from castles now? How romantic!' Lucrezia spat.

'Shut up.'

'I suppose you think you're achieving great things, charging around, creating havoc, killing whomever you wish?'

'I said, shut up.'

'But does your plan have any form? What do you think you are going to achieve? Don't you know how strong we are?'

Ezio hesitated at a staircase leading down to the next floor. 'Which way?' he asked her.

She laughed, and didn't reply.

He shook her. 'Which *way*?'

'To the left,' she replied sullenly.

She was silent for a while, then started again. This time Ezio let her ramble on. He was sure of where he was now. She squirmed in his grip, but he was concentrating on two things: keeping a firm hold of her, and being alert for any ambush by the Castel guards.

'Do you know what became of the remains of the Pazzi family in Florence once you'd brought them to their knees? Your dear friend Lorenzo the so-called *Magnifico* stripped them of all their possessions and threw them into prison. All of them! Even those who'd played no part in the conspiracy against him.' Ezio's mind turned unwillingly to the revenge Caterina had taken over a rebellion against her in Forlì. Her measures had far exceeded Lorenzo's – indeed, they made them look mild. He shook the thoughts away.

'The women were forbidden to marry and the family tombstones were erased,' Lucrezia went on. 'Wiped from the history books. Poof! Just like that!'

But they were not tortured and killed, thought Ezio. Well, it was possible that Caterina had felt justified in her actions at the time. Still, her cruelty had cost her some of the loyalty she had always been able to depend on before, and perhaps that was why Cesare had finally been able to take Forlì.

She was still an important ally, though, and that was what Ezio had to remember. That, and to suppress whatever feelings – real or imagined – he may have felt for her.

'You and your Assassin friends ignored the consequences of your actions. You were content to set things in motion, but you were never willing to see them through.' Lucrezia paused for breath and Ezio gave her a savage yank forwards, but that didn't stop her: 'Unlike you, Cesare will finish what he started, and bring peace to Italy. He kills for a higher purpose – again, unlike you.'

'The ignorant and the passive make easy targets,' retorted Ezio.

'Say what you like,' replied Lucrezia, realizing she had touched a nerve. 'In any case, my words are wasted here, you *ipocrita*.'

217

They had all but reached the cells now. 'Remember,' Ezio said, drawing his dagger, 'if you try to warn your guards, your tongue . . .'

Lucrezia breathed hard, but was silent. Watchfully, Ezio inched forward. The two new guards were seated at the table, playing cards. Throwing Lucrezia to the ground in front of him, he leapt on them and dispatched them both before they had a moment to react. Then he spun round and charged after Lucrezia, who had got to her feet and begun to run back the way she'd come, screaming for help. He caught up with her in two bounds, clapped a hand over her mouth and pulled her to him with his other arm, swinging her round and pushing her back towards Caterina's cell. She bit and tore at the gloved hand over her mouth, then, seeing she was powerless, appeared to give up and went limp.

Caterina was already at the grille, which Ezio unlatched.

'*Salute*, Lucrezia,' said Caterina, smiling unpleasantly. 'How I've missed you.'

'*Vai a farti fottere, troia* – Go fuck yourself, you whore!'

'Charming as always,' said Caterina. 'Ezio, bring her close. I'll take the key.'

She reached out as Ezio obeyed her order. He noticed that Caterina caressed Lucrezia's breasts as she reached between them and extracted the key, which hung on a black silk cord.

Caterina passed the key to Ezio, who quickly unlocked the door. The same key fitted the padlock securing the chains – Caterina had not, after all, been chained to the wall – and as Caterina divested herself of these, Ezio shoved Lucrezia into the cell.

'Guards! Guards!' screamed Lucrezia.

'Oh, shut up,' said Caterina, picking up a dirty rag from the guards' table and using it to gag her enemy. Then Ezio took some more twine and bound Lucrezia's ankles, before slamming the cell door shut and locking it securely.

Ezio and Caterina looked at each other.

'My hero,' she said drily.

Ezio ignored that. 'Can you walk?'

Caterina tried, but stumbled. 'I don't think I can – the manacles they had on me must have done some damage.'

Ezio sighed and lifted her into his arms. He'd have to drop her like a sack if they were surprised by the guards and he needed to get to his weapons quickly.

'Which way?' she asked.

'Stables first, then the quickest route out of here.'

'Why save me, Ezio? Seriously? With Forlì taken, I am useless to you.'

'You still have a family.'

'It isn't your family.'

Ezio kept walking. He remembered where the stables should be in relation to where they were. It was fortunate that Caterina seemed to be the only prisoner in this section, so there were no other guards about. Still, he trod softly and moved quickly, but not so fast as to lumber into a trap. Every so often he stopped and listened. She was light in his arms and, despite imprisonment, her hair still smelt of vanilla and roses, reminding him of happier times they had had together.

'Listen, Ezio, that night in Monteriggioni, when we . . . bathed together . . . I had to ensure your allegiance. To protect Forlì. It was in the Assassin Brotherhood's interests as much as mine, but—' she broke off. 'Do you understand, Ezio?'

'If you had wanted my allegiance, all you had to do was ask for it.'

'I needed you on my side.'

'My loyalty and my sword arm on your side weren't enough. You wanted to be sure of my heart as well.' Ezio walked on, shifting her weight in his arms. 'But, *è la politica.* Of course, I knew it. You need not explain.'

His heart felt as if it had fallen down a bottomless mineshaft. How *could* her hair still be scented?

'Caterina,' he asked, his throat dry. 'Did they . . . ? Did Cesare . . . ?'

She sensed, however dimly, what he felt, and smiled – with her lips, though, he noticed, not with her eyes. 'Nothing happened. My name must still have some small value. I was left . . . unspoiled.'

They had reached the main door of the stables. It

was unguarded, but firmly closed. Ezio put Caterina down. 'Try to walk a little. You must get the strength back in your ankles.'

He looked around for a means of opening the door, which had no bolts or handles. There had to be a way . . .

'Try over there,' said Caterina. 'Isn't that a lever of some kind?'

'Wait here,' Ezio said.

'As if I had a choice.'

He made his way over to the lever, noticing as he went a square hole in the floor with an open trap door above it. From the smell beneath it must have been some sort of grain store. And peering down, he could make out a large number of sacks, and boxes, too – boxes of what looked like gunpowder.

'Hurry,' said Caterina.

He took the lever in his hands and hauled on it. It was stiff at first, but under the strain of his muscles, it gave, a little at first, and then swung over easily. At the same time the door swung open.

There were a couple of guards in the stable, who whirled round at the sound of the door creaking on its hinges, and rushed towards it, drawing their swords.

'Ezio! *Aiuto!*'

He sped over to Caterina, picked her up and carried her towards the hole in the floor.

'What are you doing?!'

He held her over the hole.

'Don't you dare!'

He dropped her down, unable to resist a short snicker at her yell of panic. It wasn't far, and he had time to see her land safely on the soft sacks before turning to face the guards. The fight was short and sharp as the guards were heavy with fatigue and had been taken by surprise. Ezio's skills with a blade were more than a match for them. One of them managed to get a glancing blow in, but it only cut the material of Ezio's doublet and didn't reach the flesh. Ezio himself was tiring.

When it was over, Ezio reached down and hauled Caterina out.

'*Figlio di puttana*,' she swore, dusting herself down. 'Never do that to me again.'

He noticed that she seemed to be walking at least a little better already.

Quickly, he selected horses for them and soon had them saddled and ready. He helped her onto one, and leapt into the saddle of the other himself. An archway led off one side of the stables and through it he could see the main gate of the Castel. It was guarded, but it was open. Dawn was approaching, and no doubt tradesmen from the city were expected, to make deliveries.

'Ride like hell,' Ezio told her, 'before they have time to realize what's going on, across the bridge and then make for Tiber Island. You'll be safe there. Find Machiavelli. He'll be waiting for me.'

'But we *both* have to get away from here.'

'I'll follow. But for now I must stay and take care of the remaining guards, create a diversion, a delay, something.'

Caterina pulled the reins of her horse in, so that it reared. 'Get back in one piece,' she said. 'Or I will never forgive you!'

Ezio hoped she meant it as he watched her kick the horse into a gallop. She charged past the guards at the main gate, scattering them. As soon as he saw that she was clear, he rode his own horse back through the stable to the grain and powder store, seizing a torch from its sconce as he passed. This he threw into the hole, and then wheeled round and galloped back the way he had come, drawing his sword.

The guards had formed a cordon and were waiting for him, halberds raised. Ezio didn't know the horse, but he knew what he had to do: he rode straight at the line of guards, and at the last minute pulled hard on the reins and, leaning forward in the saddle, dug his heels in. At the same time as the horse charged forward, there was an almighty explosion from near the stable. He was right; it had been gunpowder. The ground shook with the explosion, and the guards instinctively ducked down. The horse, also shocked by the noise of the bang, was even more determined to make good her flight. She flew into the air, clearing the line of guards as easily as she might have cleared a fence.

Leaving panic and confusion in his wake, he rode in the direction of the rising sun. His heart swelled within him. He had saved Caterina!

26

Once he was sure he had shaken off any possible pursuers, Ezio turned his horse. He was loath to lose such a good animal, but he took it to the stables where he and Machiavelli had hired horses what seemed like a lifetime ago, and turned it over to the chief ostler there. The stables were neat and clean and clearly doing a thriving business, in a district that seemed to have shaken off Borgia control and, for the moment at least, maintained its independence. Then he made his way back towards Tiber Island on foot. The Assassin secret ferry was waiting at the bank, and once on the island itself, he hastened towards the hideout.

Inside, he found that Caterina had arrived safely. She was lying on a makeshift bed near the door, being tended by a doctor. She smiled as she saw him, and tried to sit up, but the doctor gently restrained her.

'Ezio! I am relieved to see you safe.'

He took her hand and squeezed it. 'Where is Machiavelli?' There was no return of his pressure, but perhaps she was still too weak.

'I don't know.'

La Volpe emerged from the shadows at the end of the room. 'Ezio! Good to see you again!' He embraced the younger man. 'I brought your *Contessa* here. As for Machiavelli . . .'

Just then the main door swung open and Machiavelli himself came in. He looked drawn.

'Where have you been?' asked La Volpe.

'Looking for Ezio – not that I am accountable to you,' said Machiavelli. Ezio was saddened to note the tension that still existed between his two friends. Machiavelli turned to Ezio and, without ceremony, asked, 'What of Cesare and Rodrigo?'

'Cesare left almost immediately for Urbino. As for Rodrigo, he was at the Vatican.'

'That's odd,' said Machiavelli. 'Rodrigo should have been in the Castel.'

'Very odd indeed,' put in La Volpe evenly.

If he'd noticed the dig, Machiavelli ignored it. 'What a wasted opportunity,' he mused. Then, recollecting himself, he said to Caterina. 'No offence, *Contessa*. We are glad to see you safe.'

'I take none,' she said.

'Now that Cesare has gone to Urbino, we must concentrate on building our forces here.'

Machiavelli raised his eyebrows. 'But I thought we intended to strike now! We should go after him and cut him down where he stands.'

'That would be impossible,' Caterina said. 'I have

seen his army. It is massive. You would never reach him.'

Ezio said, 'I say we work here, in Rome. Here, we have already made a good start. We should continue to erode the Borgia influence, while restoring our own. And, in fact, I want to begin immediately.'

'You speak as if you were already our leader,' said Machiavelli, 'but the post has not been discussed, let alone ratified, by our council.'

'And I say we need a leader, and we need one right away,' countered La Volpe. 'We have no time for councils and ratifications. We need to consolidate the Brotherhood once again and, for my money, Ezio is the right man for the job. Machiavelli, I appeal to you – you and I are two of the most senior Assassins left. Bartolomeo is bound to agree. Let us make this decision now – keep it secret if you like – and later we can put it to a formal vote.'

Machiavelli seemed to be on the point of speech, but then let it go and simply shrugged.

'I will not fail you,' Ezio said. 'Gilberto, I'd like you to bring Bartolomeo and my sister Claudia here. There are matters to discuss. Niccolò, please come with me.'

On his way out, Ezio paused by Caterina's bed. 'Take care of her,' he said to the doctor.

'Where are we going?' Machiavelli asked once they were back in the city centre.

'There's something I want to show you.'

He led the way to the nearest market square. Half of it was open for business; there was a baker, a butcher was swatting flies away from his wares, and a greengrocer had a selection of rather tired-looking produce on sale. Early as it was, it was the wine shops that were doing the best business. And, as Ezio expected, a small knot of Borgia guards were duffing up the hapless owner of a leather-goods stall.

'Look,' said Ezio as they blended in with the small crowd of shoppers.

'I know what is going on,' said Machiavelli.

'I know you do, Niccolò,' said Ezio. 'Forgive me, but you see the big picture. You understand what is to be done politically to break the Borgia, and I for one do not doubt your sincerity in this.' He paused. 'But we must start at a more fundamental level. The Borgia take what they want from the people with complete impunity, to maintain their power.'

They watched the guards push the man to the ground, then, laughing, help themselves to what they fancied from his stall and move on. The man picked himself up, watched them go in impotent rage and then, close to tears, began to rearrange his goods. A woman came up to comfort him, but he shook her off. Nevertheless she stayed, hovering near him, care and concern in her eyes.

'Why did you not help him?' asked Machiavelli? 'Send them packing?'

'Look,' said Ezio. 'Helping one man is good, but it will not solve the problem. They will come back, when we are not here, and they will do the same again. Look at the quality of the stuff on offer here. The vegetables are old, the meat is flyblown and the bread, no doubt, is hard. The best goes to the Borgia. And why do you think so many people are drinking?'

Machiavelli said, 'I do not know.'

'Because they are in pain,' Ezio replied. 'They are without hope and they are oppressed. They want to blot it all out. But we can *change* that.'

'How?'

'By recruiting them to our cause.' He spread his arms. 'These people – these are the ones who will form the backbone of our resistance to the Borgia.'

'We've talked of this before,' said Machiavelli sharply. 'You cannot be serious.'

'I'm going to start with that stallholder. To win this war, Niccolò, we need loyal soldiers, however they fight for us. We must sow the seeds of rebellion in their minds.' He paused, then continued earnestly, 'By recruiting those whom the bullying state has made its enemies, we arm the people who have been disarmed by the Borgia.'

Machiavelli looked at his friend long and hard. 'Go then,' he said. 'Go and recruit our first novices.'

'Oh, I intend to,' said Ezio. 'And you will see that from the group of determined men and women I gather round us, I will forge a sword capable of cutting the limbs and head from the trunk of the Borgia – and of the Templars themselves.'

27

Ezio returned to the Assassin centre of operations on Tiber Island alone. He had done a good day's work, discreetly converting a number of disaffected citizens to his cause.

Apart from the loyal attendants who staffed and guarded the place, it was deserted, and Ezio looked forward to a little quiet time, to think and plan; but as he approached, he found he had a visitor. One who wanted to be quite sure that his presence would not be noted, and one who, therefore, waited until the general staff had gone about their business elsewhere in the building before he made himself known.

'Psst! Ezio! Over here!'

'Who's there?' Ezio was instantly alert, though he already thought he knew the voice. Tall bushes grew on either side of the lane that led to their headquarters, which was known to no one outside their organization. If by any chance the secret had been penetrated . . .

'Come here!'

'Who is it?'

'It's me!'

Leonardo da Vinci, dandified and distracted as ever,

stepped out of his hiding place into the lane.

'Leo! My God!'

Ezio, remembering who Leonardo's new master was, checked his initial impulse, which had been to run and embrace his old friend.

His reaction registered with Leonardo, who looked a little older, to be sure, but who had lost none of his élan or vigorous enthusiasm. He took a step forward, but kept his head lowered. 'I'm not surprised you don't show that much enthusiasm at seeing me again.'

'Well, Leo, I must admit that you have disappointed me.'

Leonardo spread his hands. 'I knew you were behind the break-in at the Castel. It could only have been you. So I knew you were still alive.'

'Surely your new masters would have told you that?'

'They tell me nothing. I am no more than a slave to them.' There was the smallest twinkle in Leonardo's eye. 'But they have to trust me.'

'As long as you deliver.'

'I think I'm just about bright enough to stay one step ahead of them.' Leonardo took another step towards Ezio, arms half held out. 'It is good to see you again, my friend.'

'You have designed weapons for them — new guns which we will find difficult to match.'

'I know, but if you will let me explain . . .'

'And how did you find this place?'

'I can explain . . .'

Leonardo looked so contrite, and so unhappy, and he seemed so sincere that Ezio's heart warmed, despite himself, towards his old friend. He also reflected that, after all, Leonardo had come to see him, no doubt at great personal risk; and that if he sought a rapprochement, it would be a foolish leader indeed who would turn down the friendship and the partnership of such a man.

'Come here!' cried Ezio, spreading his arms wide.

'Oh, Ezio!' Leonardo hurried forward and the two men embraced warmly.

Ezio led his friend into the Assassin headquarters, where they sat down together. Ezio knew that Caterina had been moved to an inner room, where she could complete her recovery in peace and quiet, and the doctor had given orders that she was not to be disturbed. He was tempted to disobey, but there would be time enough for talk with her later. Besides, Leonardo's appearance dictated a change of priorities.

Ezio had wine and cakes brought for them.

'Tell me everything,' said Ezio.

'I will explain. First of all, you must forgive me. The Borgia commandeered my services, but under duress. If I'd refused to serve them, they would have subjected me to a long and painful death. They described what they would do to me if I refused to help them. Even now I cannot think of it without trembling.'

'You are perfectly safe now.'

Leonardo shook his head. 'No! I must go back to them. I am of far more use to you if they think I am still working for them. As it is, I have done my utmost to create the minimum possible number of new inventions to satisfy them.' Ezio was about to interrupt, but Leonardo held up a nervous hand. 'Please, this is a kind of confession, and I'd like to complete it. Then you may judge me as you think fit.'

'No one is judging you, Leonardo.'

Leonardo's manner became more intense. Ignoring the refreshments, he leant forward. 'I say I work for them under duress,' he went on, 'but it is more than that. You know I keep out of politics – I like to keep my nose clean – but men who seek power seek me out because they know what I can do for them.'

'This I do know.'

'I play along to stay alive. And why do I wish to stay alive? Because I have so much to *do*!' He took a breath. 'I cannot tell you, Ezio, how my poor brain teems!' He made a gesture that seemed partly all-embracing, partly despairing. 'There is so much to discover!'

Ezio was silent. This he also knew.

'So,' Leonardo concluded, 'now you know.'

'Why have you come here?'

'To make amends. I had to assure you that my heart is not with them.'

'And what do they want of you?'

'Whatever they can get. War machines are the main thing. They know what I am capable of.'

Leonardo produced a packet of papers, which he handed over. 'Here are some of the designs I've done for them. Look, here is an armoured vehicle capable, if correctly constructed, of moving across all terrains, and the men concealed within it can fire guns – big guns – while remaining fully protected from all assaults. I call it a tank.'

Ezio blenched as his eye scanned the drawings. 'And is it . . . under construction?'

Leonardo looked artful. 'I said, "If correctly constructed." Unfortunately, as the design stands, the thing is only able to swivel on its own axis.'

'I see,' Ezio smiled.

'And look at this.'

Ezio perused a drawing of a horseman managing two horses, harnessed side by side. Attached to their traces by long horizontal poles at front and rear, where there were also wheels, were rotating scythe-like devices, which could be used to cut down any enemy at which the horseman rode. 'A fiendish device,' he said.

'Yes, but unfortunately the horseman himself is . . . fully exposed.' Leonardo's eyes twinkled some more.

Ezio's smile broadened, then faded again. 'But what of the guns you have given them?'

Leonardo shrugged. 'One has to throw a sop to

Cerberus,' he said. 'I have to give them something of actual use or they will grow suspicious.'

'But they are very efficient guns.'

'Indeed they are, but they are not half as efficient as that little pistol I made for you once, years ago, based on the design from the Codex page. A pity really – I had trouble reining myself in on that one.'

Ezio thought sadly of his lost Codex weapons, but he would come back to them.

'What else is in this packet of papers?'

Although they were alone, Leonardo lowered his voice. 'I have copied the plans not only for the largest of the machines, but also for where they are to be used in battle.' He spread his hands ironically. 'Alas, that they should not be more efficient.'

Ezio looked at his old friend admiringly. This was the man who had designed a submarine for the Venetians to use against the Turkish galleys. If he had chosen not to build in defects to these designs, there would be no hope at all against the Borgia. How glad he was to have welcomed Leonardo as he had. This man was worth more than two armies.

'For God's sake, Leo, have a glass of wine at least. I know I can never reward you enough for all this.'

But Leonardo waved the proffered beaker away. 'There is far graver news. You know they have the Apple?'

'Of course.'

'They have given it to me to study. You and I already know something of the extent of its powers. Rodrigo knows a little less, but he has more intellect than Cesare, though Cesare is the one to watch.'

'How much information on the Apple have you given them?'

'As little as possible, but I have to give them something. Fortunately, Cesare seems satisfied, so far, with the limited applications I have vouchsafed him. But Rodrigo knows there is more and grows impatient.' He paused. 'I had considered ways of stealing it, but it is kept under close guard and I am only allowed access to it under the strictest supervision. I was able to use its powers to locate you, though. It has that facility, you know. Quite fascinating.'

'And you taught them that trick?'

'Of course not! All I want is to return it to its rightful owner.'

'Fear not, Leo. We will recover it. In the meantime, stall them as far as you can, and if you can, keep me posted on how much you have let them know.'

'I will.'

Ezio paused. 'There is something else.'

'Tell me.'

'I have lost all the Codex weapons you once fashioned for me.'

'I see.'

'Except for the original Hidden Blade. The pistol,

the Poison Blade, the Double Blade, the miraculous Bracer – all these are gone.'

'Hmm,' said Leonardo. Then he smiled. 'Well, re-creating them for you may not be a problem.'

'Really?' Ezio could scarcely believe it.

'The designs you let me have are still in Florence, well hidden with my old assistants Agniolo and Innocento. The Borgia will never have them. If they ever took Florence – heaven forfend! – or even if the French did, Agniolo has strict orders to destroy them, and even he and Innocento – not that I do not trust them absolutely – would never be able to re-create them independently of me. But I . . . I never forget a design. However—' He hesitated, almost embarrassed. 'You must pay me for the raw materials I will need. In advance.'

Ezio was astonished. 'Really? They are not paying you at *il Vaticano*?'

Leonardo coughed. 'Very . . . very little. I suppose they think that keeping me alive is payment enough. And I am not such a fool as to think that the minute my services become . . . superfluous to requirements, they will not kill me with as little reflection as they might kill a dog.'

'Hardly that,' said Ezio. 'They would rather you were dead than have you work for anyone else.'

'Yes, I've been thinking along the same lines,' said Leonardo. 'And there's really nowhere to run. Not that I want to. I want to see the Borgia crushed – I'll engage myself so far in politics as to say that. But my beloved Milan is in French hands,' he started to muse. 'Perhaps . . . later, when all this is over . . . I might even try my luck in France. They say it's a very civilized country . . .'

It was time to bring him back to reality. Ezio went to an iron-bound chest and from it produced a leather pouch, bulging with ducats. This he gave to Leonardo.

'Payment on account for the Codex weapons,' he said briskly. 'When can you have them ready?'

Leonardo considered. 'It won't be as easy as it was last time,' he said. 'I must work secretly, and alone, for I cannot wholly trust all the assistants I have working for me here.' He paused. 'Let me contact you again. As soon as possible, I promise.' He hefted the heavy bag in his hand. 'And who knows, for this much money I may even be able to throw in a couple of new weapons – my own inventions this time, of course, but effective, I think you'll find.'

'Whatever you can do for us will earn my undying gratitude and my protection, wherever you are,' said Ezio. He made a mental note to delegate a handful of his new recruits, as soon as they had finished their training, to keep a watchful eye on Leonardo and to report back regularly on him. 'Now, how shall we maintain contact?'

Leonardo said, 'I've thought of that.' He took out a

piece of chalk and, on the table between them, drew a man's right hand, pointing.

'It's beautiful,' said Ezio.

'Thank you. It's just a sketch of part of a painting I've been thinking of doing, of St John the Baptist. If I ever get round to it. Go and sit where it's pointing to.'

Ezio obeyed.

'That's it,' said Leonardo. 'Tell your men to keep their eyes peeled. If they see one of these – it'll just look like a bit of *graffiti* to anyone else – tell them to let you know, and follow the direction it's pointing in. That's how we'll rendezvous.'

'Splendid,' said Ezio.

'Don't worry, I'll make sure you're forewarned. In case you're thinking of charging off on some mission or other.'

'Thanks.'

Leonardo stood. 'I must go. Otherwise I'll be missed. But first . . .'

'First what?'

Leonardo grinned and shook the bag of money.

'First, I'm going shopping.'

28

Ezio left the hideout shortly after Leonardo, to continue his recruiting work, but also to keep himself
busy. He was impatient to have the replacement Codex
weapons back in his hands.

When, later in the day, he returned for a prearranged meeting, it was to find that Machiavelli had
preceded him. Caterina was with him, sitting in a chair,
her knees covered with a fur rug. As usual, Machiavelli
did not stand on ceremony.

'Where have you been?' he asked.

Ezio didn't like his tone. 'We all have our secrets,' he
replied, keeping his voice level. 'And, may I ask, what
have you been up to?'

Machiavelli smiled. 'I've been refining our carrier-
pigeon system. We can use it now to send orders to the
new recruits scattered about the city.'

'Excellent. Thank you, Niccolò.'

They looked at each other. Machiavelli was almost
ten years Ezio's junior, yet there was no doubting the
independence and ambition behind those veiled eyes.
Did he resent Ezio's leadership? Had he hoped it
might have fallen on him? Ezio put the thought aside

– surely the man was more of a theorist, a diplomat, a political animal. And there could be no doubt about his usefulness – or his allegiance – to the Brotherhood. If only Ezio could fully convince La Volpe of that.

As if on cue, La Volpe entered the hideout, accompanied by Claudia.

'What news?' Ezio asked him after the two had greeted one another.

'Bartolomeo sends his apologies. It seems that General Octavien has had another stab at attacking the barracks.'

'I see.'

'They redoubled their assault, but we are holding our ground.'

'Good.' Ezio turned to his sister, coldly. 'Claudia,' he said, inclining his head.

'Brother,' she rejoined with equal frostiness.

'Please sit down, all of you,' said Ezio.

Once they were settled, he continued. 'I have a plan prepared for the Borgia.'

'I suggest', Machiavelli put in immediately, 'that we go either after their supplies or after Cesare's followers.'

'Thank you, Niccolò,' said Ezio evenly. '*My* plan is to attack both. If we can cut off his funds, Cesare will lose his army and return without his men. How does he get his money?'

La Volpe said, 'We know that he depends on Rodrigo for much of his money, and Rodrigo's banker is

Agostino Chigi. But Cesare also has his own banker, whose identity has yet to be confirmed, though we have our suspicions.'

Ezio decided, for the moment, to keep his own thoughts in that direction quiet. It would be best to have them confirmed, if possible, by La Volpe's men.

'I know someone – a client of ours at The Rosa in Fiore – who owes that banker money. The senator Egidio Troche is complaining about interest rates all the time.'

'*Bene*,' said Ezio. 'Then we must follow that up.'

'There's something else,' said Machiavelli. 'We have news that they are planning to station French troops on the road that leads to Castel Sant'Angelo. Your attack must have really rattled them. And apparently Cesare is planning to return to Rome. Immediately. Quite why so soon is beyond me, but we'll find out. In any case, when he does arrive, he'll be so well guarded that you'll never get to him. Our spies tell us that he intends to keep his return secret, at least for the moment.'

'He's got something up his sleeve,' said La Volpe.

'Brilliant,' said Machiavelli, and the two men exchanged a look that wasn't friendly.

Ezio considered this. 'Our best course of action would seem to be to corner this French general of theirs, Octavien, and kill him. Once he's out of the way, Bartolomeo will have the Frenchmen on the defensive, and they'll abandon their guard duty at the Castel.'

Caterina spoke for the first time: 'Even with those troops gone, Ezio, the Papal Guard will continue to protect the bridge and the main gate.'

'Ah,' said La Volpe, 'but there's a side entrance. Lucrezia's latest plaything, the actor Pietro Benintendi, has a key.'

'Does he?' said Ezio. 'I saw him with her at the Castel.'

'I'll have my men find out where he is,' promised La Volpe. Shouldn't be too difficult.'

Caterina smiled. 'Sounds like a good idea. I'd like to help. We should be able to scare that key out of him – and he'll stop seeing Lucrezia. Anything to rob that bitch of any pleasure.'

'*Momentino, Contessa*,' said Machiavelli. 'We are going to have to do without your help.'

Caterina looked at him, surprised. 'Why?'

'Because we are going to have to get you out of the city – maybe to Florence – until we can get Forlì back for you. Your children are already safe there.' He looked around. 'Ezio's rescuing you wasn't without its consequences. There are heralds all over the city, proclaiming a rich reward for the *Contessa's* capture – alive or dead. And no bribe can shut them up.'

There was silence. Then Caterina rose, letting the rug fall to the floor. 'Then it appears that I have outstayed my welcome,' she said. 'Excuse me.'

'What are you talking about?' said Ezio, alarmed.

'Only that I am in danger here—'

'We will protect you!'

'And – more importantly – a liability to you.' She was looking at Machiavelli as she spoke. 'Isn't that so, Niccolò?'

Machiavelli was silent.

'I am answered,' said Caterina. 'I will make my preparations at once.'

29

'Are you sure you're able to ride?' Ezio asked her.

'I rode from the Castel when you rescued me, didn't I?'

'Yes, but then there was no choice.'

'Is there a choice now?'

Ezio was silent. It was the following morning and Ezio watched as Caterina and her two female attendants packed the few clothes and provisions Claudia had organized for her journey. She would leave the next day before dawn. A small escort of Ezio's men would ride with her part of the way, to see her safely out of Rome. Ezio had offered to join them, but this Caterina had refused. 'I don't like goodbyes,' she'd said. 'And the more drawn-out they are, the worse they are.'

He watched her as she bustled about her packing. He thought about the times they had had together, long ago in Forlì, and then about what he had fondly imagined was a reunion in Monteriggioni. The Assassin Brotherhood seemed to have taken over his life – and left him solitary.

'I wish you would stay,' he said.

'Ezio, I can't. You know I can't.'

'Dismiss your women.'

'I have to hurry.'

'Dismiss them. This won't take long.'

She did so, but he could see with what reluctance, and even then she said, 'Be sure to return in five minutes by the water clock.'

Once they were alone, he didn't know where to begin.

'Well?' she said, more gently, and he could see that her eyes were troubled, though by what, he could not tell.

'I . . . I rescued you,' he said lamely.

'You did, and I am grateful. But didn't you tell the others that you did so purely because I am still a useful ally – even with Forlì gone?'

'We'll get Forlì back.'

'And then I shall go there again.'

Ezio was silent again. His heart felt empty.

She came up to him and put her hands on his shoulders. 'Ezio, listen. I am no use to anyone without Forlì. If I leave now, it is to seek safety and to be with my children. Don't you want that for me?'

'Yes.'

'Well, then . . .'

'I didn't rescue you because you're valuable to the cause.'

It was her turn to be silent.

'But because—'

'Don't say it, Ezio.'

'Why not?'

'Because I cannot say it back.'

No weapon could have cut him more deeply than those words. 'You used me then?'

'That sounds rather harsh.'

'What other words would you wish me to use?'

'I tried to explain earlier.'

'You are a ruthless woman.'

'I am a woman with work to do, and a duty.'

'Then whatever serves your cause, goes.'

She was silent again, then said, 'I've tried to explain this to you already. You must accept it.' She had taken her hands from his shoulders. He could see that her mind had wandered back to her journey and that she was looking at the things yet to be packed.

He thought, recklessly, *To hell with the Brotherhood! I know what I want! Why shouldn't I live for myself, for a change?*

'I'm coming with you,' he said.

She turned to him again, her eyes serious. 'Listen, Ezio. Perhaps you are making a choice, but you are making it too late. Perhaps I have done the same thing. But you are leader of the Assassins now. Don't give up the work you have started, the great work of rebuilding after the disaster at Monteriggioni. Without you, things will fall apart again, and then who will there be to save us?'

'But you never really wanted me.'

He looked at her. She was still there, in the room with him, but her spirit had long gone. How long ago it had left him, he did not know – perhaps it had never really been there. Perhaps he had only hoped for it, or imagined it. At that moment, he felt that he was looking at the corpse of love, yet still he refused to believe in its death. But like any other death, he saw that he had no choice but to get used to the reality.

There was a knock at the door.

'Come in,' said Caterina, and her attendants returned. Ezio left them to their packing.

The next morning, Ezio was determined to resist seeing Caterina off, but he could not. It was cold, and when he got to the appointed square, in a safe district of the city, they were already mounted, the horses restless. Perhaps, even now, at the last moment, she would relent. But her eyes, though kind, were distant. He thought he could have borne things better if she hadn't looked at him with kindness. Kindness was almost humiliating.

All he could say was, '*Buona fortuna, Contessa*, and . . . farewell.'

'Let's hope it's not "farewell".'

'Oh, I think it is.'

She looked at him once more. 'Well then – *buona fortuna anche*, my Prince; and – *Vittoria agli Assassini!*'

249

She wheeled her horse round and, without another word or even a backward glance, at the head of her guardian entourage, she galloped north out of the city and out of his life. He watched them until they were mere specks in the distance, a lonely, middle-aged man who had been given a last chance at love, and missed it.

'*Vittoria agli Assassini*,' murmured Ezio tonelessly to himself, as he turned and made his way back into the still-sleeping city.

30

With Cesare's return imminent, Ezio had to put his private grief aside and get on with the work Fate had given him. In his attempt to cut Cesare off from his funds, the first step was to find and neutralize Cesare's banker, and the initial lead as to who that was would come from The Rosa in Fiore.

'What do you want?' Claudia couldn't have been less friendly if she'd tried.

'You spoke of a senator at the meeting.'

'Yes I did. Why?'

'You said he owed money to Cesare's banker. Is he here?'

She shrugged. 'You'll probably find him on the Campidoglio. Surely you don't need my help for that?'

'What does he look like?'

'Oh, let me see, average?'

'Don't play games with me, Sister.'

Claudia relented slightly. 'He's maybe sixty, lean, worried-looking, clean-shaven, grey hair, your height or a little less. Name's Egidio Troche. Stubborn type, Ezio, pessimistic, set in his ways. You'll have your work cut out trying to get round him.'

'Thank you.' Ezio looked at her hard. 'Now, I intend to track down this banker and kill him. I've a pretty shrewd idea who he is, but I need to find out where he lives. This senator could lead me to him.'

'The banker's security's pretty tight. So would yours be, if you were in a position like his.'

'You think mine isn't?'

'As if I cared.'

'Listen, Claudia, if I'm tough with you, it's because I worry about you.'

'Spare me.'

'You're doing well—'

'Thank you, kind sir—'

'But I need you to organize a big job for me. Once I have neutralized this banker, I need your girls to get his money to a place of safety.'

'Just let me know when – or should I say "if" – you succeed.'

'Just stay alert.'

In a dark mood, Ezio set off for the Capitoline Hill, the administrative centre of Rome, where he was greeted by a busy scene. There were several senators going about their business in the broad piazza around which the government buildings were arranged, accompanied by secretaries and assistants, who carried papers in leather folders and bustled after their masters as they moved from building to building, all of them trying to look as busy and important as possible. As far as he could, Ezio blended into the melee, keeping a watchful eye out for a man answering the description Claudia had given him. As he moved through the crowd, he kept his ears pricked for any hint he might pick up about his quarry. There was certainly no sign of Egidio among the senators at the moment, though he seemed to be providing his colleagues with a lively topic of conversation.

'Egidio's been asking for money again,' said one.

'When doesn't he? What's it for this time?'

'Oh, some proposal to reduce the number of public executions.'

'Ridiculous!'

Ezio moved on to another knot of senators, and there he gleaned more information. He wasn't sure, from what he heard, whether Egidio was a militant (and therefore foolish) liberal reformer, or a rather ham-fisted conman.

'Egidio's petitioning for an end to the torturing of witnesses in the criminal courts,' the leading member of the next group was saying.

'Fat chance!' replied the harassed-looking man he was talking to. 'It's just a front, anyway. All he really wants the money for is to pay off his debts.'

'And he wants to get rid of exemption licences.'

'Please! Like that's going to happen. Every citizen who feels mistreated by our laws should surely be permitted to pay for an exemption from those laws.

It's our duty. After all, it's our own Holy Father who brought the exemption licences in, and he's following the example of Christ Himself – "Blessed are the Merciful"!'

Another Borgia scam for making money, thought Ezio, while the other senator rejoined, 'Why should we give any money to Egidio? Everyone knows what he'd do with it.'

The two men laughed and went about their business.

Ezio's attention was then attracted by a small group of Borgia guards who had Cesare's personal crest – two red bulls, quartered with fleurs-de-lys – sewn onto their doublets. As this always spelt trouble, he made his way over to them and saw, as he approached, that they had surrounded one of the senators. The others were carrying on as if nothing out of the ordinary was happening, but Ezio could see that they left plenty of space between the guards and themselves.

The unfortunate senator answered Claudia's description perfectly.

'No more arguing,' the guards' sergeant was saying.

'Your payment's due,' added his corporal. 'And a debt's a debt.'

Egidio had dropped any pretence of dignity and was pleading. 'Make an exception for an old man,' he quavered. 'I beg of you.'

'No,' snarled the sergeant, nodding to two of his men, who seized Egidio and threw him to the ground.

'The banker has sent us to collect, and you know what that means.'

'Look, give me until tomorrow – this evening! – I'll have the money ready then.'

'Not good enough,' responded the sergeant, kicking the senator hard in the stomach. He stepped back and the corporal and the other two guards set about belabouring the prostrate old man.

'That won't get you your money,' said Ezio, stepping forward.

'Who are you? Friend of his?'

'I'm a concerned bystander.'

'Well, you can take your concern and mind your own fucking business!'

The sergeant, as Ezio had hoped, stepped too close, and with practised ease Ezio slipped the catch on his Hidden Blade and, raising his arm, swept it across the guard's exposed throat, just above the gorget he was wearing. The other guards watched, rooted to the spot in astonishment as their leader fell to his knees, his hands futilely scrabbling at the wound to staunch the fountain of blood. Before they could react, Ezio was upon them, and a matter of seconds later, the three of them had joined their sergeant on the Other Side, all three with their throats slit. Ezio's mission left no time for sword play, only swift, efficient killing.

During the skirmish the piazza emptied as if by magic. Ezio helped the senator to his feet. There was blood on the man's clothes and he looked – and indeed was – in a state of shock mingled with relief.

'We'd better get out of here,' Ezio said to him.

'I know a place. Follow me,' Egidio replied, and set off with remarkable speed for an alleyway between two of the larger government buildings. They hastened down it, turned left, then down some stairs into a basement area which contained a door. This the senator hastily unlocked, ushering Ezio into a small, dark, but comfortable-looking apartment.

'My bolthole,' said Egidio. 'Useful when you have as many creditors as I have.

'But one big one.'

'My mistake was to consolidate all my debts with the banker. I wasn't fully aware of his exact connections at the time. I should have stuck to Chigi. At least he's honest – as far as a banker can be!' Egidio paused. 'But what of you? A Good Samaritan in Rome? I thought they were a dying breed.'

Ezio let that go. 'You are *Senatore* Egidio Troche?'

Egidio looked startled. 'Don't tell me I owe you money as well?!'

'No, but you can help me. I am looking for Cesare's banker.'

The senator smiled thinly. 'Cesare *Borgia's* banker? Ha! And you are?'

'Just let's say I'm a friend of the family.'

'Cesare has a lot of friends these days. Unfortunately, I am not one of them. So, if you'll excuse me, I have some packing to do.'

'I can pay.'

Egidio stopped looking nervous. 'Ah! You can *pay*? *Ma che meraviglia!* He fights off guards for one *and* he offers one money! Tell me, where have you been all my life?'

'Well, I haven't descended from heaven. You help me and I'll help you. It's as simple as that.'

Egidio considered this. 'We'll go to my brother's place. They've got no quarrel with him, and we can't stay here – it's too depressing, and it's far too close to my – dare I say, our? – enemies.'

'Let's go, then.'

'But you'll have to protect me. There'll be more of Cesare's guards out after me, and they won't be especially friendly, if you know what I mean – especially after that little show you put on in the piazza.'

'Come on.'

Egidio led the way out cautiously, making sure the coast was clear before they set off by a labyrinthine route through back alleys and seedy lanes, across little *piazze*, and skirting the edges of markets. Twice they encountered pairs of guards, and twice Ezio had to fight them off, this time using his sword to full effect. It seemed that the city was on full alert for both men – and both men in flight together proved too good a bounty for the Borgia henchmen. Time was not on

Ezio's side, so when the next pair of guards appeared at the far side of a small piazza, they simply had to run for it, and Ezio, unable to take to the rooftops with the senator in tow, had to depend on Egidio's apparently exhaustive knowledge of Rome's backstreets. At last they reached the back of a new and quietly splendid villa, set in its own walled courtyard, a few blocks east of St Peter's. Egidio let them into the courtyard through a small iron-bound gate set into one of the walls, for which he produced a key.

Once inside, they both breathed more easily.

'Someone really wants you dead,' said Ezio.

'Not yet – they want me to pay them first.'

'Why only once they've got their money? By the sound of things you're something of a milch cow to them.'

'It isn't that simple. The fact is, I've been a fool. I'm no friend of the Borgia, even if I have borrowed money from them, and recently a bit of information came my way, which gave me an opportunity to do them down – if only a little.'

'And that was?'

'A few months ago, my brother Francesco, who's Cesare's chamberlain – I know, I know, don't get me started – told me a good deal about Cesare's plans for the Romagna. He plans to create a mini-kingdom there, from which he intends to conquer the rest of the country and bring it to heel. As the Romagna is on the doorstep of the Venetian territories, Venice is already unhappy about Cesare's inroads there.'

'So what did you do?'

Egidio spread his hands. 'I wrote to the Venetian ambassador, giving him all the information I'd got from Francesco. Warning him. But one of my letters must have been intercepted.'

'Won't that implicate your brother?'

'He's managed to keep himself in the clear so far.'

'But what possessed you to do such a thing?'

'I had to do something. The Senate has nothing to do, really, these days, except put its imprimatur on all the Borgia decrees. If it didn't, it would cease to exist altogether. As it is, there's no independence. Do you know what it's like not to have *un cazzo* to do?' Egidio shook his head. 'It changes a man. I admit that even I have taken to gambling and drinking . . .'

'And whoring.'

The senator looked at him. 'Oh, you're good. You're very good. What was it that gave me away? The scent of perfume on my sleeve?'

Ezio smiled. 'Something like that.'

'Hmm. Well, anyway, as I was saying, senators used to do what senators are supposed to do: petitioning about real issues, like – oh, I don't know where to start – unlawful cruelty, abandoned children, street crime, lending rates, keeping some kind of rein on Chigi and the other bankers. Now, the only legislation we are allowed to draw up independently concerns stuff like the appropriate width of the sleeves of women's dresses.'

'But not you. You try to raise money for false causes in order to pay off your gambling debts.'

'They're not false causes, my boy. As soon as we have a proper government again, and as soon as I am on an even keel financially, I intend to pursue them vigorously.'

'And when do you think that will be?'

'We must be patient. Tyranny is unbearable, but it never lasts. It's too brittle.'

'I wish I could believe that.'

'Of course you've got to stand up to it, whatever happens. You obviously have to.' He paused. 'I'm probably – what? – ten or fifteen years older than you. I must make the most of my time. Or have you never looked at a grave and thought, *This is the most significant thing I will ever do: die?*'

Ezio was silent.

'No,' continued Egidio. 'I guess not.' He turned in on himself. '*Maledette* letters! I should never have sent them to the ambassador. Now Cesare will kill me as soon as he gets a chance, debt or no debt, unless by some miracle he decides to vent his anger on someone else. God knows, he's capricious enough.'

'Someone else? Like your brother?'

'I'd never forgive myself.'

'Why not? You're a politician.'

'We're not all bad.'

'Where is your brother?'

'I've no idea. Not here, thank God. We haven't talked since he found out about the letters, and I'm enough of a liability for him. If he saw you . . .'

'Can we get down to business?' said Ezio.

'Of course. One good turn, and so on . . . Now, what was it you wanted again?'

'I want to know where Cesare's banker is. Where he works. Where he lives.'

Egidio was suddenly all briskness. 'Right, I need to arrive with the money.' He spread his hands again. 'Problem is, I have none.'

'I told you I'd get it for you. Just tell me how much, and where you are meeting this banker.'

'I never know until I'm actually there. I usually go to one of three prearranged points. His associates meet me and take me to him. I owe ten thousand ducats.'

'No problem.'

'*Sul serio?*' Egidio almost beamed. 'You have to stop this. You might actually give me hope.'

'Stay here. I'll return with the money at sunset.'

Early in the evening, Ezio returned to an increasingly incredulous Egidio. He placed two heavy leather bags in the senator's hands.

'You came back! You actually came back!'

'You waited.'

'I'm a desperate man. I cannot believe you would just . . . do this.'

'There is a condition.'

'I knew it.'

'Listen,' Ezio said. 'If you survive, and I hope you will, I want you to keep an eye on what's going on politically in this city. And I want you to report everything you find to . . .' He hesitated, then said, 'To *Madonna* Claudia, at the bordello they call The Rosa in Fiore. Especially anything you can pick up on the Borgia.' Ezio smiled inwardly. 'Do you know the place?'

Egidio coughed. 'I . . . I have a friend who sometimes frequents it.'

'Good.'

'What will you do with this information? Make the Borgia disappear?'

Ezio grinned. 'I'm just . . . recruiting you.'

The senator looked at the bags of money. 'I hate to give this to them.' He fell into a thoughtful silence, then said, 'My brother has watched my back because we're family. I hate the *pezzo di merda*, but he is still my brother.'

'He works for Cesare.'

Egidio pulled himself together. '*Va bene.* They sent me word of the meeting place this afternoon while you were gone. The timing's perfect. They're impatient for their money, so the meeting's tonight. I sweated blood, you know, when I told their messenger that I'd be sure to have their money ready for them.' He paused again. 'We should go soon. What will you do? Follow me?'

'It wouldn't look good if you didn't seem to be alone.'

Egidio nodded. 'Good. Just time for a glass of wine before we set off then. Will you join me?'

'No.'

'Well, I certainly need one.'

31

Ezio followed the senator through another maze of streets, though as these led to the Tiber, they were more familiar to him. They passed monuments, squares and fountains that were all familiar to him, as well as building works – the Borgia spent lavishly on *palazzi*, theatres and galleries in their quest for self-aggrandisement. At last Egidio halted in an attractive square formed by large private houses on two sides and a row of expensive shops on a third. On the fourth was a well-tended little park that sloped down towards the river. This was Egidio's destination. He selected a stone bench and took up a position by it in the gathering gloom, looking left and right, but apparently unruffled. Ezio admired his poise, and it was also useful. Any sign of nervousness might have put the banker's minions on their guard.

Ezio took up position by a cedar tree and waited. He didn't have to wait long. Minutes after Egidio's arrival, a tall man dressed in a livery he did not recognize came up to him. A badge on his shoulder displayed a crest; one half showed a red bull in a golden field, while the other had broad black and gold horizontal stripes. Ezio was none the wiser for this.

'Good evening, Egidio,' the newcomer said. 'It seems that you are ready to die like a gentleman.'

'That's hardly friendly of you, *Capitano*,' replied Egidio, 'as I have the money.'

The man raised an eyebrow. 'Really? Well, that makes all the difference. The banker will be most pleased. You came alone, I trust?'

'Do you see anyone else here?'

'Just follow me, *furbacchione*.'

They moved off, retracing their steps eastwards, and crossed the Tiber. Ezio followed them at a discreet distance, but staying within earshot.

'Is there any news of my brother, *Capitano*?' asked Egidio as they walked.

'I can only tell you that Duke Cesare wishes very much to interview him. As soon as he returns from the Romagna, that is.'

'I hope he's all right?'

'If he has nothing to hide, he has nothing to fear.'

They continued in silence, and at the Church of Santa Maria sopra Minerva turned north, in the direction of the Pantheon.

'What'll happen to my money?' said Egidio. Ezio realized that he was pumping the captain for Ezio's benefit. Clever man.

'*Your* money?' The Captain snickered. 'I hope all the interest's there.'

'It is.'

'It had better be.'

'Well?'

'The banker likes to be generous to his friends. He treats them well. He can afford to.'

'Treat you well, does he?'

'I like to think so.'

'How generous he is,' observed Egidio, with such heavy sarcasm that even the captain caught it.

'What did you say?' he asked threateningly, breaking his stride.

'Oh . . . nothing.'

'Come on, we're there.'

The great bulk of the Pantheon rose out of the gloom in its cramped piazza. The tall Corinthian portico of the 1500-year-old building, constructed as a temple to all the Roman gods, but long since consecrated as a church, towered above them. In its shadow three men were waiting. Two were dressed similarly to the captain, while the third was in civilian dress: a dry, tall, withered-looking man, whose fine robes sat ill on him. They greeted the captain, and the civilian nodded coldly at Egidio.

'Luigi! Luigi Torcelli!' said Egidio loudly, again for Ezio's benefit. 'It's good to see you again. Still the banker's agent, I see. Thought you'd have been promoted by now. Desk job and all that.'

'Shut up,' said the withered man.

'He's got the money,' said the captain.

266

Torcelli's eyes glittered. 'Well, well! That *will* put my master in a good mood. He's having a rather special party this evening, so I'm delivering your payment to him personally, at his palazzo. I must hurry – time is money – so give it here.'

Egidio clearly hated to comply, but the two underling guards levelled their halberds at him and he handed over the bags. 'Oof!' he said. 'It's heavy. Glad to get shot of them.'

'Shut up,' snapped the agent once again. To the guards he said, 'Hold him here until I get back.'

With that, he disappeared inside the cavernous, deserted church, closing its mighty doors firmly behind him.

Ezio needed to follow him, but there was no way he'd get through those doors, and, anyway, first he had to get past the guards undetected. Egidio must have guessed this, for he started up a line of banter with the men in uniform, irritating them, but also distracting them.

'Why not release me? I've paid up,' he said indignantly.

'What if you've sold us short?' replied the captain. 'The money has to be counted first. You must see that.'

'What? Ten thousand ducats? It'll take all night!'

'It has to be done.'

'If Luigi's late, he'll get stick. I can imagine the kind of man the banker must be!'

'Shut *up*.'

'You people certainly have a very limited vocabulary. Look, think of poor old Torcelli – if he doesn't show up with the money soon, the banker probably won't let him join in the fun. *Does* he let his lackeys join in the fun?'

The captain cuffed the senator impatiently round the head and Egidio fell silent, though he was still grinning. He'd seen Ezio slip past and begin to climb the façade of the building in the direction of the dome behind it.

Once on the roof of the circular edifice, which the classical frontage partially concealed, Ezio made his way towards the round opening – the oculus – he knew was at its centre. It would be a test of all his climbing skills, but, once inside, he would find the agent and put the next phase of the plan, which was rapidly forming in his mind, into operation. The agent was about his size and, though far less muscular, his flowing robes would hide Ezio's physique, if all went well.

The trickiest part was lowering himself through the aperture at the dome's apex, then finding some way of descending from there. He'd been to the church before, and knew that censers hanging far below were suspended by chains from this very roof. If he could reach one of them . . . If it would take his weight . . .

Well, there was no other way. Ezio knew full well that even he couldn't climb, fly-like, across the inner curve of a dome, coffered though it was, that hung 140 feet above the cold grey flagstone floor.

He hung over the edge of the oculus and peered into the gloom beneath. A pinpoint of light far below showed where the agent was, seated on a bench that ran round the edge of the wall. He'd have the money next to him and would be counting it by candlelight. Next, Ezio looked round for the chains that held the censers. None was within reach, but if he could just . . .

He changed position and lowered his legs over the edge of the circular opening, gripping it with both hands. It was a huge risk, but the chains looked solid and old, and far heavier than he'd expected. He looked at their fixings in the ceiling, and as far as he could see they were set fast in solid stone.

There was nothing for it. Pushing hard with his hands, he threw himself forwards and sideways into the void.

For a moment it seemed he was suspended in the air, as if the air was holding him up, as water does a swimmer, but then he started to fall.

His arms flailed forward and he willed his body towards the nearest chain – and caught it. The links slipped under his gloves and he slid several feet before he was able to get a firm grip, then he found himself swaying gently in the darkness. He listened. He had heard no sound, and it was too dark for the agent to see the chain swinging from where he sat far below.

Ezio looked towards the light. It still burned steadily and there were no calls of alarm.

Steadily, he lowered himself down until he was perhaps twenty feet above the floor. He was quite close to the agent, and could see his silhouette hunched over the money bags, the gold coins glinting in the candlelight. Ezio could hear the man muttering, and the gentle, rhythmic click of an abacus.

Suddenly, there was an awful, tearing sound from above. The fixing of the chain in the roof could bear the strain of his extra weight no longer, and had ripped loose. Ezio let go of the chain as it went loose in his hands and threw himself forward towards the candle. As he sailed through the air, he heard a startled, 'Who's there?' from the agent, and a seemingly unending rattle as 140 feet of chain fell snaking to the floor. Thank God the church doors were closed: their thickness would deaden any sound from within.

Ezio fell upon the agent with his full weight, knocking the breath out of him, and both men sprawled on the floor, the agent spreadeagled beneath Ezio.

He wriggled free, but Ezio had him by the arm.

'Who are you? Christ protect me!' said the agent, terrified.

'I am sorry, friend,' said Ezio, releasing the Hidden Blade.

'What? No! No!' the agent jabbered. 'Look, take the money! It's yours! It's *yours*!'

Ezio adjusted his grip and drew the man close.

'Get away from me!'

'*Requiescat in Pace*,' said Ezio.

Ezio quickly stripped the agent of his outer robes and put them on over his own, drawing a scarf over his lower face and tipping the agent's hat down low. The robes were a little snug, but they weren't a noticeably bad fit. Then he finished transferring the money from the bags into the metal box the agent had brought for the purpose, and where much of it was already neatly stacked. To it he added the account book and, abandoning the abacus and the leather bags, he tucked the heavy box under his arm and made for the door. He had heard enough of the agent's manner of speech to be able to emulate it tolerably, he hoped. Anyway, he'd have to chance it.

As he approached the door, it opened and the captain called through it, 'Everything going well in there?'

'Just done.'

'Well, hurry up, Luigi, or we'll be late.'

Ezio emerged into the portico.

'The count is complete?'

Ezio nodded.

'*Va bene*,' said the captain. Then, turning to the men who held Egidio, he crisply ordered, 'Kill him.'

'Wait!' said Ezio.

'What?'

'Don't kill him.'

The captain looked surprised. 'But that's . . . that's hardly usual procedure, is it, Luigi? Besides, do you know what this guy's *done*?'

'I have my orders – from the banker himself – this man is to be spared.'

'May I ask why?'

'Do you question the commands of the banker?'

The captain shrugged and nodded to the guards, who let go their hold of the senator.

'Lucky you,' he said to Egidio, who had the sense not to glance at Ezio before hastening off without another word.

The captain turned to Ezio. 'All right, Luigi. Lead the way.'

Ezio hesitated. He was stumped, as he had no idea where to go. He hefted the box. 'This is heavy. Have the guards carry it between them.'

'Certainly.'

He passed the box over but still didn't move.

The guards waited.

'*Ser* Luigi,' said the captain after a few moments. 'With respect, we must get this to the banker on time. Of course, I am not questioning your authority . . . but should we not hurry?'

What was the point of buying time to think? Ezio knew he'd have to work on a hunch. It was likely that the banker would live somewhere in the vicinity of either the Castel Sant'Angelo or the Vatican. But which? He plumped for the Castel Sant'Angelo, and started off in a westerly direction. His security detail looked at one another, but followed him. Even so, he sensed their disquiet, and indeed, after they had gone a little way, he heard the two guardsmen whispering, 'Is this some kind of test?'

'Not sure.'

'Perhaps we're too early?'

'Maybe we're taking a roundabout route deliberately – for some reason.'

Finally the captain tapped him on the shoulder and said, 'Luigi, are you all right?'

'Of course I am.'

'Then – again with respect – why are you taking us towards the Tiber?'

'Security reasons.'

'Ah – I did wonder. Normally we just go straight there.'

'This is a particularly important consignment,' said Ezio, hoping it was. The captain didn't bat an eyelid.

While they had stopped to talk, one of the guards muttered to the other, 'Load of rubbish, if you ask me. This kind of arsing about makes me wish I were still a blacksmith.'

'I'm starving. I want to go home,' muttered the other. 'Stuff the security. It's only a couple of blocks north of here.'

On hearing this, Ezio breathed a sigh of relief, for his mind had flashed on the location of the palazzo of the other banker, Agostino Chigi, who dealt with the Pope's affairs. That was a little to the north-east of where they were now. It stood to reason that Cesare's banker's place would not be far away – in the financial district. What a fool he'd been not to think of that before, but it had been another busy day.

'We've made enough of a detour,' he said decisively. 'We'll take a direct route from here.'

He set off towards the Palazzo Chigi, and was reassured by the sense of relief he got from his companions. After a while, the captain even decided to take the lead. They adopted a brisk pace and soon reached a district of clean, broad streets. The large well-lit marble edifice they headed for had different guards on duty at the foot of its entrance steps and in front of the imposing double front door at their head.

Evidently, Ezio's party was expected.

'Not before time,' said the leader of the new guards, who clearly outranked the captain. Turning to Ezio, he added, 'Hand over the box to my men, Luigi. I'll see the banker gets it. You'd better come, too. There's someone here who wants to talk to you.' He looked round. 'Where's Senator Troche?'

'Dealt with as ordered,' said Ezio quickly before anyone else could answer.

'Good,' replied the guard leader gruffly.

Ezio followed the box, which was now in the hands of the new guards, up the steps. Behind him, the captain made to follow.

'Not you,' said the guard leader.

'We can't go in?'

'Not tonight. You and your men are to join the patrol here. And you might send one of them to fetch another detachment. We're on full security. Orders of Duke Cesare.'

'*Porco puttana*,' growled one of Ezio's guards to his mate.

Ezio pricked up his ears. *Cesare? He's here?* he thought to himself, his mind racing as he went through the open doors into an entrance hall ablaze with light and, luckily, thronged with people.

The captain and the guard leader were still arguing about the extra patrol duty when a detachment of Papal city police came up to them on the double. They were out of breath and concern showed on their faces.

'What is it, sergeant?' the guard leader said to their commander.

'*Perdone, Colonnello*, but we've just been on the beat near the Pantheon – the doors were open . . .'

'And?'

'So we investigated. I sent some men in . . .'

'Spit it out, man.'

'We found *Messer* Torcelli, sir. Murdered.'

'Luigi?' The guard leader turned to look up at the front door through which Ezio had just disappeared. 'Nonsense. He arrived here a few minutes ago, with the money. There must be some mistake.'

32

Ezio, after having quickly and discreetly divested himself of Luigi's outer garments and hidden them behind a column, made his way through the crowd of richly attired guests, many of whom wore masks, keeping a close eye on the guards with the box of money. He drew nearer to them as they approached an attendant in fine livery, to whom they handed it.

'For the banker,' said one of the guards.

The attendant nodded and, carrying the box with ease, turned to make his way towards the back of the hall. Ezio was about to follow when he was joined by three girls who brushed against him. Their dress was as opulent as that of the other guests, but their décolleté left little to the imagination. With a shock of surprise and pleasure, Ezio recognized them as courtesans from The Rosa in Fiore. He'd obviously underestimated his sister. No wonder she was so furious with him.

'We'll take over from here, Ezio,' said one of the girls.

'It wouldn't do for you to get too close,' said a second. 'But keep us in sight.'

They swanned off after the attendant and soon

caught up with him, at which point one of them engaged him in conversation.

'Hi there,' she said.

'Hello,' replied the man guardedly. But it wasn't much fun being at such a party and yet having to be on duty.

'Mind if I walk with you? All these people! It's hard to get through them with any speed.'

'Sure. I mean, I don't mind if you want to keep me company.'

'I've never been here before.'

'Where did you come from?'

'Trastevere.' She shuddered theatrically. 'You have to pass some of the old ruins to get here. They make me nervous.'

'You're safe here.'

'With you, you mean?'

The attendant smiled. 'I could protect you, if the need arose.'

'I bet you could.' She looked at the box. 'My, what a fine chest you have there.'

'It isn't mine.'

'Oh, but you're holding it in those strong arms of yours. What muscles you must have.'

'Want to touch them?'

'*Santò cielo!* But what would I tell the priest in Confession?'

By now they had arrived at an iron-bound door

flanked by two guards. Ezio watched as one of them knocked. A moment later, the door was opened and a figure in the red robes of a cardinal appeared in the entrance, with an attendant similarly dressed to the first.

'Here is the money you were expecting, Your Eminence,' said the first attendant, handing the box to the second.

Ezio drew in his breath, his thoughts had been confirmed. The banker was none other than Juan Borgia the Elder, Archbishop of Monreale and Cardinal-Priest of Santa Susanna. The selfsame man he had seen in Cesare's company at Monteriggioni and in the stable yard at the Castel Sant'Angelo!

'Good,' said the banker, whose black eyes glittered in his sallow face. He was eyeing the girl, who stood close to the first attendant. 'I'll take her, too, I think.'

He grabbed her by the arm and pulled her to him, looking levelly at the first attendant. 'As for you, you are dismissed.'

'*Onoratissima!*' said the girl, willingly snuggling up to the banker as the attendant tried to control the expression on his face. The second attendant disappeared into the room beyond the door, closing it behind him, as the banker led the girl back into the party.

The first attendant watched them go, then gave a resigned sigh. He started to leave, but then stopped, patting himself down. 'My coin purse! What's happened to it?' he muttered, then looked in the direction the banker had gone with the girl. They were surrounded by laughing guests, amongst whom agile servants moved with silver trays loaded with food and drink. 'Oh shit!' he said to himself, and made his way back towards the front doors which, as he passed through them, closed behind him. Evidently all the guests had arrived. Ezio watched him go and thought, *If they continue to treat people like that, I should have no trouble mustering all the new recruits I need.*

Ezio turned and pushed his way through to a position close to the banker just as a herald appeared on a gallery and a trumpeter blew a short fanfare to make silence for him.

'*Eminenze, signore, signori,*' announced the herald. 'Our esteemed lord, and guest of honour, the Duke of Valence and Romagna, Captain-General of the Papal *Forze Armate*, Prince of Andria and Venafro, Count of Dyois and Lord of Piombino, Camerino and Urbino – His Grace *Messer* Cesare Borgia – is about to honour us with an address in the Great Inner Chamber.'

'Come on, my dear, you shall sit near me,' the banker said to the courtesan from The Rosa in Fiore, his bony hand snaking round her buttocks. Joining the press of people that now moved obediently through the double doors that led to the inner chamber, Ezio followed. He noticed that the other two girls were not far away, but were sensibly ignoring him. He wondered how many other allies his sister had managed to infiltrate into this gathering. If she succeeded in all he had asked her to do, he would have to do more than eat humble pie, but he also felt proud and reassured.

Ezio took a seat on an aisle near the middle of the assembly. Papal guards lined the edges of the room, and another row stood in front of the dais that had been erected at one end of it. Once everyone had settled, the women fanning themselves, for the room was hot, a familiar figure in black strode onto the dais. He was accompanied, Ezio noticed, by his father, although Rodrigo simply took a seat behind him. To his relief, Lucrezia was nowhere to be seen, though she must have been released by now.

'Welcome, my friends,' said Cesare, smiling a little. 'I know we all have a long night ahead of us.' He paused for the laughter and scattered applause. 'But I will not detain you long. My friends, I am honoured that the Cardinal of Santa Susanna has gone to so much trouble to help me celebrate my recent victories.'

Applause.

'And what better way shall I have to mark them than by joining in the brotherhood of Man? Soon we will gather here again for an even greater gala, for then we shall be celebrating a united Italy. Then, my friends, the feasting and revelry will last not one night, or two, or even five, six or seven – we shall spend *forty* days and nights in celebration.'

Ezio saw the Pope stiffen at this, but Rodrigo said

nothing; he did not interrupt. The speech, as Cesare had promised, was a short one, amounting to a list of the new city states brought under his sway, and a vague outline of his plans for future conquests. When it was over, amid loud shouts of approval and applause, Cesare turned to go, but his way was blocked by Rodrigo, who was clearly struggling to suppress his fury. Ezio made his way forward to listen to the terse conversation that had started, sotto voce, between father and son. As for the other revellers, they had begun to drift back to the main hall, their minds already on the pleasures of the party ahead.

'We did not agree to conquer all Italy,' Rodrigo was saying, his voice full of spite.

'But, *caro padre*, if your brilliant Captain-General says we can do it, why not rejoice and let it happen?'

'You risk ruining everything! You risk upsetting the delicate balance of power we have worked so hard to maintain.'

Cesare's lip curled. 'I appreciate all that you have done for me, of course, *caro padre*, but do not forget that I control the army now, and that means that I make the decisions.' He paused to let his words sink in. 'Don't look so glum. Enjoy yourself!'

With that, Cesare left the dais and went through a curtained door to one side. Rodrigo watched him go for a moment then, muttering to himself, followed.

Strut as much as you like for now, Cesare, thought Ezio.

I'll pluck you down. In the meantime, your banker must pay the price for his involvement with you.

Putting on the air of any other party guest, he sauntered in the same direction as the others. During the speech, the main hall had been transformed – beds and couches were placed around it under heavy canopies, and the floor had been covered with damask cushions and thick Persian rugs. Servants still passed among the guests, providing wine, but the guests had become more interested in one another. All over the room, men and women were shedding their clothes, in pairs, threesomes, foursomes and more. The smell of sweat rose with the heat.

Several women and not a few men, some not yet engaged in the fun and games, gave Ezio the eye, but few paid any serious attention to him as he made his way, using the columns of the room for cover, towards the banker, who had now shed his biretta, his magnificent ferraiolo and his cassock to reveal a spindly figure in a white cotton shirt and woollen long johns. He and the girl were half sitting, half lying on a canopied couch set into an alcove, more or less hidden from the view of the rest of the guests. Ezio drew near.

'And are you having a pleasant evening, my dear?' the banker was saying, his gnarled hands fiddling clumsily with the stays of her dress.

'Yes, *Eminenza*, indeed I am. There is so much to look at.'

'Oh, good. I spared no expense, you know.' His lips slobbered over her neck. He bit and sucked, moving her hand lower.

'I can tell,' she replied, her eyes meeting Ezio's over the banker's shoulder and warning him to stay back for the moment.

'Yes, sweetheart, the finer things in life make power so rewarding. If I see an apple growing on a tree, I simply pluck it. No one can stop me.'

'Well,' said the girl. 'I suppose is does depend a bit on whose tree it is.'

The banker cackled. 'You don't seem to understand: *all* the trees are owned by me.'

'Not mine, my dear.'

The banker drew back a little, and when he spoke again, frost had crept into his voice, 'On the contrary, *tesora*, I saw you steal my attendant's purse. I believe I've earned a free ride for your penance. In fact, I'm taking a free ride that'll last all night long.'

'Free?' Ezio hoped the girl wasn't pushing her luck. He glanced around the room. The few guards were stationed round its perimeter at intervals of perhaps fifteen feet, but none of them near. The banker, on his own ground, was clearly sure of himself. Perhaps a little too sure.

'That's what I said,' replied the banker, the ghost of menace in his tone. Then a new thought struck him. 'Do you have a sister by any chance?'

'No, but I have a daughter.'

The banker considered this. 'Three hundred ducats?'

'Seven.'

'You drive a hard bargain, but . . . done. A pleasure doing business with you.'

33

As the evening wore on, Ezio listened to the voices around him – 'Do it again!' 'No, no, you're hurting me!' 'No, you can't do that. I won't allow it!' – and all the sounds of pain and pleasure – the pain real, the pleasure simulated.

The banker was not running out of steam, unfortunately, and, having lost patience fumbling with her, started to tear the girl's dress off her. She still implored Ezio with her eyes to hold his ground. 'I can handle this,' she seemed to be saying to him.

He looked around the room again. Some of the servants and most of the guards had been inveigled by the guests to join in the fun, and he noticed people wielding wooden and ivory dildos, and little black whips.

Soon . . .

'Come here, my dear,' the banker was saying, pushing the girl back down onto the couch and, managing to straddle her, pushing himself into her. Then his hands closed round her neck and he started to strangle her. Choking, she struggled, then fainted.

'Oh yes! That's nice!' he gasped, the veins in his

neck bulging. His fingers tightened round the girl's neck. 'This should increase your pleasure. It certainly increases mine.' A minute later he had finished and lay heavily on her body, slipping on their sweat as he caught his breath.

He had not killed the girl. Ezio could see the rise and fall of her chest.

The banker clawed his way to his feet, leaving her prostrate form half-on, half-off the couch.

He snapped out an order to a pair of servants who were still on duty nearby: 'Get rid of her.'

As the banker moved towards the main orgy, Ezio and the servants watched him go. As soon as he was at a safe distance and otherwise occupied, the servants lifted the girl gently onto the couch, placed a carafe of water near her and covered her with a fur rug. One of them noticed Ezio. Ezio put a finger to his lips and the man smiled and nodded. At least there was some good in this fetid hellhole.

Ezio shadowed the banker as he pulled up his long johns and moved from group to group, muttering his appreciation like a connoisseur in an art gallery.

'Oh, *bellissima*,' he would say from time to time, stopping to watch, then he made for the iron-bound door he'd originally appeared from and knocked on it. It was opened from within by the second attendant, who'd almost certainly been spending all that time verifying the new accounts.

Ezio didn't give them a chance to close the door behind them; he leapt forward and pushed both men back inside. Ezio closed the door and faced them. The attendant, a little man in his shirtsleeves, burbled and fell to his knees, a dark stain flowering between his legs, before he fainted. The banker drew himself up.

'You!' he said. '*Assassino!* But not for much longer.' His arm snaked out to a bell pull, but Ezio was quicker. The Hidden Blade sprang out and slashed through the fingers of the hand the banker had extended. The banker snatched his maimed hand back as three fingers scattered onto the carpet. 'Stay back!' he screamed. 'Kill me and it'll do no good. Cesare will never let you live. But—'

'Yes?'

The man's face became sly. 'If you spare me . . .'

Ezio smiled. The banker understood. He nursed his ruined hand.

'Well,' he said, though tears of pain and rage were starting in his eyes. 'At least I have lived. The things I have seen, felt, tasted. I regret none of them. I do not regret a moment of my life.'

'You have played with the trinkets power brings. A man of real strength would be contemptuous of such things.'

'I gave the people what they wanted.'

'You delude yourself.'

'Spare me.'

'Your own debt is due, *Eminenza*. Unearned pleasure only consumes itself.'

The banker fell to his knees, mumbling half-remembered prayers.

Ezio raised the Hidden Blade.

'*Requiescat in Pace*,' he said.

He left the door open when he departed. The orgy had declined to some sleepy, smelly groping. One or two of the guests, supported by servants, were vomiting, while another pair of servants carried out a corpse: it had evidently all been too much for someone's heart. There was no one left on guard.

'We are ready,' said a voice at his elbow. He turned to see Claudia. Around the room, a dozen girls disentangled themselves and stood. Among them, dressed once more and looking shaken but otherwise fine, was the girl the banker had molested so vilely. The servants who had helped her stood beside her. More recruits.

'Get out of here,' said Claudia. 'We'll recover the money. With interest.'

'Can you—?'

'Just . . . just this once, trust me, Ezio.'

34

Though his mind remained full of misgivings about leaving his sister in charge, Ezio admitted to himself that he had, after all, asked her to do this job for him. A lot hung on it, but he had better do as she'd said and trust her.

It was cold in the small hours of the new day, and he pulled his hood up as he slipped past the dozing guards posted outside the banker's palazzo. The torches had burned low and the house itself, no longer so brilliantly lit from within, seemed old, grey and tired. He toyed with the idea of going after Rodrigo, whom he hadn't seen since his furious departure from the dais after Cesare's speech – Cesare clearly had not chosen to stay at the party – but he put the notion aside. He wasn't going to storm the Vatican single-handed and he was tired.

Ezio returned to Tiber Island to clean up and refresh himself, but he didn't linger over it. He had to find out, as soon as possible, how Claudia had fared; only then would he be able truly to relax.

The sun was appearing over the horizon, turning the rooftops of Rome gold, as he skimmed over them in the direction of The Rosa in Fiore. From his vantage point, he saw a number of Borgia patrols running about the city in a state of high excitement and agitation, but the brothel was well-hidden, and its location was a respected secret among its clients – they certainly wouldn't want to be answerable to Cesare if he got wind of it – so Ezio wasn't surprised to find no Borgia uniforms in its vicinity. He dropped down to a street not far away, and walked, trying not to hurry, towards the bordello.

As he approached, however, he tensed. Outside, there were signs of a struggle and the pavement was stained with blood. Drawing his sword, and with a pounding heart, he made his way through the door, which he found ajar.

The furniture in the reception room had been overturned and the place was a mess. Broken vases lay on the floor, and the pictures on the walls – tasteful illustrations of some of the juicier episodes in Boccaccio – were askew. But that was not all. The bodies of three dead Borgia guards lay in the entrance and there was blood everywhere. He was making his way forward when one of the courtesans – the selfsame girl who had suffered at the hands of the banker – came to greet him. Her dress and hands were covered in blood, but her eyes were shining.

'Oh, Ezio, thank God you're here.'

'What happened?' His thoughts flew to his mother and sister.

'We got away all right, but the Borgia guards must have followed us all the way back here—'

'What *happened*?!'

'They tried to trap us inside – to ambush us.'

'Where are Claudia and Maria?'

The girl was crying now. 'Follow me.'

She preceded him in the direction of the inner courtyard of The Rosa in Fiore. Ezio followed, still in great trepidation, but he noticed that the girl was unarmed and, despite her distress, she led the way without fear. What kind of massacre . . . ? Had the guards killed everyone except her – how had she escaped? – and left taking the money with them?

The girl pushed open the door leading to the courtyard, where an appalling sight greeted his eyes , though it was not the one he had expected.

There were dead Borgia guards everywhere, and those that were alive were badly wounded or dying. In their midst, by the fountain, stood Claudia, her dress drenched in blood, with a rondel dagger in one hand and a stiletto in the other. Most of the girls whom Ezio had seen at the banker's palazzo stood near her, similarly armed. To one side, protected by three of the girls, was Maria, and behind her, stacked against the wall, was not one, but seven metal boxes of the same type that Ezio had delivered to the banker.

Claudia was still on guard, as were the other women, expecting another wave of attacks.

'Ezio!' she said.

'Yes,' he replied, though he was looking at the carnage.

'How did you come here?'

'Over the rooftops, from Tiber Island.'

'Did you see any more of them?'

'Plenty, but they were running around in circles. None were near here.'

His sister relaxed slightly. 'Good. Then we must get the street outside cleaned up and the door closed. Then we must do something about this mess.'

'Did you . . . lose anyone?'

'Two – Lucia and Agnella. We have already laid them on their beds. They died bravely.'

She wasn't even trembling.

'Are you all right?' asked Ezio hesitantly.

'Perfectly,' she replied, composed. 'We'll need help disposing of this lot. Can you drum up some of your recruits to help? We left our new friends, the servants, behind at the palazzo, so that they can put anybody who asks off the scent.'

'Did any of this patrol escape?'

Claudia looked grim. She hadn't yet lowered either of her weapons. 'Not one. No news will get back to Cesare.'

Ezio was silent for a moment. Nothing could be heard but the splashing of the fountain and the song of the morning birds.

'How long ago?'

She half smiled. 'You just missed the party.'

He smiled back. 'No need for me. My sister knows how to wield a knife.'

'And I'm ready to do it again.'

'You speak like a true Auditore. Forgive me.'

'You needed to test me.'

'I wanted to protect you.'

'As you see, I can take care of myself.'

'I do see.'

Claudia dropped her weapons and made a gesture towards the treasure chests. 'Enough interest for you?'

'I see that you can totally outplay me and I am lost in admiration.'

'Good.'

Then they did what they had been wanting to do for the last five minutes, and flung themselves into each other's arms

'Excellent,' said Maria, joining them. 'It's good to see you've both come to your senses at last!'

35

'Ezio!'

Ezio hadn't expected to hear the familiar voice again so soon. A pessimistic part of him had not expected to hear it again at all. Nevertheless, he'd been pleased to get the note left for him at Tiber Island bidding him to this rendezvous, which he was keeping on his way to the Sleeping Fox, the headquarters of La Volpe's Thieves' Guild in Rome.

He looked round, but there was no one to be seen. The streets were empty, even of Borgia uniforms, for he was already in a district reclaimed by La Volpe's men.

'Leonardo?'

'Over here!' The voice came from a darkened doorway.

Ezio walked across to it and Leonardo dragged him into the shadows.

'Were you followed?'

'No.'

'Thank God. I've been sweating blood.'

'Were you . . . ?'

'No. My friend, *Messer* Salai, watches my back. I'd trust him with my life.'

'Your friend?'

'We're very close.'

'Be careful, Leo, you have a soft heart where young men are concerned and that could be a chink in your armour.'

'I may be soft-hearted, but I'm not a fool. Now, come on.'

Leonardo pulled Ezio out of the doorway after first looking up and down the street. A few yards to the right, he ducked down an alleyway that snaked between windowless buildings and featureless walls for a furlong or so, at which point it became part of a crossroads with three other alleys. Leonardo took the one on the left, and after another few yards arrived at a low, narrow door, which was painted dark green. This he unlocked. Both men had to squeeze through the entrance, but once inside Ezio found himself in a large vaulted hall. Natural light bathed the place through windows placed high in the walls, and the room was filled with trestle tables, cluttered and crowded with all manner of stuff: easels; animal skeletons; dusty books; maps, rare and precious, like all maps – the Assassin Brotherhood's own collection at Monteriggioni had been invaluable, but the Borgia in their ignorance had destroyed the map room with cannonades, and so had no use of them themselves – pencils, pens, brushes, paints, piles of papers and drawings pinned to the walls . . . In short, it was the typical, familiar and somehow comforting clutter of Leonardo's studios wherever Ezio had encountered them.

'This is my own place,' said Leonardo proudly. 'As far as possible from my official workshop near Castel Sant'Angelo. No one comes here but me. And Salai, of course.'

'Don't they keep tabs on you?'

'They did for a while, but I'm good at ingratiation when it suits me and they swallowed the act whole. I rent this place from the Cardinal of San Pietro in Vincoli. He knows how to keep a secret and he's no friend of the Borgia.'

'There's no harm in taking out a little insurance for the future?'

'Ezio, my friend, nothing, but nothing, gets past you! Now, to business. I don't know if there's anything I can offer you – there must be a bottle of wine some-where.'

'Leave it, don't worry. Just tell me why you sent for me.'

Leonardo went over to one of the trestle tables on the right-hand side of the hall and rummaged under-neath it, then produced a long, leather-bound, wooden case, which he placed on the tabletop.

'Here we are,' he said with a flourish as he opened it.

The case was lined in purple velvet – 'Salai's idea, bless him!' explained Leonardo – and contained perfect copies of Ezio's lost Codex weapons: there was the

Bracer for protecting the left forearm, the little retractable Pistol, the Double-Bladed Dagger and the Poison Blade.

'The Bracer was the biggest problem,' continued Leonardo. 'It was very hard to get a match for that extraordinary metal. From what you told me of the accident in which you lost the originals, it might have survived. If you could get it back . . . ?'

'If it did survive, it will be buried under several tons of rubble,' said Ezio. 'It might as well be at the bottom of the sea.' He slipped the Bracer on. It felt a little heavier than the first, but it looked as if it would serve very well. 'I don't know how to thank you,' he said.

'That's easy,' replied Leonardo. 'With money! But these are not all.' He delved under the table again and brought out another case, larger than the first. 'These are new, and may come in handy from time to time.'

He opened the lid to reveal a lightweight crossbow with a set of bolts, a set of darts and a mailed leather glove.

'The darts are poisoned,' said Leonardo, 'so don't ever touch the points with your bare hands. If you can retrieve them from your – ahem – target, you'll find they are re-usable up to a dozen times.'

'And the glove?'

Leonardo smiled. 'I'm rather proud of that. It'll enable you to climb on any surface with ease. Almost as good as becoming a gecko.' He paused, troubled.

'We haven't actually tested it on glass, but I doubt if you'll ever encounter a surface *that* smooth.' He paused. 'The crossbow's just a crossbow, but it's very compact and light. What makes it special is that it's just as powerful as those heavy things which are now being superseded by my wheel-locks – forgive me – and of course the advantage it has over a gun is that it's more or less silent.'

'I can't carry these with me now.'

Leonardo shrugged. 'No problem. We'll deliver them. To Tiber Island?'

Ezio considered. 'No. There's a bordello called The Rosa in Fiore. It's in the *rione* Montium et Biberatice, near the old forum with the column.'

'We'll find it.'

'Leave them there with my sister, Claudia. May I?' Ezio took a sheet of paper and scribbled something on it. 'Give this to her. I've sketched its location, as it's hard to find. I'll get the money to you as soon as possible.'

'Five thousand ducats.'

'*How* much?'

'Not cheap, these things . . .'

Ezio pursed his lips. 'Fine.' He took back the note and wrote an additional line. 'We have recently come into some new and . . . unexpected funds. My sister will pay you. And listen, Leo, I have to trust you. Not a word to anyone else.'

'Even Salai?'

'Salai if you have to. But if the brothel's location is discovered by the Borgia, I will kill Salai, and I will kill you, my friend.'

Leonardo smiled. 'I know these are very troubled times, my dear, but when – when – have I *ever* let you down?'

Content with that, Ezio took leave of his friend and continued on his way to the Sleeping Fox. He was running late, but the meeting with Leonardo had been more than worth it.

He went through the courtyard, pleased to see that business still seemed to be booming, and was about to announce himself to the thieves standing guard on either side of the door marked *Uffizi* when La Volpe himself appeared, apparently out of nowhere – he was good at that.

'*Buongiorno*, Ezio!'

'*Ciao*, Gilberto!'

'I'm glad you've come. What is it you want?'

'Let's sit somewhere quiet.'

'In the *Uffizi*?'

'Let's stay here. What I have to say is for your ears alone.'

'That's good, for I have something to say to you, too, which should stay between us – for now.'

They settled down at a table in an otherwise empty bar inside the inn, away from the gamblers and drinkers.

'It's time to pay a visit to Lucrezia's lover, Pietro,' said Ezio.

'Good. I've already got men out looking for him.'

'*Molto bene*, but a working actor shouldn't be that hard to find, and this one's famous.'

La Volpe shook his head. 'He's famous enough to have minders of his own. And we think he may have gone to ground because he's frightened of Cesare.'

'That makes sense. Well, do your best. Now, what is it you have on your mind?'

La Volpe wrestled with himself for a moment, then said, 'It's delicate . . . Ezio, if I may . . .'

'What is it?'

'Someone has warned Rodrigo to stay away from the Castel Sant'Angelo.'

'And you think that someone is . . . Machiavelli?'

La Volpe was silent.

'Do you have proof?' Ezio pressed him.

'No, but . . .'

'I know that Machiavelli troubles you, but listen, Gilberto, we must not be split apart by suspicion.'

At that moment the door banged open and they were interrupted by the arrival of a wounded thief, who staggered into the room. 'Bad news!' he cried. 'The Borgia know the whereabouts of our spies!'

'Who told them?' thundered La Volpe, rising.

'Maestro Machiavelli was asking about our search for the actor, Pietro, earlier today.'

La Volpe's hand tightened into a fist. 'Ezio?' he said quietly.

'They've got four of our men under guard,' said the thief. 'I was lucky to get away.'

'Where?'

'Not far from here, near Santa Maria dell'Orto.'

'Come on!' La Volpe yelled to Ezio.

Within minutes, La Volpe's men had readied two horses and the two Assassins rode out of the stables of the Sleeping Fox at breakneck speed.

'I still do not believe Machiavelli has turned traitor,' insisted Ezio as they rode.

'He went quiet for a bit, to allay our doubts,' La Volpe hurled back. 'But look at the facts: first the attack on Monteriggioni, then the business at the Castel Sant'Angelo, and now this. He is behind it all.'

'Just ride! Ride like the devil! We may still be in time to save them.'

They galloped helter-skelter through the narrow streets, reining in and thrusting forward as they strove to avoid injuring the people and smashing down the market booths in their path. Citizens and chickens alike scattered in their path, but when Borgia guards tried to block their way, halberds raised, they simply rode them down.

They reached the place the wounded thief had indicated within seven minutes, and saw the Borgia uniforms preparing to pack the four captured thieves onto a covered wagon, hitting them with the pommels of their swords and taunting them as they did so. In a moment, Ezio and La Volpe were upon them like avenging Furies.

Swords drawn, they steered their mounts skilfully among the guards, cutting them off from their prisoners and dispersing them about the square in front of the church. Grasping his sword firmly in his right hand, La Volpe let go of his reins with his left and, holding on with his thighs, wheeled the horse towards the wagon, seized the driver's whip from him and struck hard at the flanks of the horses in the shafts. They reared and neighed, then stampeded off, as the waggoner strove in vain to control them. Hurling the whip aside, and almost falling, La Volpe grabbed his reins again and swung his horse round to join Ezio, who was surrounded by five guards, who were stabbing at his horse's chest and quarters with their halberds. Flailing them with his sword, La Volpe gave Ezio enough time to break free of the trap and slice open the midriff of the closest guard. Turning the horse round in a tight circle, he swiped again with his sword and neatly severed the head from the body of another. Meanwhile, La Volpe had despatched the last of the guards, while the rest either lay wounded or had fled.

'Run, you swine!' La Volpe yelled at his men. 'Back to base! Now! We'll join you there!'

The four thieves pulled themselves together and darted down the main street out of the square, ducking and diving through the small crowd that had gathered to watch the fight. Ezio and La Volpe rode after, shepherding them to make sure they all got back in one piece.

They made their way into the Sleeping Fox by a secret side entrance and had soon assembled in the bar, which now had a 'Closed' sign on its door. La Volpe ordered beer for his men, but did not wait for it to arrive before he started his interrogation.

'What were you able to find out?'

'Boss, there's a plan to kill the actor this evening. Cesare is sending his "butcher" to see to it.'

'Who's that?' asked Ezio.

'You've seen him,' replied La Volpe. 'Micheletto Corella. No one could ever forget a face like that.'

Indeed, Ezio's inner eye flashed on the man he'd seen at Cesare's right hand at Monteriggioni, and again in the stables of the Castel Sant'Angelo. A cruel, battered face that looked much older than its owner's age warranted, with hideous scars near his mouth, giving him the appearance of wearing a permanent, sardonic grin. Micheletto Corella. Originally *Miguel* de Corella. Corella – did that region of Navarre, which produced such good wine, really also produce this torturer and murderer?

'He can kill a person one hundred and fifty different

ways,' La Volpe was saying, 'but his preferred method is strangulation.' He paused. 'He's certainly the most accomplished murderer in Rome. No one escapes him.'

'Let's hope tonight will be the first time,' said Ezio.

'Where this evening? Do you know?' La Volpe asked the thieves.

'Pietro's performing in a religious play this evening. He's been rehearsing at a secret location.'

'He must be scared. And?'

'He's playing Christ.' One of the thieves snickered at this. La Volpe glared. 'He's to be suspended from a cross,' continued the man who'd been talking. 'Micheletto will come at him with a spear and pierce his side – only it won't be make-believe.'

'Do you know where Pietro is?'

The thief shook his head. 'I cannot tell you that. We couldn't find out. But we do know that Micheletto will wait at the old Baths of the Emperor Trajan.'

'The Terme di Traiano?'

'Yes. We think the plan is this: Micheletto intends to disguise his men in costumes, and make the killing look like an accident.'

'But where's the performance taking place?'

'We don't know, but it can't be far from where Micheletto will be waiting for his men to gather.'

'I'll go there and shadow him,' Ezio decided. 'He'll lead me to Lucrezia's lover.'

'Anything else?' La Volpe asked his men.

They shook their heads. A serving man came in then, bringing a tray containing beer, bread and salami, which the thieves fell on gratefully. La Volpe drew Ezio to one side.

'Ezio, I am sorry, but I am convinced that Machiavelli has betrayed us.' He held up a hand. 'Whatever you say will not convince me otherwise. I know we would both wish to deny it, but the truth is now clear. In my opinion, we should . . . do what needs to be done.' He paused. 'And if you don't, I will.'

'I see.'

'And there's another thing, Ezio. God knows I'm loyal, but I also have the welfare of my men to consider. Until this thing is settled, I'm not putting them at unnecessary risk any more.'

'You have your priorities, Gilberto, and I have mine.'

Ezio left, to prepare himself for his evening's work. Borrowing a horse from La Volpe, he made his way straight to The Rosa in Fiore, where Claudia greeted him.

'You've had a delivery,' she said.

'Already?'

'Two men, both very dapper. One quite young and a bit shifty-looking, but handsome in a pretty sort of way. The other, maybe fifty – a few years older than you, anyway. Of course, I remembered him – your old friend Leonardo – but he was quite formal. He gave me this note and I paid him.'

'That was quick.'

Claudia smiled. 'He said he thought you might appreciate an *express* delivery.'

Ezio smiled back. It would be good to encounter tonight's villains – he imagined Micheletto's men would be trained to a very high standard – armed with a few of his old friends, the Codex weapons. But he'd need backup, too, and from La Volpe's attitude, he knew he couldn't depend on the loan of a contingent of thieves.

His thoughts turned to his own militia of new recruits. It was time to put a few of them through their paces.

36

Unknown to Ezio, *Messer* Corella had one other small piece of business to conclude for his boss before the main event of the evening. But it was still quite early.

He stood silently on a deserted dock by the Tiber. A few barges and two ships rode at anchor, gently moving with the river's flow. The ships' grubby furled sails rippled slightly in the wind. A group of guards wearing Cesare's insignia were coming towards them, half hauling, half carrying a blindfolded man between them. At their head was Cesare himself.

Micheletto recognized the man, without surprise, as Francesco Troche.

'Please,' Francesco was whimpering, 'I have done nothing wrong.'

'Francesco, my dear friend,' said Cesare. 'The facts are plain. You told your brother about my plans in the Romagna, and he contacted the Venetian ambassador.'

'It was an accident. I am still your servant and your ally.'

'Are you demanding that I discount your actions and rely on mere friendship?'

'I am . . . asking, not demanding.'

'My dear Francesco, in order to unite Italy I must have every institution under my control. You know what higher organization we serve — the Order of Templars, of which I am now head.'

'I thought your father . . .'

'And if the Church does not fall in line,' continued Cesare firmly, 'I will eliminate it entirely.'

'But you know that I really work for you, not the Pope.'

'Ah, but do I, Troche? There's only one way I can be unconditionally sure of that now.'

'Surely you can't intend to kill me, your most loyal friend?'

Cesare smiled. 'Of course not.'

He snapped his fingers. Noiselessly, Micheletto approached from behind Francesco's back.

'You are . . . you are letting me go?' Relief flooded into Troche's voice. 'Thank you, Cesare. Thank you from my heart. You will not regret—'

But his words were cut short as Micheletto, a thin cord twisted between his hands, leant forward and bound it tightly round his neck. Cesare watched for a moment, but even before Francesco was completely dead, he turned to the captain of the guard and said, 'Have you got the costumes for the play ready?'

'Yessir!'

'Then give them to Micheletto when he's finished.'

'Yessir!'

'Lucrezia is mine and mine alone. I didn't think she was that important to me, but when I got that message in Urbino, from one of her own men, that that wretched toad of an actor had been pawing her, slobbering over her, I came back immediately. Can you understand a passion like that, captain?'

'Yessir!'

'You're a fool. Have you done, Micheletto?'

'*Messere*, the man is dead.'

'Then weigh him down with stones and dump him in the Tiber.'

'I obey, Cesare.'

The captain had given orders to his men, and four of them had gone to fetch two large wicker hampers, which they now carried between them.

'Here are the costumes for your men. Make doubly sure the work is done correctly.'

'Indeed, *Messere*.'

Cesare stalked off, leaving his subordinate to make his arrangements. Motioning to the guards to follow him, Micheletto led the way towards the Baths of Trajan.

Ezio and his band of recruits were already at the baths, hidden in the shelter of a ruined portico. He had noticed a number of men in black already gathered, and he watched them closely as Micheletto appeared. The guards put the baskets of costumes down and Micheletto motioned them to depart. The shadows were deep, and Ezio nodded to his men to prepare themselves. He had strapped the Bracer to his left forearm, and the Poison Blade to his right.

Micheletto's men formed a line, and as each man came up to his leader, he was handed a costume – they were uniforms in the style of those worn by Roman legionaries at the time of Christ. Ezio noticed that Micheletto himself wore the costume of a centurion.

As each man stepped away to don his costume, Ezio stood ready. Silently, he extended the concealed Poison Blade that Leonardo had re-crafted for him. The unsuspecting thugs went down without a whisper, then his own recruits put on the theatrical clothes, and pulled Micheletto's henchmen's bodies out of sight.

Absorbed in his work, Micheletto was unaware, once everyone was in costume, that the men he now commanded were not his own. He led them, with Ezio close behind, in the direction of the Colosseum.

A stage had been erected in the ruins of the old Roman amphitheatre where, since the time of the Emperor Titus, gladiators had fought each other to the death, *bestiarii* had dispatched wild animals in their tens of thousands, and Christians had been thrown to the lions. It was a gloomy place, but the gloom was dispersed somewhat by the hundreds of flickering torches that illuminated the stage, while the audience, ranged on benches on a wooden grandstand, were absorbed in watching a play on the subject of Christ's Passion.

'I seek Pietro Benintendi,' Micheletto said to the doorkeeper, showing him a warrant.

'He acts onstage, *signore*,' replied the doorkeeper. 'But one of my men will take you to where you may wait for him.'

Micheletto turned to his 'companions'. 'Don't forget,' he told them. 'I will be wearing this black cloak with the white star on its shoulder. Cover my back and wait for your cue, which will be Pontius Pilate's order to the centurion to strike.'

I must get to Pietro before he does, thought Ezio, tagging along at the back of the group as they followed their leader into the Colosseum.

Onstage, three crosses had been erected. He watched as his recruits disposed themselves according to Micheletto's orders and Micheletto himself took his place in the wings.

The play was reaching its climax:

'My God, my God, why hast thou forsaken me?' cried Pietro from the cross.

'Hark,' said one of the actors playing the Pharisees. 'How he crieth upon Elijah to deliver him!'

One, dressed as a Roman legionary, dipped a sponge in vinegar and placed it on the tip of his spear. 'Wait and see whether Elijah dare come here or not.'

'My thirst is great; my thirst is great,' cried Pietro.

The soldier raised the sponge to Pietro's lips.

'Yea, thou shalt drink no more,' said another Pharisee.

Pietro raised his head. 'Mighty God in Majesty,' he declaimed. 'To work Thy Will I shall never cease. My spirit I betake to Thee; receive it, O Lord, into Thy hands.' Pietro gave a great sigh. '*Consummatum est!*'

His head dropped. Christ had 'died'.

On cue, Micheletto strode onto the stage, his centurion's uniform glittering under the thrown-back black cloak. Ezio, watching, wondered what had become of the actor originally playing the centurion, but imagined that he had met a fate similar to that of most of Micheletto's victims.

'Lords, I say unto you,' recited Micheletto boldly, 'this was indeed the Son of God the Father Almighty. I know it must be so. I know by the manner of his cry that He has fulfilled the prophecy, and the godhead is revealed in Him!'

'Centurion,' said the actor playing Caiaphas, 'as God gives me speed, thy folly is great indeed. Thou dost not understand! When thou seest His heart bleed, then we shall see what thou wilt say. Longinus, take this spear into thy hand.'

Caiaphas handed a wooden spear to the actor playing the Roman legionary, Longinus, a large man with flowing locks — *clearly a favourite of the audience and doubtless*, thought Ezio, *a bitter rival of Pietro's*.

'Take this spear and take good heed,' added one of

the Pharisees for good measure. 'Thou must pierce the side of Jesus Nazarenus that we shall know He is truly dead.'

'I will do as thou biddest me,' declaimed Longinus, 'but on your heads be it. Whatever the consequence, I wash my hands of it.'

He then made a great show of stabbing Jesus' side with the prop spear and, as the blood and water spilled forth from a hidden sac concealed in Pietro's loincloth, so Longinus began his big speech. Ezio could see the beady glint in the 'dead' Jesus' eyes as Pietro watched him jealously.

'High King of Heaven, I see Thee here. Let water be thrown onto my hands and onto my spear, and let my eyes be bathed, too, that I may see thee more clearly.' He made a dramatic pause. 'Alas, alack and woe is me! What is this deed that I have done? I think that I have slain a man, sooth to say, but what manner of man I know not. Lord God in Heaven, I cry you mercy, for it was my body which guided my hand, not my soul.' Allowing himself another pause for a round of applause, he ploughed on. 'Lord Jesus, much have I heard spoken of Thee – that Thou hast healed, through Thy pity, both the sick and the blind. And, let Thy Name be praised! – Thou hast healed me this day of my own blindness – my blindness of spirit. Henceforward, Lord, Thy follower will I be. And in three days Thou shalt rise again to rule and judge us all.'

The actor who was playing Joseph of Arimathea, the wealthy Jewish leader who donated his own tomb – which had already been built – for the housing of Christ's body, then spoke: 'Ah, Lord God, what heart had You to allow them to slay this man that I see here dead and hanging from a cross, a man who ne'er did aught amiss? For surely, God's own Son is He. Therefore, in the tomb that is made for me, therein shall His body buried be – for He is King of Bliss.'

Nicodemus, Joseph's colleague in the Sanhedrin and a fellow sympathizer, added his voice: '*Ser* Joseph, I say surely, this is God's Son Almighty. Let us request His body of Pontius Pilate, and nobly buried He shall be. And I will help thee to take Him down devotedly.'

Joseph then turned to the actor playing Pilate and spoke again: '*Ser* Pilate, I ask of thee a special boon to grant me as thou may. This prophet that is dead today – allow me of his body custody.'

While Micheletto took up position very near the central cross, Ezio slipped backstage. There, he rummaged swiftly through a costume skip and found a rabbinical robe, which he hurriedly put on. He returned to the stage from backstage left, managing to slip in just behind Micheletto without anyone noticing or the action skipping a beat.

'Joseph, if indeed Jesus Nazarenus is dead, as the centurion must confirm, I will not deny you custody.'

Turning to Micheletto, Pilate spoke again: 'Centurion! Is Jesus dead?'

'Ay, *Ser* Governor,' said Micheletto flatly, and Ezio noticed him draw a stiletto from under his cloak. Ezio had replaced his Poison Blade, now exhausted of venom, with his trusty Hidden Blade, and with it he now pierced Micheletto's side, holding him upright and manoeuvring him offstage, in the direction he had come. Once backstage, he laid the man down.

Micheletto fixed him with a glittering look. 'Hah!' he said. 'You cannot save Pietro. The vinegar on the sponge was poisoned. As I promised Cesare, I made doubly sure.' He fought for breath. 'You had better finish me.'

'I did not come here to kill you. You helped your master rise and you will fall with him. You don't need me; you are the agent of your own destruction. If you live, well, a dog always returns to its master, and you will lead me to my real quarry.'

Ezio had no time for more; he had to save Pietro.

As he rushed back onstage, he was greeted by a scene of chaos. Pietro was writhing on the cross and vomiting as he turned the colour of a peeled almond. The audience was in uproar.

'What's going on? What's happening?' cried Longinus, as the other actors scattered.

'Cut him down!' Ezio yelled to his recruits. Some threw keenly aimed daggers to slice through the ropes that bound Pietro to the cross, while others stood ready to catch him. Still more were fighting back the Borgia guards who had appeared from nowhere and were storming the stage.

'This wasn't in the script!' gurgled Pietro as he fell into the arms of the recruits.

'Will he die?' asked Longinus hopefully. One rival less is always good news in a tough profession.

'Hold off the guards!' shouted Ezio, leading the recruits off stage and carrying Pietro in his arms across a shallow pool of water in the middle of the Colosseum, disturbing dozens of drinking pigeons, which flew up and away in alarm. The very last glimmer from the setting sun bathed Ezio and Pietro in a dull red light.

Ezio had trained his recruits well, and those bringing up the rearguard successfully fought off the pursuing Borgia guards as the rest made their way out of the Colosseum and into the network of streets to the north. Ezio led the way to the house of a doctor of his acquaintance. He hammered on the door and, having been granted reluctant admission, had Pietro laid on a table covered with a palliasse in the doctor's consulting room, from whose beams a baffling number of dried herbs hung in organized bunches, giving the room a pungent smell. On shelves, unidentifiable or unmentionable objects, creatures and parts of creatures floated in glass bottles filled with cloudy liquid.

Ezio ordered his men outside to keep watch. He wondered what any passers-by might think if they saw a bunch of Roman soldiers. They'd probably think they were seeing ghosts and run a mile. He himself had shed his Pharisee outfit at the first opportunity.

'Who are you?' murmured Pietro. Ezio was concerned to see that the actor's lips had turned blue.

'Your saviour,' said Ezio. To the doctor he said, 'He's been poisoned, *Dottore* Brunelleschi.'

Brunelleschi examined the actor quickly, shining a light into his eyes. 'From the pallor, it looks like they used cantarella. The poison of choice for our dear masters, the Borgia.' To Pietro, he said, 'Lie still.'

'Feel sleepy,' said Pietro.

'Lie still! Has he been sick?' Brunelleschi asked Ezio. 'Yes.'

'Good.' The doctor bustled about, mixing fluids from the different-coloured glass bottles with practised ease and pouring the mixture into a phial. This he handed to Pietro, propping his head up.

'Drink this.'

'Hurry up,' said Ezio urgently.

'Just give him a moment.'

Ezio watched anxiously, and after what seemed an age, the actor sat up.

'I think I feel slightly better,' he said.

'*Miracolo!*' said Ezio in relief.

'Not really,' said the doctor. 'He can't have had

much, and for my sins I've had quite a bit of experience with cantarella victims — it's enabled me to develop a pretty effective antidote. Now,' he continued judiciously, 'I'll apply some leeches. They will lead to a full recovery. You can rest here, my boy, and very soon you'll be as right as rain.' He bustled some more and produced a glass jar full of black, wriggling creatures. He scooped out a handful.

'I cannot thank you enough,' said Pietro to Ezio. 'I—'

'You *can* thank me enough,' replied Ezio briskly. 'The key to the little gate you use for your trysts at the Castel Sant'Angelo with Lucrezia. Give it to me. Now!'

Misgiving appeared on Pietro's face. 'What are you talking about? I'm simply a poor actor, a victim of circumstance . . . I . . .'

'Listen, Pietro, Cesare knows about you and Lucrezia.'

Now misgiving was replaced by fear. 'Oh God!'

'But I can help you. If you give me the key.'

Mutely, Pietro delved into his loincloth and handed it over. 'I always keep it with me,' he said.

'Wise of you,' said Ezio, pocketing the key. It was reassuring to have it, for it would guarantee him access to the Castel whenever he had need of it.

'My men will fetch your clothes and get you to a place of safety. I'll detail a couple of them to keep watch over you. Just keep out of sight for a while.'

'But . . . my public!' wailed the actor.

'They'll have to make do with Longinus until it's safe for you to put your head above the parapet again,' grinned Ezio. 'I shouldn't worry. He isn't a patch on you.'

'Oh, do you really think so?'

'No question.'

'Ouch!' said Pietro, as the first leech went on.

In the wink of an eye, Ezio had disappeared outside. There he gave the necessary orders to his men. 'Get out of those costumes as soon as you can,' he added. 'The Baths of Trajan aren't far. With any luck, your street clothes will still be where you left them.'

He departed on his own, but he hadn't gone far when he noticed a figure skulking in the shadows. As soon as the man felt Ezio's eyes on him, he cut and ran. But not before Ezio had recognized Paganino, the thief who'd been determined to stay behind at the sack of Monteriggioni.

Hey!' Ezio shouted, giving chase. '*Un momento!*'

The thief certainly knew his way around these streets. Ducking and diving, he was so adroit that Ezio all but lost him in the pursuit, and more than once had to leap to the rooftops to scan the streets below in order to locate the man again. Leonardo's magical glove came in surprisingly handy at such times, he found.

At last he managed to get ahead of his prey and cut off his line of escape. The thief went for his dagger, an ugly-looking cinquedea, but Ezio quickly wrested it out of his hand so that it clattered harmlessly to the pavement.

'Why did you run?' asked Ezio, pinioning the man. Then he noticed a letter protruding from the man's leather belt-pouch. The seal was unmistakeable: it was that of Pope Alexander VI – Rodrigo – the Spaniard!

Ezio let out a long breath as a series of suspicions fell into place. Long ago Paganino had been with Antonio de Magianis' Thieves' Guild in Venice. He must have been offered enough money by the Borgia to switch sides, and then he'd infiltrated La Volpe's group here – the Borgia had had a mole at the heart of the Assassin organization all along.

Here was the traitor – not Machiavelli at all!

While Ezio's attention was distracted, the thief wrenched himself free and, in a flash, seized his fallen weapon. His desperate eyes met Ezio's.

'Long live the Borgia!' he cried, and thrust the cinquedea firmly into his own breast.

Ezio looked down at the fallen man as he thrashed about in his death agonies. Well, better this death than a slow one at the hands of his masters – Ezio well knew the price exacted by the Borgia for failure. He stuffed the letter into his doublet and made off. *Merda*, he thought to himself. *I was right. And now I have to stop La Volpe before he gets to Machiavelli.*

37

As Ezio made his way across the city, he was accosted by Saraghina, one of the girls from The Rosa in Fiore.

'You must come quickly,' she said. 'Your mother wants to see you urgently.'

Ezio bit his lip. There should be time. 'Hurry,' he said.

Once at the bordello, he found Maria waiting for him, and her face betrayed her anxiety.

'Ezio,' she said. 'Thank you for coming to see me.'

'I have to be quick, Mother.'

'There's something amiss.'

'Tell me.'

'The old proprietor of this establishment—'

'*Madonna* Solari?'

'Yes.' Maria collected herself. 'It turns out she was a cheat and a liar. We've discovered that she was playing *il doppio gioco*, and she had close ties with the Vatican. Worse, several of those still employed here may be—'

'Don't worry, *Madre*. I'll root them out. I'll send my most trusted recruits to interview the girls. Under Claudia's direction, they will soon get at the truth.'

'Thank you, Ezio.'

'We will ensure that only girls loyal to us remain here. As for the rest . . .' The expression on Ezio's face was harsh.

'I have other news.'

'Yes?'

'We have word that ambassadors from King Ferdinand of Spain and from the Holy Roman Emperor, Maximilian, have arrived in Rome. It seems they seek an alliance with Cesare.'

'Are you sure, Mother? What need have they of him?'

'I don't know, *figlio mio*.'

Ezio's jaw was set. 'We had better be safe rather than sorry. Ask Claudia to investigate for me. I give her a full mandate to give orders to the recruits I will send.'

'You trust her for this?'

'Mother, after the business with the banker, I would trust the two of you with my life. I am ashamed not to have done so before, but it was only my anxiety for your safety that—'

Maria held up a hand. 'You do not need to explain. And there is nothing to forgive. We are all friends again now. That is what matters.'

'Thank you. Cesare's days are numbered. Even if the ambassadors gain his support, they will soon find it is worthless.'

'I hope your confidence is well-founded.'

'Believe me, Mother, it is. Or will be – if I can save Machiavelli from La Volpe's misguided suspicion.'

38

Borrowing a horse from the stables he had liberated, Ezio rode post-haste to the Sleeping Fox. It was crucial that he get there before anything happened to Machiavelli. Lose him and he'd lose the best brains in the Brotherhood.

Although the hour was not that late, he was alarmed to see that the inn was closed. He had his own key and let himself in through the wicket gate.

The scene that met his eyes told him that he had arrived not a moment too soon. The members of the Thieves' Guild were all present. La Volpe and his principal lieutenants stood together, busily discussing something that appeared to be of great importance, and it looked as though judgement had been reached, since La Volpe, a baleful look on his face, was approaching Machiavelli, a businesslike basilard in his right hand. Machiavelli, for his part, looked unconcerned, seemingly without any idea about what was happening.

'Stop!' shouted Ezio, bursting in on the scene and catching his breath after his headlong ride.

All eyes turned to him, while La Volpe stood rooted to the spot.

'Stay your hand, Gilberto!' commanded Ezio. 'I have discovered the real traitor.'

'What?' said La Volpe, shocked, against a background of excited murmuring from his people.

'He is – was – one of your own men: Paganino! He was present at the attack on Monteriggioni, and now I see his mischief in many of our recent misfortunes.'

'Are you sure of this?'

'He himself revealed his guilt.'

La Volpe's brow darkened. He sheathed his dagger. 'Where is he now?' he growled.

'Where no one can touch him any more.'

'Dead?'

'By his own hand. He was carrying this letter.' Ezio held the sealed parchment aloft and passed the letter to La Volpe. Machiavelli came up as the thieves' leader broke the seal and opened the paper.

'My God!' said La Volpe, scanning the words.

'Let me see,' said Machiavelli.

'Of course,' La Volpe said, crestfallen.

Machiavelli was scanning the letter. 'It's from Rodrigo to Cesare. Details of our plans for the French general, Octavien – amongst other things.'

'One of my own men!'

'This is good news,' Machiavelli said to Ezio. 'We can substitute this letter with another containing false information – put them off the scent . . .'

'Good news indeed,' replied Ezio, but his tone was cold. 'Gilberto, you should have listened to me.'

'I am once again in your debt, Ezio,' said La Volpe, humbly.

Ezio also allowed himself a smile. 'What debt can there be amongst friends who trust – who *must* trust – one another?'

Before La Volpe could reply, Machiavelli put in: 'And congratulations, by the way. I gather you resurrected Christ three days early.'

Ezio laughed, thinking of his rescue of Pietro. How did Machiavelli find out about things so *fast*?!

La Volpe looked around at the men and women of the Guild gathered around them. 'Well, what are you staring at?' he said. 'We're losing business here.'

Later, after Machiavelli had left to deal with the intercepted letter, La Volpe drew Ezio aside. 'I'm glad you are here,' he said, 'and not just because you prevented me from making a total fool of myself.'

'More than that,' said Ezio lightly. 'Do you know what I would have done to you if you had killed Niccolò?'

La Volpe grunted. 'Ezio . . .' he said.

Ezio clapped him on the back. 'But all's well. No more quarrels. Within the Brotherhood, we cannot afford them. Now, what is it you wanted to say to me? Do you have need of my assistance?'

'I do. The Guild is strong, but many of my men are

young and untested. Look at that kid who nicked your purse. Look at young Claudio . . .'

'And your point is . . . ?'

'I was coming to that. Generally, the thieves in Rome are young men and women – skilled in their trade, sure, but young and prone to rivalries. Damaging rivalries.'

'Are you speaking of another gang?'

'Yes. One in particular, which may pose a threat. I need reinforcements to deal with them.'

'My recruits?'

La Volpe was silent, then he said, 'I know I refused you help when my suspicions about Niccolò were at their height, but now . . .'

'Who are they?'

'They call themselves the *Cento Occhi* – the One Hundred Eyes. They are creatures of Cesare Borgia and they cause us significant trouble.'

'Where is their base?'

'My spies have located it.'

'Where?'

'Just a moment. They are angry and they are spoiling for a fight.'

'Then we must surprise them.'

'*Bene!*'

'But we must be prepared for retaliation.'

'We will strike first, then they will have no opportunity for retaliation.' La Volpe, now more his old self, rubbed his hands in anticipation. 'The main thing is to take out their leaders. They alone have direct contact with the Borgia. Remove them and we will have beheaded the *Cento Occhi*.'

'And you really need my help for this?'

'You broke the power of the Wolfmen.'

'Without your help.'

'I know.'

'The man who helped me break the Wolfmen was . . .'

'I *know*!'

'Listen, Gilberto. We will combine forces and do this together – have no fear of that. Then, I presume, your Guild will be the dominant cartel in Rome.'

'That is true,' agreed La Volpe reluctantly.

'If I help you in this,' said Ezio slowly, 'there is a condition.'

'Yes?'

'That you shall not, again, threaten the unity of the Brotherhood. For that is what you almost did.'

La Volpe bowed his head. 'I am schooled,' he said meekly.

'Whether we succeed in this venture of yours or fail.'

'Whether we succeed or fail,' agreed La Volpe. 'But we won't.'

'Won't what?'

La Volpe gave his friend a Mephistophelean grin. 'Fail,' he said.

39

Having detailed a group of his growing recruit-militia
to help La Volpe in his efforts against the *Cento Occhi*,
Ezio made his way back to his lodgings. He refilled the
Poison Blade's inner phial with the venom Leonardo
had prepared especially, and checked and cleaned the
retractable Pistol, the Double Blade, and the new
crossbow and poison darts.

His work was interrupted by a messenger from
Bartolomeo, bidding him come to the mercenaries'
barracks as quickly as possible. Sensing trouble, and
worried about it – he had hoped that Bartolomeo and
his *condottieri* had the French in check – Ezio packed
the Codex weapons he judged he might need into a
saddlebag and made his way to the stables, where he
rented his favourite horse and set off. It was a fine day,
and the road was more or less dry, since rain had held
off for about a week. The countryside seemed a little
dusty as he rode through it, taking care to choose a
route obscure enough not to be monitored by Borgia
troops, and taking the odd short cut through the
woods and across fields, where cows raised their heads
idly from their grazing to watch him pass.

It was afternoon by the time he reached the barracks, and all seemed quiet. He noticed that, since their renovation, the ramparts and walls had taken a slight bruising from French cannonades, but the damage wasn't serious, and a handful of men were busy on scaffolding or slung in baskets from the battlements, repairing the gouges and cracks the cannonballs had made.

He dismounted and handed the bridle to an ostler who came running up, gently wiping the little flecks of foam from his horse's mouth – he hadn't ridden her hard. Ezio patted her muzzle before making his way, unannounced, across the parade ground in the direction of Bartolomeo's quarters.

His mind was on his next step, now that Cesare's banker had been removed, and he was considering what counter-action his enemy might take to ensure that there was no cessation in his supply of funds, so he was surprised to find himself nose to the tip with Bianca, Bartolomeo's great sword.

'Who goes there?' bellowed Bartolomeo.

'*Salve* to you, too,' rejoined Ezio.

Bartolomeo gave vent to a huge belly laugh. 'Got you!'

'Teach me to be on my toes.'

'Actually,' Bartolomeo gave a theatrical wink, 'I was expecting my wife.'

'Well, well.'

Bartolomeo lowered his sword and embraced Ezio.

When he released him from the bear hug, his expression was more serious.

'I'm glad you've come, Ezio.'

'What's the matter?'

'Look.'

Ezio followed his friend's gaze to where a platoon of wounded mercenaries were entering the parade ground.

'The French *puttane* have got us under pressure again,' said Bartolomeo, answering Ezio's unspoken question.

'I thought you'd barked the shins of their general – what's his name?'

'Octavien de Valois thinks he's some kind of descendant of the noble house of Valois. Some wretched spawn of a bastard, if you ask me.'

Bartolomeo spat as another contingent of wounded men appeared.

'Looks serious,' said Ezio.

'King Louis must have sent reinforcements to back up Cesare after we gave Valois a bashing.' Bartolomeo scratched his beard. 'I suppose I should be flattered.'

'How bad is it?'

'They've got their tower back,' said Bartolomeo grumpily.

'We'll get it back. Where's Valois now?'

'You're right.' Bartolomeo ignored the question. 'Of course we'll get it back again! We'll have the scoundrels in retreat before you can say *fottere*! It's only a matter of time.'

Just then, a bullet whizzed past their ears and embedded itself in the wall behind them.

'It was so quiet when I rode up,' said Ezio, looking at the sky. The sun had gone behind large clouds, which had suddenly rolled across the sky.

'*Seemed* so quiet, you mean. They're sneaky bastards, the French. But I'll have Valois by the throat soon enough, mark my word.' He turned to yell an order to a sergeant who'd come running up. 'Close the gates! Get those men off the outer walls! *Move!*'

Men ran hither and thither, manning the battlements and priming the cannon.

'Don't worry, friend,' said the big *condottiero*. 'I've got the situation well in hand.'

At that moment a large cannonball crashed into the ramparts nearest the two men, sending dust and shards of stone flying in all directions.

'They seem to be getting closer!' yelled Ezio.

Bartolomeo's men fired a salvo from the barracks' main cannon by way of reply and the walls seemed to shake with the report from the great guns. The response from the French artillery was just as ferocious: the thunder of two score guns tore at the air, and this time the balls found their marks more accurately. Bartolomeo's men were still desperately trying to restore defensive orders when another huge salvo from the French rocked the walls of the barracks. This time the French seemed to be focusing their efforts on the main gate and two of the gatekeepers fell dead, having been caught up in the bombardment.

'CLOSE THE FUCKIN' GATES!' roared Bartolomeo.

The well-trained soldiers under Bartolomeo's command rushed forward to repel the sortie of French troops who, without warning, had appeared at the main entrance of the barracks. The French had clearly been holding back for this surprise attack and unfortunately, thought Ezio to himself, they had managed to gain the upper hand. Bartolomeo's fortress had been caught unprepared for an attack.

Bartolomeo jumped down from the battlements and ran towards the gate at full tilt. Whirling Bianca, he towered above the Frenchmen, and the great broadsword sliced viciously into their ranks. The French soldiers seemed to halt in trepidation at Bartolomeo's arrival. Meanwhile Ezio directed the musketeers to cover those men who strove to push the gates closed before the enemy could gain a surer foothold inside the barracks. The Assassin troops rallied with the presence of their leader and succeeded in pushing the gates closed, but only seconds later there was an almighty crash and the wooden bar that held the gates shut bowed ominously. The French had succeeded in manoeuvring a battering ram to the main gates while the defenders' attention was focused on the French soldiers who'd breached the barrack walls.

'We should have built a fuckin' moat!' yelled Bartolomeo.

'There wasn't time for that!'

Ezio shouted at the musketeers to divert their fire outside the walls at the gathering French forces. Bartolomeo leapt up the ramparts and stood next to Ezio, who was watching the scene unfolding – French troops had appeared from nowhere, and in great numbers.

'We're surrounded!' cursed Bartolomeo, without exaggeration.

Behind them, one of the minor gates caved in with a crash and a splintering of timber, and before any of the defenders could do anything to prevent it, a large unit of French infantry stormed in, swords drawn and seemingly willing to fight to the death. This sudden infiltration succeeded in cutting Bartolomeo's quarters off from the rest.

'Oh my God, what are they up to now?' shouted Bartolomeo. The Assassin soldiers were better trained than the French – and usually more resolved to their cause – but the sheer weight of numbers and the suddenness of the attack had caught them unawares. It was all they could do to hold the line and slowly try to move the French squadron back. The air was thick with the chaos of close-quarters hand-to-hand combat. The space was so crowded that in places the battle had turned into a straightforward fist fight as there was no longer room to wield weapons.

The atmosphere was hot and claustrophobic with the brewing storm – it was as if the gods were frowning on the scene as great storm clouds oppressed the sky overhead. The dust of the parade-ground floor rose up like a mist, and the day, which had been so fine only moments earlier, turned dark. Soon afterwards, the rain began to fall in torrents and the pitched battle turned into a confused rout, in which the two opposing forces could barely see what they were doing. The ground turned to mud and the fighting became more and more desperate and chaotic.

Then suddenly, as if the enemy had achieved some purpose, the French trumpets sounded a retreat and Valois's men withdrew as swiftly as they had arrived.

It took a while to restore order, and Bartolomeo's first concern was to order carpenters to replace the shattered gate with a new one. Naturally they had one ready in case of just such an eventuality, but it would take an hour to install it. Meanwhile, he led Ezio in the direction of his quarters.

'What the hell were they after?' he asked no one in particular. 'My maps? They're precious, those maps!'

He was interrupted by another French fanfare. With Ezio close behind, he ran up one of the stairways leading to a high rampart above the main gate. There, only a short distance away on the scrubby, cypress-scattered plain in front of the barracks, sat the Général Duc Octavien de Valois himself, on horseback, surrounded by a knot of his officers and infantry. Two of the infantrymen were holding a prisoner, whose body was obscured by a sack thrown over the head.

'*Bonjour, Général d'Alviano*,' smarmed the Frenchman, looking up at Bartolomeo. '*Êtes-vous prêt à vous rendre?* Are you ready to surrender?'

'Why don't you come a little closer and say that, you crummy little Frog?'

'Tut, tut, *mon Général.* You really ought to learn French. That might help mask your barbaric sensibilities, *mais franchement, je m'en doute.*' Smilingly, he looked around at his officers, who tittered appreciatively.

'Perhaps you could teach me,' Bartolomeo hollered back. 'And I would instruct *you* in fighting, since you seem to do so little of it – at least, fair and square, like a gentleman should.'

Valois smiled thinly. 'Hmm. Well, *cher ami*, as amusing as this little parley has been, I see I must repeat my request: I'd like your unconditional surrender by sunrise.'

'Come and get it. My Lady Bianca will whisper it in your ear.'

'Ah! I believe another lady might object to that.'

He nodded to his infantrymen, who pulled the sack off their prisoner. It was Pantasilea!

'*Il mio marito vi ammazzerà tutti*,' she spluttered defiantly, spitting pieces of hemp and dust. 'My husband will murder you all!'

It took Bartolomeo a moment to recover from the

shock. Ezio grasped his arm, while his men looked at one another, aghast.

'I'll kill you, *fotutto Francese*!' he screamed.

'Dear me, calm down,' sneered Valois. 'For your wife's sake. And rest assured that no Frenchman would ever harm a woman – unnecessarily.' His tone became more businesslike. 'But even a dunderhead like you can imagine, I think, what will happen if you do not accede to my terms.' He kicked his horse's flanks and prepared to turn away. 'Come to my headquarters at dawn – unarmed – and bone up on a little French. Soon all Italy will be speaking it.'

He raised his hand. The infantrymen threw Pantasilea across the back of one of the officer's horses and the whole party cantered off, the infantry following in its wake.

'I'll get you, you *pezzo di merda figlio di puttana*!' Barlomeo shouted impotently after them. 'That whoreson piece of shit,' he muttered to Ezio before charging off.

'Where are you going?' Ezio yelled after him.

'To get her back!'

'Bartolomeo! Wait!'

But Bartolomeo ploughed on, and by the time Ezio caught up with him, he was in the saddle, ordering the gates to be opened.

'You can't do this alone,' pleaded Ezio.

'I'm not alone,' replied the *condottiero*, patting Bianca, which hung at his side. 'Come with me if you wish, but you'll have to hurry.' He spurred on his horse and headed for the now-open gates.

Ezio didn't even watch him go. He shouted brisk orders to Bartolomeo's Captain of Cavalry and, within minutes, he, Ezio and a mounted unit of *condottieri* were galloping out of the barracks in hot pursuit of their leader.

40

General de Valois's headquarters were situated within the ruins of the fortified ancient Roman barracks of the old emperors' personal brigade, the Praetorian Guard. It was located in the eighteenth *rione*, on the north-eastern edge of Rome, which was now outside the shrunken city Rome had become. In its heyday, 1500 years earlier, Rome was vast – the greatest city in the world by far – boasting one million inhabitants.

Ezio and his troop had caught up with Bartolomeo on the road, and now they were gathered together on a small rise near the French base camp. They'd attempted an attack, but their bullets had bounced uselessly off the strong modern walls de Valois had had built on top of the old ones. Now they had moved out of range of the responding hail of gunfire that had been the French response to their foray. All Bartolomeo could do was hurl imprecations at his enemies.

'You cowards! What, steal a man's wife and then go and hide inside a fortress? Hah! Nothing hangs between your thighs, do you hear me? *Nothing! Vous n'avez même pas une couille entre vous tous!* There, that good enough French for you, you *bastardi*? In fact, I don't think you have any balls at all.'

The French fired a cannon. They were within range of that and the shot hammered into the ground a few feet from where they were standing.

'Listen, Barto,' said Ezio. 'Calm down. You'll be no good to her dead. Let's re-group, then we'll storm the gates, just like we did at the Arsenale that time in Venice when we were chasing down Silvio Barbarigo.'

'It won't work,' said Bartolomeo glumly. 'The entrance is thicker with Frenchmen than the streets of Paris.'

'Then we'll climb the battlements.'

'They can't be scaled. And even if you could, you'd be so outnumbered, even *you* wouldn't be able to hold out.' He brooded. 'Pantasilea would know what to do.' He brooded some more, and Ezio could see that his friend was becoming positively despondent. 'Maybe this is the end,' he continued gloomily. 'I'll just have to do what he says: enter their camp at dawn, bearing propitiatory gifts, and just hope the sod spares her life. Wretched coward!'

Ezio had been thinking, and now he snapped his fingers excitedly. '*Perché non ci ho pensato prima*? Why didn't I think of it before?'

'What? Did I say something?'

Ezio's eyes were shining. 'Back to your barracks.'

'What?'

340

'Call your men back to barracks. I'll explain there. Come on!'

'This had better be good,' said Bartolomeo, giving his men the order, 'Fall back!'

It was night by the time they got back. Once the horses had been stabled and the men stood down, Ezio and Bartolomeo went to the map room and sat down in conference.

'So, what's this plan of yours?'

Ezio unrolled a map, which showed the Castra Praetoria and its surroundings in detail. He pointed inside the fortress.

'Once inside, your men can overpower the camp's patrols, am I correct?'

'Yes, but—'

'Especially if they are taken completely by surprise?'

'*Ma certo*. The element of surprise is always—'

'Then we need to get hold of a lot of French uniforms. And their armour. Fast. At dawn, we'll walk right in, bold as brass; but there's no time to lose.'

Comprehension dawned on Bartolomeo's rugged face – comprehension, and hope: 'Hah! You crafty old scoundrel! Ezio Auditore, you truly are a man after my own heart. And thinking worthy of my Pantasilea herself. *Magnifico!*'

'Give me a few men. I'm going to make a sortie to their tower now, get in, and fetch what we need.'

'I'll give you all the men you need; they can strip the uniforms from the dead French troops.'

'Good.'

'And Ezio.'

'Yes?'

'Be sure to kill them as cleanly as possible. We don't want uniforms covered in blood.'

'They won't feel a thing,' said Ezio. 'Trust me.'

As Bartolomeo was detailing men for the job in hand, Ezio collected his saddlebag, and from it selected the Poison Blade.

They rode silently up to the Borgia Tower, which the French commanded, their horses' hooves muffled with sacking. Dismounting a short way off, Ezio bade his men wait while he scaled the outer wall with the skill of a denizen of the distant Alps and the grace and cunning of a cat. A scratch from the Poison Blade was enough to kill, and the over-confident French had not posted many guards – those that there were, he took completely unawares and they were dead before they even knew what had happened to them. Once the guards were out of the way, Ezio opened the main gate, which groaned on its hinges, making Ezio's heart race. He paused to listen, but the garrison slept on. Without a sound, his men ran into the tower, entered the garrison and over-came its inmates with barely a struggle. Collecting the uniforms took a little longer, but within an hour they were back at the barracks, mission accomplished.

'Bit of blood on this one,' grumbled Bartolomeo, sifting through their booty.

'He was the exception as he was the only man who was truly on his toes – I had to finish him the conventional way, with my sword,' said Ezio, as the men detailed for the operation ahead changed into the French uniform.

Bartolomeo said, 'Well, you'd better bring me a suit of their perverted mail, too.'

'You're not wearing one,' said Ezio, as he put on a French lieutenant's uniforms.

'What?'

'Of course you aren't! The plan is that you gave yourself up to us. We are a French patrol, bringing you to the Général Duc de Valois.'

'Of course.' Bartolomeo thought hard. 'Then what?'

'Barto, you can't have been paying attention. Then your men attack – on my signal.'

'*Bene!*' Bartolomeo beamed. 'Get a move on,' he said to those of his men who hadn't yet finished dressing. 'I can smell the dawn already, and it's a long ride.'

The men rode hard through the night, but left their horses at a little distance from the French HQ, in the charge of their squires. Before leaving them, Ezio first checked Leonardo's little Codex pistol – the design had been improved so he could fire more than one shot before reloading – and discreetly strapped it

343

to his arm. He and his group of 'French' soldiers then proceeded on foot in the direction of Castra Praetoria.

'De Valois thinks Cesare will allow the French to rule Italy,' explained Bartolomeo as he and Ezio marched side by side. Ezio was playing the part of the senior officer of the patrol, and would hand Bartolomeo over himself. 'Silly fool! He's so blinded by the trickle of royalty in his blood that he can't see the plan of the battlefield – blasted little inbred runt that he is!' He paused. 'But you know and I know that, whatever the French may think, Cesare intends to be the first king of a united Italy.'

'Unless we stop him.'

'Yes.' Bartolomeo reflected. 'You know, brilliant though your plan is, personally I don't like using this kind of trick. I believe in a fair fight – and may the best man win.'

'Cesare and de Valois may have different styles, Barto, but they both fight dirty, and we have no choice but to fight fire with fire.'

'Hmm! "There will come a day when men no longer cheat each other. And on that day we shall see what Mankind is truly capable of."' he quoted.

'I've heard that somewhere before.'

'You should have! It's something your father wrote.'

'Psst!'

They had drawn close to the French encampment,

and up ahead Ezio could see figures moving about –
French perimeter guards.

'What'll we do?' asked Bartolomeo, sotto voce.

'I'll kill them – there aren't many of them – but we
must do it noiselessly and without fuss.'

'Got enough poison left in that gadget of yours?'

'This lot are alert and they're quite widely spaced
apart. If I kill one and I'm noticed, I may not be able
to prevent some getting back and raising the alarm.'

'Why kill them at all? We're in French uniforms.
Well, you lot are.'

'They'll ask questions. If we make an entrance with
you in chains . . .'

'Chains?!'

'Shh! If we make an entrance, de Valois will be so
tickled it won't occur to him to ask where we sprang
from. At least, I hope it won't.'

'That chicken brain? No worries!' But how are we
going to get rid of them? We can hardly shoot them.
The gunfire would be as good as a fanfare.'

'I'm going to shoot them with this,' said Ezio, producing Leonardo's compact, quick-load crossbow.
'I've counted. There are five of them and I have six
bolts. The light's still a bit dim for me to aim properly
from here, so I'll have to get a bit closer. Just you hang
on here with the rest.'

Ezio slipped forward until he was within twenty
paces of the nearest French sentry. Cranking back the

string, he placed the first bolt in the groove and, lifting the tiller to his shoulder, took a quick bead on the man's breast and fired. There was a muted snap and a hiss, and the man toppled to the ground instantly, like a puppet whose strings had been cut. Ezio was already on his way through the bracken to his next victim; the twang of the crossbow was barely audible. The small bolt hit the man's throat, and he made a strangulated gargling sound before his knees gave way beneath him. Five minutes later, it was all over. Ezio had used all six bolts, since he'd missed on the first shot at his last man, causing him to lose his resolve momentarily, but he'd reloaded and fired successfully before the soldier had had time to react to the strange, dull noise he'd heard.

He had no more ammunition for the bow now, but he gave silent thanks to Leonardo. He knew this weapon would prove more than useful on another occasion. Ezio quietly hauled the fallen French soldiers to some sparse cover, hoping it would be enough to hide them from anyone who happened to pass by. As he did so he retrieved the used bolts for another time – recalling Leonardo's advice – then, stowing the crossbow, made his way back to Bartolomeo.

'All done?' the big man asked him.

'All done.'

'Valois next,' Bartolomeo vowed. 'I'll make him squeal like a stuck pig.'

The sky was lightening, and dawn, clad in a russet mantle, was walking over the dew on the distant hills to the east.

'We'd better get going,' said Bartolomeo.

'Come on, then,' replied Ezio, clapping manacles on his wrists before he could object. 'Don't worry, they're spring-loaded fakes. Just make a sudden tight fist and they'll drop off. But for God's sake wait for my signal. And by the way, the "guard" just to your left will stay close to you. He's got Bianca under his cloak. All you have to do is reach across and . . .' Ezio's voice took on a warning note, 'But only *at my signal.*'

'Aye, aye, sir,' smiled Bartolomeo.

At the head of his men, Bartolomeo two paces behind him with a special escort of four, Ezio marched boldly in the direction of the main gate of the French headquarters. The rising sun glittered on their chain mail and breastplates.

'*Halte-là!*' ordered a sergeant-commander at the gate, who was backed up by a dozen heavily armed sentries. His eyes had already taken in the uniforms of his fellow soldiers so he ordered, '*Déclarez-vous!*'

'*Je suis le lieutenant Guillemot, et j'emmène le général d'Alviano ici présent à Son Excellence le Duc-Général Monsieur de Valois. Le général d'Alviano s'est rendu, seul et sans armes, selon les exigences de Monsieur le Duc,*' said Ezio fluently, causing Bartolomeo to raise an eyebrow.

'Well, Lieutenant Guillemot, the general will be

pleased to see that General d'Alviano has come to his senses,' said the Captain of the Guard, who had hurried up to take charge. 'But there's something – just a trace – about your accent, which I cannot place. Tell me, what part of France are you from?'

Ezio drew a breath. 'Montréal,' he replied firmly.

'Open the gates,' the Captain of the Guard said to his sergeant.

'Open the gates!' shouted the sergeant.

Within seconds, Ezio was leading his men into the heart of the French headquarters. He fell back a step so as to have Bartolomeo, and the 'prisoner's' escort, at his side.

'I'll kill the lot of them,' muttered Bartolomeo, 'and eat their kidneys fried for breakfast. By the way, I didn't know you spoke French.'

'Picked it up in Florence,' Ezio replied casually. 'Couple of girls there I knew.' He was quietly glad his accent had passed muster.

'You rogue! Still, they say that's the best place to learn a language.'

'What, Florence?'

'No, you fool – *bed*!'

'Shut up.'

'You sure these manacles are fakes?'

'Not *yet*, Barto. Be patient, and shut up!'

'It's taking all my patience. What are they saying?'

'I'll tell you later.'

It was just as well that Bartolomeo's French was limited to a few words, thought Ezio, as he listened to the jibes being hurled at his friend: '*Chien d'Italien*' – 'Italian dog'; '*Prosterne-toi devant tes supérieurs*' – 'Bow down before your betters'; '*Regarde-le, comme il a honte de ce qu'il est devenu!*' – 'Look at him, how ashamed of himself he is at his own downfall!'

The ordeal was soon over, though, as they arrived at the foot of the broad stairway leading up to the entrance of the French general's quarters. De Valois himself stood at the head of a group of officers, his prisoner Pantasilea at his side. Her hands were tied behind her back, and she wore loose manacles on her ankles, which allowed her to walk, but only in small steps. At the sight of her, Bartolomeo could not resist an angry growl. Ezio kicked him.

De Valois held up his hand. 'No need for violence, Lieutenant, though I do congratulate you on your zeal.' He turned his attention to Bartolomeo. 'My dear general, it seems that you have seen the light.'

'Enough of your crap!' snarled Bartolomeo. 'Release my wife, and get these cuffs off me.'

'Oh dear,' said de Valois. 'Such high-handedness, and from someone born with absolutely nothing to his name.'

Ezio was about to give the signal, when Bartolomeo retorted to Valois, raising his voice, 'My name is worth its currency. Unlike yours, which is counterfeit!'

The surrounding troops fell silent.

'How dare you?' said de Valois, white with rage.

'You think that commanding an army in itself grants you status and nobility? True nobility of spirit comes from fighting alongside your men, not by kidnapping a woman to cheat your way out of a battle.'

'You savages never learn,' said de Valois malevolently and, producing a pistol, he cocked it and pointed it at Pantasilea's head.

Ezio knew he had to act fast, so he took out a pistol and fired one shot into the air. At the same time, Bartolomeo, who'd been dying for this moment, bunched his fists so the manacles flew off.

Pandemonium followed. The disguised *condottieri* accompanying Ezio immediately attacked the startled French soldiers, and Bartolomeo, seizing Bianca from the 'guard' still on his left, bounded up the stairway. De Valois was too quick for him, though. Keeping a tight hold on Pantasilea, he backed into his quarters and slammed the door behind him.

'Ezio!' implored Bartolomeo. 'You have to save my wife. Only you can do it. That place is built like a strongbox.'

Ezio nodded and tried to give his friend a reassuring smile. He scanned the building from where he stood. It wasn't large, but it was a strong new structure, built by French military architects and designed to be impregnable. There was nothing for it but to try to gain entry from the rooftops, where no one would be expecting an assault, and where, therefore, the weak points *might* be.

Ezio leapt up the stairs and, taking advantage of the melee below, which was diverting everyone else's attention, he looked for a place to climb. Suddenly, a dozen Frenchmen started after him, keen swords flashing in the early morning sun, but in a flash Bartolomeo was standing between Ezio and them, flourishing Bianca menacingly.

The walls of de Valois's quarters might have been designed to be unassailable, but there were enough nooks and crannies in them for Ezio to be able to plot a route with his eyes, and within a couple of moments he was on the roof. It was flat and made of wood overlaid with tile, and there were five French sentries stationed there, who challenged him as he sprang over the parapet, demanding a password. When he could not give one, they ran towards him, halberds lowered. It was lucky they weren't armed with muskets or pistols! Ezio shot the first one, then drew his sword and gave battle to the other four; they put up a desperate struggle, surrounding and jabbing him mercilessly with the points of their weapons. One slashed his sleeve open, nicking his elbow and drawing blood, but the blade slid harmlessly off the metal Bracer on his left forearm.

Using the Bracer and his sword, he was able to defend himself against the increasingly frenetic blows.

Ezio's skill with his blade was offset by having to tackle four opponents at once, but thoughts of Bartolomeo's beloved wife spurred him on – he knew that he could not fail; he must not fail. Eventually the tide of the fight turned in his favour; he ducked under two swords that were slashing towards his head, and engaged another with his Bracer, leaving him free to smash aside the fourth man's blade. The manoeuvre gave him the opening he needed, and a lethal slash across the man's jaw felled him. Three to go. Ezio stepped close to the nearest Frenchman, inside his guard, which threw the man, giving him no room to wield his sword. He then flicked his Hidden Blade forward into the man's abdomen. Two left – both of whom were looking nervous. It took just a couple of minutes to defeat the remaining two French guards, who no longer had the advantage of numbers. Their swordplay was simply no competition for Ezio's mastery of the blade. Breathing heavily and leaning on his sword for a moment, Ezio stood in the midst of his five vanquished foes.

The roof gave way in its centre to a large square opening. After reloading his pistol, Ezio approached it cautiously. As he'd expected, he found himself looking down into a courtyard, undecorated and bare of any plants, chairs or tables, though there were two or three stone benches arranged around a dry fountain and pool.

As he looked over the edge, a shot cracked and a bullet zinged past his left ear, causing him to draw back. He didn't know how many pistols de Valois had. If only one, he calculated that it would take the General perhaps ten seconds to reload. He regretted the crossbow, but there was nothing to be done about that. Tucked into the back of his belt were five of the poison darts. But he'd have to be fairly close range to use them, and he didn't want to do anything to endanger Pantasilea.

'Don't come any nearer!' yelled de Valois from below. 'I'll kill her if you do.'

Ezio hovered near the edge, looking down into the courtyard, but his line of vision was limited by the rim of the roof. He could see no one down there, but he could sense the panic in de Valois's voice.

'Who are you?' the General called. 'Who sent you? Rodrigo? Tell him it was all Cesare's plan.'

'You'd better tell me all you know, if you want to get back to Burgundy in one piece.'

'If I tell you, will you let me go?'

'We'll see. The woman must not be harmed. Come out where I can see you,' commanded Ezio.

Below him, de Valois stepped warily out from the colonnade that surrounded the courtyard and took up position near the dry fountain. Pantasilea's hands were tied behind her back, and he held her by a bridle which was attached to a halter round her neck. She had been crying, Ezio could see, but she was silent now and tried to keep her head held high. The look she gave de Valois was so withering that, had it been a weapon, it would have eclipsed all the Codex armaments combined.

How many men were hidden down there with him, Ezio wondered? Though the fearful tone of his voice suggested that the general had run out of options and was feeling cornered.

'Cesare has been bribing the cardinals to get them away from the Pope and onto his side. Once he had subdued the rest of the country for Rome, I was supposed to march on the capital and seize the Vatican, together with anyone else who opposed the Captain-General's will.'

De Valois waved his pistol around wildly and, as he turned, Ezio saw that he had two more stuck in his belt.

'It wasn't my idea,' continued de Valois. 'I am above such scheming.' A trace of the old vanity was creeping back into his voice. Ezio wondered if he'd allowed the man too much latitude. He moved into view and boldly leapt down into the courtyard, landing in a panther-like crouch.

'Stay back!' screamed de Valois. 'Or I'll—'

'Harm one hair of her head and my archers above will fill you fuller of arrows than Santo Sebastiano,' Ezio hissed. 'So, you noble little soul, what was in it for you?'

'As I am of the House of Valois, Cesare will give me Italy. I will rule here, as befits my birthright.'

Ezio almost laughed. Bartolomeo had not been exaggerating – quite the opposite – when he'd called this popinjay a chicken brain! But he still had Pantasilea, so he was still dangerous.

'Good. Now, let the woman go.'

'Get me out first. Then I'll let her go.'

'No.'

'I have King Louis's ear. Ask for what you want in France and it shall be yours. An estate, perhaps? A title?'

'Those things I already have. Here. And you are never going to rule over them.'

'The Borgia have tried to overturn the natural order,' wheedled de Valois, changing tack. 'I intend to set it right again. Royal blood should rule, not the foul, tainted stuff that runs in their veins.' He paused. 'I know you are not a barbarian, like them.'

'Neither you, nor Cesare, nor the Pope, nor anyone who does not have peace and justice on his side will ever rule Italy while I have life in my body,' said Ezio, moving slowly forward.

Fear seemed to have frozen the French General to the spot. The hand that now held the pistol to Pantasilea's temple, trembled, and he did not retreat. Evidently they were alone in his quarters, unless the only other occupants were servants who'd had the sense to hide.

They could hear a steady, heavy noise, as of deliberate, slow blows being struck, and the outer doors of the quarters vibrated. Bartolomeo must have routed the French and brought up battering rams.

'Please . . .' quavered the General, all his urbanity gone. 'I will kill her.' He glanced up at the opening in the roof, trying to catch a glimpse of Ezio's imaginary archers, not even reflecting, as Ezio had feared he might when he'd first mentioned them, that such soldiery had been all but superseded in modern warfare, though the bow was still far quicker to reload than the pistol or musket.

Ezio took another step forward.

'I'll give you anything you want. There's money here, plenty of it; it's to pay my men with, but you may have it all. And I . . . I . . . I will do anything you want of me.' His voice was pleading now, and he cut such a pathetic figure that Ezio could barely bridle his contempt. This man actually saw himself as King of Italy!?

It hardly seemed worth killing him.

Ezio was close to him now and the two men looked each other in the eye. Ezio slowly took first the pistol, and then the bridle, out of the General's nerveless hands. With a whimper of relief, Pantasilea hobbled back out of the way, watching the scene with wide eyes.

'I . . . I only wanted respect,' said the General, faintly.

'But real respect is earned,' said Ezio, 'not inherited, or purchased. And it cannot be gained by force. "*Oderint dum Metuant*" must be one of the stupidest sayings ever coined. No wonder Caligula adopted it: "Let them hate, as long as they fear." No wonder our modern Caligula lives by the same saying. And you serve him!'

'I serve my King, Louis XII.' De Valois looked crestfallen. 'But perhaps you are right. I see that now.' Hope sparked in his eyes. 'I need more time . . .'

Ezio sighed. 'Alas, friend. You have run out of that.' He drew his sword as de Valois, understanding, and acting with dignity at last, knelt and lowered his head.

'*Requiescat in Pace*,' said Ezio.

With a mighty crash, the outer doors of de Valois's quarters splintered and fell open, revealing Bartolomeo, dusty and bloody but uninjured, standing at the head of a troop of his men. He rushed up to his wife and hugged her so tightly he knocked the breath out of her, before busying himself about getting the halter off her neck; his fingers were so nervous and clumsy that Ezio had to do it for him. He cut the manacles from her feet with two mighty blows of Bianca, and, calmer now, untied the cords that bound her wrists.

'Oh, Pantasilea, my love, my heart, my own. Don't you ever dare disappear like that again. I was lost without you.'

357

'No you weren't. You rescued me.'

'Ah,' Bartolomeo looked embarrassed. 'No. Not I – it was Ezio! He came up with a—'

'*Madonna*, I am glad you are safe,' interrupted Ezio.

'My dear Ezio, how can I thank you? You saved me.'

'I was but an instrument, just a part of your husband's brilliant plan.'

Bartolomeo looked at Ezio with an expression of confusion and gratitude on his face.

'My prince!' said Pantasilea, embracing her husband. 'My hero!'

Bartolomeo blushed and winked at Ezio, saying, 'Well, if I'm your prince, I'd better earn that title. Mind you, it wasn't *all* my idea, you know.'

As they turned to go, Pantasilea brushed by Ezio and whispered, 'Thank you.'

41

A few days later, after Bartolomeo had rounded up the remains of de Valois's dispirited army, Ezio fell in with La Volpe, both on their way to a convocation Ezio had ordered of the Brotherhood at the Assassin hideaway on Tiber Island.

'How do things stand now here in Rome?' was Ezio's first question.

'Very good, Ezio. With the French army in disarray, Cesare has lost important support. Your sister Claudia tells us that the Spanish and the Holy Roman ambassadors have left hurriedly for home, and my men have routed the *Cento Occhi*.'

'There is still much to do.'

They arrived at their destination and found the rest of their companions already gathered in the inner room of the hideout, where a fire blazed on a hearth in the middle of the floor.

After they had greeted each other and taken their places, Machiavelli stood and intoned in Arabic, '*Laa shay'a waqi'un moutlaq bale kouloun moumkine*' – the Wisdom of our Creed is revealed through these words – 'We work in the Dark, to serve the Light. We are Assassins.'

Then Ezio stood and turned to his sister: 'Claudia. We dedicate our lives to protecting the freedom of Humanity. Mario Auditore, and our father Giovanni, his brother, once stood at a similar fire to this one, engaged in the same task. Now, I offer the choice to you: of joining us.'

He extended his hand and she placed hers in his. Machiavelli withdrew from the fire the familiar branding iron ending in two small semicircles like the letter 'C', which could be brought together by means of a lever in the handle.

'Everything is permitted. Nothing is true,' he said gravely. The others – Bartolomeo, La Volpe and Ezio – repeated the words after him.

Just as Antonio de Magianis had once done to Ezio, so Machiavelli now solemnly applied the branding iron to Claudia's ring finger and closed the clamp, so that the mark of a ring was burnt there forever.

Claudia winced, but did not cry out. Machiavelli removed the iron and put it safely to one side.

'Welcome to our Order – our Brotherhood,' he told Claudia formally.

'Sisterhood too?' she asked, rubbing a soothing ointment onto her branded finger from a little phial Bartolomeo had proffered her.

Machiavelli smiled. 'If you like.'

All eyes were on him now as he turned to Ezio.

'We have not seen eye to eye on many issues—'

'Niccolò—' Ezio interrupted, but Machiavelli held up a hand to stay him.

'But ever since the epiphany in the vault under the Sistine Chapel, and even before then, you have proved again and again that you were exactly what our order needed. You have led the charge against the Templars, carried our *gonfalon* proud and high, and steadily rebuilt our Brotherhood after the debacle at Monteriggioni.' He looked around. 'The moment has come, my friends, to appoint formally Ezio to the position he already occupies by common consent: that of our Leader. I present to you Ezio Auditore di Firenze, the Grand Master of our order.' He turned to Ezio. 'My friend, from henceforth you will be known as *il Mentore*, the guardian of our Brotherhood and of our secrets.'

Ezio's head swam with emotion, though a part of him still wanted to wrench itself away from this life which demanded every waking hour and allowed few even for sleep. Still, he stepped forward and austerely repeated the words central to the Creed: 'Where other men are limited by morality and law, we must, in quest of our sacred goals, always remember: Everything is permitted. Nothing is true. Nothing is true. Everything is permitted.'

The others repeated the formula after him.

'And now it is time,' said Machiavelli, 'for our newest member to take her leap of faith.'

They made their way to the church of Santa Maria

in Cosmedin and climbed its bell tower. Carefully guided by Bartolomeo and La Volpe, Claudia fearlessly threw herself into the void just as the golden orb of the sun broke free of the eastern horizon, catching the folds in her silver dress in its light and turning them golden too. Ezio watched her land safely and walk with Bartolomeo and La Volpe in the direction of a nearby colonnade. Now Machiavelli and Ezio were left alone. Just as Machiavelli was about to make his leap, Ezio stopped him.

'Why the sudden change of heart, Niccolò?'

Machiavelli smiled. 'What change of heart? I have always stood by you. I have always been loyal to the cause. My fault is independent thinking. That is what caused the doubts in your mind – and in Gilberto's. Now we are free of all that unpleasantness. I never sought the leadership. I am . . . more of an observer. Now, let us take our leap of faith together, as friends and fellow warriors of the Creed!'

Machiavelli held out his hand and, smiling, Ezio took it firmly in his grasp. Then they threw themselves off the roof of the *campanile* together.

Scarcely had they landed and rejoined their companions than a courier rode up. Breathless, he announced, '*Maestro* Machiavelli, Cesare has returned to Rome alone from his latest foray in the Romagna. He rides for the Castel Sant'Angelo.'

'*Grazie*, Alberto,' said Machiavelli, as the courier

wheeled his horse round and sped back the way he had come.

'Well?' Ezio asked him.

Machiavelli showed his palms. 'The decision is yours, not mine.'

'Niccolò, you had better not stop telling me what you think. I now seek the opinion of my most trusted advisor.'

Machiavelli smiled. 'In this case you know my opinion already. It hasn't changed. The Borgia must be eradicated. Go, and kill them, *Mentore*. Finish the job you have started.'

'Good advice.'

'I know,' Machiavelli looked at him appraisingly.

'What is it?' Ezio asked.

'I had been thinking of writing a book about Cesare's methods. Now, I think I will balance it with an examination of yours.'

'If you're writing a book about me,' said Ezio, 'better make it a short one!'

42

Ezio arrived at the Castel Sant'Angelo to find that a crowd had gathered on the opposite bank of the Tiber. Blending in with the gathered masses, he made his way to the front, and saw that the French troops guarding the bridge that led to the Castel, and the Castel itself, were in total disarray. Some soldiers were already packing up their equipment, while officers and lieutenants moved frantically among them, issuing orders to unpack again. Some of the orders were contradictory, and, as a result, here and there fights had broken out. The Italian crowd was watching, Ezio noted, with quiet pleasure. Though he carried his own clothes in a satchel slung over his shoulder, Ezio had taken the precaution of once more donning the French uniform he had worn in the attack on Castra Praetoria, and he now shed the cloak he'd been wearing to cover it, and walked quickly onto the bridge. No one paid him any attention, but as he passed among the French troops, he gleaned useful snippets of conversation.

'When are we expecting the attack from d'Alviano and his mercenaries?'

'They say he's on his way now.'

'Then why are we packing? Are we retreating?'

'I hope so! *Tout cela, c'est rien qu'un tas de merde.*'

A private spotted Ezio. 'Sir! Sir! What are our orders?'

'I'm on my way to see,' replied Ezio.

'Sir!'

'What is it?'

'Who's in charge now, sir? Now that General de Valois is dead?'

'No doubt the King is sending a replacement.'

'Is it true, sir, that he died valorously in battle?'

Ezio smiled to himself. 'Of course it's true. At the head of his men.'

He moved on towards the Castel itself.

Once inside, he found his way up to the ramparts, and from his vantage point looked down to the courtyard, where he spotted Cesare talking to a captain of the Papal Guard who was posted at the door of the inner citadel.

'I need to see the Pope!' Cesare said urgently. 'I need to see my father *now*!'

'Of course, Your Grace. You will find His Holiness in his private apartments at the top of the Castel.'

'Then get out of my way, you fool!' Cesare thrust past the hapless captain as the latter gave hasty orders for a wicket gate in the main door to be opened to admit him. Ezio watched for a moment, then made his way around the circumference of the Castel until he came to the place where the secret gate was located. He dropped to the ground and let himself through with Pietro's key.

Once inside, he looked around warily, then, seeing no one, he dived down a stairway in the direction of the cells from which he'd rescued Caterina Sforza. Finding a quiet spot, he swiftly shed the French lieutenant's uniform and changed back into his own clothes, which were designed for the work he had to do. He checked his weapons quickly, strapping on the Bracer and the Poison Blade, and checking that he had a supply of poison darts safely stowed in his belt. Then, hugging the walls, he made off in the direction of the stairway that led to the top of the Castel. The way was guarded and he had to send three soldiers to their Maker before he could proceed.

At last he arrived at the garden where he had watched Lucrezia and her lover keep their tryst. In daylight he could see that her apartments were part of a complex. Larger and even grander ones stood beyond, and he guessed these to be the Pope's. But as he was making off in that direction he was interrupted by a conversation coming from within Lucrezia's rooms. He made his way stealthily to the open window, where the voices were coming from, and listened. He could just see Lucrezia, apparently none the worse for wear after her ordeal in the cells, talking to the same attendant he'd seen her entrust with the information about her affair with Pietro, which he had passed on to her jealous brother, with evident success to judge by Cesare's fast return to Rome.

'I don't understand it,' Lucrezia was saying irritably. 'I ordered a fresh batch of cantarella only last night. Toffana was to have delivered it to me personally by noon. Did you see her? What's going on?'

'I'm terribly sorry, *mia signora*, but I've just heard that the Pope intercepted the delivery. He's taken it all for himself.'

'That old bastard. Where is he?'

'In his rooms. *Madonna*, There's a meeting—'

'A meeting? With whom?'

The attendant hesitated. 'With Cesare, *Madonna*.'

Lucrezia took this in, then said, half to herself, 'That's strange. My father didn't tell me Cesare was back here again.'

Deep in thought, she left the room.

Alone, the attendant started to tidy up, rearranging tables and chairs and muttering under his breath.

Ezio waited a moment to see if there would be any more useful information imparted, but all the attendant said was, 'That woman gives me so much trouble . . . Why didn't I stay in the stables, where I was well off? Call this promotion?! I put my head on the block every time I run an errand. *And* I have to taste her food for her every time she sits down to a bloody meal.' He paused for a moment. Then added, 'What a family!'

43

Ezio left before he heard those last words. He slipped through the garden towards the Pope's apartments and, since the single entrance was heavily guarded and he did not want to draw attention to himself – it wouldn't be long before the bodies of the guards he'd killed below stairs were discovered – he found a place where he could climb up to one of the principal windows of the building unobtrusively. His hunch that this would be a window giving on to the Pope's chamber paid off, and it had a broad external sill where he could perch at one end whilst remaining out of sight. Using the blade of his dagger, he was able to prise a side light open a fraction so that he could hear anything that might be said inside.

Rodrigo – Pope Alexander VI – was alone in the room, standing by a table on which lay a large silver bowl of red and yellow apples, whose position he adjusted nervously as the door opened and Cesare entered, unannounced. He was clearly angry, and without preamble, he launched into a bitter diatribe.

'What the hell is going on?' he began.

'I don't know what you mean,' replied his father with reserve.

'Oh yes you do. My funds have been cut off and my troops dispersed.'

'Ah. Well, you know that after your banker's tragic ... demise, Agostino Chigi took over all his affairs ...'

Cesare laughed mirthlessly. '*Your* banker! I might have known. And my men?'

'Financial difficulties strike all of us from time to time, my boy, even those of us with armies and overweening ambition.'

'Are you going to get Chigi to release money to me or not?'

'No.'

'We'll see about that!' Angrily, Cesare snatched an apple from the bowl. Ezio saw that the Pope was watching his son carefully.

'Chigi won't help you,' said the Pope levelly. 'And he's too powerful for you to bend him to your will.'

'In that case,' said Cesare, sneering, 'I'll use the Piece of Eden to get what I want. It will render your help unnecessary.' He bit into the apple with a mean smile.

'That has been made abundantly clear to me already,' said the Pope drily. 'By the way, I suppose you are aware that General de Valois is dead?'

Cesare's smile disappeared in a flash. 'No. I have only just returned to Rome.' His tone became threatening. 'Did you ... ?'

The Pope spread his hands. 'What possible reason

would I have had to kill him? Or was he plotting against me, perhaps, with my own, dear, brilliant, *treacherous* Captain-General?'

Cesare took another bite of the apple. 'I do not have to stand for this!' he snarled as he chewed.

'If you must know, the Assassins murdered him.'

Cesare swallowed, his eyes wide. Then his face went dark with fury. 'Why did you not stop them?'

'As if I could.' It was your decision to attack Monter- iggioni, not mine. It's high time you took responsibility for your misdeeds – if it's not too late.'

'My *actions*, you mean,' replied Cesare proudly. 'Despite the constant interference of failures like you.'

The younger man turned to go, but the Pope hurried round the table to block his way to the door.

'You're not going anywhere,' Rodrigo growled. 'And you are deluded. *I* have the Piece of Eden.'

'Liar. Get out of my way, you old fool.'

The Pope shook his head sadly. 'I gave you every- thing I could, and yet it was never enough.'

At that instant, Ezio saw Lucrezia burst into the room, her eyes wild.

'Cesare!' she shrieked. 'Be careful! He intends to poison you!'

Cesare froze. He looked at the apple in his hand, spitting out the chunk he had just bitten, his face a mask. Rodrigo's own expression changed from one of triumph to one of fear. He backed away from his son, putting the table between them.

'Poison me?' said Cesare, his eyes boring into his father's.

'You would not . . . listen to reason,' stammered the Pope.

Cesare smiled as he advanced, very deliberately, on Rodrigo, saying, 'Father. Dear Father. Do you not see? I control everything. *All* of it. If I want to live, despite your efforts, I shall live. And if there is anything – *anything* – I want, I take it.' He came close to the Pope and seized him by the collar, raising the poisoned apple in his hand. 'For example, if I want you to die, you *die!*'

Pulling his father close he shoved the apple into his open mouth before he had time to close it and, grabbing him by the head and jaw, forced his lips together and held them shut. Rodrigo struggled and choked on the apple, unable to breathe. He fell to the floor in agony and his two children coldly watched him die.

Cesare wasted no time and, kneeling, searched his dead father's robes. There was nothing. He stood and bore down on his sister, who shrank from him.

'You . . . you must seek help. The poison is in you,' she cried.

'Not enough,' he barked hoarsely. 'Do you really think I am such a fool as not to have taken a prophylactic antidote before coming here? I know what a devious old toad our father was, and how he would react if he thought for a moment that real power was slipping in my direction. Now, he said he had the Piece of Eden.'

'He ... he ... was telling the truth.'

Cesare slapped her. 'Why was I not told?'

'You were away ... he had it moved ... he feared the Assassins might—'

Cesare slapped her again. 'You plotted with him!'

'No! No! I thought he had sent messengers to tell you.'

'Liar!'

'I am telling the truth. I really thought you knew, or at least had been informed, of what he'd done.'

Cesare slapped her again, harder this time, so that she lost her balance and fell.

'Cesare,' she said as she struggled for breath, panic and fear in her eyes, 'are you mad? I am Lucrezia. Your sister. Your friend. Your lover. Your queen.' Rising, she put her hands timidly to his cheeks to stroke them. But Cesare's response was to grab her round the throat and shake her, as a terrier shakes a ferret.

'You're nothing but a bitch.' He brought his face close to hers, thrusting it at her aggressively. 'Now tell me,' he continued, his voice dangerously low. 'Where is it?'

Disbelief showed in her voice when she replied, gagging as she struggled to speak, 'You ... never loved me?'

His response was to let go of her throat and hit her again, this time close to the eye, with a closed fist.

'Where is the Apple? THE APPLE!' he screamed. 'Tell me!'

She spat in his face and he took her arm and threw her to the floor, kicking her hard as he repeated his question over and over again. Ezio tensed, forcing himself not to intervene – after all, he had to know the answer – though he was appalled at what he was witnessing.

'All right. All right,' she said at last, in a broken voice.

He pulled her to her feet and she placed her lips close to his ear, whispering, to Ezio's fury.

Satisfied, Cesare pushed her away. 'Smart decision, little sister.' She tried to cling to him, but he pushed her away with a gesture of disgust and strode from the room.

As soon as he had gone, Ezio smashed through the window and landed close to Lucrezia who, the spirit drained from her, slumped against the wall. Ezio quickly knelt by Rodrigo's inert body and felt for a pulse.

There was none.

'*Requiescat in Pace*,' whispered Ezio, rising again and confronting Lucrezia. Looking at him she smiled bitterly, a little of the fire returned to her eyes at the sight of him.

'You were there? All the time?'

Ezio nodded.

'Good,' she said. 'I know where the bastard is going.'

'Tell me.'

'With pleasure. Saint Peter's. The pavilion in the courtyard.'

'Thank you, *Madonna*.'

'Ezio.'

'Yes?'

'Be careful.'

44

Ezio raced along the Passetto di Borgo, which ran through the *rione* of Borgo and connected the Castel Sant'Angelo with the Vatican. He wished he'd been able to bring some of his men with him, or that he'd had time to find a horse, but urgency lent his feet wings, and any guards he encountered were swiftly thrown aside in his headlong rush.

Once in the Vatican, Ezio made his way to the pavilion in the courtyard, where Lucrezia had indicated the Apple would be. With Rodrigo gone, there was a fair chance that there would be a new Pope on whom the Borgia could have no influence, since the College of Cardinals, apart from those members who'd been well and truly bought, were fed up and disgusted at being pushed around by this foreign family.

But for now Ezio had to stop Cesare, before he could get hold of the Apple and use its power – however dimly he might understand it – to regain all the ground he had lost.

Now was the time to strike his enemy down for good – it was now or never.

Ezio reached the courtyard only to find it deserted.

He noticed that at its centre there was, instead of a fountain, a large sandstone sculpture of a pine cone in a stone cup on a plinth. It stood perhaps ten feet high. He scanned the rest of the sunlit courtyard, but it was bare, with a dusty white floor that burnt his eyes with its brightness. There wasn't even a colonnade, and the walls of the surrounding buildings had no decoration at all, though there were rows of narrow windows high up and, at ground level, one plain door on each side, all of which were closed. It was an unusually austere place.

He looked again at the pine cone and approached it. Looking closely, he could just discern a narrow gap between the dome of the cone and its body, running round the whole circumference. Climbing up the plinth, he found he was able to steady himself by gripping with his toes and, holding on with one hand, he ran the other round the rim of the cone where the gap was, feeling carefully for any possibly imperfection that might disclose a hidden trigger or button.

There! He'd found it. Gently, he pressed it, and the top of the cone sprang open on hitherto hidden bronze hinges, firmly screwed into the soft stone and strengthened with cement. In the centre of the hollow space that was now revealed, he saw a dark green leather bag. He fumbled at its drawstring with his hand, and the faint glow he saw within its depths confirmed his hopes; he had found the Apple!

His heart was in his mouth as he carefully lifted the

bag free – he knew the Borgia, and there was no guarantee that it might not be booby-trapped, but he had to take that risk.

Where the hell was Cesare? The man had had a good few minutes' start on him, and had doubtless ridden here on horseback.

'I'll take that,' cried a cold, cruel voice behind him. Bag in hand, Ezio dropped lightly to the ground and turned to confront Cesare, who had just burst through the southern wall door, followed by a troop of his personal guard, who fanned out round the courtyard, surrounding Ezio.

Of course, Ezio thought, he hadn't reckoned on competition so had wasted time collecting backup.

'Beat you to it,' he taunted Cesare.

'It won't do you any good, Ezio Auditore. You've been a thorn in my side too long. But it ends here. Now. My sword will take your life.'

He drew a modern schiavona with a basket hilt and took a step towards Ezio. But then, suddenly, he turned grey and clasped his stomach, dropping his sword as his knees buckled. Evidently it had not been a strong enough antidote, thought Ezio, breathing a sigh of relief.

'Guards!' croaked Cesare, struggling to stay on his feet.

There were ten of them, five armed with muskets. Ezio ducked and dived as they fired at him, the balls from their muskets cannoning into the floor and walls as Ezio skittered to cover behind a pillar. Whisking out the poison darts from his belt, he sprang from his cover, drawing close enough to the musketeers to hurl the darts one by one. Cesare's men weren't expecting an assault, and looked at each other in surprise. Ezio threw his darts, and each one found its fatal mark. Within seconds, three guards were down, the poison in the darts quickly having mortal effect.

One of the musketeers regained his composure for a moment and hurled his weapon like a club, but Ezio ducked and the weapon went spiralling over his head. He quickly loosed the next two darts, until the musketeers were all down. Ezio had no time to retrieve his darts as Leonardo had suggested.

The five swordsmen, after recovering from their initial shock – for they'd assumed that their comrades with guns would have made short work of the Assassin – closed in quickly, wielding heavy falchions. Ezio almost danced among them as he avoided their clumsy blows – the swords were too heavy for fast work or much manoeuvrability – releasing the newly recrafted Poison Blade and drawing his dagger. Ezio knew he didn't have much time to engage the soldiers before Cesare made a move, so his fighting technique was more sparse and efficient than usual, preferring to lock his opponents' blade with his dagger and use the Poison Blade to finish the job. The first two fell without a whisper, at which point the remaining three decided to attack all at once. Ezio pulled back five quick paces and extended his dagger up full and high, charging forward at the nearest of the three oncoming guards. As he drew into range, Ezio skidded to his knees, sliding across the ground and under the blade of one baffled guard. The Poison Blade nicked the man's thigh as Ezio skidded past, barrelling towards the remaining guards, while his dagger slashed at the tendons of their lower legs. Both men shrieked as Ezio's blade found its target and the men fell, their legs useless.

Cesare watched all this in quiet disbelief, and as Ezio careened towards the last three guards, Cesare decided not to wait for the outcome of the fight. He recovered himself enough to turn and flee.

Hemmed in by the guards and unable to follow, Ezio watched him go out of the corner of his eye.

No matter, though, for he still had the Apple, and he remembered enough of its power – how could he forget? – to use it, after the melee was over, to guide him back through the Vatican by a different route from that by which he'd come, reckoning, as he did, that Cesare would have wasted no time in securing the Passetto di Borgo. Glowing from within the leather bag, the Apple indicated on its surface a way through the high painted halls and chambers of the offices of the Vatican towards the Sistine Chapel, and thence by a southward-leading corridor into St Peter's itself. Its power was such that passing monks and priests within the Vatican turned away from Ezio, avoiding him, and Papal guards remained rigidly at their posts.

Ezio wondered how soon news of the Pope's death would filter down through the hierarchy of the Vatican. The confusion that would follow in its wake would need a strong hand to control it, and he prayed that Cesare would not have the opportunity to take advantage of any uncertainty to stake his own claim, if not to the Papacy – surely that was out of his reach – then to influencing the election in order to place a new Pope, friendly to his ambitions, on St Peter's throne.

Passing young Michelangelo's brilliant new sculpture of the Pietà on his left, Ezio left the basilica and blended into the crowds milling about in the shabby old square that lay in front of the east entrance.

45

By the time he reached the Assassin hideout on Tiber Island, church bells had begun to ring out all over Rome. They were sounding the Pope's death knell.

He found his friends waiting for him.

'Rodrigo is dead,' he announced.

'We guessed as much from the bells,' said Machiavelli. 'Magnificent work!'

'It was not by my hand, but Cesare's.'

It took a moment for this to sink in. Then Machiavelli spoke again: 'And what of Cesare?'

'He lives, though the Pope tried to poison him before he died.'

'The serpent is biting its own tail,' said La Volpe.

'Then the day is saved!' cried Claudia.

'No.' said Machiavelli. 'If he's freed himself of the restraint of his father, Cesare may yet regain the ground he has lost. We must not allow him to assemble his remaining supporters. The coming weeks will be critical.'

'With your aid I will hunt him down,' said Ezio firmly.

'Niccolò is right; we must act fast,' La Volpe put in.

'Do you hear those trumpets? They are a summons to the Borgia forces to gather.'

'Do you know where?' asked Bartolomeo.

'It's likely that they'll rally their troops in the piazza in front of Cesare's palace in Trastevere.'

'My men will patrol the city,' said Bartolomeo, 'but we'd need a full army to do it properly.'

Ezio carefully produced the Apple from its bag. It glowed dully. 'We have one,' he said. 'Or something just as good.'

'Do you know how to use it?' asked Machiavelli.

'I remember enough from when Leonardo experimented with it long ago in Venice,' replied Ezio. He held the strange artefact aloft and, concentrating, tried to project his thoughts at it.

There was no response for several minutes, and he was about to give up when, slowly at first, and then with increasing energy, the Apple began to glow more and more brightly, until the light emanating from it made them cover their eyes.

'Stand back!' bawled Bartolomeo as Claudia gasped in alarm, and even La Volpe started back.

'No,' said Machiavelli. 'Science – but something out of our reach.' He looked at Ezio. 'If only Leonardo were here.'

'As long as it serves our purpose,' said Ezio.

'Look,' said La Volpe. 'It's showing us the *campanile* of Santa Maria in Trastevere. That's where Cesare must be.'

'You were right,' cried Bartolomeo. 'But look at the number of troops he still has.'

'I'm going. Now,' said Ezio, as the projected scene faded and the Apple became inert.

'We're coming with you.'

'No.' Ezio held up a hand. 'Claudia, I want you to go back to The Rosa in Fiore and get your girls to find out all they can about Cesare's plans, then mobilize our recruits. Gilberto, get your thieves to fan out all over the city and bring word of any Templar chapters that may be reorganizing. Our enemies are fighting for their very lives. Bartolomeo, organize your men and have them ready to move at a moment's notice.'

He turned to Machiavelli. 'Niccolò. Get over to the Vatican. The College of Cardinals will be going into conclave soon to elect a new Pope.'

'Indeed. And Cesare will certainly try to use what influence he has left to elevate a candidate favourable to him to the Papal Throne – or at least someone he can manipulate.'

'But Cardinal della Rovere wields great authority now, and he is the Borgia's implacable enemy, as you know. If only—'

'I will go and talk to the Cardinal *Camerlengo*. The election may be long and drawn out.'

'We must take every advantage we can of the inter-regnum. Thank you, Niccolò.'

'How will you manage on your own, Ezio?'

'I'm not on my own,' said Ezio, gently replacing the Apple in its bag. 'I'm taking this with me.'

'Just as long as you know how to keep it under control,' said Bartolomeo mistrustfully. 'If you ask me, it's a creation straight out of Beelzebub's workshop.'

'In the wrong hands, perhaps. But as long as we have it—'

'Then don't let it out of your sight, let alone your grasp.'

They broke up then, each hastening away to attend to the duties Ezio had assigned them. Ezio himself crossed to the west bank of the river and sprinted the short distance to the church La Volpe had recognized in the vision accorded them by the Apple.

The scene had changed by the time he reached it, though he saw units of soldiers in Cesare's livery making their way out of the square in organized groups, as if under orders. These were disciplined men who understood that failure would spell their ruin.

There was no sign of Cesare, but Ezio knew that he must still be sick from the effects of the poison. His rallying call to the troops must have taken it out of him. There was only one place he would think of retreating to: his fortified *palazzo*, not far away. Ezio set off in its direction.

He blended in with a group of Borgia attendants who wore Cesare's personal crest on the shoulders of their cloaks. They were too agitated to have noticed him, even if he hadn't been using the Apple to render himself as good as invisible. Using the guards as cover, he slipped through the palazzo's gates, which opened quickly for them and then, just as quickly, clanged shut again behind them.

Ezio slipped into the shadows of the courtyard's colonnade and glided along the perimeter of the inner walls, stopping to peer in at each unshuttered window. Then, ahead, he saw a door with two guards posted outside it. He looked around. The rest of the courtyard was deserted. He approached silently, releasing his Hidden Blade, and fell upon the guards before they knew what was happening. One, he killed instantly. The other managed to get a blow in, which would have severed his left hand from his arm had it not been for the Bracer. While the man recovered from his astonishment at what appeared to be witchcraft, Ezio plunged the Blade into the base of his throat, and he fell like a sack to the ground.

The door was unlocked and its hinges, when Ezio warily tried them, proved well-oiled, so that he could slide into the room noiselessly.

It was large and gloomy. Ezio took refuge behind an arras near the door, set there to exclude draughts, and watched the men seated around a large oak table at its centre. The table was spread with papers and illuminated by candles in two iron candelabra. At its head sat Cesare, his personal doctor, Gaspar Torella, at his side.

His face was grey and he was sweating prodigiously as he glared at his officers.

'You must hunt them down,' he was saying, grasping the arms of his chair tightly in an effort to stay upright.

'They are everywhere and nowhere at once,' declared one helplessly.

'I don't care how you do it, just do it!'

'We cannot, *signore*, not without your guidance. The Assassins have regrouped. With the French gone, or in disarray, our own forces are scarcely able to match them. They have spies everywhere, and our own network is no longer able to root them out. Ezio Auditore has turned vast numbers of the citizenry to his cause.'

'I am ill, *idioti*! I depend on your initiative.' Cesare sighed, falling back in his chair. 'I was damned nearly killed, but I still have teeth.'

'Sir . . .'

'Just hold them at bay, if that's the best you can do.' Cesare paused to catch his breath, and Doctor Torella mopped his brow with a lint cloth soaked in vinegar, or some other strong-smelling astringent, muttering soothingly to his patient as he did so. 'Soon,' Cesare continued, 'Soon, Micheletto will reach Rome with my own forces from Romagna and the north, and then you will see how quickly the Assassins will crumble into dust.'

Ezio stepped forth and revealed the Apple. 'You

delude yourself, Cesare,' he said in a voice of true authority.

Cesare started from his chair, fear in his eyes. 'You! How many lives do you have, Ezio? But this time you will surely die. Call the guard! Now!' he bellowed at his officers as he allowed his doctor to hurry him from the room to safety through an inner door.

Lightning-fast, one of the officers made for the door to raise the alarm while the others drew pistols and levelled them at Ezio, who just as swiftly withdrew the Apple from its bag and held it aloft, concentrating hard and pulling the hood of his tunic down low to shield his eyes.

The Apple began to pulsate and glow, and the glow turned to an incandescence that gave out no heat, but which was as bright as the sun. The room turned white.

'What sorcery is this?' shouted one of the officers, firing wildly. By chance his shot hit the Apple, but it had no more effect on it than a handful of dust.

'Truly, this man has God Himself on his side!' another bawled, vainly trying to shield his eyes and staggering blindly in what he thought he thought was the direction of the door.

As the light increased, the officers blundered up against the table, covering their eyes with their hands.

'What's happening?'

'How is this possible?'

'Do not smite me, Lord!'

'I cannot *see*!'

His lips pressed together in concentration, Ezio continued to project his will through the Apple, but even he dared not look up from under the protecting peak of his cowl. He had to judge the moment to cease. When he did so, a wave of exhaustion hit him as the Apple, invisible within its own light, suddenly went dead. There was no sound in the room. Cautiously, Ezio lifted his hood and saw that the room was almost as it was before. The candles on the table cast a pool of light at the centre of the gloom, burning on, almost reassuringly, as if nothing had happened. Their flames were steady, as there was no hint of a breeze.

The tapestry on the arras was bleached of all its colour, and all the officers lay dead around the table, save the one who had first been making for the door; he was slumped against it, his hand still on the latch. Ezio went over to him and had to move him aside in order to leave.

As he rolled the man over, he inadvertently looked into his eyes. He wished he hadn't – it was a sight he would never forget.

'*Requiescat in Pace*,' said Ezio, acknowledging the chill realization that the Apple did indeed have powers which, if unleashed without check, could control the minds of men and open up undreamed-of possibilities and worlds.

It could wreak destruction so terrible as to be beyond the power of imagination itself.

46

The conclave was undecided. Despite the efforts of Cardinal della Rovere to outwit him, Cesare clearly still had enough clout to hold him in check. Fear, or self-interest, kept the cardinals wavering. Machiavelli guessed what they were trying to do – they would find a candidate to elect who might not last long, but who would be acceptable to all parties. An interim Pope, if you like a caretaker until the balance of power resolved itself.

Bearing this in mind, Ezio was pleased when, after weeks of deadlock, Claudia brought news to Tiber Island.

'The Cardinal of Rouen – a Frenchman, Georges d'Amboise – has revealed under . . . duress . . . that Cesare has planned a meeting with Templar loyalists in the countryside, outside Rome. The cardinal himself attends.'

'When is it?'

'Tonight.'

'Where?'

'The location is to be kept secret until the last minute.'

'Then I will go to the cardinal's residence and follow him when he leaves.'

'They have elected a new Pope,' said Machiavelli, coming in hurriedly. 'Your pet French cardinal, Claudia, will take the news to Cesare tonight. In fact, a small delegation of them, still friendly to the Borgia, is going with him.'

'Who is the new Pope?' asked Ezio

Machiavelli smiled. 'It is as I thought,' he said. 'Cardinal Piccolomini. He's not an old man – he's sixty-four – but he's in poor health. He's chosen to be known as Pius III.'

'Whom does he support?'

'We don't know yet, but all the foreign ambassadors put pressure on Cesare to leave Rome during the election. Della Rovere is furious, but he knows how to wait.'

Ezio spent the rest of the day in consultation with Bartolomeo, and between them they put together a combined force of recruits and *condottieri* strong enough for any battle that might ensue with Cesare.

'It's just as well you didn't kill Cesare back at his *palazzo*,' said Bartolomeo. 'This way, he'll draw all his supporters to him and we can smash the lot of them.' He looked at Ezio. 'I've got to hand it to you, my friend. You might almost have planned it this way.'

Ezio smiled and returned to his lodgings, where he

strapped on the Pistol, and put the Double Blade into the wallet on his belt.

With a small group of hand-picked men, Ezio made up the advance guard, leaving the rest to follow some way behind. When the Cardinal of Rouen rode out in the late afternoon with his fellows and their entourage, Ezio and his horsemen followed at a safe distance. They did not have a long ride before the Cardinal stopped at a large country estate whose mansion was set behind fortified walls near the shores of Lake Bracciano.

Ezio scaled the walls of the mansion alone and shadowed the delegation of cardinals as it made its way to the Great Hall, blending in with the Borgia's hundred or so leading officers. There were many other people present from other lands, whom Ezio did not recognize, but knew must be members of the Templar Order. Cesare, fully recovered now, stood on a raised dais in the centre of the crowded hall. Torches flickered in their sconces on the stone walls, making shadows leap and giving the congress more of an air of a witches' coven than a gathering of military forces.

Outside, Borgia soldiers were gathering in numbers that surprised Ezio, who had not forgotten Cesare's remark about Micheletto bringing his remaining troops out of the provinces to back him up. He was worried that even with Bartolomeo's men and his own recruits, who had drawn up a couple of hundred yards from the mansion, they might find their match in this assembly. But it was too late now.

Ezio watched as a pathway was made between the serried ranks in the hall to allow the cardinals to approach the dais.

'Join me and I will take back Rome for us,' Cesare declaimed as the Cardinal of Rouen made his appearance with his fellow prelates. Seeing them, Cesare broke off.

'What news of the conclave?' he demanded.

The Cardinal of Rouen hesitated. 'Good news – and bad,' he said.

'Spit it out!'

'We have elected Piccolomini.'

Cesare considered this. 'Well, at least it isn't that fisherman's son, della Rovere!' He turned on the Cardinal. 'But it's still not the man I wanted. I wanted a puppet. Piccolomini may have one foot in the grave, but he can still do me a lot of damage. I paid for your appointment. Is this how you thank me?'

'Della Rovere is a powerful foe.' The Cardinal hesitated again. 'And Rome is not what it once was. Borgia money has become tainted.'

Cesare looked at him coldly. 'You will regret this decision,' he said frostily.

The Cardinal bowed his head and turned to go, but as he did so, he spotted Ezio, who had made his way forward in order to see more clearly.

'It's the Assassin!' he yelled. 'His sister put me to the Question. That's how he got here. Run! He'll kill us all!'

The cardinals took to their heels as one amidst a general panic. Ezio followed them and, once outside, fired his pistol. The sound carried to his advance guard, posted just outside the walls, and they in turn fired muskets as a signal to Bartolomeo to attack. They arrived just as the gates in the walls were opened to allow the fleeing cardinals to depart. The defenders had no time to close the gates before being over-powered by the advance guard, who managed to hold the gate until Bartolomeo, whirling Bianca above his head and roaring his war cry, came up with the main Assassin force. Ezio fired his second shot into the belly of a Borgia guard, who came screaming up, flailing an evil-looking mace, but he had no time to reload. In any case, for close fighting, the Double Blade was the perfect weapon. Finding an alcove in the wall, he took shelter in it and, with practised hand, exchanged the Pistol for the Blade. Then he rushed back into the hall, looking for Cesare.

The battle in the mansion, and the area within its encircling walls, was short and bloody. The Borgia and Templar troops were unprepared for an attack of this magnitude, and they were trapped within the walls. They fought hard, and many a *condottiero* and Assassin recruit lay dead by the time it was over. The Assassins had the advantage of being already mounted, though, and few of the Borgia faction got to their horses before they were cut down.

It was late by the time the dust had settled. Ezio, bleeding from a flesh wound in his chest, had laid about him so furiously with the Double Blade that it had sliced through his own glove and cut his hand deeply. Around him lay a host of bodies, half, perhaps, of the assembly – those who had not been able to flee and ride off north into the night.

Cesare was not among them, though. He, too, had fled.

47

Much occurred in the weeks that followed. The Assassins sought Cesare frantically, but in vain. He did not return to Rome, and indeed Rome seemed purged of all Borgia and Templar influence, though Ezio and his companions remained on the alert, knowing that as long as the enemy lived, there was danger. They suspected there were still pockets of diehard loyalists just waiting for a signal.

Pius III proved to be a bookish and deeply religious man. Sadly, though, after a reign of only twenty-six days, his already frail health succumbed to the additional pressures and responsibilities the Papacy placed on it and, in October, he died. He had not, as Ezio had feared, been a puppet of the Borgia. Rather, during the short span of his supremacy, he set in motion reforms within the College of Cardinals that swept away all the corruption and sensuality fomented by his predecessor. There would be no more selling of cardinalates for money, and no more accepting of payments in order to let well-off murderers escape the gallows. Alexander VI's pragmatic doctrine of 'Let them live in order to repent' no longer held currency.

Most importantly, however, he had issued a warrant throughout the Papal States for the arrest of Cesare Borgia.

His successor was elected immediately and by an overwhelming majority. Only three cardinals opposed him – one of them being Georges d'Amboise, the Cardinal of Rouen, who vainly hoped to gain the Triple Tiara for the French. Following the check in his career caused by the election of Pius III, Giuliano della Rovere, Cardinal of San Pietro in Vincoli, had wasted no time in consolidating his supporters and assuring himself of the Papacy at the next opportunity, which he knew would come soon.

Julius II, as he styled himself, was a tough man of sixty, still vigorous, mentally and physically. He was a man of great energy, as Ezio would soon learn, a political intriguer and a warrior, and proud of his humble origins as the descendant of fishermen – for had not St Peter himself been a fisherman?

The Borgia threat still cast its shadow, though.

'If only Cesare would show himself,' growled Bartolomeo as he and Ezio sat in conference in the map room of his barracks.

'He will. But only when he's ready.'

'My spies tell me he plans to gather his best men to attack Rome through one of its principal gates.'

Ezio considered this. 'If Cesare's coming from the north, as seems almost certain, he'll try to get in by the gate near the Castra Praetoria. He might even try to retake the Castra itself as it's in a strong strategic position.'

'You're probably right.'

Ezio stood. 'Gather the Assassins. We'll face Cesare together.'

'And if we cannot?'

'That's fine talk from you, Barto! If we can't, I will face him alone.'

They parted company, arranging to meet in Rome later in the day. If there were going to be an attack, the Holy City would be ready for it.

Ezio's hunch proved right. He'd told Bartolomeo to summon the others to a church piazza near the Castro, and when they arrived, they made their way to the northern gate. It was already heavily defended, as Julius II had shown himself perfectly happy to accept Ezio's advice. The sight that met their eyes, a couple of hundred yards distant, was a sobering one. There was Cesare, on a pale horse, surrounded by a group of officers wearing the uniform of his own private army, and behind him was at least a battalion of his own troops.

Even at that distance, Ezio's keen ears could pick out Cesare's bombast – the odd thing was, why did people still fall for it?

'All of Italy shall be united, and you will rule at my side!' Cesare was proclaiming.

He turned and spotted Ezio and his fellow Assassins ranged along the ramparts of the gate. Then he rode alone a little closer, though not close enough to be within crossbow- or musket-range.

'Come to watch my triumph?' he shouted up at them. 'Don't worry. This isn't all my strength. Soon, Micheletto will arrive with my armies, but you will all be dead by then. I have enough men to deal with you.'

Ezio looked at him, then turned to look down at the mass of Papal troops, Assassin recruits and *condottieri* ranged beneath him inside the gate. He raised a hand, and the gatekeepers drew back the wooden staves that kept the gates shut. They stood ready to open them at his next signal. Ezio kept his hand raised.

'My men will never fail me!' cried Cesare. 'They know what awaits them if they do! Soon you will pass from this Earth, and my dominions will return to me.'

Ezio wondered if the New Disease had affected the balance of his mind. He let his hand drop, and below him the gates swung open and the Roman forces streamed out, cavalry first, infantry running behind. Cesare yanked at his reins, desperately, forcing the bit hard into his horse's mouth as he wheeled the steed round. The violence of his manoeuvre made his mount stumble, though, and he was quickly overtaken. As for his battalion, it broke and ran at the sight of the oncoming Roman brigades.

Well, well, thought Ezio. My question is answered.

These men were prepared to fight for money, but not from loyalty. You can't buy loyalty.

'Kill the Assassins!' yelled Cesare frantically. 'Uphold the honour of the Borgia!' It was all in vain, though. He was surrounded.

'Throw down your arms, Cesare,' Ezio called to him.

'Never!'

'This is not your city any more. You are no longer Captain-General. The Orsini and the Colonna families are on the side of the new Pope, and when some of them paid lip service to you, that was all it was – lip service. They were just waiting for the chance to reclaim the cities and estates you stole from them.'

A small deputation rode out through the gates now. Six knights in black armour, one of them bearing Julius II's crest – a sturdy oak tree – on a pennant. At their head, on a dapple-grey palfrey (the very opposite of a war horse) rode an elegantly dressed man whom Ezio instantly recognized as Fabio Orsini. He led his men straight up to the still-proud Cesare.

Silence fell.

'Cesare Borgia, called Valentino, sometime Cardinal of Valencia and Duke of Valence,' Orsini proclaimed – Ezio could see the triumphant twinkle in his eye – 'by order of His Holiness, Pope Julian II, I arrest you for the crimes of murder, betrayal and incest!'

The six knights fell in next to Cesare, two on each

side, one before and one behind. The reins of his horse were taken from him and he was tied to the saddle.

'No, no, no, *no*!' bawled Cesare. 'This is not how it ends!'

One of the knights flicked at Cesare's horse's rump, and it started forward at a trot.

'This is *not* how it ends!' Cesare yelled defiantly. 'Chains will not hold me!' His voice rose to a scream. 'I will not die by the hand of Man!'

Everybody heard him, but nobody was listening.

'Come on, you,' said Orsini crisply.

48

'I wondered what had happened to you,' Ezio said. 'Then I saw the chalk drawing of a pointing hand, and I knew you were signalling me, which is why I sent you a message. And now, here you are! I thought you might have slipped away to France.'

'Not me – not yet!' said Leonardo, brushing some dust off a chair at the Assassin's Tiber Island hideaway before sitting down. Sunlight streamed in through the high windows.

'I'm glad of it. Even gladder that you didn't get caught in the dragnet the new Pope has organized to capture any remaining Borgia supporters.'

'Well, you can't keep a good man down,' replied Leonardo. He was as finely dressed as ever, and didn't appear to have been affected by recent events at all. 'Pope Julius isn't a fool – he knows who'd be useful to him and who wouldn't, never mind what they've done in the past.'

'As long as they are truly repentant.'

'As you say,' Leonardo answered drily.

'And are you prepared to be useful to me?'

'Haven't I always been?' smiled Leonardo. 'Is there

anything to worry about, now that Cesare's under lock and key? It's only a matter of time before they take him out and burn him at the stake. Look at the list of arraignments! It's as long as your arm.'

'Maybe you're right.'

'Of course, the world wouldn't be the world without trouble,' said Leonardo, going off on another tack. 'It's all very well that Cesare's been brought down, but I've lost a valuable patron, and I see they're thinking of bringing that young whippersnapper Michelangelo here from Florence. I ask you! All he can do is knock out sculptures.'

'He's a pretty good architect, too, from what I hear. And not a bad painter either.'

Leonardo gave him a black look. 'You know that pointing finger I drew? One day soon, I hope, it's going to be at the centre of a portrait of a man – John the Baptist – pointing towards heaven. Now *that* will be a painting!'

'I didn't say he was as good a painter as you,' added Ezio quickly. 'And as for being an inventor . . .'

'He should stick to what he knows best, if you ask me.'

'Leo, are you jealous?'

'Me? Never!'

It was time to bring Leonardo back to the problem that was bothering Ezio, and the reason he'd responded to Leonardo's message that he was seeking him out.

He just hoped he could trust him, though he knew Leonardo well enough to understand what made him tick.

'Your former employer . . .' he began.

'Cesare?'

'Yes. I didn't like the way he said, "Chains will not hold me."'

'Come on, Ezio. He's in the deepest dungeon of the Castel Sant'Angelo. How the mighty are fallen, eh?'

'He still has friends.'

'A few misguided creatures may still think he has a future, but since Micheletto and his armies don't seem to have materialized, I can't see that there's any real danger.'

'Even if Micheletto failed to keep the remains of Cesare's forces together, which seems likely, since none of our spies in the countryside have reported any troop movements—'

'Look, Ezio, when news reached them of della Rovere's elevation to the Papacy, and of Cesare's arrest, the old Borgia army will have scattered like ants from a nest when you pour boiling water into it.'

'I won't rest easy until I know Cesare is dead.'

'Well, there is a way to find out.'

Ezio looked at Leonardo. 'Do you mean the Apple?'

'Where is it?'

'Here.'

'Then get it, let's consult it.'

Ezio hesitated. 'No, it's too powerful. I must hide it from Mankind for ever.'

'What, a valuable thing like that?' Leonardo shook his head.

'You said yourself, many years ago, that it should never be allowed to fall into the wrong hands.'

'Then all we have to do is keep it out of the wrong hands.'

'There is no guarantee that we can always do that.

Leonardo looked serious. 'Look, Ezio, if you ever decide to bury it somewhere, promise me one thing.'

'Yes?'

'Well, two things. First, hang on to it for as long as you need it. You should have everything on your side if your goal is to eradicate the Borgia and the Templars for ever. But when you are done, and you do hide it from the world, then think of it as a seed to be planted. Leave some kind of clue as to its whereabouts for such as may be able to find it. Future generations – perhaps future Assassins – may have need of the Apple's power one day, to use on the side of good.'

'And if it fell into the hands of another Cesare?'

'Back on Cesare, I see. Listen, why not put yourself out of your misery and see if the Apple can offer you any guidance?'

Ezio wrestled with himself for a few moments longer, then said, 'All right. I agree.'

He disappeared for a moment and then returned,

holding a square lead-covered box with a massive lock. From within his tunic, he took a key, tied to a silver chain around his neck, and opened the box. There, on a bed of green velvet, lay the Apple. It looked drab and grey, as it always did when inert, the size of a small melon and with a curiously soft and pliant texture, much like human skin.

'Ask it,' urged Leonardo, his eyes keen as he saw the Apple again. Ezio knew his friend was fighting down a desire to grab the thing and run, and he understood how great the temptation was for the polymath, whose thirst for knowledge at times threatened to overwhelm him and never let him rest.

Ezio held the Apple up and closed his eyes, concentrating his thoughts as he formulated questions. The Apple began to glow almost at once, and then it began to throw images onto the wall.

They came thick and fast and did not last long, but Ezio – and Ezio alone – saw Cesare escape from his prison and Rome. That was all, until the inchoate images on the wall coalesced to show a busy seaport, the water shining and glittering beneath a southern sun, and a fleet in the harbour. The vision dissolved, and then there was a view of a distant castle, or perhaps a fortified hill town, which Ezio somehow knew was far away – from the landscape and heat of the sun, it was certainly not in the Papal States of Italy. The architecture, too, looked foreign, but neither

Ezio nor Leonardo could place it. Then Ezio saw Mario's citadel at Monteriggioni, and the picture moved and shifted, taking him to Mario's secret study – the Sanctuary – where the Codex pages had been assembled. The concealed door to it was closed, and on the outside of it Ezio could see arcane figures and letters written. Next it was as if he were an eagle flying over the ruins of the Assassin former stronghold. Then, abruptly, the Apple went dead, and the only light in the room was once again provided by calm sunlight.

'He will escape! I have to go!' Ezio dropped the Apple back into its box and stood so abruptly he knocked over his chair.

'What about your friends?'

'The Brotherhood must stand, with or without me. That is how I have built it.' Taking it from its box again, Ezio placed the Apple in its leather bag. 'Forgive me, Leo, I have no time to waste.' He already had his Hidden Blade and his Bracer strapped on, and he packed the Pistol and some ammunition in his belt-wallet.

'Stop. You must think. You must plan.'

'My plan is to finish Cesare. I should have done it long ago.'

Leonardo spread his hands. 'I see that I cannot stop you. But I have no plans to leave Rome, and you know where my studio is.'

'I have a gift for you,' said Ezio. There was a small

strongbox on the table between them. Ezio laid a hand on it. 'Here.'

Leonardo rose. 'If this is goodbye, then keep your money. I do not want it.'

Ezio smiled. 'Of course it isn't goodbye, and of course you want it. You need it, for your work. Take it. Think of *me* as your patron, if you like, until you find a better one.'

The two men hugged each other.

'We shall see each other again,' said Ezio. 'You have my word. *Buona fortuna*, my oldest friend.'

What the Apple had predicted could not be amended, for the Apple showed the future as it would be, and no man or woman could alter that, any more than he or she could change the past.

As Ezio approached the Castel Sant'Angelo, he could see Papal guards, the new ones who wore the livery of Julius II, running out of the ancient fortress and dispersing in organized bands across the river and down the surrounding streets. Bells and trumpets rang out a warning. Ezio knew what had happened, even before a breathless captain he stopped told him:

'Cesare's escaped!'

'When?'

'The guards were being changed. About half an hour ago.' Half an hour! Exactly the time the Apple had shown it happening!

'Do you know how?'

'Unless he can walk through walls, we have no idea. But it looks as if he had friends on the inside.'

'Who? Lucrezia?'

'No. She hasn't stirred from her apartments since all this happened. The Pope has had her under house arrest since he took power. We've arrested two guards who used to work for the Borgia. One's a former blacksmith and he might have been able to jemmy the lock, though there's no sign of damage to the cell door, so they probably just used the key . . . if they're guilty.'

'Is Lucrezia giving us any trouble?'

'Strangely, not. She seems . . . resigned to her fate.'

'Don't trust her. Whatever you do, don't be lulled into a sense of false security by her manner. When she's quiet, she's at her most dangerous.'

'She's being guarded by Swiss mercenaries. They're hard as rocks.'

'Good.'

Ezio thought carefully. If Cesare had any friends left in Rome, and evidently he had, they'd get him out of the city as fast as they could. But the gates would already have been sealed, and from what he had seen, Cesare, bereft of the Apple and unskilled in Assassin techniques, would not be able to escape the dragnets and cordons being set up all over Rome.

That left one possibility.

The river!

The Tiber flowed into Rome from the north and left it to the west, where it flowed into the sea only a few miles away, at Ostia. Ezio remembered the slave traders he had killed, and that they had been in Cesare's pay. They would not have been the only ones! They could get him on a boat, or a small sea-going ship, disguised as a mariner or concealed under tarpaulin amongst the cargo. It wouldn't take long for a ship under sail or oars, going with the current, to reach the Tyrrhenian Sea, and from there – well, that depended on what Cesare's plans were. The thing was to catch him before he could put them into effect.

Ezio made his way by the quickest route down to the mid-town docks, which were closest to the Castel. The quays were chock-a-block with boats and ships of all shapes and sizes. It would be like looking for a needle in a haystack. Half an hour. He'd barely have had time to cast off yet, and the tide was only just rising.

Finding a quiet spot, Ezio crouched down and, without hesitation this time, took the Apple out of its pouch. There was nowhere here for it to project its images, but he felt that, if he trusted it, it would find another way of communicating with him. He held it as close to him as he dared, and closed his eyes, willing it to respond to his question.

It did not glow, but he could feel it grow warm through his gloves, and it began to pulse. As it did, strange sounds came from it, or were they sounds within his head? He wasn't sure. A woman's voice, oddly familiar though he could not place it, and seemingly quite distant, said softly but clearly, 'The small caravel with red sails at Pier Six.'

Ezio ran down to the quay. It took him a little time, pushing his way through a throng of busy, cursing mariners, to locate Pier Six, and when he did so, the boat that answered the Apple's description was just casting off. It, too, seemed familiar. Its decks were stacked with several sacks and boxes of cargo – boxes large enough to conceal a man – and on deck Ezio recognized, with a shock, the seaman he had left for dead after his abortive rescue of *Madonna* Solari. The man was limping badly as he approached one of the boxes and, with a mate, shifted its position. Ezio noticed that the box had holes bored along each side near the top. He ducked behind a rowing boat, which was raised on trestles for repainting, to keep out of sight, as the sailor he had lamed turned to look back towards the quay, scanning it, perhaps to check for pursuers.

He watched helplessly for a moment as the caravel pushed out into midstream, raising one of its sails to catch the stiff breeze out there. Even on horseback, he couldn't follow the little ship along the river's bank, since the path was often blocked or interrupted by buildings that came right up to the water. He had to find a boat for himself.

He made his way back to the quays and walked hastily along them. The crew of a shallop had just finished unloading, and the boat itself was still rigged. Ezio approached the men.

'I need to hire your boat,' he said urgently.

'We've just put in.'

'I'll pay handsomely.' Ezio delved into his purse and showed them a handful of gold ducats.

'We've got to get the cargo seen to first,' said one crew member.

'Where d'you want to go?' asked another.

'Downstream,' said Ezio, 'and I need to go now.'

'See to the cargo,' said a newcomer, approaching. 'I'll take the *signore*. Jacopo, you come with me. It won't take more than the two of us to sail her.'

Ezio turned to thank the newcomer and recognized, with a shock, that it was Claudio, the young thief he'd rescued from the Borgia.

Claudio smiled at him. 'One way of thanking you, *Messere*, for saving my life. And keep your money, by the way.'

'What are you doing here?'

'I wasn't cut out for thievery,' said Claudio. 'La Volpe saw that. I've always been a good sailor, so he lent me the money to buy this boat. I'm the master, and I do a good trade between here and Ostia.'

'We need to hurry. Cesare's Borgia's escaped.'

Claudio turned and barked out an order to his mate.

Jacopo sprang aboard and began to prepare the sails, then he and Ezio embarked, and the rest of the crew cast them off.

The shallop, free of cargo, felt light in the water. Once they reached midstream, Claudio put on as much sail as he could, and soon the caravel, which was more heavily laden, ceased to be a speck in the distance.

'Is that what we're after?' asked Claudio.

'Yes, please God,' replied Ezio.

'Better get your head down,' said Claudio. 'We're well-known on this stretch, but if they see you, they'll know what's up. I know that craft. It's run by an odd bunch; they don't socialize.'

'D'you know how many crew there are?'

'Five, usually. Maybe fewer. But don't worry. I haven't forgotten what La Volpe taught me – it still comes in handy, sometimes – and Jacopo here knows how to use a blackjack.'

Ezio sank beneath the low gunwale, raising his head from time to time just to check the closing distance between them and their objective. The caravel was a faster vessel than the shallop, though, despite it's heavier load, and Ostia was in sight before Claudio could draw alongside. Nevertheless he boldly hailed the caravel.

'You look pretty heavily laden,' he called. 'What you got on board – gold bullion?'

'None of your business,' the master of the caravel

snarled back from his place near the wheel. 'And back off. You're crowding my water.'

'Sorry, mate,' said Claudio, as Jacopo brought the shallop right alongside, bumping the caravel's fenders. Then he cried to Ezio, '*Now!*'

Ezio leapt from his hiding place across the narrow gap dividing the two ships. Recognizing him, the lame sailor gave out a strangled roar and lunged at him with a bill hook; it caught on Ezio's Bracer, and Ezio was able to pull him close enough to finish him with a deep thrust of the Hidden Blade into his side. While he'd been so engaged, he'd failed to notice another crewman stealing up on him from behind, brandishing a cutlass. He turned in momentary alarm, unable to avoid the descending blade, when a shot rang out and the man arched his back, letting his cutlass fall to the deck before crashing overboard himself.

'Look out!' yelled Jacopo, who was holding the shallop alongside as the master of the caravel strove to get clear. A third seaman had emerged from below decks and was using a crowbar to prise open the upright crate with holes along its top sides, while a fourth was crouching at his side, covering him with a wheel-lock pistol. No ordinary sailor would have access to such a gun, thought Ezio, remembering the battle with the slave-traders. Claudio leapt from the shallop onto the caravel's deck and threw himself on the man with the crowbar, while Ezio darted forward and skewered the wrist of the hand holding the gun with his Hidden Blade. It fired harmlessly into the deck and the man retreated, whimpering, holding his wrist, trying to stop the blood pulsing out of the ante-brachial vein.

The master of the boat, seeing his men routed, pulled a pistol himself and fired at Ezio, but the caravel lurched in the current at the crucial moment and the shot went wide, though not wide enough, as the ball sliced a nick in Ezio's right ear, which bled heavily. Shaking his head, Ezio levelled his gun at the master and shot him through the forehead.

'Quick!' he said to Claudio. 'You take the wheel of this thing and I'll deal with our friend here.'

Claudio nodded and ran to bring the caravel under control. Feeling the blood from his ear soak his collar, Ezio twisted his opponent's wrist hard to loosen his grip on the crowbar. Then he brought his knee up into the man's groin, seized his collar and half dragged, half kicked him to the gunwales, where he tossed him overboard.

In the silence that followed the fight, furious and confused shouts and imprecations could be heard coming from the crate.

'I will kill you for this. I will twist my sword in your gut and give you more pain than you could ever dream possible.'

'I hope you're comfortable, Cesare,' said Ezio. 'But

if you're not, don't worry. Once we get to Ostia, we'll arrange something a little more civilized for your return trip.'

'It's not fair,' said Jacopo from the shallop. 'I didn't get a chance to use my blackjack!'

PART TWO

Everything is permitted. Nothing is true.

Dogma Sicarii, I, i.

49

It was late in the spring of the Year of Our Lord 1504. The Pope tore open the letter a courier had just brought him, scanned it, then banged a meaty fist down on his desk in triumph. The other hand held up the letter, from which heavy seals dangled.

'God bless King Ferdinand and Queen Isabella of Aragon and Castile!' he cried.

'Good news, Your Holiness?' asked Ezio, seated in a chair across from him.

Julius II smiled darkly. 'Yes! Cesare Borgia has been safely delivered into one of their strongest and most remote *rocca*!'

'Where?'

'Ah, that's classified information, even to you. I can't take any chances with Cesare.'

Ezio bit his lip. Had Julius guessed what he'd do if he knew the location?

Julius continued reassuringly: 'Don't look so downcast, dear Ezio. I can tell you this: it's a massive fortress, lost in the plains of central north-eastern Spain, and totally impregnable.'

Ezio knew that Julius had had his reasons for not

having Cesare burned at the stake – in case it made a martyr of him – and he acknowledged that this was the next best thing. But still Cesare's words haunted him: 'Chains will never hold me.' Ezio felt in his heart that the only thing that would hold Cesare securely was Death. But he smiled his congratulations anyway.

'They've got him in a cell at the top of the central keep, in a tower one hundred and forty feet high,' Julius continued. 'We don't have anything more to worry about, as far as he's concerned.' The Pope looked at Ezio keenly. 'What I've just told you is *also* classified information, by the way, so don't go getting any ideas. In any event, at a word from me, they'll switch the location, just in case anyone goes looking for him and I get wind of it.'

Ezio let it go and changed tack. 'And Lucrezia? Do we have any news from Ferrara?'

'Well, her third marriage seems to be doing her good, though I must admit I was worried at first. The d'Este family are such a bunch of snobs that I thought the old Duke would never accept her as a suitable wife for his son. Marrying a Borgia! Talk about marrying beneath you! To them, it would be a bit like you getting hitched to your scullery maid!' The Pope laughed heartily. 'But she's settled down. Not a peep out of her. She's taken to exchanging love letters and even poems with her old friend Pietro Bembo – all above board, of course' – here Julius winked broadly – 'but she is basically a good and faithful wife to Duke Alfonso; she even goes to church and embroiders tapestries. Of course, there's no question of her coming back to Rome – *ever*! She'll end her days in Ferrara, and she should be thankful she's got away with her head still on her shoulders. All in all, I think it's safe to say that we've got that flock of Catalan perverts out of our hair for good.'

Ezio wondered if the Vatican spy ring was as well informed about the Templars as they were about the Borgia. Cesare had been their leader and continued to be so, even from prison. But about this the Pope kept his counsel.

He had to admit that the affairs of Italy had seen worse days than these. They had a strong Pope, who'd had the sense to retain Agostino Chigi as his banker, and the French were on the back foot. King Louis hadn't left Italy, but he had at least withdrawn to the north, where he seemed content to dig in. In addition, the French king had ceded Naples to King Ferdinand of Aragon.

'I hope so, Your Holiness.'

Julius looked at Ezio keenly. 'Listen, Ezio, I'm not a fool, so don't take me for one. Why do you think I brought you in as my counsellor? I know there are still pockets of Borgia loyalists around the countryside – and even a few diehards left in the city – but I have *other* enemies than the Borgia to worry about these days.'

'The Borgia could still pose a threat.'

'I don't think so.'

'And what are you doing about your other enemies?'

'I'm reforming the Papal Guard. Have you seen what good soldiers the Swiss are? Best mercenaries of the lot! And since they won independence from the Holy Roman Empire and Maximilian five or six years ago, they've been putting themselves out to hire. They're totally loyal and not very emotional – such a change from our own dear fellow countrymen – and I'm thinking of getting a brigade of them put together as my personal bodyguard. I'll arm them with the usual halberds and stuff, but I'm also issuing them with Leonardo's muskets.' He paused. 'All I need is a name for them.' He looked at Ezio quizzically. 'Any ideas?'

'How about the Swiss Guard?' suggested Ezio, who was a little tired.

The Pope considered this. 'Well, it's not startlingly original, Ezio. Frankly, I rather favoured the Julian Guard, but one doesn't like to sound too egotistical.' He grinned. 'All right, I'll use what you propose. It'll do for the time being, at any rate.'

They were interrupted by the sound of hammering and other building works, coming from above their heads, and other parts of the Vatican.

'Wretched builders,' commented the Pope. 'Still, it has to be done.' He crossed the room to a bell pull. 'I'll get someone to go and shut them up until we've finished. Sometimes I think builders are the greatest destructive force Man has yet invented.'

An attendant arrived at once and the Pope gave him his orders. Minutes later, amid muffled swearing, tools were downed, noisily.

'What are you having done?' asked Ezio, knowing that architecture vied with warfare as the Pope's two greatest passions.

'I'm having all the Borgia apartments and offices boarded up,' replied Julius. 'Far too sumptuous. More worthy of a Nero than the Leader of the Church. And I'm razing all their buildings on the roof of the Castel Sant'Angelo. I'll turn it into one big garden – I might even stick a little summer house up there.'

'Good idea,' said Ezio, smiling to himself. The summer house would doubtless be a real pleasure dome, fit, if not for a king, at least for trysts with one or other of the Pope's mistresses – female or male. The Pope's private life didn't concern Ezio. What mattered was that he was a good man and a staunch ally. And compared with Rodrigo, his corruptions were about as significant as a child's tantrums. Furthermore, he'd steadily continued the moral reforms of his predecessor, Pius III.

'I'm having the Sistine Chapel done up as well,' continued the Pope. 'It's so *dull*! So I've commissioned that bright young artist from Florence, Michelangelo what's-his-name, to paint some frescoes on the ceiling. Lots of religious scenes, you know the kind of thing. I thought of asking Leonardo, but his head's so full of ideas that he scarcely ever finishes a big painting. It's a pity. I rather liked that portrait he did of Francesco del Giocondo's wife . . .'

Julius interrupted himself and looked at Ezio. 'But you didn't come here to talk about my interest in modern art.'

'No.'

'Are you *sure* you're not taking the threat of a Borgia revival too seriously?'

'I think we *should* take it seriously.'

'Look – my army has regained most of the Romagna for the Vatican. There's no army left for the Borgia to fight with.'

'Cesare is still alive! With him as a figurehead—'

'I hope you're not questioning my judgement, Ezio? You know my reasons for sparing his life. In any case, where he is now, he's as good as buried alive.'

'Micheletto is still at large.'

'Pah! Without Cesare, Micheletto is nothing.'

'Micheletto knows Spain well.'

'He's nothing, I tell you.'

'He knows Spain. He was born in Valencia. He's the bastard nephew of Rodrigo.'

The Pope, who, despite his years, was a large and vigorous man still in the prime of his life, had been pacing the room during this last exchange. Now, he returned to the desk, placed his large hands on it and leant threateningly over Ezio. His manner was convincing.

'You are letting your worst fears run away with you,'

he said. 'We don't even know whether Micheletto is still alive or not.'

'I think we should find out, once and for all.'

The Pope pondered Ezio's point and relaxed slightly, sitting down again. He tapped the heavy signet ring on his left hand with the index finger of his right.

'What do you want to do?' he asked heavily. 'Don't expect any resources from me. The budget's over-stretched as it is.'

'The first thing is to locate and destroy any last diehards in the city of Rome itself. We may find someone who knows something about Micheletto – his whereabouts or his fate – then . . .'

'Then?'

'Then, if he's still alive . . .'

'You'll destroy him?'

'Yes.' *Unless he turns out to be more useful to me alive*, Ezio thought.

Julius sat back. 'I am impressed by your determination, Ezio. It almost frightens me. And I am glad I'm not an enemy of the Assassins myself.'

Ezio looked up sharply. 'You know about the Brotherhood?'

The Pope made a tent of his fingers. 'I always needed to know who the enemies of my enemy were. But your secret is safe with me. As I told you, I am not a fool.'

50

'Your instinct is right. I will guide you and guard you, but I do not belong to you and soon you must let me go. I have no power over him that controls me. I must obey the will of the Master of the Apple.'

Ezio was alone in his secret lodgings, holding the Apple in his hands as he tried to use it to help him locate his quarry in Rome, when the mysterious voice came to him again. This time he could not tell if the voice was male or female, or whether it came from the Apple or somewhere in his mind.

Your instinct is right. But, also, *I have no power over him that controls me.* Why then had the Apple shown him only hazy images of Micheletto – just enough to tell him that Cesare's henchman was still alive. And it could not – or would not – pinpoint Cesare's location. At least for now.

Suddenly Ezio realized something his inner self had always known: that he should not abuse its power by overusing it and that he should not become dependent on the Apple. Ezio knew that it was his own will that had blurred the answers he sought. He must not be slothful. He must fend for himself. One day he would have to again, anyway.

He thought of Leonardo. What could that man not do if he had the Apple? And Leonardo, the best of men, nevertheless invented weapons of destruction as easily as he produced sublime paintings. Might the Apple not only have the power to help Mankind, but to corrupt it? In Rodrigo's or Cesare's hands — if either of them had ever been able to master it — it could have become the instrument, not of salvation, but destruction!

Power is a potent drug, and Ezio did not want to fall victim to it.

He looked at the Apple again. It seemed inert in his hands now, but as he placed it back in its box, he found he could hardly bear to close the lid. What paths could it not open up for him?!

No, he must bury it. He must learn to live by the Code without it. But not yet!

He had always sensed in his heart that Micheletto lived. Now he knew it for a fact. And while he lived, he would do his utmost to free his evil master, Cesare.

Ezio had not told Pope Julius his full plan: he intended to seek out Cesare and kill him, or die in the attempt.

It was the only way.

He would use the Apple only when he had to. He had to keep his own instincts and powers of deduction sharp, in anticipation of the day when the Apple would no longer be in his possession. He would hunt down the Borgia diehards in Rome without it. Only if he failed, within three days, to unearth them, would he resort to its power again. He still had his friends – the girls of The Rosa in Fiore, La Volpe's thieves and his fellow Assassins – and with their help, how could he fail?

Ezio knew that the Apple would, in ways he could not fully comprehend, help him, as long as he respected its potential. Perhaps that was its secret. Perhaps no one could ever fully master it, except a member of the race of ancient Adepts who had left the world in trust to Humanity, to make or break it, as their will elected.

He closed the lid and locked the box.

Ezio summoned a meeting of the Brotherhood on Tiber Island that night.

'My friends,' he started, 'I know how hard we have striven, and I believe that victory may be in sight, but there is still work to do.'

The others, all except Machiavelli, looked at each other in surprise.

'But Cesare is muzzled!' cried La Volpe. 'For good!'

'And we have a new Pope, who has always been an enemy of the Borgia,' added Claudia.

'And the French are driven back,' put in Bartolomeo. 'The countryside is secure. And the Romagna is back in Papal hands.'

Ezio held out a hand to quieten them. 'We all know that a victory is not a victory until it is absolute.'

'And Cesare may indeed be muzzled, but he lives,' said Machiavelli quietly. 'And Micheletto . . .'

'Exactly,' Ezio said. 'And as long as there are pockets of Borgia diehards, both here and in the Papal States, there is still seed from which a Borgia revival may grow.'

'You are too cautious, Ezio. We have won,' cried Bartolomeo.

'Barto, you know as well as I do that a handful of city states in the Romagna remain loyal to Cesare. They are strongly fortified.'

'Then I'll go and sort them out.'

'They will keep. Caterina Sforza's army is not strong enough to attack them from Forlì, but I have sent messengers requesting that she keep a close eye on them. I have a more pressing job for you.'

Oh God, thought Ezio, *why does my heart still skip a beat when I mention her name?*

'Which is?'

'I want you to take a force to Ostia and keep watch on the port. I want to know about any suspicious ships coming in and out of the harbour. I want you to have messengers on horseback ready to bring news to me here the instant you have anything to report.'

Bartolomeo snorted. 'Sentry duty! Hardly the sort of work for a man of action like me.'

'You will get as much action as you need when the time is right to move against the rebel city states I've mentioned. In the meantime, they live in hope, waiting for a signal. Let them live in hope, it'll keep them quiet. Our job is to snuff out that hope – for ever.'

Machiavelli smiled. 'I agree with Ezio,' he said.

'Well, all right. If you insist,' Bartolomeo replied grumpily.

'Pantasilea will enjoy the sea air after her ordeal.'

Bartolomeo brightened. 'I hadn't thought of that.'

'Good.' Ezio turned to his sister. 'Claudia, I imagine the change of regime hasn't affected business at The Rosa in Fiore too badly?'

Claudia grinned. 'It's funny how even princes of the Church find it hard to keep the devil between their loins in abeyance – however many cold baths they say they take.'

'Tell your girls to keep their ears to the ground. Julius has the College of Cardinals firmly under his control, but he still has plenty of enemies with ambitions of their own, and some of them might just be mad enough to think that if they could free Cesare, they could use him as a means of furthering their own ends. And keep an eye on Johann Burchard, too.'

'What? Rodrigo's Master of Ceremonies? Surely he's harmless enough. He hated having to organize all those orgies. Isn't he just a functionary?'

'Nevertheless, anything you hear – especially if it's about diehard factions still at large here in Rome – let me know.'

'It'll be easier now that we no longer have Borgia guards breathing down our necks every minute of the day.'

Ezio smiled a little absently. 'I have another question to ask. I have been too busy to visit, and it troubles me, but how is our mother?'

Claudia's face clouded. 'She keeps the accounts, but, Ezio, I fear she is failing. She seldom goes out. She speaks more and more often of Giovanni, and of Federico and Petruccio.'

Ezio fell silent for a moment, thinking of his lost father and brothers. 'I will come when I can,' he said. 'Give her my love and ask her to forgive my neglect.'

'She understands the work you have to do. She knows that you do it not only for the good of us all, but for the sake of our departed kinsmen.'

'The destruction of those who killed them shall be their monument,' said Ezio, his voice hard.

'And what of my people?' asked La Volpe.

'Gilberto, your people are vital to me. My recruits remain loyal, but they see that life returns to normal, and most of them long to return to the lives they led before we persuaded them to join us in the struggle to throw off the Borgia yoke. They retain their skills, but they are not sworn members of the Brotherhood, and I cannot expect them to bear the yoke that we bear, for it is a yoke that only death will relieve us of.'

'I understand.'

'I know the men and women under your command are city-bred. Some country air will make a change.'

'How do you mean?' asked La Volpe suspiciously.

'Send your best people into the towns and villages around Rome. There will be no need to go further out than Viterbo, Terni, L'Aquila, Avezzano and Nettuno. I doubt if, beyond the rough circle round Rome that those towns define, we'd find much. There can't be many diehards left, and those there are will want to be within striking distance of Rome.'

'They'll be hard to find.'

'You must try. You know yourself how even a small force in the right place can do untold damage.'

'I'll send out my best thieves and disguise them as peddlers.'

'Report anything you find back to me, especially news of Micheletto.'

'Do you really think he's still out there somewhere? Mightn't he have gone back to Spain, or at least the Kingdom of Naples? If he isn't dead already, that is.'

'I am convinced he's still alive.'

La Volpe shrugged. 'That's good enough for me.'

When the others had gone, Machiavelli turned to Ezio and said, 'What about me?'

'You and I will work together.'

'Nothing would give me greater pleasure, but before we go into details, I have a question.'

'Go ahead.'

'Why not use the Apple?'

Ezio, sighing, explained as best he could.

When he'd finished Machiavelli looked at him, took out his little black notebook and wrote in it at length. Then he stood up, crossed the room and sat down next to Ezio, squeezing his shoulder affectionately as he did so. Any such gesture from Machiavelli was as rare as hen's teeth.

'Let's get down to business,' he said.

'This is what I have in mind,' said Ezio.

'Tell me.'

'There are women in this city who may help us. We must seek them out and talk to them.'

'Well, you picked the right man for the job. I am a diplomat.'

Gaining access to the first was easy – Pope Julius had seen to that – but getting her to talk wasn't.

She received them in a sumptuous parlour on the *piano nobile* of her large house, whose windows (on four sides) provided sublime vistas of the once-great city, now part crumbling, but also part magnificent, after the last few Popes had poured money into self-aggrandisement.

'I don't see how I can help you,' she said after listening to them, although Ezio noticed that she didn't meet their eyes.

'If there are pockets of diehards in the city, we need

to know about them, *Altezza*, and we need your help,' said Machiavelli. 'If we find out later that you have held out on us . . .'

'Don't threaten me, young man,' retorted Vannozza. '*Dio mio!* Do you know how long ago it is since Rodrigo and I were lovers? Well over twenty years!'

'Perhaps your children . . . ?' asked Ezio.

She smiled grimly. 'I expect you are wondering how a woman like me could have produced such a brood,' she said. 'But I tell you there is very little Cattanei blood in them. Well, in Lucrezia, perhaps; but Cesare . . .' She broke off and Ezio could see the pain in her eyes.

'Do you know where he is?'

'I know no more than you do, and I don't care to. It's years since I've even seen him, though we lived in the same city. He is dead to me.'

Clearly the Pope was being very careful to keep Cesare's whereabouts secret. 'Perhaps your daughter knows?'

'If I don't, why should she? She lives in Ferrara now. You could go and ask her, but it's a long way north, and the Holy Father has forbidden her ever to return to Rome.'

'Do you see her?' asked Machiavelli.

Vannozza sighed. 'As I said, Ferrara's a long way north. I don't care to travel much these days.'

She looked around the room, glancing at the servants

who stood near the door, and occasionally at the water clock. She had offered them no refreshment and seemed eager for them to go. An unhappy woman, she seemed ill at ease and constantly kneaded her hands together, but was that because she was concealing something, or because she was being forced to talk about people she'd clearly rather not discuss?

'I have – or rather *had* – eight grandchildren,' she said unexpectedly. Ezio and Machiavelli knew that Lucrezia had had several children by her various husbands, but few had survived childhood. People said that Lucrezia had never taken pregnancy very seriously, and that she had a habit of partying and dancing right up to the moment of her accouchement. Had that alienated her from her mother? Cesare had a daughter, Louise, who was a child of four.

'Do you see any of them?' asked Machiavelli.

'No. Louise is still in Rome, I think, but her mother has made sure that she's more French than Italian.'

She rose then, and the servants, as if on cue, opened the room's ornate double doors.

'I wish I could be of more assistance . . .'

'We thank you for your time,' said Machiavelli drily.

'There are other people you might like to talk to,' said Vannozza.

'We intend to visit the *Princesse* d'Albret.'

Vannozza pressed her lips together. '*Buona fortuna*,' she said, without conviction. 'You'd better hurry, too.

435

I hear she's making preparations to leave for France. Perhaps, if I'm lucky, she'll come and say goodbye.'

Ezio and Machiavelli had risen, too, and made their farewells.

Once outside in the street, Machiavelli said, 'I think we'll have to use the Apple, Ezio.'

'Not yet.'

'Have it your own way, but I think you're a fool. Let's go and see the princess. Lucky we can both speak French.'

'Charlotte d'Albret won't be leaving for France today – I've got men watching her *palazzo*. There's someone else I want to see first. In fact, I'm surprised Vanozza didn't mention her.'

'Who?'

'Giulia Farnese.'

'Doesn't she live in Carbognano these days?'

'My spies tell me she's in town, so we ought to take advantage of that.'

'What makes you think we'll get any more out of her than we got out of Vannozza?'

Ezio smiled. 'Giulia was Rodrigo's last mistress and he was passionate about her.'

'I remember when the French captured her. He was beside himself.'

'And then the French foolishly ransomed her for three thousand ducats. He'd have paid twenty times that amount to get her back. He'd probably have struck any kind of deal they wanted. But I guess that's what happens when your mistress is over forty years younger than you are: you get besotted.'

'It didn't stop him dumping her when she turned twenty-five, though.'

'Yes. She was too old for him by then! Let's hurry.'

They made their way north, through the narrow streets in the direction of the Quirinale.

On the way, Machiavelli noticed that Ezio was becoming increasingly ill at ease.

'What's the matter?' he asked.

'Have you not noticed anything?'

'What?'

'Don't look round!' Ezio was terse.

'No.'

'I think we're being followed . . . by a woman.'

'Since when?'

'Since we left Vannozza's *palazzo*.'

'One of her people?'

'Perhaps.'

'Alone?'

'I think so.'

'Then we'd better shake her.'

Impatient though they were to get on, they slowed their pace, looking in shop windows and even pausing at a wine booth. There, over the rim of his beaker, Ezio caught sight of a tall, athletically built blonde woman dressed in a good, but unassuming dark green robe of a lightweight material. She'd be able to move fast in clothes like that if the need arose.

'I've got her,' he said.

They both scanned the wall of the building against which the booth was erected. It was a new place, constructed in a fashionably rusticated style of large roughened slabs of stone separated by sunken joints. At intervals, iron rings for tethering horses had been let into the wall.

It was perfect.

They made their way to the back of the booth, but there was no way out there.

'We'll have to be quick,' said Machiavelli.

'Watch me!' replied Ezio, putting his beaker down on a table near the entrance. A few seconds later he was halfway up the wall, with Machiavelli close behind him. Bystanders gaped as the two men, their capes fluttering in the breeze, disappeared over the rooftops, leaping across alleyways and streets, sending tiles skeetering down to smash on the cobbles, or flop in the mud of unmade lanes as the people below ducked or jumped out of the way.

Even if she'd been able to, the woman couldn't climb vertical walls in a long skirt, but Ezio saw that her dress had a carefully disguised slit to the thigh on one side, enabling her to run, and she was tearing through the streets after them, thrusting aside anyone who got in her way. Whoever she was, she was well-trained.

At last they lost her. Breathing hard, they came to a halt on the roof of Sant Niccolò de Portiis, and lay down flat, keenly scanning the streets below. There seemed to be no one unduly suspicious amongst the citizens in the streets, though Ezio thought he recognized two of La Volpe's thieves working the crowd, using sharp little knives to cut purses. Presumably they were two who hadn't been selected to go out into the surrounding countryside, but he'd have to ask Gilberto about that later.

'Let's go down,' suggested Machiavelli.

'No, it's easier to stay out of sight up here and we haven't far to go.'

'She didn't seem to have much trouble following us. Lucky for us there was that roof with a high wall round it, where we could change direction without her noticing.'

Ezio nodded. Whoever she was, she'll be reporting back by now. He wished she were on their side. As things stood, they'd have to get to the large apartment Giulia kept in Rome, and then get out of the Quirinale district fast. Maybe he should detail a couple of his recruits to watch their backs on any future forays. The Borgia diehards were lying low under the new Pope's tough regime, but only to lull the authorities into a false sense of security.

Giulia's first husband, Orsino Orsini, had been happy to turn a blind eye to the affair his nineteen-year-old wife had embarked on with the sixty-two-year-old Rodrigo Borgia. She had a daughter, Laura, but no one knew if she was the child of Orsino or Rodrigo. Rodrigo, despite being a Valencian by birth, had risen through the Church until he controlled the Vatican's purse strings, and he had shown his gratitude to his delicious young mistress by installing her in a brand-new house (which she'd long since been obliged to quit) conveniently close to the Vatican, and by making her brother Alessandro a cardinal. The other cardinals called him 'the Cardinal of the Skirts' behind his back, though of course never in Rodrigo's presence. Giulia they called 'the Bride of Christ'.

Ezio and Machiavelli dropped to the ground in the *piazza* onto which the princess's apartment block fronted. A couple of Papal Guards stood nearby, but otherwise the square was deserted. The guards' tunics bore, on their shoulders, the crest of the della Rovere family: a massive oak tree, root and branch, now surmounted by the Triple Tiara and the keys of Saint Peter. Ezio recognized the men – six months earlier they'd been in Borgia livery. How times had changed, as now they saluted him and he acknowledged them.

'Fuckers,' said Machiavelli under his breath.

'A man's got to work,' said Ezio. 'I'm surprised that you, of all people, can take issue with such a bagatelle.'

'Come on.'

They'd arrived without due notice and it took some

trouble to convince the Farnese attendants – six blue fleurs-de-lys ranged on a yellow background on their capes – to admit them, but, as Ezio knew, *signora* Farnese was at home. She received them in a room that was half as gaudy but twice as tasteful as La Vannozza's. At thirty, she had more than retained the beauty of her youth and the intelligence that informed it. Despite them being unexpected guests, the *signora* had *Moscato* and *panpetati e mielati* served for them immediately.

It soon became clear that she knew nothing and was innocent of any Borgia taint, despite her previous closeness to that execrable family (as Machiavelli called them). Machiavelli saw that she had moved on, and when he and Ezio asked her about her once close friendship with Lucrezia, all she said was, 'What I saw of her was her good side. I think she fell too much under the bullying sway of her father and brother. I thank God she is rid of them.' She paused. 'If only she had met Pietro Bembo earlier. Those two were soul mates. He might have taken her to Venice and saved her from her dark side.'

'Do you see her still?'

'Alas, Ferrara is so far to the north, and I have my hands full, running Carbognano. Even friendships die, Ezio Auditore.'

An image of Caterina Sforza blew into his mind before he had a chance to extinguish it. Ah, God, how the thought of her caught at his heart still.

441

It was late afternoon by the time they left. They kept a close eye out for anyone shadowing them, but there was nobody.

'We must use the Apple,' said Machiavelli again.

'This is but the first day of three. We must learn to trust ourselves and our own intelligence, and not lean on what has been vouchsafed us.'

'The matter is pressing.'

'One more appointment today, Niccolò. Then, perhaps, we shall see.'

The *Princesse* d'Albret, *Dâme* de Chalus, Duchess of Valentinois' was, according to the gatekeepers of her opulent villa in the Pinciano district, not at home. But Ezio and Machiavelli, impatient and tired, pushed past anyway, and encountered Charlotte in her *piano nobile*, engrossed in packing. Huge chests full of costly linen and books and jewellery stood about the half-empty room, and in a corner, the confused little four-year-old Louise, Cesare's only legitimate heir, played with a wooden doll.

'You are damned impertinent,' said the cold-looking blonde who confronted them, her dark brown eyes flashing fire.

'We have the imprimatur of the Pope himself,' lied Ezio. 'Here is his warrant.' He held up a blank parchment, from which impressive-looking seals hung.

'Bastards,' said the woman coolly. 'If you think I know where Cesare is imprisoned, you are fools. I never

442

want to see him again, and I pray that none of his *sang maudit* has passed into the veins of my innocent little daughter.'

'We also seek Micheletto,' said Machiavelli implacably.

'That Catalan peasant,' she spat. 'How should I know?'

'Your husband told you how he might escape, if taken,' suggested Machiavelli. 'He depended on you.'

'Do you think so? I don't! Perhaps Cesare confided in one of his dozens of mistresses. Perhaps the one that gave him the *malattia venerea*?'

'Do you—?'

'I never touched him after the first pustules appeared, and he at least had the decency to keep away from me and wallow in the gutter with his whores from then on. And father eleven brats by them. At least I am clean, and my daughter, too. As you see, I am getting out of here. France is a far better country than this wretched hellhole. I'm going back to La Motte-Feuilly.'

'Not to Navarre?' asked Machiavelli slyly.

'I see you are trying to trick me.' She turned her cold, bony face towards them and Ezio noticed that her beauty was marred – or enhanced – by a dimple in the middle of her chin. 'I do not choose to go to that province merely because my brother married the heiress to the throne and thereby became king.'

'Does your brother remain faithful to Cesare?' asked Ezio.

443

'I doubt it. Why don't you stop wasting my time and go and ask him?'

'Navarre is far away.'

'Exactly. Which is why I wish you and your saturnine friend were on your way there. And now it is late and I have work to do. Please leave.'

'A wasted day,' commented Machiavelli as they took to the streets again, the shadows lengthening.

'I don't think so. We know that none of those closest to Cesare are harbouring or protecting him.' Ezio paused. 'All the most important women in his life hated him, and even Giulia had no time for Rodrigo.'

Machiavelli grimaced. 'Imagine being fucked by a man old enough to be your grandfather.'

'Well, she didn't do too badly out of it.'

'We still don't know where Cesare is. Use the Apple.'

'No, not yet. We must stand on our own feet.'

'Well,' sighed Machiavelli. 'At least God gave us good minds.'

At that moment, one of Machiavelli's spies came running up out of breath. He was a small, bald man with alert eyes and a wild face.

'Bruno?' said Machiavelli, surprised and concerned.

'*Maestro*,' panted the man. 'Thank God I've found you.'

'What is it?'

'The Borgia diehards! They sent someone to follow you and *Maestro* Ezio—'

'And?'

'Sure that you were out of the way, they have taken Claudia!'

'My sister! Sweet Jesus – how?' gasped Ezio.

'She was in the square outside Saint Peter's – you know those rickety wooden colonnades the Pope wants to tear down?'

'Get on with it!'

'They took her – she was organizing her girls, getting them to infiltrate . . .'

'Where is she now?'

'They have a hideout in the Prati – just to the east of the Vatican. That's where they've taken her.' Bruno quickly gave them the details of where Claudia was being held prisoner.

Ezio looked at Machiavelli.

'Let's go!' he said.

'At least we've found out where they are,' said Machiavelli, drily as ever, as the two of them bounded up to the rooftops again, running and leaping across Rome until they came to the Tiber, where they crossed the *ponte* della Rovere and made haste again towards their goal.

The place Machiavelli's spy, Bruno, had indicated was a ramshackle villa just north of the Prati district market. But its crumbling stucco belied a brand-new iron-bound front door, and the grilles on the windows were new and freshly painted.

Before Machiavelli could stop him, Ezio had gone up to the door and hammered on it.

The judas set into it opened and a beady eye regarded them, then, to their amazement, the door swung smoothly back on well-oiled hinges.

They found themselves in a nondescript courtyard where there was no one about. Whoever had opened the door – and closed it firmly behind them – had disappeared. There were doors on three sides of the yard. The one opposite the entrance was open And above it was a tattered banner bearing a black bull in a golden field.

'Trapped,' said Machiavelli succinctly. 'What weapons do you have?'

Ezio had his trusty Hidden Blade, his sword and his dagger. Machiavelli carried a light sword and a stiletto.

'Come in, gentlemen, you are most welcome,' said a disembodied voice from a window overlooking the courtyard somewhere high up in the wall above the open door. 'I think we have something to trade with.'

'The Pope knows where we are,' retorted Machiavelli loudly. 'You are lost. Give yourselves up. The cause you serve is dead.'

A hollow laugh was his rejoinder. 'Is it indeed? I think not. But come in. We knew you'd take the bait. Bruno has been working for us for a year now.'

'Bruno?'

'Treachery runs in families, and dear Bruno's is no

exception. All Bruno wanted was a little more cash than you were giving him. He's worth it. He managed to inveigle Claudia here, in the hope of meeting one of the English cardinals. They sit on the fence, as the English always do, and Claudia hoped to swing him to your side and get a little information out of him. Unfortunately, Cardinal Shakeshaft met with a terrible accident – he was run over by a carriage and died on the spot – but your sister, Ezio, is still alive – just – and I am sure she is longing to see you.'

'*Calma,*' said Machiavelli as the two men looked at each other. Ezio's blood boiled. He'd spent a day trying to trace the diehards only to be led straight to them.

He dug his fingernails into his palms.

'Where is she, *bastardi*?' he yelled.

'Come in.'

Cautiously, the two Assassins approached the dark entrance.

There was a dimly lit hall, in whose centre, on a plinth, was a bust of Pope Alexander VI by Adkingnono (as Machiavelli guessed), the coarse features – the hooked nose, the weak chin, the fat lips – done to the life. There was no other furniture, and again there were three doors leading off the three walls facing the entrance; only that facing the entrance was open. Ezio and Machiavelli made for it and, passing through the door, found themselves in another bleak room. There was a table, on which various rusty surgical instruments were arrayed on a stained cloth, glittering under the light of a single candle. Next to it was a chair, and on it Claudia was seated, half undressed and bound, her hands in her lap, her face and breasts bruised, a gag in her mouth.

Three men detached themselves from the shadows that obscured the back wall. Ezio and Machiavelli were aware of others, too, men and women, behind them and on either side. Those they could see in the dim light wore the now grubby colours of the Borgia and all were heavily armed.

Claudia's eyes spoke to Ezio's. She managed to wrestle her branded finger free enough to show him: she had not given in, despite the torture. She was a true Assassin. Why had he ever doubted her?

'We know how you feel about your family,' said the chief diehard, a gaunt man of perhaps fifty summers whom Ezio did not recognize. 'You let your father and brothers die. Your mother we need not bother about as she is dying anyway. But you can still save your sister. If you wish. She's already well struck in years and doesn't even have any children, so perhaps you won't bother.'

Ezio controlled himself. 'What do you want?'

'In exchange? I want you to leave Rome. Why don't you go back to Monteriggioni and build the place up again? Do some farming. Leave the power game to those who understand it.'

Ezio spat.

'Oh dear,' said the thin man. He seized Claudia by the hair and, producing a small knife, cut her left breast.

Claudia screamed.

'She's damaged goods at the moment, but I'm sure she'll recover under your tender care.'

'I'll take her back and then I'll kill you. Slowly.'

'Ezio Auditore! I gave you a chance, but you threaten me – and you are in no position to threaten. If there's any killing to be done, it will be by me. Forget Monteriggioni – a sophisticated lady like *Madonna* Claudia would doubtless hate it there anyway – your destiny is here: to die in this room.'

The men and women on each side closed in, drawing swords.

'I told you – we're trapped,' said Machiavelli.

'At least we've found the bastards,' replied Ezio, as each man looked the other in the eye. 'Here!' He flung a handful of poison darts to his companion. 'Make them work.'

'You didn't tell me you came prepared.'

'You didn't ask.'

'I did.'

'Shut up.'

Ezio fell into a crouch as the diehards advanced. Their leader held the thin knife to Claudia's throat.

'Let's go!'

As one, they drew their swords. And with their other hands they threw the poison darts with deathly aim.

The Borgia supporters toppled on either side, as Machiavelli closed in, slicing and slashing with his sword and dagger, pushing against the diehards who tried to crush him – in vain – by force of numbers.

Ezio had one goal – to kill the thin man before he could rip open Claudia's throat. He leapt forward, seizing the man by the gizzard, but his adversary was as slippery as an eel and wrenched himself to one side without letting go of his victim.

Ezio finally managed to wrestle him to the floor and, grasping his right hand in his left, forced the point of the thin knife the man was holding close to his own throat. Its point touched the jugular artery.

'Have mercy,' babbled the diehard leader. 'I served a cause I thought was true.'

'How much mercy would you have shown my sister?' asked Ezio. 'You filth! You are finished.'

There was no need to release the Hidden Blade. 'I told you it would be a slow death,' said Ezio, drawing the knife down to the man's groin, 'but I am going to be merciful.' He slid the knife back up and sliced the man's throat open. Blood bubbled in the man's mouth. '*Bastardo!*' he gurgled. 'You will die by Micheletto's hand!'

'*Requiescat in Pace,*' said Ezio, letting the man's head

fall, though for once he spoke the words without much conviction.

The other diehards lay dead or dying about them as Machiavelli and Ezio hastened to untie the harsh cords that bound Claudia.

She had been badly beaten, but the diehards had at least drawn a line at leaving her honour intact.

'Oh, Ezio.'

'Are you all right?'

'I hope so.'

'Come on. We must get out of here.'

'Gently.'

'Of course.'

Ezio took his sister in his arms and, followed by a sombre Machiavelli, walked out into the dying light of day.

'Well,' said Machiavelli, 'at least we know for sure that Micheletto is still alive.'

51

'We've found Micheletto,' said La Volpe.

'Where?' Ezio's voice was urgent.

'He's holed up in Zagarolo, just to the east of here.'

'Let's get him then.'

'Not so fast. He's got contingents from the Romagna towns still loyal to Cesare. He'll put up a fight,' La Volpe warned.

'Let him.'

'We'll have to organize.'

'Then let's do it. Now!'

Ezio, with Machiavelli and La Volpe, summoned a meeting on Tiber Island that night. Bartolomeo was still in Ostia, watching the port, and Claudia was resting up at The Rosa in Fiore, tended by her ailing mother after her terrible ordeal. There were enough thieves and recruits to muster a force of one hundred men and women able to bear arms, and there was no need of other *condottieri* to back them up.

'He's encamped in the old gladiatorial school, Ludus Magnus, and he's got maybe two hundred and fifty men with him.'

'What does he intend to do?' Ezio wondered.

'No idea. Break out, head for safety in the north with the French, who knows?'

'Whatever his plans are, let's nip them in the bud.'

By early dawn, Ezio had gathered a mounted force. They rode out the short distance to Zagarolo and had surrounded Micheletto's encampment by sunrise. Ezio bore his crossbow on one arm, over the Bracer, and, on the other, his Poison Blade. There would be no quarter taken, though he wanted to take Micheletto alive.

The defenders put up a fierce fight, but in the end Ezio's forces were victorious, scattering the diehards under Micheletto's command like chaff.

Among the wounded, dead and dying, Micheletto stood proud, defiant to the last.

'We take you, Micheletto da Corella, as our prisoner,' said Machiavelli. 'No more shall you infect our nation with your schemes.'

'Chains will never hold me,' snarled Micheletto. 'Any more than they will hold my master.'

They took him in chains to Florence, where he took up residence in the cells of the Signoria, in the very cell where Ezio's father Giovanni had spent his last hours. There, the governor of the city, Piero Soderini, together with his friend and adviser Amerigo Vespucci, and Machiavelli, interrogated and tortured him, but they could get nothing out of him and so, for the moment, they left him to rot. His days as a killer seemed done.

Ezio, for his part, returned to Rome.

'I know you are a Florentine at heart, Niccolò,' he told his friend at their parting, 'but I shall miss you.'

'I am also an Assassin,' replied Machiavelli. 'And my first loyalty will always be to the Brotherhood. Let me know when you next have need of me and I will come to you without delay. Besides,' he added darkly, 'I haven't given up all hope of squeezing information out of that vile man.'

'I wish you luck,' said Ezio.

He wasn't so sure they'd break him. Micheletto might be an evil man, but he was also very strong-willed.

52

'Ezio, you must put Micheletto out of your mind,'
Leonardo told him as they sat in the Ezio's studio in
Rome. 'Rome is at peace. This Pope is strong. He has
subdued the Romagna. He is a soldier as much as he is
a man of God, and perhaps under him all Italy will
find peace at last. And although Spain controls the
south, Ferdinand and Isabella are our friends.'

Ezio knew that Leonardo was happy in his work.
Pope Julius had employed him as a military engineer
and he was tinkering with a host of new projects,
though he sometimes pined for his beloved Milan,
which was still in French hands, and talked in his more
depressed moments of going to Amboise, where he
had been offered all the facilities he needed whenever
he wanted them. He often talked of going once he had
finished Pope Julius's commissions.

As for the Romagna, Ezio's thoughts turned often
to Caterina Sforza, whom he still loved. A letter he'd
received from her told him that she was now involved
with the Florentine ambassador. Ezio knew her life
remained in turmoil and that, despite Julius's support,
she had been dismissed from Forlì by her own people

on account of the cruelty she had displayed when putting down the rebellion against her late intractable second husband, Girolamo Feo, and that she was growing old in retirement now, in Florence. At first his letters to her were angry, then remonstrative, then pleading, but she replied to none of them, and finally he accepted that she had used him and that he would never see her again.

Thus it was with relationships between men and women. The lucky ones last, but too often when they end, they end for good, and deep intimacy is replaced by a desert.

Ezio was hurt and humiliated, but he didn't have time to wallow in his misery. His work in Rome consolidating the Brotherhood, and above all holding it in readiness, kept him busy.

'I believe that as long as Micheletto lives, he will do his best to escape, free Cesare Borgia, and help him rebuild his forces,' Ezio maintained.

Leonardo had problems of his own, regarding his feckless boyfriend, Salai, and barely listened to his old friend. 'No one has ever escaped from the prison in Florence,' he said. 'Not from those cells.'

'Why don't they kill him?'

'They still think they might get something out of him, though personally I doubt it,' said Leonardo. 'In any case, the Borgia are finished. You should rest. Why don't you take your poor sister and return to Monteriggioni?'

'She has grown to love Rome and would never return to such a small place now, and, in any case, the Brotherhood's new home is here.'

This was another sadness in Ezio's life. After an illness, his mother, Maria, had died. Claudia, after her abduction at the hands of the Borgia diehards, had given up The Rosa in Fiore, and the brothel was now controlled by Julius's own network of spies, who used different girls. La Volpe had negotiated with his colleague Antonio in Venice to send Rosa, now older and statelier but no less fiery than she had been when Ezio knew her in La Serenissima, to Rome to run it.

There was also the problem of the Apple.

So much had changed, and when Ezio was summoned to the Vatican for an interview with the Pope, he was unprepared for what he would hear.

'I'm intrigued by this device you've got,' said Julius, coming as always straight to the point.

'What do you mean, Your Holiness?'

The Pope smiled. 'Don't prevaricate with me, my dear Ezio. I have my own sources and they tell me you have something you call the Apple which you found under the Sistine Chapel some years ago. It seems to have great power.'

Ezio's brain raced. How had Julius found out about the Apple? Had Leonardo told him? Leonardo could be curiously innocent at times, and he had wanted a new patron very badly. 'It was vouchsafed to me, in a manner

457

I find hard to explain to you, by a force from an antique world to help us. And it has, but I fear its potential. I cannot think that the hands of Man are ready for such a thing, but it is known as a Piece of Eden. There are other pieces, some lost to us and others perhaps left hidden.'

'It sounds very useful. What does it do?'

'It has the ability to control men's thoughts and desires. But that is not all: it is able to reveal things undreamed of.'

Julius pondered this. 'It sounds as if it might be very useful to me. Very useful indeed. But it could also be used *against* me in the wrong hands.'

'It is what the Borgia were misusing when they tried to gain total ascendancy. Luckily, Leonardo, to whom they gave it to research, kept its darkest secrets from them.'

The Pope paused once again in thought. 'Then I think it better if we leave it in your care,' he said at last. 'If it was vouchsafed to you by such a power as you describe, it would be rash to take it away from you.' He paused again. 'It seems to me that, when you feel you have no further use for it, you should hide it in a safe place, and maybe, if you wish, leave some kind of clue for any worthy successor – possibly a descendant of yours – who perhaps alone will be able to understand it, so that it may once more have a use in the world for future generations. For I do believe, Ezio Auditore –

and perhaps I am being guided by God in this – that in our time, no one but you should have custody of it. It may be that there is some unique quality, some sense that enables you to withstand using it irresponsibly.'

Ezio bowed and said nothing, but in his heart he acknowledged Julius's wisdom, and he couldn't have agreed more with his judgement.

'By the way,' Julius said, 'I don't care for Leonardo's boyfriend – what's his name? Salai? He seems very shifty to me and I wouldn't trust him. It's a pity Leo seems to, for apart from that one little weakness the man is a genius. Do you know, he's developing some kind of lightweight, bulletproof armour for me? I don't know where he gets his ideas from.'

Ezio thought of the Codex Brace Leonardo had re-created for him and he smiled to himself. Well, why not? Now he could guess the source of the Pope's information about the Apple, and he knew that Julius had revealed it deliberately. Fortunately, Salai was more of a fool than a knave, but he'd have to be watched all the same, and, if necessary, removed.

After all, he knew what the nickname Salai meant: 'little satan'.

53

Ezio made his way back to Leonardo's studio soon after his audience with the Pope, but he failed to find Salai at home, and Leonardo was shamefaced about him. He had sent Salai into the country and no amount of persuasion would get him to reveal where. This would have to be a problem for La Volpe and his Thieves' Guild to deal with. It was clear that Leonardo was embarrassed. Perhaps he would learn to keep his mouth shut in front of the boy in future, for he knew that Ezio could get Leonardo into a deal of trouble. Fortunately Leonardo was still more of a help than a hindrance, and a good friend, too, and Ezio made this very clear to him. But if there were any more breaches of security – well, no one was indispensable.

Leonardo wanted to make it up to Ezio, though.

'I've been thinking about Cesare,' he said, with his usual eagerness.

'Oh?'

'In fact I'm very glad you've come. I've found someone I think you should meet.'

'Does he know where Cesare is?' asked Ezio.

If he did, thought Ezio, Micheletto would cease to matter. If he didn't, Ezio might even consider letting Micheletto escape from prison – for Ezio knew the *Signoria* well – and using the man to lead him to his master. It was a dangerous plan, he knew, but he wasn't going to use the Apple except as a last resort. He found the burden of the Piece of Eden increasingly disturbing, having had a series of strange dreams, of countries and buildings and technology that couldn't possibly exist . . . Then he remembered the vision of the castle, the remote castle in a foreign land. That at least was a recognizable building of his own time. But where could it be?

Leonardo brought him back from his musings.

'I don't know if he knows where Cesare is. But he's called Gaspar Torella, and he was Cesare's personal physician. He's got some ideas I think are interesting. Shall we go and see him?'

'Any lead is a good one.'

Dottore Torella received them in a spacious surgery on the Appenine, whose ceiling was hung with herbs, but also with strange creatures such as dried bats, the little corpses of desiccated toads and even a small crocodile. Torella was wizened and a little bent in the shoulders, but he was younger than he looked, his movements were quick, almost lizard-like, and the eyes behind his spectacles were bright. He was also another Spanish expatriate, but he was reputed to be brilliant, so Pope Julius had spared him – he was, after all, a scientist with no interest in politics.

What he was interested in, and talked about at length, was the New Disease.

'You know, both my former master and his father Rodrigo had it. It's very ugly indeed in its final stages, and I believe it affects the mind, and may have left both Cesare and the former Pope affected in the brain. Neither had any sense of proportion, and it may still be strong in Cesare – wherever they've put him.'

'Do you have any idea?'

'My guess is somewhere as far away as possible, and in a place he could never escape from.'

Ezio sighed. So much was surely obvious.

'I have called the disease the *morbus gallicus* – the French disease,' Dr Torella plunged on enthusiastically. 'Even the present Pope has it in the early stages and I am treating him. It's an epidemic, of course. We think it came from Columbus's sailors, and probably Vespucci's too, about seven or eight years ago when they brought it back from the New World.'

'Why call it the French disease then?' asked Leonardo.

'Well, I certainly don't want to insult the Italians, and the Portuguese and the Spanish are our friends. But it broke out first among French soldiers in Naples. It starts with lesions on the genitals and it can deform the hands, the back and the face, indeed the whole head. I'm treating it with mercury, to be drunk or rubbed on the skin, but I don't think I've found a cure.'

'That is certainly interesting,' said Ezio. 'But will it kill Cesare?'

'I don't know.'

'Then I must still find him.'

'Fascinating,' said Leonardo, excited by yet another new discovery.

'There is something else I've been working on,' said Torella, 'which I think is even more interesting.'

'What is it?' asked his fellow scientist.

'It's this: that people's memories can be passed down – preserved – from generation to generation in the bloodline. Rather like some diseases. I like to think I'll find a cure for *morbus gallicus*, but I feel it may be with us for centuries.'

'What makes you say that?' said Ezio, strangely disturbed by the man's remark about memories being passed down through the generations.

'Because I believe it's transmitted, in the first instance, through sex – and we'd all die out if we had to do without that.'

Ezio grew impatient. 'Thank you for your time,' he said.

'Don't mention it,' replied Torella. 'And by the way, if you really want to find my former master, I think you could do worse than look in Spain.'

'In Spain? Where in Spain?'

The doctor spread his hands. 'I'm a Spaniard, so is Cesare. Why not send him home? It's just a hunch. I'm sorry I can't be more specific.'

Ezio thought, *It would be like looking for a needle in a haystack* . . . But it may be a start.

54

Ezio no longer kept the location of his lodgings a total secret, but only a few knew where they were. One of them was Machiavelli. One night Ezio was awoken by him at four in the morning when there was a deliberate, urgent knocking at the door.

'Niccolò! What are you doing here?' Ezio was instantly alert, like a cat.

'I have been a fool.'

'What happened? You were working in Florence – you can't be back so soon.' Ezio already knew something grave must have happened.

'I have been a fool,' Machiavelli repeated.

'What's going on?'

'In my arrogance, I kept Micheletto alive,' sighed Machiavelli. 'In a secure cell, to question him.'

'You'd better tell me what's going on.'

'He has escaped! On the eve of his execution!'

'From the *Signoria*? How?'

'Over the roof. Borgia diehards climbed onto it during the night and killed the guards, then they lowered a rope. The priest who gave him his last confession was a Borgia sympathizer – he's being burnt at the

-stake today – and he smuggled a file into his cell. Micheletto sawed through just one bar on the window. He's a big man, but it was enough for him to squeeze out and climb up. You know how strong he is. By the time the alarm was raised, he was nowhere to be found in the city.'

'We must seek him out, and' – Ezio paused, suddenly seeing an advantage in this adversity – 'having found him, see where he runs. He may yet lead us to Cesare. He is insanely loyal, and without Cesare's support his own power is worthless.'

'I have light cavalry scouring the countryside even now, trying to hunt him down.'

'But there are plenty of small pockets of Borgia die-hards – like those who rescued him – willing to shelter him.'

'I think he's in Rome. That's why I've come here.'

'Why Rome?'

'We have been too complacent. There are Borgia supporters here too. He will use them to make for Ostia and try to board a ship there.'

'Bartolomeo is in Ostia; no one will escape him and his *condottieri* there. I'll send a rider to alert him.'

'But where will Micheletto go?'

'Where else but Valencia, his home town.'

'Ezio, we must be sure. We must use the Apple, now, this minute, to see if we can locate him.'

55

Ezio turned and, in the bedroom of his lodgings, out of sight of Machiavelli, he drew the Apple from its secret hiding place. Carefully, he took it out of its container with gloved hands and placed it on the table in his bedroom. Then he concentrated. Very slowly the Apple began to glow, and then its light brightened until the room was filled with a cold illumination. Next, images – dim at first and indistinct – flickered onto the wall and resolved themselves into something it had shown Ezio before.

'It's a strange, remote castle in a brown, barren landscape; very old, with a massive outer barbican, four main towers and an impregnable-looking square keep at its centre,' he explained to Machiavelli.

'Where is that *rocca*? What is the Apple telling us?' Machiavelli shouted from the other room.

'It could be anywhere,' Ezio muttered to himself. 'From the landscape, Syria perhaps? Or,' he said, as with a sudden rush of excitement he remembered Doctor Torella's words, 'Spain!' he shouted to Machiavelli. 'Spain!'

'Micheletto can't be in Spain.'

'I am certain he plans to go there.'

'Even so, we don't know where this place is. There are many, many castles in Spain, and many similar to this one. Consult the Apple again.'

But when Ezio tried again, the image remained unchanged: a solidly built castle on a hill, a good 300 years old, surrounded by a little town. The image was monochrome and all the houses, the fortress and the countryside were an almost uniform brown. There was only one spot of colour, a bright flag on a pole on the very top of the keep.

Ezio squinted at it.

A white flag with a red, ragged cross in the form of an 'X'.

His excitement mounted. 'The military standard of King Ferdinand and Queen Isabella of Spain!'

'You can see their standard!' yelled Machiavelli from the other room, his voice contracting with excitement. 'Good. Now we know what country. But we still don't know where it *is*. Or why we're being shown it. Is Micheletto on his way there? Ask the Apple again.'

The vision faded and was replaced by a fortified hill town, from whose fort flew a white flag crisscrossed with red chains, their links filled in yellow, which Ezio recognized as the flag of Navarre. Then there was a third and final picture: a massive, wealthy seaport, with ships drawn up on a glittering sea and an army gathering. But no clue about the exact location of any of these places.

Everyone was in place. Couriers rode daily between the points where the Brotherhood had set up bases. Bartolomeo was beginning to enjoy Ostia, and Pantasilea loved it. Antonio de Magianis still held the fort in Venice. Claudia had returned, for the time being, to Florence to stay with her old friend Paola, who kept an expensive house of pleasure on which The Rosa in Fiore had been modelled, and La Volpe and Rosa watched over Rome.

It was time for Machiavelli and Ezio to go hunting.

Leonardo was reluctant to let Ezio and Machiavelli enter his studio, but eventually he allowed them in. 'Leo, we need your help,' Ezio said, coming straight to the point.

'You weren't very pleased with me last time we met.'

'Salai shouldn't have told anyone about the Apple.'

'He got drunk in a wine booth and blurted it out to impress. Most of the people around him didn't know what he was talking about, but there was an agent of Pope Julius within earshot. He is very contrite.'

'Where is he now?' asked Ezio

Leonardo squared his shoulders. 'If you want my help, I want payment.'

'What are you talking about? What kind of payment?'

'I want you to leave him alone. He means a lot to me, he is young, with time he will improve.'

'He's a little sewer rat,' said Machiavelli.

'Do you want my help or don't you?'

Ezio and Machivelli looked at each other.

'All right, Leo, but keep him on a very close rein, or by God we'll show no mercy next time.'

'All right. Now, what do you want me to do?

'We're having problems with the Apple. It isn't as acute as it was. Could there be something wrong with it mechanically?' asked Machiavelli.

Leonardo stroked his beard. 'You have it with you?'

Ezio produced the box. 'Here.' He took it out and placed it carefully on Leonardo's work table.

Leonardo examined it with equal care. 'I don't really know what this thing is,' he conceded finally. 'It's dangerous, it's a mystery and it's very, very powerful, and yet only Ezio seems able to control it. God knows, when it was in my power in the old days under Cesare, I tried, but I only partially succeeded.' He paused. 'No, I don't think the word "mechanical" describes this thing. If I weren't more of a scientist than an artist, I'd say it had a mind of its own.'

Ezio remembered the voice that had come from the Apple. What if Leonardo were right?

'Micheletto is on the run,' said Ezio urgently. 'We need to locate him, and fast. We need to pick up his trail before it's too late.'

'What do you think he's planning?'

'We are almost certain that Micheletto has decided to go to Spain to locate and liberate his master Cesare, and they will then attempt to return to power. We need to stop them,' said Machiavelli.

'And the Apple?'

'Shows an image of a castle. It must be somewhere in Spain because it flies the Spanish flag, but the Apple doesn't – or won't, or can't – give its location. We also saw an image of a town flying the Navarrese flag, and a seaport with an army gathering to embark there, but the Apple gave us nothing on Micheletto at all,' said Ezio.

'Well,' said Leonardo. 'Cesare can't have jinxed it because no one's that clever, so it must – how can I put this? – have *decided* not to be helpful.'

'But why would it do that?'

'Why don't we ask it?'

Ezio once again concentrated, and this time a most divine music, sweet and high, came to his ears. 'Can you hear it?' he asked.

'Hear what?' replied the others.

Through the music came the voice he had heard before: 'Ezio Auditore, you have done well, but I have more than played my part in your career and you must now return me. Take me to a vault you will find under the Capitoline, and leave me there to be found by future members of your Brotherhood. But be quick! You must then ride post-haste to Naples, where Micheletto is embarking for Valencia. This knowledge is my last gift to you. You have more than enough power of your own to have no further need of me. I will lie in the ground until future generations have need of me, so you must leave a sign to indicate my burial place. Farewell, Mentor of the Brotherhood! Farewell! Farewell!'

The Apple ceased to glow and looked dead, like an old leather-bound ball.

Swiftly, Ezio told his friends what had been imparted to him.

'Naples? Why Naples?' Leonardo asked.

'Because it's in Spanish territory and we have no jurisdiction there.'

'And because he knows – somehow – that Bartolomeo is policing Ostia,' said Ezio. 'We must make all speed. Come!'

Dusk was falling as Machiavelli and Ezio carried the Apple in its box down into the catacombs below the Colosseum, and, passing through the dreadful gloomy rooms of the remains of Nero's Golden House, carried torches before them as they made their way through a maze of tunnels under the old Roman Forum to a spot near the church of San Nicola in Carcere. There they found a secret door within the crypt, and behind it was a small vaulted room, in the centre of which stood a plinth. On this they placed the Apple in its box and withdrew. Once closed, as if by magic the door ceased to be visible, even to them, but they knew where it was and near it they drew the sacred, secret symbols that only a member of the Brotherhood would understand. The same symbols they inscribed at regular intervals along their way back, and again at the mouth of the entrance near the Colosseum from which they emerged.

After meeting Leonardo again, who had insisted on joining them, they rode hard to Ostia, where they took a ship for the long coastal journey south to Naples. They arrived on Midsummer's Day, 1505 – Ezio's forty-sixth birthday.

They didn't go into the teeming, hilly town, but remained among the fortified docks, splitting up to search among the sailors, tradesmen and travellers busy about their fishing smacks, their shallops and their caravels, carracks and cogs, visiting the taverns and brothels, and all in frantic haste, for no one, Spanish, Italian or Arab, seemed to have an answer to their question: 'Have you seen a tall, thin man, with huge hands and scars on his face, seeking passage to Valencia?'

After an hour of this, they regrouped on the main quay.

'He's going to Valencia. He must be,' said Ezio through gritted teeth.

'But if he isn't?' put in Leonardo. 'And we charter a ship and sail to Valencia anyway, we might lose days and even weeks, and so lose Micheletto altogether.'

'You're right.'

The Apple didn't lie to you. He was – or, if we're lucky – *is* here. We just have to find somebody who knows for sure.'

A whore sidled up, grinning. 'We're not interested,' snapped Machiavelli.

She was a pretty blonde woman of about forty years of age – tall and slim, with dark brown eyes; long, shapely legs; small breasts; broad shoulders; and narrow hips. 'But you *are* interested in Micheletto da Corella.'

Ezio swung round on her. She looked so like Caterina that for a moment his head swam. 'What do you know?'

She snapped back with all the hardness of a whore, 'What's it worth to you?' Then came the professional smile again. 'I'm Camilla, by the way.'

'Ten ducats.'

'Twenty.'

'Twenty! You'd earn less than that in a week on your back!' snarled Machiavelli.

'Charmer. Do you want the information or not? I can see you're in a hurry.'

'Fifteen then,' said Ezio, pulling out his purse.

'That's better, *tesoro*.'

'Information first,' said Machiavelli as Camilla held out her hand for the money.

'Half first.'

Ezio handed over eight ducats.

'Generous with it,' said the woman. 'All right. Micheletto was here last night. He spent it with me and I've never earned my money harder. He was drunk, he abused me and he ran off at dawn without paying. Pistol in his belt, sword, ugly-looking dagger. Smelt pretty bad, too, but I know he had money because I guessed what he'd do and took my fee out of his purse when he finally fell asleep. Of course, the bouncers

475

from the brothel followed him, though I think they were a little scared, so they kept their distance a bit.'

'And?' said Machiavelli. 'None of this is of any use to us so far.'

'But they kept him in sight. He must have chartered a ship the night before because he went straight to a carrack called the *Marea di Alba*, and sailed on the dawn tide.'

'Describe him,' said Ezio.

'Big, huge hands – I had them round my neck so I should know – broken nose, scarred face, some of the scars seemed to make him look like he had a permanent grin. He didn't talk much.'

'How d'you know his name?'

'I asked, just to make conversation, and he told me,' she answered simply.

'And where was he going?'

'One of the bouncers knew one of the seamen and asked him as they were casting off.'

'Where?'

'Valencia.'

Valencia. Micheletto was going back to his birthplace – which was also the home town of a family called Borgia.

Ezio handed her seven more ducats. 'I'll remember you,' he said. 'If we find you're lying, you'll regret it.'

It was already midday. It took them another hour to find a fast caravel available for charter and agree the price. Another two hours were needed to victual and prepare the ship, then they had to wait for the next tide. A caravel is faster than a carrack, but, even so, it was early evening before the sails were raised. And the sea was choppy and the wind against them.

'Happy birthday,' said Leonardo to Ezio.

58

The Fates were against them, too. Their ship sailed well, but the sea remained rough and they encountered squalls that took the sails aback. The hoped-for chance of catching up with Micheletto at sea was long gone when, five days later, their battered caravel put into port at Valencia.

It was a prosperous and booming place, but none of the three – Ezio, Leonardo or Machiavelli – were familiar with it. The recently built Silk Exchange vied in grandeur with the Bell Tower, the Torres de Quart and the Palau de la Generalitat. It was then a powerful Catalan city, one of the most important trading ports in the Mediterranean Sea, but it was also confusing and teeming with Valencianos, who mingled in the busy streets with Italians, Dutch, English and Arabs, creating a babel of languages in the streets.

Fortunately the *Marea di Alba* was moored near to where the caravel docked, and the two captains were friends.

'*Ciao*, Alberto!'

'*Ciao*, Filin!'

'Bad voyage?' said Alberto, a stout man of thirty, as

he stood on the poop deck of his vessel, supervising the loading of a mixed cargo of silk, and rare, expensive coffee, for the return journey.

'*Brutissimo*.'

'So I see from the state of your ship. But there'll be a good sea and a fair wind for the next week, so I'm hurrying back as soon as I can.'

'I won't be so lucky. When did you get in?'

'Two days ago.'

Ezio stepped up. 'And your passenger?'

Alberto spat. '*Che tipo brutto* – but he paid well.'

'Where is he now?'

'Gone. I know he was in the town, asking questions, but he's well-known here and he has many friends, believe it or not.' Alberto spat again. 'Not of the best sort, either.'

'I'm beginning to wish I hadn't come,' whispered Leonardo. 'One thing I am not is a man of violence.'

'Where has he gone, do you know?'

'He was staying at the Lobo Solitario, you could ask there.'

They disembarked and made straight for the Lone Wolf Inn, after Alberto had given them directions and added, darkly, 'It is not a place for gentlemen.'

'What makes you think we are gentlemen?' said Machiavelli.

Alberto shrugged.

Ezio scanned the busy quay. Out of the corner of his

eye he saw three or four shady characters watching them, causing him to check his Bracer and Hidden Blades. He slung his bag over his shoulder, leaving his arms free for his sword and dagger. Noticing this, Machiavelli did the same while Leonardo looked askance.

Together they made their way into the town, remaining on the alert even though the shady characters had disappeared.

'Shall we stay at the same place as our quarry?' suggested Ezio. 'It'll be the best place to be to find out where he is.'

The inn was located in a narrow street of tall tenements, which twisted away from one of the main thoroughfares. It was a low, dark building, in contrast to the sparkling newness of most of the rest of the town. The dark wooden door was open, giving onto a dark interior. Ezio entered first; Leonardo, reluctantly, last.

They had reached the centre of the vestibule in which furniture and a long, low counter could only just be made out, when the door behind them banged shut. The ten men who had been lurking in the shadows, their eyes already accustomed to the dark, now pounced, flinging themselves on their victims with guttural cries. Ezio and Machiavelli immediately threw down their bags and, in one movement, Machiavelli drew his sword and dagger and closed on his first assailant. The glint of blades flashed in the semi-darkness of the room, which was big enough for there to be plenty of space to move, helping both sides.

'Leonardo!' shouted Ezio. 'Get behind the counter, and catch this.'

He threw his sword to Leonardo, who caught it, dropped it and picked it up again in the space of a second. Ezio unleashed the Hidden Blade as one of the men fell on him, stabbing him with it in the side and penetrating his guts. The man stumbled, clutching his belly, blood bubbling between his hands. Meanwhile, Machiavelli strode forward, holding his sword aloft. Quick as a flash he thrust his sword into the throat of his first opponent, while simultaneously slicing into the groin of a second with his other blade. The man fell to the floor with an anguished roar, fumbling vainly at his wound, while twitching with agony. Machiavelli closed in and glanced briefly at his victim, kicking out viciously and silencing the man in an instant.

The assailants drew back for a moment, surprised that their ambush had not achieved its purpose, and at the alacrity of their intended victims, then they renewed their attack with redoubled vigour. There was a cry from Machiavelli as he was cut in his sword arm from behind, but in a moment Ezio was upon his friend's assailant, plugging his dagger straight into the man's face.

The next thing Ezio knew, a big man, who smelt of prison straw and stale sweat, crept up behind him and threw a garrotte around his neck. Ezio choked and dropped his dagger, raising his hand to tear at the rope being tightened on his windpipe. Machiavelli leapt over and stabbed at the big man, cutting into him and causing him to cry out in sudden pain, but Machiavelli had missed his mark and the man was able to thrust him away. It was enough to make him lose his grip on the garrotte, though, so that Ezio was able to spring free.

The light was too dim to make out the black-cloaked forms of the surviving attackers, but the failure of their immediate assault seemed to have unnerved them.

'Get them!' an unpleasant, guttural voice said. 'We are still five against three.'

'*Sancho dieron en el pecho!*' shouted another as Ezio smashed his heavy dagger into the sternum of one flabby creature, splitting it as neatly as if it were a chicken breast. 'We are four against three. *Nos replegamos!*'

'No!' ordered the first man who had spoken. '*Aguantels mentres que m'escapi!*'

The man spoke in Catalan. The big man who had tried to strangle him. The man who still had the stink of prison clinging to him. Micheletto!

Moments later the door to the street was flung open and slammed shut again as Micheletto made his escape, momentarily silhouetted in the streetlight. Ezio rushed after him, but his path was blocked by one of the three surviving attackers, who was holding a scimitar aloft ready to bring it down on his head. Ezio was too close to wield either of his weapons effectively, so he threw himself to the side, out of the way. As he rolled to safety, the scimitar came swinging down, but the man had struck so violently, expecting the sword's path to be interrupted by a body, that it continued its trajectory, burying itself in the man's genitals. With a howl, he dropped the sword and fell to the ground, clutching his manhood in an attempt to stop the fountaining blood, and writhing in agony.

The last two men struggled with each other to reach the door in order to escape, and one succeeded; but the second, already wounded in the fight, was tripped by Machiavelli and crashed to the ground as Leonardo threw himself across him to prevent his rising. When it became clear he would not, Leonardo stood clear and Ezio knelt and turned him over, pressing the point of the Hidden Blade into his nostril.

'I am Ezio Auditore, Mentor of the Assassins,' he said. 'Tell me where your master is bound and I will show you mercy.'

'Never!' croaked the man.

Ezio pressed the point of the Blade in further. Its razor-sharp edges slowly beginning to slit the man's nose.

'Tell me!'

'All right! He is going to the Castillo de la Mota.'

'What is there?'

'That is where Cesare is held prisoner.'

Ezio pushed the Blade.

'Have mercy! I speak the truth, but you will never succeed in thwarting us. The Borgia will return to power and rule all Italy with an iron fist. They will swarm into the south and throw the filthy Spanish monarchy out, and then they will destroy the Kingdoms of Aragon and Castile and rule them too.'

'How do you know where Cesare is? It is a dark secret known only to Pope Julius and his Council, and to King Ferdinand and his.'

'Do you not think we have spies of our own? Even in the Vatican? They are good, these spies. This time, better than yours.'

With a sudden movement, the man brought up his right arm. In it was a small knife, which he aimed at Ezio's heart. Ezio just had time to block the blow with his left arm, and the knife skeetered harmlessly off his Bracer and onto the floor.

'Long Live the Royal House of Borgia!' the man cried.

'*Requiescat in Pace*,' said Ezio.

'Welcome to Valencia,' Leonardo muttered.

59

The Lone Wolf Inn was deserted but there were beds of a sort, and as it was late by the time Ezio and his companions had recovered from the bloody tussle with Micheletto's diehards, they had no choice but to spend the night there. They found wine, water and food – bread, onions and some salami – and even Leonardo was too hungry to refuse it.

The following morning, Ezio rose early, eager to find horses for the journey ahead. Their ship's captain, Filin, was at the docks seeing to the refitting of his battered ship. He knew of the remote Castle of La Mota, and gave them directions, as far as he could, as to how to find it, but it would be a long and arduous journey of many days. Filin also helped organize their horses, but preparations still took another forty-eight hours, since they had to provision themselves as well. The journey would take them north-west across the brown sierras of central Spain. There were no maps, so they travelled from one town or village to another, using the list of names Filin had given them.

They passed out of Valencia, and after several days' hard riding on their first set of horses – Leonardo complaining bitterly – they entered the beautiful mountain country around the tiny hill town of Cuenca. Then down again onto the flat plain of Madrid, and through the royal city itself, where the bandits who tried to rob them soon found themselves dead on the road. From there they went north to Segovia, which is dominated by its Alcázar, where they spent the night as the guests of the seneschal of Queen Isabella of Castile.

They continued on through open country where they were attacked and almost robbed by a gang of Moorish highwaymen, who had somehow slipped through the fingers of King Ferdinand and survived in open country for twelve years. Ferdinand, King of Aragon, Sicily, Naples and Valencia, was founder of the Spanish Inquisition and scourge of the Jews – with dire consequences for his nation's economy – through his Grand Inquisitor, Tomás de Torquemada; but through marriage to his equally ugly wife, Isabella, he had united Aragon and Castile and begun the road to making Spain a single nation. Ferdinand had ambitions on Navarre, too, though Ezio wondered how far the bigoted king's designs would have an impact on that country, where Cesare had such close family ties, being the brother-in-law of its French king.

Fighting weariness, they rode on, praying that they would be in time to thwart Micheletto's plan. But despite all the haste they had made, he had had a good start on them.

60

Micheletto and his small band of diehards reined in their horses and stood up in their stirrups to look at the castle of La Mota. It dominated the small town of Medina del Campo, and had been built to protect it from the Moors.

Micheletto had good eyesight, and even from that distance he could see the red scarf that Cesare had hung from his cell window. It was the topmost window in the central tower and there was no need for bars because no one had ever escaped from La Mota. You could see why. The walls had been crafted by skilled eleventh-century masons and the stone blocks were so skilfully laid that the surface was as smooth as glass.

It was good that they had devised this plan using the red scarf, otherwise it might have been hard for Micheletto to find his master. The go-between, a La Mota sergeant-of-the-guard, who'd been recruited to the Borgia cause in Valencia some time earlier, was perfect, and, once bribed, he had proved totally dependable.

Getting Cesare out was going to be difficult, though. His cell door was permanently watched by two Swiss Guards from a troop on loan from Pope Julius, all of whom were totally inflexible and incorruptible. So getting Cesare out the easy way was impossible.

Micheletto measured the height of the central tower with his eyes. Once inside the place, they'd have to scale an impossible wall to a cell 140 feet up. So, that was out. Micheletto considered the problem. He was a practical man, but his speciality was killing, not problem solving, and his thoughts led him to reflect on the main tool of his trade: rope.

'Let's ride a little closer,' he said to his companions. They'd all dressed in hunting outfits, rather than their customary black, in order to arouse little or no suspicion. He had ten men with him, and each of them carried, as part of their standard equipment, a length of rope.

'We don't want to get too close,' said his lieutenant, 'or the guards on the ramparts will see us.'

'And what will they see? A hunting party coming to Medina to revictual. Don't worry, Girolamo.'

The remark gave Micheletto the germ of an idea and he continued, 'We'll ride right up to the town.'

It was about half an hour's ride, during which Micheletto was more than usually silent, his battered brow deeply furrowed. Then, as they approached the walls of the city, his face cleared.

'Rein in,' he said.

They did so and Micheletto looked them over. The youngest, a man of eighteen called Luca, had no hair on his chin and a tip-tilted nose. He was already a hardened killer, but his face had the innocence of a cherub.

'Get out your ropes and measure them.'

They obeyed. Each rope measured twelve feet – 120 feet when tied securely together. Add Micheletto's own and you had 130 feet. Cesare would have to drop the last ten feet or so, but that would be nothing to him.

The next problem was getting the rope to Cesare. For that they'd have to contact their recruit, the sergeant-of-the-guard, Juan, which wouldn't be too hard as they knew Juan's movements and hours of duty. That would be Luca's job, since, as an innocent-looking young man, he'd attract the least attention – the rest of his band, though dressed like hunters, looked like the men they were: hardened thugs. Juan's palm would have to be greased, but Micheletto always carried a contingency fund of 250 ducats, and a tenth of that should do it. For the whole job.

Juan could gain access to Cesare's cell and deliver the rope – the Swiss Guards wouldn't suspect him. Micheletto might even fake a letter with an official-looking seal on it, to be delivered to Cesare as cover.

The outer barbican was massive, though, and once Cesare was at the foot of the central tower, he'd have to cross the inner courtyards and get out – somehow – through the only gate.

The one good thing was that La Mota's main function

these days was to guard its single prisoner. Its original purpose had been to ward off attacks from the Moors, but that threat had long since been removed and the massive place was, in every sense other than guarding Cesare, redundant, so he knew from Juan that it was a fairly cushy posting.

They'd have to take a change of clothes to Cesare from time to time, so Micheletto thought through the possibilities of Juan organizing delivery of a 'change of clothes' for Cesare – a disguise to fool the guards – then maybe it might work. He could think of no other way, apart from fighting their way in, and getting Cesare out by force.

'Luca,' he said finally. 'I have a job for you.'

It turned out that Juan wanted fifty ducats for the whole job, and Micheletto beat him down to forty, though he didn't waste time with too much bartering. It took Luca three trips to and fro to set the whole thing up, but finally he reported back: 'It's arranged. He's going to take the rope and a guard's uniform to Cesare when he accompanies the man who takes him his evening meal at six o'clock. The postern gate will be guarded by Juan, who's going to take the midnight-to-six gate-watch. It's a five-minute walk from the castle to the town . . .'

Cesare Borgia's left leg hurt from the lesions of the New Disease, but not much, just a dull ache that made him limp slightly. At 2 a.m., once he had changed into the guard's uniform, he tied one end of the rope firmly to the central mullion of the window of his cell and carefully lowered the rest out into the night. When it was all paid out, he slung his good leg over the windowsill, hauled the other one after it and took a firm grip on the rope. Sweating, despite the coolness of the night, he descended hand over hand until his ankles felt the end of the rope. He dropped the last ten feet, feeling the pain in his left leg when he landed, but he shook it off and limped across the deserted inner courtyard and through the outer one, where the sleepy guards paid him no attention, thinking him one of their own.

At the gate he was challenged, at which point his heart went to his mouth. But then Juan came to his rescue.

'It's all right. I'll take him to the guardhouse.'

What was going on? So near and yet so far.

'Don't worry,' said Juan under his breath.

The guardhouse was occupied by two sleeping guards. Juan kicked one of them into life.

'Wake up, Domingo. This man has a warrant for town. They forgot to order more straw for the stables and they need some before they ride out on the dawn patrol. Take him back to the gate, explain to the guards there and let him out.'

'Yessir!'

Cesare followed the guard out through the postern, which was then firmly locked behind him, and limped through the moonlight into the town. What joy to feel the cool night air around him after so long. He'd been confined in this dump since 1504, but he was free now. He was still only thirty; he'd get it all back, and he'd take such vengeance on his enemies, especially the Assassin Brotherhood, that he'd make Caterina Sforza's purges at Forlì make her look like a nursemaid.

He heard and smelt the horses at the appointed rendezvous. Thank God for Micheletto. Then he saw them; they were all there, in the shadows of the church wall. They had a fine black beast ready for him. Micheletto dismounted and helped him into the saddle.

'Welcome back, *Excellenza*,' he said. 'And now we must hurry. That bastard *Assassino*, Ezio Auditore, is on our heels.'

Cesare was silent. He was thinking about the slowest death he could devise for the Assassin.

'I've put matters in hand already at Valencia,' continued Micheletto.

'Good.'

They rode off into the night, heading south-east.

61

'He's *escaped*!?' Ezio had ridden the last miles to La Mota without sparing himself, his companions or their horses, but with an ever-deepening sense of apprehension. 'After more than two years?' *How?*'

'It was carefully planned, *signore*,' said the hapless lieutenant of the castle, a plumpish man of sixty with a very red nose. 'We are holding an official enquiry.'

'And what have you come up with?'

'As yet . . .'

But Ezio wasn't listening. He was looking around at the Castle of la Mota. It was exactly as the Apple had depicted it. And the thought led him to remember another vision it had vouchsafed him: the gathering army at a seaport . . . The seaport had been Valencia!

His mind raced frantically.

He could think only of getting back to the coast as fast as possible.

'Get me fresh horses!' he yelled.

'But, *signore* . . .'

Machiavelli and Leonardo looked at each other.

'Ezio, whatever the urgency, we must rest, at least for a day,' said Machiavelli.

'A week,' groaned Leonardo.

As matters turned out, they were delayed because Leonardo fell ill. He was exhausted and missed Italy badly. Ezio was almost tempted to abandon him, but Machiavelli counselled restraint.

'He is your old friend, and they cannot gather an army and a fleet in under two months.'

Ezio relented.

Events were to prove him right – and to prove Leonardo invaluable.

62

Ezio and his companions were back in Valencia within a month, where they found the city in a state of uproar. Machiavelli had underestimated the speed with which things could happen in such a wealthy town.

Men had been secretly mustering and now, just outside Valencia, there was a huge camp of soldiers, maybe a thousand men. The Borgia were offering mercenaries good wages, and word had got round fast. Budding soldiers were coming in from as far away as Barcelona and Madrid, and from all over the provinces of Murcia and La Mancha. Borgia money ensured that a fleet of perhaps fifteen ships – quickly run-up troop ships with half a dozen small warships to protect them – was in the process of being built.

'Well, we don't need the Apple to tell us what our old friend Cesare is planning,' said Machiavelli.

'That's true.' He doesn't need a vast army to take Naples, and once he's established a bridgehead there, he'll recruit many more men to his cause. His plan is to conquer the kingdom of Naples, and then all Italy.'

'What are Ferdinand and Isabella doing about this?' asked Machiavelli.

'They'll be getting a force together to crush it. So we'll enlist their aid.'

'It will take too long. Their army has to march from Madrid. The garrison here must have been put out of action. But you can see that Cesare's in a hurry,' rejoined Machiavelli.

'It might not even be necessary,' mused Leonardo.

'What do you mean?'

'Bombs.'

'Bombs?' asked Machiavelli.

'Quite little bombs, but effective enough to, say, wreck ships or disperse a camp.'

'Well, if they'll do that for us . . .' said Ezio. 'What do you need to make them?'

'Sulphur, charcoal and potassium nitrate. And steel. Thinnish steel. Flexible. And I'll need a small studio and a furnace.'

It took them a while, but, fortunately for them, Captain Alberto's ship, the *Marea di Alba*, was tied up at its usual quay. He greeted them with a friendly wave.

'Hello again,' he said. 'Those people I told you about . . . the ones who aren't gentlemen. I don't suppose you heard about the fracas at the Lone Wolf shortly after you arrived?'

Ezio smiled and told him what they needed.

'Hmm. I know a man here who might be able to help you.'

'When do you return to Italy?' asked Leonardo.

'I've brought over a cargo of grappa, and I'm taking back silk again. Maybe two, three days. Why?'

'I'll tell you later.'

'Can you get what we need arranged quickly?' asked Ezio, who had a sudden sense of foreboding, though he couldn't blame Leonardo for wanting to leave.

'Certainly!'

Alberto was as good as his word, and within a few hours everything had been arranged and Leonardo settled down to work.

'How long will it take you?' asked Machiavelli.

'Two days, since I don't have any assistants. I've enough material here to make twenty, maybe twenty-one, bombs. That's ten each.'

'*Seven* each,' said Ezio.

'No my friend, ten each – one lot for you, and one for Niccolò here. You can count me out.'

Two days later, the bombs were ready. They were about the shape and size of a grapefruit, encased in steel and fitted with a catch at the top.

'How do they work?'

Leonardo smiled proudly. 'You flip this little catch – actually, it's more of a lever – you count to three, then you throw them at your target. Each of these is enough to kill twenty men and, if you hit a ship in the right place, to disable it completely, perhaps even sink it.' He paused for a moment. 'It's a pity there isn't time to build a submarine.'

'A what?'

'Never mind. Just throw it after a count of three. Don't hold on to it any longer or you'll be blown to pieces yourself!' He rose. 'And now, goodbye and good luck.'

'What?'

Leonardo smiled ruefully. 'I've had quite enough of Spain, so I've booked a passage with Alberto. He sails on this afternoon's tide. I'll see you back in Rome – if you make it.'

Ezio and Machiavelli looked at one another, then solemnly embraced Leonardo.

'Thank you, my dear friend,' said Ezio.

'Don't mention it.'

'Thank God you didn't build these things for Cesare,' said Machiavelli.

After Leonardo had gone, they carefully packed the bombs – there were exactly ten each – into linen bags, which they slung over their shoulders.

'You take the mercenaries' encampment, I'll take the port,' said Ezio.

Machiavelli nodded grimly.

'When we've done the job, we'll meet at the corner of the street where the Lone Wolf is,' said Ezio. 'I reckon the Lone Wolf is where Cesare will have his centre of operations. Once the chaos has started, he'll go there to regroup with his inner circle. We'll try to corner them before they can make their escape – again.'

'For once I'll back your hunch,' grinned Machiavelli. 'Cesare is so vainglorious he won't have thought to change the Borgia diehards' hideout. And it's more discreet than a *palazzo.*'

'Good luck, friend.'

'We'll both need it.'

They shook hands and parted to go on their separate missions.

Ezio decided to head for the troop ships first. Blending in with the crowd, he made his way down to the port and, once on the quay, selected his first target. He took out the first bomb, fighting down the insidious doubt that it might not work, and, aware that he'd have to be fast, flipped its catch, counted to three and flung it.

He was working at close range and his aim had deadly accuracy. The bomb landed with a clatter in the belly of the ship. For a few moments nothing happened, and Ezio cursed inwardly – what if the plan failed? – but then there was an almighty explosion, the ship's mast cracked and fell, and splintered wood was tossed high in the air.

Amid the chaos that followed, Ezio darted along the quay, selecting another ship and throwing the next bomb. In several cases, the first explosion was followed by a mightier one, as some of the troop ships had already been laden with casks of gunpowder. In one case, an exploding ship carrying gunpowder destroyed its two neighbours.

One by one, Ezio wrecked twelve ships, but the chaos and panic that ensued were of equal value. In the distance he could hear explosions, shouts and screams as Machiavelli did his work, too.

As Ezio made his way to their rendezvous, he hoped his friend had survived.

All Valencia was in uproar, but pushing his way against the flow of the crowd, Ezio made the appointed meeting place in ten minutes. Machiavelli wasn't there, but Ezio didn't have long to wait. Looking a bit shabby, and with a blackened face, his fellow Assassin soon came running up.

'May God reward Leonardo da Vinci,' he said.

'Success?'

'I have never seen such pandemonium,' replied Macchiavelli. 'The survivors are running away out of town as fast as they can. I think most of them will prefer the plough to the sword after this.'

'Good! But we still have work to do.'

They made their way down the narrow street and arrived at the door of the Lone Wolf to find it closed. Silently as cats, they climbed onto the roof. It was a one-storey building, bigger than it appeared from the front, and near the top of the pitched roof there was an open skylight. They approached it and cautiously looked over the edge.

It was a different room from the one in which they had been ambushed, with two men down below:

Micheletto stood at a table, and facing him, seated, was Cesare Borgia. His once handsome face, now lacerated by the New Disease, was white with fury.

'They have destroyed my plans! Those damned Assassins! Why did you not destroy them? Why did you fail me?'

'*Excellenza*, I—' Micheletto looked like a whipped dog.

'I must make good my escape. I'll go to Viana, in Navarre, just across the border. Let them try to recapture me then. I'm not waiting here for Ferdinand's men to come and haul me back to La Mota. My brother-in-law is king of Navarre and he will surely help me.'

'*I* will help you, as I have always helped you. Only let me come with you.'

Cesare's cruel lips curled. 'You got me out of La Mota, sure, and you built up my hopes. But now look where you have got me!'

'Master, all my men are dead. I have done what I could.'

'And failed!'

Micheletto went white. 'Is this my reward? For all my years of faithful service?'

'You dog, get out of my sight. I discard you! Go and find some gutter to die in.'

With a cry of rage, Micheletto hurled himself at Cesare, his huge, strangler's hands flexed to close on his former master's throat. But they never got there. With lightning speed, Cesare whipped out one of the two pistols he had in his belt and fired at point blank range.

Micheletto's face was destroyed beyond all recognition. The rest of his body crashed over the table. Cesare sprang back, out of his chair, to avoid being covered in blood.

Ezio had drawn back, so as to be invisible but not out of earshot, and was preparing to leap from the roof and grab Cesare as he came out of the front door of the inn. But Machiavelli had craned forward to get a better view of the dreadful showdown, and now he inadvertently kicked a tile loose, alerting Cesare.

Cesare looked up swiftly and drew his second pistol. Machiavelli didn't have time to draw back before Cesare fired, shooting him through the shoulder and smashing his collarbone before he fled.

Ezio thought of pursuit, but only for an instant. He had heard Cesare say that he intended to go to Viana, and he would follow him there, but not before he had seen to his wounded friend.

Machiavelli groaned apologies of all things, as Ezio managed to haul him off the roof. At least he could walk, though the wound was bad.

Once they reached the main thoroughfare, Ezio accosted a passer-by, having to stop the man by force as the chaos raged around them.

'I need a doctor,' he said urgently. 'Where can I find one?'

'Many people need a doctor!' replied the man.

Ezio shook him. 'My friend is badly wounded. Where can I find a doctor? Now!'

'Let go of me! You could try *el médico* Acosta. His rooms are just down the street. There's a sign outside.'

Ezio grabbed the near-fainting Macchiavelli and supported him. He took his scarf from his tunic and with it staunched the wound as best he could. Niccolò was losing a lot of blood.

The minute he saw the wound, Acosta had Machiavelli sit in a chair. He took a bottle of alcohol and some swabs and carefully dressed it.

'The ball went right through the shoulder,' he explained in broken Italian. 'So at least I won't have to dig it out. And it's a clean wound. But as for the collarbone, I'll have to reset it. I hope you're not planning on travelling at any time soon?'

Ezio and Machiavelli exchanged a glance.

'I have been a fool again,' said Machiavelli, forcing a grin.

'Shut up, Niccolò.'

'Go on. Get after him. I'll manage.'

'He can stay here with me. I have a small annexe that needs a patient,' said Acosta. 'And when he's healed, I'll send him after you.'

'How long?'

'Perhaps two weeks, maybe more.'

'I'll see you in Rome,' said Machiavelli.

'All right,' replied Ezio. 'Take care of yourself, my friend.'

'Kill him for me,' said Machiavelli. 'Though at least he spared us the trouble of Micheletto.'

PART THREE

We have reached the last era in prophetic song.
Time has conceived, and the great sequence of
the ages starts afresh. Justice, the virgin, comes
back to dwell with us, and the rule of Saturn is
restored. The Firstborn of the New Age is
already on his way from high heaven down to
earth.

Virgil, *Eclogues, IV*

63

Ezio once again travelled across Spain on a long and lonely journey, almost due north to Viana. He arrived there in the month of March, in the year of Our Lord 1507. The city that he saw, a mile or so distant, looked exactly like the one in the vision accorded him by the Apple, with strong walls and a well-fortified citadel at its centre, but there was a difference.

Even before he crossed the border into Navarre, Ezio's practised eyes told him the city was under siege. When he came to a village, most of the locals just shook their heads dumbly when questioned, but when he sought out the priest, with whom he was able to converse in Latin, he learned the whole picture.

'You may know that our King and Queen have designs on Navarre. It's a rich land and they want to incorporate it into Spain.'

'So they want to take Viana?'

'They've already taken it. It's occupied by the Count of Lerin on their behalf.'

'And the besiegers?'

'They are Navarrese forces. I think they will be the victors.'

'What makes you say that?'

'Because they are under the command of the brother-in-law of the King of Navarre, and he is an experienced general.'

Ezio's heart beat faster, but he still needed confirmation: 'His name?'

'He's very famous, apparently. The Duke of Valence, Cesare Borgia. They say he once commanded the army of the Pope himself. But the Spanish troops are brave. They have taken the fight out to the enemy, and there have been bloody battles in the fields outside the town. I would not go any further in that direction, my son; there lies only devastation and blood.'

Ezio thanked him and spurred his horse forward.

He arrived at the scene to find a pitched battle going on right in front of him, while a fog swirled around them. In its midst, Cesare Borgia took a stand, hacking down any foe who came at him. Suddenly Ezio himself had to fight another horseman – a Navarrese, with his crest bearing a red shield crisscrossed with yellow chains. Ezio slashed at the man with his sword, but his foe ducked just in time to miss the blade and Ezio nearly toppled over from the momentum. Recovering just in time, Ezio manoeuvred his horse round and back towards the man. The horseman was pulling his sword arm back to strike a blow at Ezio's open flank, but Ezio lunged at him with a lightning flick of his sword arm. The tip of his sword slashed into the man's chest, and he pulled back in pain, allowing Ezio to deliver a mighty blow downwards, splitting his foe's right shoulder down to his chest. He fell without a cry and was finished off by the Spanish infantrymen.

Cesare was on foot, and Ezio decided that it would be easier to get close to him undetected if he were also on foot, so he dismounted and ran through the fray towards him.

At last he stood face to face with his deadly foe. Cesare's face was streaked with blood and dust and strained with exertion, but when he saw Ezio his expression took on a new determination.

'Assassin! How did you find me?'

'My thirst to avenge Mario Auditore led me to you.'

They sliced at each other with their swords until Ezio managed to knock Cesare's weapon out of his hand. Then, sheathing his own, he flung himself on the Borgia, putting his hands around his throat. Cesare had learnt a few things from Micheletto about the art of strangling, though, and he managed to free himself by thrusting Ezio's arms away. Ezio unleashed the Hidden Blade, but Cesare caught the blow, once again successfully defending himself, as the battle raged about them.

It was then that the Spanish trumpets sounded the retreat. Triumphant, Cesare yelled to the nearest Navarrese troops, 'Kill him! Kill the Assassin. Tear the *maldito bastardo* into pieces!' As the fog increased, so Cesare melted into it and the Navarrese soldiers closed in on Ezio. He fought them off long and hard before exhaustion overwhelmed him, then he fell to the ground, almost unnoticed as the melee and fog swirled around him and the soldiers left him for dead.

When Ezio came to, some time later, he was lying on his back in the middle of the battlefield; he had to push a corpse off him before he could sit up.

The battlefield lay under a cloudy, blood-red sky, and, in the distance, the sun burned angrily. Dust hung in the air over a wide, unmade road, littered with the dead.

Ezio saw a crow standing on a corpse's chin, pecking hungrily at its eye. A riderless horse stampeded by, driven mad by the smell of blood. Broken banners snapped in the breeze.

Groaning with the effort, he stood up and, painfully at first, walked through the field of dead. He found that he had lost his sword and dagger, though the Hidden Blade and the Bracer had not been found and looted.

His first job was to replace his weapons. Near him, he noticed a peasant sifting through the spoils of battle. The peasant looked at him.

'Help yourself,' he said. 'There's more than enough to go round.'

Ezio looked for fallen officers and knights, as they would be better armed, but in every case someone had got there before him. At last he found a dead captain with a fine sword and a dagger similar to his own. These he took gratefully.

Next he went in search of a horse as it would be quicker to get around that way. He was in luck. Not half a mile from the edge of the battlefield, well away from the Navarrese camp, he came across a fully saddled and bridled warhorse, its back bloodstained, but not with its own blood, grazing in a green field. Talking to it gently, he mounted it. It kicked a little at first, but he soothed it quickly, then rode it back the way he had come.

Back on the battlefield, he encountered more peasants recovering what they could from the bodies. He passed them and galloped uphill towards the sound of another fight. The crest of the hill revealed a level plain below it where the battle had been rejoined, close to the battlemented walls of the town, from where cannon-fire issued.

64

Ezio steered his horse to one side of the battle, through some olive groves, where he encountered a patrol of Navarrese troops. Before he had time to turn round, they had fired their muskets at him, missing him, but cutting his horse down from under him.

He managed to escape amongst the trees and continued on foot, taking care to avoid the Spanish troops, who were prowling everywhere. Creeping closer, he came to a clearing, in which he saw one Spanish soldier lying wounded on the ground while another did his best to comfort him.

'*Por favor*,' said the wounded man. 'My legs. Why won't the bleeding stop?'

'*Compadre*, I have done all I can for you. Now you must trust in God.'

'Oh, Pablo, I'm afraid! *Mis piernas! Mis piernas!*'

'Quiet now, Miguel. Think of all the money we'll get when we've won the battle. And the booty!'

'Who is this old man we are fighting for?'

'Who? *El Conde de* Lerin?'

'Yes. We are fighting for him, aren't we?'

'Yes, my friend. He serves our King and Queen, and we serve him, so we fight.'

'Pablo, the only thing I'm fighting for now is my life.'

A patrol arrived on the other side of the clearing.

'Keep moving,' said its sergeant. 'We must outflank them.'

'My friend is wounded,' said Pablo. 'He cannot move.'

'Then leave him. Come on.'

'Give me a few more minutes.'

'Very well. We head north. Follow us. And be sure no Navarrese sees you.'

'Will we know when we have outflanked them?'

'There will be gunfire. We'll cut them down where they least expect it. Use the trees for cover.'

'Just a moment, sir.'

'What is it?'

'I will follow now.'

'Immediately?'

'Yes, sir. My comrade Miguel is dead.'

Once they had gone, Ezio waited for a few minutes, then made his way north before veering east, in the direction he knew Viana lay. He left the olive groves and saw that he had passed the field of battle and was skirting it on its northern side. He wondered what had become of the Spanish soldiers, for there was no sign of any successful outflanking movement and the battle seemed to be going to the Navarrese.

On his way lay a shattered village. He avoided it, as he could see Spanish snipers concealed behind some of the charred and broken walls, using long-muzzled wheel-locks to fire on any Navarrese troops at the edge of the battle.

He came across a soldier, his tunic so bloodstained that Ezio could not tell what side he was on, sitting with his back to a stray olive tree and hugging himself in agony, his whole body shaking, his gun abandoned on the ground.

Reaching the outskirts of the town, among the settlements that crouched beneath its bastions, Ezio finally saw his quarry ahead of him. Cesare was with a Navarrese sergeant and was clearly assessing the best way of breaching or undermining Viana's massive walls.

The Spanish, who had taken Viana, had been confident enough to allow some of their camp followers to settle in the houses here, but they were evidently not powerful enough to protect them now.

Suddenly a woman came out of one of the cottages and ran towards them, screaming and blocking their path.

'*Ayúdenme!*' she cried. 'Help me! My son! My son is wounded!'

The sergeant went up to the woman and, seizing her by the hair, dragged her out of Cesare's way.

'*Ayúdenme!*' she yelled.

'Shut her up, will you?' said Cesare, surveying her coldly.

The sergeant drew his dagger and slit the woman's throat.

65

As Ezio shadowed Cesare, he witnessed further scenes of brutality doled out by the Navarrese troops on the hated Spanish interlopers.

He saw a young woman being roughly manhandled by a Navarrese trooper.

'Leave me in peace!' she cried.

'Be a good girl,' the soldier told her brutally. 'I will not hurt you! In fact, you might even enjoy it, you Spanish whore.'

Further along, a man, a cook by the look of him, stood in despair as two soldiers held him and forced him to watch two others set fire to his house.

Worse still was a man – doubtless a wounded Spanish soldier who had had his legs amputated – being kicked out of his cart by a pair of Navarrese squaddies. They stood there laughing as he desperately tried to drag himself away from them along a footpath.

'Run! Run!' said one.

'Can't you go any faster?' added his comrade.

The battle had obviously gone to the Navarrese, because Ezio could see them bringing siege towers up to the walls of the city. Navarrese troops were swarming up them and there was fierce fighting on the battlements already. If Cesare were anywhere, it would be at the head of his men, for he was as ferocious and fearless as he was cruel.

Somewhere behind him, a Spanish preacher intoned to a despairing congregation: 'You have brought this on yourselves through sin. This is how the Lord punishes you. Ours is a just God and this is His justice. Praise the Lord! Thank you, God, for teaching us to be humble. To see our punishment for what it is, a call to spirituality. The Lord giveth and the Lord taketh away. So is the Truth written. Amen!'

The only way into the city is up one of those towers, thought Ezio. The one nearest him had just been pushed up to the wall and, running, Ezio joined the men rushing up it, blending in with them, though there was scarcely any need, for amidst all the roaring and bellowing of the pumped-up besiegers, who scented victory at last, he would not have been noticed.

The defenders were ready for them now, though and began pouring the mixture of pitch and oil they call Greek Fire down onto the enemy below. The screams of burning men came up to those already on the tower, Ezio among them, and the rush upwards, away from the flames burning the base of the tower became frantic. Around him, Ezio saw men push their fellows out of the way in order to survive, and some soldiers fell, howling, into the flames below.

Ezio knew he had to get to the top before the flames caught up with him. Reaching it, he took a great leap of faith onto the battlements just as the blazing tower collapsed behind him, causing murderous chaos beneath.

There was fierce fighting on the ramparts, but already hundreds of Navarrese soldiers had got down into the town itself, and the Spanish trumpets were sounding the retreat into the citadel at the centre of Viana. The town seemed as good as retaken.

Cesare would be triumphant, and his wealthy brother-in-law would doubtless reward him richly. Ezio would not allow that to happen.

Running along the high wall, Ezio ducked and dived among the fighting soldiers as the Navarrese cut down the Spanish troops who had been left behind in the retreat. Ezio located Cesare, cutting his way through enemy troops as a child uses a stick to smash through tall grass. Cesare was impatient to take the citadel and, once clear of the men who attempted to block his way, he sped down a stairway on the inner wall and through the town, with Ezio seconds behind him.

Ahead of them, the citadel had already opened its doors. All the fight had gone out of the Spanish, and the Count of Lerin was ready to parlay. But Cesare was not a merciful man.

'Kill them! Kill them all!' he shouted to his troops.

With superhuman speed, he ran into the citadel and up the narrow stone staircases within it, cutting down anyone who got in his way.

Ezio kept pace with him until they reached the topmost battlements of the citadel, where Cesare stood alone, cutting down the flagpole bearing the Spanish flag. When he turned there was but one way out, and there stood Ezio, blocking it.

'There is nowhere for you to run, Cesare,' said Ezio. 'It is time to pay your debts.'

'Come on then, Ezio!' snarled Cesare. 'You brought down my family. Let's see how you settle *your* debts.'

Such was their impatient fury, they closed on each other immediately, man to man, using only their fists as weapons.

Cesare got the first blow in, his right fist swinging wildly at Ezio's head. Ezio ducked under the punch, but a fraction too late, so that Cesare's knuckles glanced off the Assassin's temple. Ezio staggered, giving Cesare cause to cry out in triumph: 'No matter what you do, I will conquer all, but first I will kill you and everyone you hold dear. As for me, I cannot die. *Fortuna* will not fail me!'

'Your hour is come, Cesare,' Ezio replied. Recovering his composure and stepping back, he drew his sword.

Cesare loosed his own blade in response and the two men began to fight in earnest. Ezio swung his blade viciously towards his foe's head, the blade sweeping a lethal flat arc through the air. Cesare was shocked by the speed of the attack, but managed to raise his own blade in a clumsy parry, his arm shuddering with the impact. Ezio's sword bounced away and Cesare thrust with his own attack, his balance and focus regained. The men circled on the parapet, flicking the tips of their swords in a swift burst of swordplay. Ezio stepped quickly forward, leading Cesare's blade off to the right, then twisting his wrist and aiming the point of his sword towards Cesare's exposed left flank. Cesare was too quick, though, and slapped Ezio's sword aside. Then he used the opening to flick his blade at Ezio, who responded by raising his wrist and using the Bracer to deflect the blow. Both men stepped back, wary once again. Cesare's skill as a swordsman had clearly not been hampered by the New Disease.

'Pah, old man. Your generation is finished. It is my turn now, and I will not wait any longer. Your antiquated systems, your rules and hierarchies – all of them must go.'

Both men were tiring, and they confronted each other, panting.

Ezio replied, 'Your new regime will bring tyranny and misery to all.'

'I know what is best for the people of Italy, not a bunch of old men who wasted their energy fighting to get to the top years ago.'

'Your mistakes are worse than theirs.'

'I do not *make* mistakes. I am the Enlightened One!'

'Enlightenment comes through years of thought, not through blind conviction.'

'Ezio Auditore, your time has come!'

Cesare slashed with his sword, striking an unexpected and cowardly blow, but Ezio was just quick enough to parry, carry through and, catching Cesare off-balance, seize his wrist and wrench the sword from his grip, sending it clattering to the flagstones.

They were on the edge of the battlements, and, far below, Navarrese troops were beginning to celebrate. There was no looting, though, for they had regained a town which was their own.

Cesare went for his dagger, but Ezio slashed at his opponent's wrist with his sword, cutting into the tendons so that it hung limply, disabled. Cesare staggered back and his face grimaced with pain and anger.

'The throne was mine!' he said, like a child who has lost a toy.

'Wanting something does not give you the right to have it.'

'What do you know? Have you never wanted something that much?'

'A true leader empowers the people he rules.'

'I can still lead Mankind into a new world.'

Seeing that Cesare was standing inches from the edge, Ezio raised his sword: 'May your name be blotted out. *Requiescat in Pace.*'

'You cannot kill me! No man can murder me!'

'Then I will leave you in the hands of Fate,' replied Ezio.

Dropping his sword, Ezio seized Cesare Borgia and, with a single deft movement, threw him off the battlements. He plunged onto the cobblestones a hundred feet below, but Ezio did not look down – the weight of his long fight against the Borgia was lifted from his heart.

66

It was Midsummer's Day again – Ezio's forty-eighth birthday. Ezio, Machiavelli and Leonardo were gathered in the newly refurbished Tiber Island headquarters, which was now a proud building for all to see.

'It's a very small birthday party,' commented Leonardo. 'Now, if you had let me design something for you, a real pageant . . .'

'Save that for two years' time,' smiled Ezio. 'We have invited you for another reason.'

'Which is?' asked Leonardo, full of curiosity.

Machiavelli, sporting a slightly crooked but fully healed shoulder, said, 'Leo, we want to extend an invitation to you.'

'Another one?'

'We want you to join us,' said Ezio solemnly. 'To become a fellow member of the Brotherhood of the Assassins.'

Leonardo smiled gravely. 'So my bombs were a success.' He was silent for a moment, then said, 'Gentlemen, I thank you, and you know that I respect your goals and will support them for as long as I live. I will never disclose the secrets of the Assassins to anyone,' he paused. 'But I tread a different path, and it is a solitary one. So forgive me.'

'Your support is almost as valuable as your becoming one of us. But can't we persuade you, old friend?'

'No, Ezio. Besides, I am leaving.'

'Leaving? Where are you going?'

'I shall return to Milan, and then I am going to Amboise.'

'To France?'

'They say it is a noble country, and it is there I choose to end my days.'

Ezio spread his hands. 'Then we must let you go, old friend.' He paused. 'This, then, is a parting of the ways.'

'How so?' asked Leonardo.

'I am returning to Florence,' replied Machiavelli. 'My work there is far from done.' He winked at Ezio. 'And I still have that book to write.'

'What will you call it?'

Machiavelli looked levelly at Ezio. '*The Prince*,' he replied.

'Send Claudia back to me.'

'I will. She misses Rome, and you know she'll support you as long as you continue your work as Mentor of the Brotherhood.'

Machiavelli glanced at the water clock.

'It is time.'

The three men rose as one and embraced each other solemnly.

'Goodbye.'

'Goodbye.'

'Goodbye.'

List of Characters

Mario Auditore: Ezio's uncle and head of the
  Brotherhood of the Assassins
Ezio Auditore: Assassin
Maria Auditore: Ezio's mother
Claudia Auditore: Ezio's sister
Angelina Ceresa: friend of Claudia's
Federico: Mario's stable master
Annetta: Auditore family housekeeper
Paola: sister of Annetta and an Assassin
Ruggiero: master sergeant in Mario Auditore's guards

Niccolò di Bernardo dei Machiavelli: Assassin,
  philosopher and writer, 1469–1527
Leonardo da Vinci: artist, scientist, sculptor, etc.,
  1452–1519
Antonio: Assassin
Fabio Orsini: Assassin
Bartolomeo d'Alviano: Italian Captain and Assassin
  (1455–1515)
Pantasilea Baglioni: Bartolomeo's wife
Baldassare Castiglione: Associate Assassin
Pietro Bembo: Associate Assassin

Gilberto the Fox, la Volpe: Assassin and head of the
    Thieves' Guild
Benito: member of the Thieves' Guild
Trimalchio: member of the Thieves' Guild
Claudio: thief and son of Trimalchio
Paganino: thief at the sacking of Monteriggioni

Madonna Solari: brothel keeper and Assassin accomplice
Agnella: prostitute from The Rosa in Fiori
Lucia: prostitute from The Rosa in Fiori
Saraghina: prostitute from The Rosa in Fiore.
Margherita deghli Campi: Roman aristocrat and Assassin
    sympathizer
Jacopo: sailor
Camilla: Naples prostitute
Filin: ship's captain
Captain Alberto: captain of the *Marea di Alba*
Acosta: Valencian doctor
Count of Lerin: Spanish count (1430–1508)
Caterina Sforza: The Countess of Forlì, daughter of
    Galeazzo (1463–1509)
Lorenzo de' Medici: 'Lorenzo the Magnificent', Italian
    statesman (1449–92)
Governor Piero Soderini: governor of Florence
    (1450–1522)
Amerigo Vespucci: friend and advisor to Soderini
    (1454–1512)

Rodrigo Borgia: Pope Alexander VI (1431–1503)
Cesare Borgia: son of Rodrigo (1476–1507)

Lucrezia Borgia: daughter of Rodrigo (1480–1519)
Vannozza Cattanei: mother of Cesare and Lucrezia
Borgia (1442–1518)
Giulia Farnese: Rodrigo's mistress (1474–1524)
Princesse Charlotte d'Albret: wife of Cesare (1480–1514)
Juan Borgia: Archbishop of Monreale and Cesare's
banker (1476–1497)
Général Duc Octavien de Valois: French general and
Borgia ally
Micheletto da Corella: Cesare's right-hand man
Luca: Micheletto's diehard
Agostino Chigi: Pope Alexander's banker (1466–1520)
Luigi Torcelli: Cesare's banker's agent
Toffana: Lucrezia's servant
Gaspar Torella: Cesare's personal doctor
Johann Burchard: Pope Alexander VI's Master of
Ceremonies
Juan: Guard at La Mota

Egidio Troche: Roman senator
Francesco Troche: Egidio's brother and Cesare's
chamberlain

Michelangelo Buonarotti: artist, sculptor etc.
(1475–1564)
Vinicio: Machiavelli's contact
Cardinal Giuliano della Rovere (1443–1513)
Cardinal Ascanio Sforza (1455–1505)
Agniolo and Innocento: assistants to Leonardo da Vinci
Pietro Benintendi: Roman actor

Dottore Brunelleschi: Roman doctor

The Cardinal of Rouen: Georges d'Amboise (1460–1510)

Pope Pius III: Cardinal Piccolomini (1439–1503)

Pope Julius II: Giuliano della Rovere, Cardinal of San Pietro in Vincoli (1443–1513)

Bruno: a spy

Glossary of Italian, French Spanish and Latin Terms

aiutateme! help me!
aiuto! help!
albergo hotel
altezza highness
altrettanto a lei also to you
andiamo let's go
arrivederci goodbye
Assassini Assassins
attenzione be careful
ayúdenme help me

bastardo, bastardi bastard/s
bellissima very beautiful
bene good, well
bestiarii gladiators
birbante rascal, rogue
bordello brothel
brutissimo most horrible, ugliest
buona questa good one
buona fortuna good luck
buona sera good evening
buongiorno, fratellino good morning, little brother

calma / calmatevi calm down
campione champion
capisci? do you understand?
capitano captain
caro padre dear father
cazzo prick/shit
che cosa fate qui? what are you doing here?
cher ami dear friend
che tipo brutto what a brute
che diavolo? what the devil?
comè usciamo di qui? how do we get out of here?
commendatore commander
campanile bell tower
compadre comrade
condottieri mercenaries
con piacere with pleasure
consummatum est it is finished
contessa Countess
corri! run!
cosa diavolo aspetti what the devil are you waiting for?
Curia the Roman law courts

déclarez-vous declare yourself
diavolo devil
dio mio my god
dio, ti prego, salvaci Lord, I beg you, save us
dottore doctor

Excellenza Excellence
el médico the doctor
Eminenze Eminence

figlio mio my son
figlio di puttana son of a whore
Firenze Florence
fortune fortune
forze armate armed forces
fottere fuck
fotutto Francese fucking Frenchman
furbacchione cunning old devil

gonfalon banner
graffito graffito
grazie, Madonna thanks to Our Lady
Halte-là stop there

idioti idiots
il Magnifico the Magnificent
insieme per la vittoria together for victory
intesi certainly/understood
ipocrita hypocrite

ladro thief
lieta di conoscervi pleased to meet you
luridi codardi filthy cowards

ma certo but of course
ma che meraviglia but what a marvel
Madonna my lady
madre mother
maestro master
mais franchement, je m'en doute but frankly, I doubt it

malattia venerea venereal illness
maldito bastardo damned bastard
maledette cursed
mausoleo mausoleum
medico doctor
merda shit
messer sir
mille grazie a thousand thank yous
miracolo miraculous
mis piernas my legs
molto bene very good
molte grazie thank you very much
momentino, Contessa one moment, Contessa
morbus gallicus French Disease

nessun problema no problem
Borgia nomenklatura influential Borgia
nos replegamos fall back

onoratissima most honoured one
ora, mi scusi, ma excuse me

padrone father
papa Pope
palazzo palace
perdone, Colonnello sorry, Colonel
perdonatemi, signore sorry, sir
perfetto perfect
pezzo di merda piece of shit
piano nobile the principal floor of a large house

piazze square(s)
pollo ripieno stuffed chicken
por favor please
pranzo lunch
presidente president
puttana whore

requiescat in Pace rest in Peace
rione district
rocca fortress

salve, messere hello, sir
sang maudit blood curse
scorpioni scorpions
Senatore Senator
sì yes
Signoria governing authority
signore sir
signora lady
si, zio mio yes, my uncle
sul serio? seriously?

tesora mia my treasure
tesora, tesoro sweetheart, treasure
torna qui, maledetto cavallo come here, damned horse

un momento one moment

va bene all right
vero true

vittoria agli Assassini victory to the Assassins
virtù virtue
Volpe Addormentata, La The Sleeping Fox

zio uncle

Author's Note

Most of the translations from foreign languages in the text are my own, but for the quotations from Machiavelli's *The Prince* and Virgil's *Eclogues* (though I have adapted the latter very slightly). I am indebted to the late scholars George Bull (1929–2001) and E. V. Rieu (1887–1972) respectively.

Oliver Bowden, Paris, 2010

Acknowledgements

Special thanks to

Yves Guillemot
Jeffrey Yohalem
Corey May
Ethan Petty
Matt Turner
Jean Guesdon

And also

Alain Corre
Laurent Detoc
Sebastien Puel
Geoffroy Sardin
Sophie Ferre-Pidoux
Xavier Guilbert
Tommy François
Cecile Russeil
Christele Jalady
The Ubisoft Legal Department
Charlie Patterson
Chris Marcus
Eric Gallant
Maria Loreto
Guillaume Carmona